CONTENTS

CATHERINE BUCHAN

By the Northern Sea

CATHERINE BUCHAN

ISBN: 9798359050234

DEDICATION

For Liz, who first read this long ago.

CHAPTER ONE: THE FIRST WEEK

Few are wholly dead

Blow on a dead man's embers

And a live flame will start.

Robert Graves, "To Bring the Dead to Life"

The door screeched on the scarred linoleum as Joyce wrenched it open. Autumnal sunshine poured in, but she hardly noticed. Grabbing the pint of milk standing on the doorstep, she hastily turned and made for the ground-floor flat. Lifting the tarnished brass knocker, she let it drop lightly on the flaking green door.

No answer.

She knocked again, then shouted, "Miss Murdoch, your milk!" Then she tried the door.

Usually Miss Murdoch had the door unlatched and called out an imperious summons. Today Joyce was running late, so the old lady ought to be impatiently waiting for her. The screech on the linoleum should have alerted her. But the door was locked and there was no response.

Setting down the milk, Joyce turned again and ran upstairs to her own flat: she had a key.

Even as she hurried, her own concerns beating frantically at her mind, she remembered being given this key. It was two years ago when she came to live in Windmill Road. Miss Murdoch had at first been very aloof and withdrawn, scarcely seeming to see the post-graduate student to whom she had let out her upper storey. But one day Joyce had come into the house bearing a small posy of Sweet Williams. The flowers were a gift from a fellow-student, a thank-you for helping to chase a reference for an overdue essay. Joyce was allergic to flowers in confined spaces, and her flat was very much a confined space. As she had wondered what to do with them, impulsively she had seized the knocker on Miss Murdoch's door and given a sharp rap. The gift of flowers had marked the beginning of a gradual unbending, spiritually speaking. As their acquaintance grew, one thing which soon emerged was that physically unbending was difficult for the old lady. She could, she explained, bend down, but straightening up involved time, effort and pain. Not that she was complaining. At her (unspecified) age, one must expect some trouble.

So Joyce had got into the habit of delivering the milk. "And I will give you a key, Miss Cunningham" (Miss Murdoch didn't believe in first names except for intimate friends and family) "Since it is possible that at my age that one day I may be ill and unable to reach the door."

Joyce had offered to do other favours for her landlady, but all of them had been politely declined. Miss Murdoch wanted, needed, to do her own shopping. The short walk was good for her and the necessity kept her looking forwards. The key had never been used, and Joyce hoped it was still where she had left it, in a kitchen drawer. She raked through a loose assortment of cutlery with little thought for possible cut fingers. Grabbing the key, she returned downstairs.

The living-room of the downstairs flat was tolerably familiar:

shabby armchairs, occasional tables and a fantastic display of china from all over the world.

"Miss Murdoch!"

The kitchen was tidy, sparkling clean. Its owner wasn't one to leave dirty dishes in the sink. The old-fashioned wooden draining board was dry.

"Miss Murdoch!"

She must be in the bedroom. Joyce had never been there. But again, all was tidy, the bed made with all the blankets tucked in: the pot-plants lifting up their heads to the sunshine; clothes folded over a chair.

"Miss Murdoch." As she saw the clothes, Joyce's voice died to a whisper. Her haste dropped from her. Slowly, oh slowly, she turned to the bathroom.

A few minutes later a young woman could be seen carefully emerging from a door in Windmill Road. Gently she pulled the door closed, using all her skill to prevent the linoleum squeaking. Her wavy brown hair lay unusually still on her shoulders as swiftly, but soberly, she walked up the hill towards the university. There was a tutorial she had to lead on the religious beliefs of the Nuer tribe in Nigeria. She tried to turn her mind towards this subject, one with which she should, perhaps, have been a little more familiar than she was. She would, however, almost certainly know more than any of her first-year students.

Alexander Melville strode into his office, a sheaf of paper under his arm and an abstracted look on his face. Hargreaves, his partner in their newly fledged firm, looked up with a cheery smile, opened his mouth in facetious greeting and then let the words die, unsaid. He watched as Melville idly flung down the rolled documents and abstracted a paper from his briefcase. Still in grim silence, he began to work.

The office phone rang. Hargreaves picked it up. "Hargreaves and Melville, architects" he intoned. It sounded good but, of course, that it was he answering betrayed the fact that they were as yet architects in a small way, unable to afford the wages or with enough work to justify of a receptionist. Hargreaves swivelled on his chair. "It's for you. Sandy."

"Hello?" Then the voice softened a little. "Oh Joyce. What's up? What? When? Well, I'm not sure either. An undertaker? Or a minister? Yes, listen, did she go to church do you know? Which one? Well, why not contact the minster? He'll know what to do, I'm sure. No, I don't suppose it will matter, though really, must a tutorial come before matters of life and death? I'm sorry. No doubt you're right. I don't understand – again. I've got to be here today, but would you like me to come round tonight? About eight-ish? O.K. I'll see you then. Don't worry, I'm sure you'll do the right thing. Or what you think is right," he added after he hung up. He swung round on Hargreaves.

"That was Joyce. Apparently she found her land-lady dead in the bathroom this morning. Not Joyce's bathroom," he added quickly, seeing his partner's lips twitch. "And please don't try to be funny about this. I'm not in the mood."

"You never are these days," muttered Hargreaves, but he had the wisdom to do so quietly.

Back in her flat Joyce turned the contents of her desk upside down looking for the telephone directory. Locating it eventually, acting as a platform for the monitor of her computer, she first looked up C for churches. Not finding anything helpful under that heading, she tried M for Martyrs Church of Scotland, the establishment where Miss Murdoch had worshipped. There was no entry.

With an exasperated sigh, Joyce made her way outside and set off to walk to the church. Really, how did these churches expect to be found by people, she wondered. Even as her mind was occupied with such questions, her ruthless honesty was trying not to be aware of the relief she felt at having something to do. She wasn't glad that Miss Murdoch was dead, but she was relieved by the busyness of death which seemed to have come her way.

The church, a nineteenth century grey sandstone edifice, was directly opposite the St. Salvator's College Quad. The heavy doors were closed and did not yield to Joyce's pressure. She tried hammering on first one door then the other. Nothing. Obviously no one was there. Spying the notice board, Joyce noted the minister's name: Rev. B. McKay.

Reunited once more with her telephone directory, the Rev. B. McKay's phone number was easily located. A woman's voice answered the phone.

"Martyr's manse."

"Could I speak to the minister, please?"

"Speaking," replied the voice, and Joyce gave herself a mental shake at her feeling of surprise. What sort of feminist was she, anyway?

"I'm sorry to bother you, but I live in the same building as Miss Murdoch; I think she is one of your parishioners?"

"Charlotte Murdoch? That's right."

"Well, I'm so sorry, but I found her dead this morning. I don't know the proper procedures. I don't even know if she has family, and I thought you might be able to advise me."

"Charlotte's gone." The voice sounded hesitant, almost as

though the minister was at a loss. "I'm so sorry to hear that. It's sudden too, isn't it? I can tell you about her family: there isn't any. Charlotte often told me she was alone in the world. Alone and last." There was a pause. "You said you live in Windmill Road – would that be in the upstairs flat?"

"That's right."

"And your name is?"

"Joyce Cunningham. I should have mentioned it before."

"You must be the Miss Cunningham that Miss Murdoch told me about. You're a post-grad and always take in her milk."

"Yes, that's how I came to find her." Suddenly Joyce found herself shaking. She stopped.

"I'm sorry," said the minister's voice. "I can tell this had been a shock for you. As for me. Listen, I'll phone the doctor and the undertaker and then, if you don't mind, I think I'll come round. Is that all right? You're not rushing out or anything?"

"That's O.K. That'll be fine," stammered Joyce.

"Good. See you soon." And the Rev. B McKay hung up.

March 3rd 1930

The doctor has gone. The minister had gone. I am alone in the house. Alone. It's the first time. I am thirty years old, and I have never been alone in my home before. Do I like it? I'm not sure. Am I uneasy? Scared? No. What is there to be frightened of? This is my home where I have always lived. In one sense I am not alone, of course; Mother's body is in the bedroom. But that is just a body. I have no sense of her living presence, no sense of her spirit anywhere near.

I tried not to shock the doctor and Mr. Brown, the minister. Especially I tried to be appropriate with the minister, because I value his opinion. It strikes me that this is strange, yet it is true. Fortunately, the good man assumed that I was stunned with grief; that I hadn't really taken it in yet. Well perhaps that is true, but I don't think so. I just feel free, so free. I could get up and go down to the beach and run in the waves for freedom – even though they must be very cold. Mother's life is over. Now it's my turn.

Of course, I couldn't really run on the beach. Not now, not yet. Someone might see me, and oh, the scandal that would cause! But this I promise myself, on this day of my mother's death: somewhere there is a beach which I will run on; somehow, somewhere I, Charlotte Murdoch, will live.

Joyce found the waiting slow. She tried to read but couldn't concentrate. She thought about tidying the flat, or washing dishes, just to give herself an occupation. Instead, she found herself pacing back and forth with a rhythmic squeak in the floorboards. She was surprised at herself; normally she was very self-contained, able to put herself outside any problem. But then, she had never encountered death close-up before. She poured herself a glass of red wine, then jumped as the doorbell rang, spilling the wine in her white blouse. The drops lay "like blood" she thought in wild cliché.

Running downstairs, she wrenched open the front door, unheeding of its protestations. "I'm so glad you've come!" she began, impulsively. The elderly man on the doorstep indubitably was not the Rev. B. McKay.

"I'm sorry," she stammered. "I was expecting someone." Really, where was her poise?

"Weren't you expecting me then?" asked the man. "I'm Dr. Marr."

"I had no idea you would get here so quickly," Joyce replied. "Do come in Doctor."

"Miss Murdoch's in her own flat, I suppose. It's a while since I was here, or since she came to the surgery. She was aye a healthy lady for her age. We may have to go to the Fiscal, just for form's sake. Still, she was old: as old as the century. Now, where is she?"

As he talked, he entered the flat and made for the bedroom.

"No, she's not there." Joyce turned to the bathroom door, opened it, and stood back. "She's in here." Dr. Marr shot her a shrewd look, then turned into the bathroom.

"You only just found her?" His voice sounded muffled.

"No, not exactly." Joyce spoke softly.

"What's that? I can't hear.

"No," flatly. "I found her at about quarter to nine this morning."

There was a short silence and the doctor's head re-appeared. "And? Why the delay?"

"I had a tutorial," Joyce began quickly. She was interrupted by the screech of the front door. Into the flat slipped a short woman in her late thirties, wearing jeans and a sweatshirt. Her fair hair, now losing its brightness, hung curly to below her ears.

"Joyce Cunningham?" asked the newcomer. "I'm Bridget McKay. Hello, Dr Marr. You made good time."

"Car-phones are a wonderful help to a doctor out on his rounds, even to one as far past retirement age as me," replied the doctor with a smile.

"I suppose there's nothing that can be done for poor Charlotte?"

The smile faded. “Indeed no, since she had been here since before 8.45 a.m. Miss Cunningham was just about to tell me why a doctor was not sent for at once.”

“She was dead!” exclaimed Joyce. “What good could a doctor have done?”

“And how do you know she was dead? Did you try her pulse or see if she was stiff? Or was it just that she felt cold?”

“I didn’t actually touch her. But you see the position she’s lying in. And she wasn’t breathing and looked a terrible colour. I knew she was dead.”

“You’ve seen many corpses in your short life, I take it?” The doctor was relentless.

“No, none.” The truth slipped out. Angrily Joyce added, “Look, she was my landlady, not family. I had a tutorial I had to attend. I didn’t have time to find out what to do.”

“A tutorial? Couldn’t your professor have excused you for once?”

“You don’t understand: I was teaching the tutorial.”

“That would be up North Street somewhere, I suppose? Could you not at least have alerted the police on your way?”

“The police! But it’s not a suspicious death, is it?”

“No, but the police can cope with other emergencies too.” Suddenly the doctor lost his temper. “Look, Miss, you don’t know when this happened. Nor do I. But you also don’t know but that a doctor could have helped Miss Murdoch this morning. Perhaps she wasn’t dead! Perhaps she was in a coma. Now we’ll never know, because you couldn’t take a minute to think of someone other than yourself.”

The doctor turned back to the bathroom. Joyce, with a gasp which caught under her ribs and heart, turned, and ran up to her flat.

Bridget McKay was left rooted to the spot, shaken and at a loss.

At eight o'clock that evening, Alexander Melville's car drew up in front of the grey sandstone house in Windmill Road. The driver drew his fingers through his wiry black hair, then bounded out of the car and up the path. He rang Joyce's bell and tried the front door, usually kept unlocked. Tonight it was locked fast, not merely sticking on the linoleum. Melville wondered at this. He would never have described Joyce as the nervous type.

On entering, "Your room looks different," was his first comment. The familiar academic order was disturbed. Usually piles of books and papers covered the desk, and often overflowed onto chairs and floor. It looked a little muddled at times, but in fact Joyce always knew exactly what was in each pile and had been known to snap at people who tried to move any of her things. For this reason they met more often at his place, in Cupar, or most often, they went out, meeting at a pre-arranged rendezvous.

Tonight the piles had been put aside, and by no very careful hand. There was an untidy heap on the desk, where assorted papers had been swept together, and all of the chairs were uniquely free of literature. And Joyce? She looked pale and exhausted. There were dark circles under her eyes, yet the eyes themselves were glowing with excitement. Clearly she was not nervous, nor in mourning.

"Oh Alex," she exclaimed, "I'm sorry the door was locked. Bridget must have done that on her way out."

"Bridget?" He thought he knew all her friends, at least by name.

"Bridget McKay. She's Miss Murdoch's minister."

"So you found the minister. Did everything get sorted out all right?"

Joyce hesitated – there had been that unpleasant doctor – then her excitement overcame her shame. "Well, the doctor was a bit abrasive, and I didn't see the undertaker. But then Bridget came up here. Oh, Alex, it's so exciting!"

Melville could see little to be excited at in the death of an old lady. "What's exciting? The minister?"

"Well perhaps," smiled Joyce. "She wasn't at all what I'd expected. But even better – look!"

She pranced over to her desk and picked up an old, rather faded notebook. It's her journal. Or at least it's the first volume. There are about a hundred more downstairs."

"Her journal? Miss Murdoch's, you mean? But Joyce, you've no business reading that."

"Joyce's eyes flashed, and she echoed, "No business? And who are you to tell me what my business is and is not? Don't set yourself up as my judge, Alex Melville."

Melville bit his lip and crossed over to look out of the window. It had been a long, disappointing day. Joyce also fell silent, busy re-living the discussion she and Bridget McKay had had on the very issue which Melville had raised.

Bridget had come up and knocked on the door of the upper flat about half an hour after Joyce had quite Miss Murdoch's rooms. The knock was tentative, and the smile on the minister's face was really a question mark.

"Miss Cunningham? I don't want to disturb you, but I thought you would be glad to know that the doctor's finished and the undertaker's been and gone, taking Miss Murdoch's body with him."

Her voice shook and Joyce could see tears in her eyes. She opened the door wider. "You cared about her."

"Yes, I did. I didn't know her very well, but she was always kind to me, and encouraging. I think she understood the difficulties of my job more than most."

"And now she's gone."

"She's gone. So suddenly. I can't take it in." By now the elder woman was crying openly. Joyce led her into the living-room, swept a chair clear for her and produced a glass of red wine.

"This may help the shock."

The minister drank and sat silent for a while. Then she offered a watery smile. "I'm sorry. I don't usually do that. I'm supposed to be comforting you."

"If I need comfort," said Joyce.

"Yes."

"And who can you go to for comfort and counsel? Do you have to find another minister?"

Bridget's smile grew stronger. "No, I go to my husband. He's a tower of strength."

Joyce was aware that many of her vague conceptions about the clergy were being revolutionised. Here was a married woman who had shown her own weakness – and she was a minister. Without thinking she said, "I didn't know woman ministers could marry."

"Why not?" flashed Bridget. "Men can."

"I know. It's just, well, there's a given role for a minister's wife. What does a minister's husband do?"

"Mine's a teacher. No, I know what you mean. Everyone wonders about that, including Ian. When we were first married, I used to tell him he had to be like Dennis Thatcher and carve out his own role. He's not the only one in that situation."

A short silence fell while Bridget sipped her wine. "In the middle of the afternoon – I feel so decadent," she giggled. Then she glanced curiously at the younger woman. "How often were you in Miss Murdoch's flat?" she asked.

"Every day, ever since I began taking in the milk."

"But these weren't proper visits, were they? I mean, you didn't sit down and talk every day, surely?"

"Oh no. We never talked in the mornings, only if we met each other later in the day. Why?"

"I just wondered how well you knew Miss Murdoch, that's all."

"I told you when I phoned that I didn't know her well. I didn't even know anything about her family. You did."

"Yes, but I didn't know her well either. I always wanted to ask her all about herself, but she wasn't the kind to invite personal conversation, was she?" Bridget dropped her gaze. "I couldn't help noticing a shelf full of notebooks when I was in her bedroom. The spines are labelled with years, starting at 1930. I think they're her diaries. I was never in the bedroom before, of course. Did she ever mention them to you?"

"No never. Did you look at them?"

"Of course not! Though I admit the thought crossed my mind. They would be so very interesting."

"Well, they might be. That depends what she wrote. Do you want to go and see? They might be full of sex and scandal!"

"Joyce!" Bridget protested, laughing. "No, I don't want to go and see. Well, I'd like it, as I said, but it wouldn't be right. We certainly wouldn't do such a thing when Miss Murdoch was alive. No, I just wondered if you knew anything about her life. She was such a steadfast Christian lady that I'm sure something specific must have happened to bring her to her faith."

"Well, if you won't look and see, you'll never know, will you?"

"No, I won't. Oh well, I must be off. I'm glad I got to meet you, Joyce. Shall I let you know about the funeral?" And Bridget had taken herself off.

It was only minutes later that Joyce had found the key of Miss Murdoch's flat, still in her pocket. Without giving the matter even half a thought, she slipped downstairs, into the bedroom, and took the first of the notebooks off the shelf. Soon she was absorbed in it, reading on from page to page with exultation. The young Charlotte Murdoch had been neither patient nor pious. That minister had been so sure of herself and her parishioner. She must let her see these thoughts some day.

Melville blinked out at the darkness. Joyce's sitting room looked out into the back garden, and all that could be seen was the remorseless radiance of a few distant streetlights, glimpsed between houses. His reflection stared back into the room, sombre, and slightly exasperated. Her neighbours all seemed to be out. It was Friday night. He wouldn't mind being out somewhere himself. But first, he knew, Joyce would have an apology. He turned back towards the room.

"I'm sorry I tried to interfere," he said, trying and failing to meet her eyes. "You know how stupid I can be about respecting your autonomy. I'm trying though."

Joyce gave him a charming smile. "Dear Alex, you give me

hope. The leopard can change his spots, if given enough time to do so."

Relieved, Melville grinned back. "And become what? A tiger, all stripes, or a lion with no marking?"

"No, no. A lovely, cuddly kitten." Joyce was laughing now. "Thank you for coming round. Have you been busy today?"

"Yes, but in the wrong way. I've not been busy designing lovely houses, as I'd like. No, I'm tired and out of sorts because I've been trying to persuade people to use my services." He sighed then shrugged. "It's just the usual story. But your day was anything but normal. Why don't we go off to Kate's for a quiet drink and you can tell me all about it."

"I've told you before, it's not called "Kate's" any more."

"Never mind, it was Kate's when I first went there, and when I met you there. So it will always be Kate's to me."

Joyce turned to pick up her jacket. Over her shoulder she quipped, "I am a man; I am set in my ways; I cannot face change."

"Right. So don't you ever get tired of me, Joyce. Because I'm going to keep coming to see you anyway."

He pulled her into his arms and kissed her brown, wind-blown hair. Then hand in hand they left the flat. At the bottom of the stairs Joyce paused. "We never locked this front door because Miss Murdoch always said she would hear if anyone opened it. But I'd better use the Yale now." In the faint light of moon and streetlight she looked up at Alex. "This is one change I really hate," she whispered.

Sunday morning sunshine blazed through the stained-glass windows of Martyrs Church, dropping rainbows into the dust motes that hung over the empty pews. Splashes of faint colour painted the woodwork and stained the milk-white linen of the communion cloth. The elder on duty finished polishing the sacramental silver and began laying the elements ready on the table. In the centre was a large loaf of bread, which he carefully turned over and cut nearly through on the underside, so that the cut would not show on the top, but it could be easily torn in two. This he placed on the platter, with smaller plates standing beside it, ready to receive the divided body. Flanking these were about two hundred tiny glasses for wine, stacked in special trays. In the sunshine the wine glowed like the blood it represented. The elder smiled. Today at least it would be proper communion, not the monthly informal gathering after the main service, but the quarterly pomp of black-suited elders and solemn propriety. It was proper communion with real wine and none of the grape juice nonsense: he had seen to it himself. He knew that the minister had her reasons for preferring to serve the non-alcoholic stuff, to do with not putting temptation before any alcoholics present (and you certainly couldn't tell who that might be: alcoholics were not all down-and-outs: he knew that). But still, he liked the old ways. He also liked Bridget McKay, though at one time he had been loud in condemning her call to the church – a woman! But they had long since made their peace.

"Dr. Marr." He jumped. Bridget had come in quietly.

"Good morning, my dear. How are you today?"

Bridget winced. She hated his paternalism, although she tried hard not to hear it as patronising. At least he was speaking to her now, and speaking kindly. There had been a time when James Marr had been unable to acknowledge her presence. This was a positive change, she reminded herself. Positive.

"To be honest, I'm a little tired. It's been a busy weekend, what with the Sunday School teachers training yesterday and

Miss Murdoch's funeral to think about as well. However, at least no one can say my job's boring!" She smiled brightly. There, she thought, I've managed to be honest, vulnerable and cheerful. She wasn't sure that she really liked James Marr, and consequently bent over backwards to be more than civil to him.

"Miss Murdoch, aye." The elder squinted up at the sunshine, careful not to catch Bridget's eye. "I suppose you think I was a wee bit harsh with that girl who found her." He paused, but before Bridget could think what to say, went on, "You'd be right. I was. But Charlotte Murdoch was good to me once, and I didn't like seeing her dead and lying in such an undignified way." He cleared his throat explosively. "Maybe what I said wasn't fitting in a church Elder."

Recovering her wits, Bridget reassured the man. Then she moved to the pulpit and checked that everything was in order: order of worship, hymn book, Bible open at the proper place, visual aids for the children's talk and notes for the sermon. Satisfied, she returned to the vestry to prepare for worship, while Dr. Marr went to unbolt the front door and ensure that the ushers knew what they were doing. Some of them were just young students, after all. Could they really be trusted to smile and give everyone a hymnbook?

The sermon was over, thank goodness. Bridget loved her church, but she hated to preach with the sun in her eyes. It stopped her seeing the faces and read their expressions which was so useful in helping her gauge her communication. Had they understood this point? Should she repeat it? Did they see this irony? Did they mark this application? She looked forward to the grey days of winter.

"We worship God with our offerings, in dedication of which, let us pray." A rustle, a shuffle, a couple of coughs. As the elders took up the money a cloud came over the sun, and in the sudden dim clarity, Bridget saw a woman slip into the sanctuary and look around her helplessly. It was Joyce Cunningham, Miss Murdoch's tenant, and obviously she was unused to church. Bridget looked around for someone who would take care of Joyce. She would like to go and greet her herself, but that would only embarrass Joyce and shock the congregation. Ah! One of the young ushers had seen her. Even better, he was going to sit with her. Some of these students were worth their weight in gold. The organ finished playing, the offering was brought forward in bulging red velvet bags, and the service proceeded.

The sun had re-emerged from behind ominous October clouds when Bridget came out of the church and stood on the steps, shaking hands with the retreating congregation. She kept a weather eye open for Joyce and she smiled, greeted and questioned. Eventually the flow of people slowed down. Last in, first out was a pattern which Bridget had come to look for, but in this case it hadn't applied. She'd seen no sign of Joyce, and there was no other door open. Eventually she bade farewell to Dr. Marr and locked the doors. She must have slipped out behind someone tall or wide.

"Reverend McKay." The voice was soft and hesitant. Bridget turned. There was Joyce, in the doorway between sanctuary and vestibule. Seen close to, Bridget noticed how smartly she was dressed, in a short-skirted, long-jacketed black suit with a crisp cream blouse beneath. Her high-heeled black shoes gleamed, as did her matching handbag.

Bridget suppressed a smile. On Friday Joyce had been in jeans and a bright-coloured jersey. In dressing up for church she had overdone it, making herself far smarter than the other worshippers, and thus revealing both her nervousness and her unfamiliarity with "ordinary" worship. She was dressed for a wedding, or, more likely, a funeral.

"Joyce," she replied, warmly. "I thought I had missed you. I'm glad you waited, because I want to speak to you. In fact, I had been planning to come to Windmill Road this afternoon."

"I wanted to see you too," said Joyce, examining her fingernails. "I wondered when the funeral will be for Miss Murdoch."

"On Tuesday morning, at eleven. Will you be able to come?"

Joyce still didn't look up. "Yes, thank goodness, I'm free then." She hesitated. "I'm sorry I was late for church this morning. I felt so rude and stupid coming in half-way through things." Suddenly she looked up and smiled. "I didn't mean to miss your sermon."

"I wouldn't blame you if you had. But really, no one would notice you coming in – except me, of course, since I was looking that way."

"Daniel Jardine noticed."

"You know Danny?" Bridget was surprised.

"He was one of the students I tutored on Friday. He's heard my views on objectivity and how an anthropologist mustn't have personal beliefs, but he was good enough not to seem obviously surprised at my turning up here." Another smile. "Better Daniel than Dr. Marr! I saw him gathering up hymnbooks at the end, but I managed not to attract his attention."

Now Bridget laughed. "If he did see you, he was probably as anxious to avoid a meeting as you could be. I gather he's sorry for Friday's outburst.

They were back in the sanctuary, and Bridget ran up to the pulpit to gather her papers and books. "It's amazing how things disappear if I leave them in the pulpit. You'd think it might be the one place where they'd be safe from prying eyes. All sorts of people are in the building all week, and I sometimes think everyone comes up here to imagine themselves preaching instead of listening – or sleeping."

"Perhaps," whispered Joyce.

"What? Speak up!" Then seeing Joyce's face, "Really, it's all right; you needn't whisper in here." She saw the way Joyce was looking at her. "Do you want to come up here? You get a fine view."

Suddenly Joyce seemed to relax. Gaily she ran up the steps and slipped into the pulpit. "Wow, you must feel so powerful up here! I bet that's why people come up, to get that feeling of authority and control."

Bridget looked troubled. "You're probably right. When I first came here, I wanted to preach from the communion table down there. I didn't want to wear robes either. But it was made clear to me that certain things just wouldn't do. Perhaps I should have stuck to my guns. This pulpit may make me look powerful, but believe me, a church is no autocracy – especially this one."

She seized her piled papers. "Come into the vestry with me while I disrobe. I wanted to ask you about Miss Murdoch," she added over her shoulder, as a startled Joyce began to follow her. "I need anything I can get for her funeral. It seems everyone loved her, but no one knows much about her." Bridget shrugged off her gown and hood and reached up behind her neck to unfasten the Geneva bands and collar. "She was St. Andrews born, in your house, actually, and she had been living there for at least the last thirty years. But she was away from the town for a long time, and no one seems to know where. What did she do with her life? She must have done something – she's that sort of person. I mean she was. She never seemed to waste any time. She would always be there when anything deeded done, and there with practical help: often food. Did you realise that she had no T.V.? She once told me that she had no time to sit and watch; though she liked the radio, because she could listen and do something else at the same time. She was well-read and well-educated, and I got the impression that she was far from conventional, despite her very conventional shell. But it was only an impression. I don't think I really knew her at all, although like everyone else, I liked what I knew."

Joyce shook her head. "You asked me on Friday, and I told you what I knew then. She never spoke about herself, though she liked to know about me. I don't mean that she was a nosy landlady. It was different than that. She really seemed interested in me as a person. Of course, there are these diaries...."

Bridget sighed. "No, Joyce, it wouldn't be right."

"For you, perhaps," insinuated Joyce. "But I could read them and tell you. I don't believe in life after death, so my conscience wouldn't trouble me. She's dead, after all. Nothing can hurt her now."

"Hurt her? I never thought that there would be anything in her life that she would be hurt by others knowing – why should you think that? I just think it would be an affront to her dignity." By now Bridget had her coat on, ready to leave. "I'd better go. Ian and the kids will have lunch ready. What's going to happen to your flat? Do you know?"

Joyce shook her head. "Believe it or not that question only occurred to me this morning. I'm going to Macpherson's the solicitors tomorrow to ask. I know that my lease was drawn up by them, so they should know."

It had not been her own idea to contact the solicitors. In a phone call that morning Sandy Melville had raised the question of Joyce's tenancy and suggested she try the solicitors who drew up the lease. But there was no need to go into all that now.

A remorseless ringing wakened Joyce the next morning. Without opening her eyes, she stretched out a hand to the alarm clock and pressed down the button. The ringing continued. Slowly it dawned on her sleep-fuddled brain that it was the telephone. Her first reaction was to pull the duvet over her head. Monday was her day for sleeping late, a weekly indulgence in a disciplined existence. The telephone was still ringing. She opened one eye to a slit and observed the sunshine edging round the thick green curtains. Her clock showed 9.05 a.m. Sighing, she reached for the phone.

"Hello?" She made no attempt to sound other than sleep and cross.

"Miss Cunningham?" The female voice was horribly alert. "Is this Miss Joyce Cunningham?"

"Ms," growled Joyce. "Yes."

"Good morning," the voice chirped brightly, "This is Fiona from Macpherson's the solicitors. We were wondering if you could come and see us this morning. We have something to tell you."

"Can't you just tell me and save both our time?"

"I'm afraid not, Miss Cunningham."

"Ms."

"Yes, well, I'm sorry, but I'm only the receptionist. Mr Macpherson will need to see you himself. He will be free in half an hour, if you're not busy yourself then."

"And if I am?"

"Oh, I don't know. His diary's really full today, but I've cancelled his 9.30 appointment so that he can see you. He said it was most important. You can come, can't you?"

"Very well." Joyce gave in but made sure she sounded grudging. "I'll re-arrange things and be there at 9.30 or soon after." She liked that "re-arrange things". No need to say that all she would be altering was her projected time of rising. All the same, she had planned to see the solicitors herself that day. She wondered what was the significance of their summoning her. Surely they wouldn't be asking her to move out already, before the funeral had taken place? As always, she had left a mug of strong coffee in the microwave, just waiting to be re-heated. Hurrying into her clothes she gulped this down and began to feel the stimulant taking effect on her sleepy mind, so that she remembered to take the front door key and her lease agreement with her.

It was another fine autumn day and the grey town seemed to glow golden as the sun gleamed on richly turning trees and glinted from windows. Hurrying up the hill towards the bus station Joyce turned as she always did, and took in the view of the sparkling, white-flecked sea, and the velvet greens of the Old Course. But today she didn't linger over the prospect. The town Church clock was already striking the half hour, and she was going to be late for the busy, important Mr Macpherson.

Later that morning the phone rang in Bridget's manse. Even as Joyce had, so did Bridget will it to be silent and go away – in vain. Monday was her day off. There was no long lie for her, as for Joyce, however, because the children and Ian needed to be up and on their way as usual. In theory Ian could handle this, and indeed his idea had been that Bridget should have a long lie on Mondays. But it had never worked. Bridget, as she had explained carefully to her husband, didn't have it in her to lie in bed, listening to the daily pre-school rush and panic, and not try to help. By the time the phone rang she had a washing hanging out to dry, had cleaned and tidied upstairs, and had done half of the dusting downstairs. By lunch-time her housework should be completed, and she had a new Colin Dexter novel awaiting an afternoon of leisure.

But first the phone had to be answered.

"Hello, Martyrs Manse."

"Oh Reverend McKay, is that you? This is Joyce Cunningham." Her voice sounded breathless and excited.

"Joyce, how are you?"

"I'm fine, I'm wonderful. I've just been seeing Mr Macpherson, the solicitor.

"And is the flat still yours?" asked Bridget, hoping to expedite the conversation.

"Oh yes. Miss Murdoch left an amazing will. She said her estate was to go to various charities – I think your church was one of them – but that no money was to be divided until the house was sold. And then she added an appendix to say that the house was not to be sold until I wish to move. The solicitors can put someone into the lower flat, and I'll go on paying the same rent to them, so her money can keep earning interest."

"Well, that's very satisfactory. Charlotte was a very practical person."

"Yes, I thought you'd like to know that. But there's something else. Let me read it to you – Mr Macpherson gave me a copy. *'I have travelled in several parts of the world and seen many wonderful things, and, more importantly, people. I leave all my diaries, excepting the first volume which is to be burned unread, to Miss Joyce Cunningham, my tenant, in hopes that they may help her in her anthropological studies..'* Reverend McKay, there are piles of them. I'm so excited. And also, I wondered if you'd like a look at them. It can't be wrong now that she's given permission. Perhaps you'd like to skim over some pages before the funeral?"

"Oh Joyce, that's great! I don't have much time, though. Could I come round this afternoon and maybe dip into a volume or so?" All thoughts of Inspector Morse were gone.

"That would be fine by me. I'll look out for you – about two?"

June 14th 1934 Cologne

I travelled here from Bonn yesterday. Another charming mediaeval city, quite dominated by its cathedral. My Gasthaus is Die Vogel, which seems a strange name. It is hard to imagine a Scottish boarding house with such an airy, non-descriptive name. I asked the Hausfrau, Frau Kellner, why it was so named, but she couldn't say. Apparently the name came with the building when her husband bought it. It doesn't come from "time immemorial" though, as the building can't be more than sixty years old. Having been introduced to my small room, my cynical thought is that perhaps it refers to the guests. Are we seen as small captives in tiny cages singing, or paying, for our supper? Probably I'm being fanciful now.

Frau Kellner was most insistent that first of all I should see the cathedral. I told her I would rather see people, because that's why I'm travelling. But she persisted, and it wasn't worth the fuss and disappointment if I returned to Die Vogel without going. So off I went to the Dom, consoling myself that there would be plenty of people there.

There were.

The cathedral itself is, of course, a majestic building. It soars, Gothically, to the sky. The windows are miracles of twisted lead and coloured glass. The interior has the chill echo of holiness and the alien odour of incense and candle-ends. What can I say? It's magnificent, but it hasn't taught me to like churches. It is a superb example of human skill and vision, but it didn't show me God. I stood in the nave and looked at the beauty rioting around me, and all I could hear was Mother. "You must go to church Charlotte. Such a naughty, ungrateful girl needs to confess her sins to God. Sit still and don't wriggle, Lottie; God doesn't like little girls who squirm. Be grateful that you have a church to go to, Lottie; many little girls run wild on a Sunday." On and on went the voice. I took a quick look round for details to mention to Frau Kellner and marched back to the human bustle of the city.

The bustle seemed centred on the market-place and the cafés that surround it. I sat at one with a genteel cup of tea, absorbing the atmosphere in lady-like seclusion. The I remembered that Mother is dead and I am mistress of my own destiny, and I crossed the square to a livelier – rowdier, Mother would have said – café and had a wonderful frothy mug of beer, my first ever. It was a little strange at first. My taste-buds are used to cold liquids either tasting of nothing (water) or being very sweet. The beer wasn't sweet, though it wasn't savoury either. I don't have wide enough gastronomic experience to make comparisons, so that if I ever come across a similar taste I shall no doubt say, "It tastes like beer." Beer has joined sweet, sour, bitter, spicy, and bland as a generic descriptive word.

June 17th, Cologne

Sunday. Church bells filled the air. I still find it hard not to go to church on Sunday, habit being so strong. Up until today I've never been to a service since Mother's funeral, but it has been a battle. Today I decided I'd made the break too quickly; my Pavlovian conscience can't cope. It may be better to go to church once in a while, even (especially) if it means being bored to tears.

So I saluted the bells cheerfully and went down to breakfast in my most respectable dress, a hat and white gloves. Frau Kellner obviously approved. Indeed it had been worth dressing up just to see her beaming like an ecstatic Dutch doll. To add to her pleasure I asked her advice as to where I should attend worship. To my horror she advised the Dom. "Ach nein" I protested. I'd been there. I'd rather go somewhere more "gemütlich". But she was adamant. Today, the Dom. Normally she would take me to her own little church, but today the Reichsbischof was preaching in the cathedral. Indeed she was going there herself.

I managed to avoid going with her. Certainly the Dom was packed out. My seat was at the end of a pew in the middle of the nave. It was only after I was seated that I noticed a small Nazi flag hanging near the pulpit. I don't think it was there before.

The service, contrary to expectation, was not boring. It was too terrible for that. Terrible. It struck me with terror – not full-blown, because this is not my country – but terror none the less. The music was splendid, at times aethereal, at times triumphant, but always shiveringly good. But Ludwig Muller, the Reichsbischof, made me shiver too. He's a middle-aged man, and obviously intelligent. He read the "Scripture" from a version of Matthew's Gospel he's currently translating. "Blessed are the Aryan in spirit, for theirs is the kingdom of God."

Then he preached. He preached on the idea of the promised land. In a few unemotional sentences he informed us that the Jews were wrong to claim God's promise for themselves. Hadn't God scattered them over the earth and even taken their land from them? Besides, Israel was never the promised land – a desert like that? No, the temperate climate and fertile, varied landscape of the Fatherland , this is what God give the people who delight him.

Looking around, no one seemed to disagree.

Now, hours later, I am still shaken. Why? I know that he was corrupting the ancient Christian traditions, but I have never adhered to the Christian faith, because my life has been meshed in its cloying bondage. So why should I worry that some German bishop comes along with a new interpretation?

The answer, I think, is because it is this interpretation. This is dangerous, because it is giving people a right to do anything they want in the name of their country. As a foreigner I am offended and afraid. I dislike religion, but I do not deny its power. Indeed, much of my dislike is caught up in my understanding that it is a powerful force in the world. Is Nazism a new religion? I hadn't thought of it that way, but now I must look closer and see. I must become an anthropologist, trying to understand the world that I meet. As an anthropologist I shall attend religious services, for I can do that while preserving my intellectual distance. As an anthropologist I shall ask the questions that I want answered. After all, words can't hurt me.

The lamp shone on two heads, one brown and smooth, the other fair and curly. As they read the pages together the silence in the room was absolute. Now Joyce turned her head and watched Bridget's troubled face.

"An anthropologist? Is that why she was faithful to your church, Reverend McKay?"

"We are gathered here today to mourn the passing and celebrate the life of Charlotte Murdoch. We have all known her, and in knowing her have had our lives enriched. We are here because Charlotte Murdoch gave to us: she gave time, advice, confidence, and love. As someone said to me coming into the church today, 'When God made Miss Murdoch, he broke the mould. She was the last of the great ladies.' We must hope she wasn't the last, but certainly she was a lady, and indeed she showed herself to be great."

Bridget's voice was sombre, and she spoke slowly, giving her words time to penetrate and linger in the minds of the people. The church was almost full, and many of those present were unknown to the minister. Because there was no known family, she had taken it upon herself to greet people as they arrived at the church. No one had claimed to be a relation.

Joyce was there, sitting near the back, once more dressed in her smart black suit. Her face showed only a decorous sorrow. Inside she was marvelling at herself: twice in church within a week. Strangely, she wished that Alex was there. Why was this? Allowing her mind to depart from the funeral service she considered the question. She wasn't bowed down with grief, though she was sorry she couldn't talk with Miss Murdoch, especially now that she was reading her life-story. And Alex had never met the woman. And she wasn't in love with him, of course, because, well, she wasn't. She didn't want him with her twenty-four hours a day, so why did she want him now? Leaving the question, she returned to the service. Would the Reverend McKay – Bridget – refer to what they'd read in the diaries?

"We all knew Miss Murdoch, but how well did we know her? Probably many of you know that she was born here in St. Andrews, in the very house where she also died. But what did she do with her life between? Did you ever wonder? I did. It's only since her death that I've learned that she was a traveller and a student of human behaviour. Hers was not a placid domestic life, nor was her mind calm and accepting. Miss Murdoch was a lover of adventure, physical, mental, and spiritual. These adventures are what went to make her the great lady the great Christian lady, that we knew."

Was there a slight emphasis on the word "Christian"? Did Bridget glance at Joyce as she made this statement? Perhaps.

After the service was over, Bridget found Joyce. "Are you coming to the graveside?"

"No, I think that's a little bit too 'Christian' for me," replied Joyce, meaningly.

Bridget was not stupid. "Joyce, I can't stop now to talk, but I really want to talk to you and ask a favour of you. Can I come round tonight?"

"O.K. I'll expect you Reverend McKay."

"Bridget."

"Yes, well, see you tonight."

It was another grim day in the architects" office. By 3 p.m. there was nothing left for Sandy Melville to do. He had made all the phone calls he could think of. He had read papers and journals, seeking a project for which he might offer a design. There was a house being built to his plans a few miles away, but he had been there on Thursday, and couldn't pretend, even to himself, that he need go again so soon. Besides builders know that an architect who is too often at the site is an architect without enough to do, and the word soon gets round. Sandy sighed and reached for Friday's paper, to bin it. It was time to stop fooling himself; he wasn't making it on his own. There was only enough work for one in this office, and he wasn't the one it came to. He retrieved the paper from the bin and turned to the recruitment pages with a sigh. Sometimes reality is very bitter.

He didn't want to move away. The Melvilles were an old Cupar family, not landed or rich, but respectable. For generations they had been labourers on various farms in the district. Now some of these farmlands had been built on, while others had been amalgamated into larger, labour-efficient enterprises, specialising in vegetables or soft fruit. Alexander, Sandy's grandfather and namesake, had been the first of the family to leave the land. He had apprenticed himself to a grocer in Kirkcaldy, but after a few years had returned and opened a small shop in Cupar. It had prospered, and Alexander Melville had been able to buy one of the town's large, yellow sandstone houses, overlooking the park, not far from what had then been an active cattle-market. There his son, James had been born, James who had become a solicitor and was now on the point of retiring. The senior Alexander still lived in that yellow house, accompanied now by his grandson, whom he, like the rest of the family and all his friends, called Sandy.

It was a happy arrangement. Sandy needed to be away from his parents in order to preserve tranquil family relationships. He had spent several years in Edinburgh, doing his training, and though he had never wanted anything but to come home to Cupar, he knew he could not adapt himself to being the son of the house once more. He had begun to look around for a suitable flat of his own, quietly, so that he might present his parents with a fait accompli. But he had reckoned without his grandfather.

There was nothing that went on in the former county town about which Alexander Melville was ignorant. "Or nothing that matters, about the people who belong here," the old man would say, with deliberate snobbery. He was still a well-known and well-respected figure in the town. So when Sandy put in a quiet inquiry about flats at the other solicitors' – not his father's – it was only normal that Mr Morrison should telephone Mr Melville and let him know. Mr Morrison claimed that he couldn't get hold of Sandy at his number – "Which is good, if it means he's busy, Mr Melville," and asked his grandfather to tell Sandy of a flat which he thought might suit.

Old Alexander asked about the flat then got hold of his grandson. "You can't stay in a little box like that, Sandy," he blustered. "The walls are made of cardboard – the roof too, I expect – and there wouldn't be room to swing a cat." The old man's snobbery was offended. He hadn't bettered himself and given the family status to see his grandson go all down-market on him. So he proposed that Sandy move in with him. "I'll tell your mother that I don't like to be alone, so she'll think you're doing me a favour. That way she'll raise no objections.

The house is big enough that we need only share kitchen and bathroom, so we can both be independent old – and young – men. You will pay me rent, of course, and get your own phone line." Sandy's grandmother had died when he was nine years old.

Mr Melville had met Joyce. It had not been a success. Joyce had assumed that to be old was to be a bit slow, mentally as well as physically, and what she intended as kindness unfortunately came across as condescension. Alexander Melville, on his part, put the girl down as a superior fool. The conflict was made verbal over the younger Alexander's name. Joyce, as ever, called him Alex. When they were alone together for a few minutes, Mr Melville challenged her.

"Why do you call him Alex? His name's Sandy, always has been."

Joyce smiled brightly. "But his name's Alexander, isn't it?" She patted Alex/Sandy's knee.

"Lassie, you don't understand. He is Sandy. He was christened Alexander, of course, but that was because he is Sandy. He was, even then. What's wrong with giving him his name?"

"But I am giving him his name, in a different way." Her smile was still determinedly bright. "Alex is the name of the man I know. You know Sandy. It probably means he relates to each of us in different ways, which is good. After all, you're his grandfather."

"And you are what?"

"His girlfriend. Don't worry, I shan't ask Alex to renounce his other names or the people who gave him them. But Alex is such a lovely name – crisp, decisive, modern, adaptable, cosmopolitan."

"Aye, I've known foreign girls called Alex. Who are you, miss, to reject who Sandy has always been? Who are you to try to make him give up his Scottish name for something with no roots? I suppose you want to change who he is, too?"

The conversation and the visit had ended there, with Joyce unwilling to upset the "poor old man" any more. But ever after Mr Melville had referred to her as "that damn condescending, posturing, rootless female."

All of this went through Sandy's mind as he sat scanning the jobs listed in "The Scotsman". He was sorry about the misunderstanding, but he wouldn't stop seeing Joyce, which was what his grandfather wanted; nor would he stop living in the family home, which, he suspected, Joyce would like, although she had never said so. Joyce attracted and intrigued him. She wasn't like other girls he had known, who had all been over-eager to please him. Sandy had always known he was attractive, but Joyce didn't fawn over him; rather, she challenged him. She made him think through and defend his opinions; she lost her temper and shouted at him; she laughed at and with him. There was no predicting her, which was part of the challenge. Unspoken at the back of his mind was the idea that he would never know her well enough to second-guess her. He hoped not, as the challenge of her personality was stimulating.

She was physically attractive as well. Sandy loved the snap in her grey eyes, the way her thick, wavy hair was held off her face by an Alice band. He liked her figure, especially her knees, and he sometimes thought he could hear the music of the sea in her voice. So far, they had not slept together. He wanted to, of course, but was also afraid of it. With Joyce, who was such an intensely vibrant person, making love would surely signify a great depth of commitment. More than with other girls he had known, Sandy was sure it would change their relationship for ever. He knew that relationships must change as they grew, but he was still delighted with where they were. What Joyce thought on this matter, he didn't know. But if she wanted to sleep with him, she would probably say so.

No, Sandy didn't want to change things with Joyce. But if he moved away, even to Edinburgh, they would change, because he simply wouldn't see her so often. Perhaps he could find a job in Dundee, that would be commutable. He closed the paper with a sigh. There were no jobs for him anywhere that he could see. It was a pity he wasn't an accountant, or a sales rep. as they seemed to be in demand everywhere. Never mind, Tuesday was one of his evenings with Joyce, and perhaps something would turn up tomorrow.

"I feel like Mr McCawber," he thought with a smile and brief remembrance of English classes as school. Then Hargreaves blew into the office, and Sandy had to concentrate on looking pleased about his partner's busyness.

When he arrived in Windmill Road, the lights from Joyce's flat shone out warm and welcoming. This time the front door was unlocked and gave its familiar screech as he forced it open. "It's only me!" he called out, bounding up the stairs and reaching the door just as it opened. Joyce stood framed in the entryway, the lamplight behind her creating an aureole around her, burnishing her hair and displaying her long, slim legs beneath a short skirt. Sandy bent to kiss her, but she peered round him.

"Is it just you, Alex?" she asked.

Taken aback, he said, "Who else should it be?"

"Bridget – Reverend McKay. She said she'd come round this evening. No doubt she'll be here soon."

Now she turned to face him and reached up to kiss him. Sandy smiled. All would be well.

It was half an hour later when Bridget appeared, long enough for Joyce to tell Sandy of what had been said at the funeral, and a little of how it had made her feel. Sandy was intrigued by the whole thing and found himself very much looking forward to meeting the minister. When she arrived, he was struck chiefly by the apprehensive look on her face. What had she to be nervous about? Joyce introduced Sandy to her, somewhat apologetically.

"I hope you don't mind. Alex and I always meet on Tuesdays, but I'm afraid I had forgotten that when I spoke to you earlier.

"I'm delighted to meet Alex," smiled Bridget, a little absently. Turning to Joyce she continued, "But really, Joyce I must explain to you about the service today. I could see your face, you know, and it seemed to me that you weren't happy when I said that Miss Murdoch was a "great Christian lady"?

"Well, I did wonder if you were giving people what they wanted to hear, at the expense of the truth. You did read these pages from her diary."

"I did, and I don't mind telling you they were shocking to me. Not shocking in an abstract way, but I was appalled that I could be so ignorant of one of my own parishioners. I couldn't believe that her piety was simply a self-imposed watching brief."

"But whether you were shocked or not, shouldn't you have told people the truth? Wasn't it unfair to Miss Murdoch that she be misrepresented at her own funeral?" Bridget sighed and looked away from Joyce's flushed face towards the dark mirror of the un-curtained window.

"I knew you would take it that way. Listen, Joyce, that's more or less how I thought myself at first. But then I put my own reactions aside, my shock and my instinctive defence of a "truth" and thought again. Would Miss Murdoch want to be exposed as the chiel amang us making notes? I don't know anyone who experienced her as anything other than a gracious Christian." She turned bright eyes back to Joyce again. "And that means one of two things. Either her "cover" was impregnable, so that only God would really know whether or not in her heart she was Christian." Joyce fidgeted. "Or else at some time she had a change of heart. That was a diary from 1934 we were reading, after all.

"I liked Miss Murdoch. She was gracious and helpful to me. That may or may not have been a guide to her true character, but it is still a fact. And so, because I liked her, I had no desire to unmask her. If she has been faking us, she has done it very well, and deserves to keep her secret.

"Personally, I don't believe she was fooling us. I believe she underwent a change of heart regarding the Christian faith."

"You want to think that." Joyce sounded sceptical.

"Yes, I do. But I can't prove it. I'm haunted and fascinated by Miss Murdoch now. I took her funeral as I thought she would like, telling what I knew from personal experience: her devotion to her mother, her travel, her neighbourliness, and her piety. But I find I can't bury her and go on. I want to know her better. Joyce, will you let me read the diaries with you?"

"Read them with me? But she left them to me to assist my research. She didn't say anyone else should see them."

"No, she didn't. But she wasn't stupid. I'm sure she was aware that you will hope to publish your research, and so my may be publishing extracts from her writings. If that's the case other people will read them. She was always helpful to me, and if I could read the diaries she could still help me. Besides, I've seen one of them – I suppose it was number two?

"No, it was the first one," said, Joyce, absently.

"The first – you mean after the one which was to be burned?"

"No, it was the first. I saw no point in burning something I had already started to read before the will was explained to me." Joyce lifted her head defiantly. "Say I was wrong if you like, but it's done now – and you've been part of it too."

Bridget looked troubled but said nothing.

"I don't see how reading the diaries would help you, apart from pandering to your curiosity." It was Sandy who spoke, his tone much calmer than his words. Both women started slightly, and he realised that they had been so involved in their conversation that they had forgotten his existence.

Now Bridget looked at him intently, as though she hadn't really seen him before. She paused, considering her words, then nodded slightly as she replied.

"It could help in one of two ways depending on what we discover. If Miss Murdoch was an implacable sceptic all her life then it will be good for me to know it, because it will teach me about the people I minister to. Who knows that there are not other unconvinced observers amongst them? If there are, she may, accidentally, show me how to reach them or how to spot them. That would be useful.

"If, on the other hand, she did convert and become the convinced Christian she seemed, then I really want to hear in her own words how it happened. You see, Alex, I grew up in a Christian home – actively Christian, I mean – and I came to my faith early, as a natural part of growing up. Oh, I've had doubts and questions since then, but I've never been totally sceptical. I don't think I have it in me. I'm not a person with a strong imagination, and I think that's a weakness in my job. It means I'm not good at empathy with those coming at the faith from different perspectives. If Miss Murdoch can show me a personality coming from a different direction it will give me a broader base for my work." She faltered. "I'm not putting this well, but you do see that it's not just idle curiosity?"

Sandy nodded. "Yes, I do. But it's not really my opinion that counts here."

Joyce looked at the two of them and then down at the floor. "I suppose you have a point, Reverend McKay. O.K., you can read them too."

"Please call me Bridget, Joyce, or else I shall have to call you Miss Cunningham. In any case Reverend McKay is an Americanism. The British usage is to talk about me as reverend, but address me as Mrs. But I prefer Bridget. Anything else makes me think you must be cross with me. How shall we do this reading?"

"Can you set aside a couple of evenings a week?"

Bridget made a face. "Not always, I'm afraid."

"Well look, come when you can, and we'll read together. If you don't come for a while, I'll read on then give you the books to catch up on your day off."

Sandy watched the pact being formed and said nothing. In this matter he knew himself to be an outsider. He had long been concerned at Joyce's apparent lack of close friends, and it had puzzled him. She was always open and welcoming to people but seemed to find it hard to get beyond that point with anyone. He had managed it and had done so before he realised quite what a feat had been accomplished (whether by himself or by Joyce he couldn't say). Now it seemed there was a chance for Joyce to make a friend of a woman. Certainly their shared interest and regular meetings would give the opportunity. Looking at Bridget he wondered about her. What sort of woman was she? What sort of person would become a minister, and what sort of woman? Was she a rabid feminist, determined to live in a world that was still traditionally masculine? Was she a religious fanatic? Who else would devote their entire life to the church? Perhaps a control freak, someone hungry for power? He wished he could see past the short, squat figure, the fair curls and blue eyes. Her conversation seemed sensible, but he wished he knew her history and motivations.

If asked, Bridget would have said that her history was simple, straightforward, "rather ordinary really". She was the product of a 'good Christian home', though not of the Church of Scotland. Her parents brought her up with church, family prayers and daily Bible reading as an accepted centre of life. Quite naturally she had come early in life to embrace her parents' religious faith as her own. It wasn't until much later that the Christianity of her parents and her childhood church was not the way in which every self-professed Christian believed. Her upbringing had clung firmly to a literal interpretation of Biblical writings. Her family's morality was what some might have labelled 'Victorian', though, of course, they just thought of it as eternally God-given. "And if it is Victorian" her parents would say, "That simply says that last century's society had a better grasp on eternal truth than we do now." At church the teaching was very much opposed to reducing Christianity to a formula of 'pie in the sky when you die', but for all that Bridget was left in no doubt that the salvation of the soul was immeasurably more important than the needs of the body. She had attended prayer meetings and evangelical rallies. Out of school she had mixed almost solely with like-minded folk, while in school she headed the clique which ran the Christian Union.

Bridget was far from unintelligent, however, and unlike some with whom she mixed, she did not close her eyes to the needs of society around her. Her understanding of the causes of the social problems she witnesses were perhaps naïve, even for her age, but when she left school at eighteen, she knew she wanted to do something to help. And so she had entered the church, idealistically believing that there she could be of use.

At New College in Edinburgh her deeply held theological beliefs – those things to which she clung as self-evident truths – came under attack. Her first year there had not been an easy time, but she had survived, and with integrity. Bridget Wallace (as she was then) had decided carefully to examine her truths against other versions, to see if they stood up. It was probably the bravest thing she had ever done, for she allowed, at least in theory, for the possibility that she might be wrong. A cynical onlooker (of which there were none, for Bridget kept this quest very private) might not have been surprised to find that her beliefs and her approach to her faith came out largely intact. To Bridget it was a vindication and a relief, and it gave her the confidence to pursue her studies, to convince the church boards of her genuine calling, to undertake her various church placements, and to preach her first sermons.

Such was the 'rather ordinary' background of the woman now offering Joyce Cunningham a shared interest, the history behind the professionally cheerful face. Marriage and years of ministry had rounded out her character, but the core of her identity remained unassailed, and her professional modus operandi was still largely tied up in her childhood convictions.

CHAPTER TWO: DIPPING INTO THE DIARY

To go abroad has something of the same sense that death brings. I am no longer of ye – what ye say now of me is of no consequence."   Mark Twain, Notebook.

June 30th, 1934 Schaffhausen.

I arrived here last night, in the dark. The hotel is clean and comfortable, although it was a little startling to be offered cake for breakfast. A more delightful surprise came when I opened my curtains this morning and looked out on a fairy-tale picture of snow-capped mountains, blossoming orchards (although most of the blossom is on the grass by now) and greening fields in between. My room has a balcony, and from it I can hear the sound of rushing water, although I can't actually see the famous Rhein Falls, as they are on the other side of the building and a few hundred yards away.

This is a fantastic country, in the colloquial sense. Now I'm in Switzerland and closer to Austria than before, so I imagine I'm probably in countryside similar to that in which Adolf Hitler (or whatever he was called then) grew up. I don't agree with him in his goals and fanaticism, but this land does something to me. I can see why it might be called a chosen land. And if I take into consideration the whole of Germany, then it seems to have almost everything: great rivers, mountains, flat, fertile plains, rolling hills and valleys full of vineyards, lakes, forests, stately cities and charming towns and villages. It also has a proud, though short, history – short as a unified country, I mean. It is a land to stick up for and be glad to belong to, objectively I can see that. And the people have used the resources well. There are great factories, exquisite china and pottery, good sensible farming and famous beers and wines. I could love such a land.

But I begin to think there is little genuine affection and contentment. It seems to me that if you scratch below the surface of an urbanely smiling German face, you will find either someone greedy for more wealth, land and glory, someone fanatical; or else you will meet a person disturbed by the official and popular distortion of all that the country has been. There seems to be no comfortable, reasonable pride left, just vainglory or 'angst' – that superbly descriptive German word.

Both viewpoints, as I am discovering, claim religious backing.

The so-called Christianity of Nazism was made plain to me in Cologne, when I attended the cathedral. On my journey yesterday I met with the other view, one that is less openly voiced.

When I boarded the train at Cologne I was fortunate to find a compartment to myself. The train was unusually quiet, but a couple of stops further on a grey-haired man in a greenish suit entered my compartment. He had a lot of luggage with him, and I helped him haul it aboard and settle it. While we were thus occupied he realised that I am a foreigner, and as the train pulled out we fell into conversation. I should have liked to ask him why he had all his baggage with him, instead of entrusting it to the guard's van, but I feared such an enquiry might be rude, and might give the impression that I was complaining about its presence in the compartment. Instead, I asked him if he knew Bonn, explaining that all I knew of the city was that Beethoven had some connection with it (I believe he was born there). My companion, who never told me his name, told me a little about the city. Being polite, I said it sounded as though it must be as beautiful as other German towns I have visited and complemented him on the scenic nature of his country. (We were at that time travelling beside the great river Rhein with its barges and steamers, and vineyards blanketed the hills on either side.) At that the man told me that in fact he was Swiss not German. He hesitated a little before he indicated his luggage and said he was leaving Germany and returning home to Berne.

How long had he been in Germany?

Twenty years! He had come to do a Doctoral degree in theology and had stayed on to teach.

And now he was leaving?

He looked a little embarrassed and fiddled with a signet ring on his finger. He said that he didn't know if he should talk of it. A pause. But I was a foreigner. Another pause. What did I think of Hitler? The question was almost abrupt, like a change of conversation, but I sensed that for my companion it was relevant.

I explained that I don't like dictators and I don't like fanatics and unfortunately the two often go together. What I should have liked to say, but hadn't the German, was that if a man has sole power in a country, it can only work well for the people if he is broad-minded, intellectual, open to new ideas and always listening to other voices. And then he wouldn't want the power. This is not the way of the fanatic, and it certainly is not Hitler's way. I did say that as a woman I am particularly alarmed at the idea of relegating women to their 'proper' sphere. Kinder, Kirche, Küche, or whatever order they put them in, is a very euphonious slogan, but I have experience of two of the three, and a very dreary bondage I found them.

My answer must have re-assured my companion. At any rate, he told me why he was leaving. He was afraid. He didn't agree with Nazi philosophy and was furious at the 'blasphemies' of

Nazi theology. Had I come across these?

I told him I had, and mentioned Ludwig Müller, the Reichsbischof. He snorted.

He could not, would not teach such diabolical distortions, but – he looked away, the fire dying out of his face – he was afraid to declare this openly and continue teaching the 'truth'.

I told him I wasn't surprised he hesitated to defy the Reich. There are whispers about what happens to those who do. But this failed to console him for what he obviously regarded as a lapse of courage.

"Yes," he said, "I can run away. I am an Auslander. I can take up my life elsewhere. But what of those who cannot?"

I said, what of them? Would they just lie low for a while and see what develops?

Some would, he was sure, and some were so frightened that they might even take the official line. But the great ones would fight. They would fight from their pulpits, from their lecture halls, from their studies. They would write the truth, speak the truth and live the truth. IF their churches and academic posts were taken from them, which is quite likely, yet they would fight.

He lowered his voice. Some of them might even be prepared to embrace violence. Hitler should watch his back. They looked back to the early Christians, persecuted by the Roman Empire; they looked back to Martin Luther and the heroes of the Reformation; they would not show themselves less daring than these, their forefathers.

I began to like my green-suited companion. His admiration for his heroes was simple and wholehearted, and his self-esteem correspondingly low. I tried a tiny piece of mischief. Martin Luther, I repeated, so it wasn't true that the German Christians needed to advance their doctrines to fulfil what Luther had hoped for? This was what I had heard.

"Nein, nein!" The man forgot himself and almost shouted, then looked around him, as though he could see invisible eyebrows raised in adjoining compartments.

I left off teasing him then. He had no sense of humour on this matter, and my German isn't really good enough for levity. I have a good vocabulary, but so much of meaning and comprehension is in intonation, and there I have much to learn. I still speak lamentably Scottish German.

July 6th 1943: Schaffhousen

The past few days I have been travelling around the countryside. When I decided to give myself a 'Grand Tour' I never intended to do the traditional thing and move from city to city. I want the rural parts of Europe to be more to me than simply land through with the train passes. So four days ago, after a leisurely couple of days in the town, spent largely marvelling at the waterfalls – beyond description - I hired a bicycle. It is an ancient thing, quite possibly Edwardian, and very heavy, but it has been well maintained, isn't too rusty and has good brakes. Of course, this is a hilly area, but I have been pleasurably surprised to find that I don't have to get off and push as much as I had expected. The downhills are glorious: much as I imagine a fun-fair ride to be. I've never been to a fun-fair, even though the Lammas Market comes annually to St. Andrews. Mother held it to be 'common' (like so much else that looked like fun) and kept me away.

Perched high on my bicycle, I have been enjoying myself. I still want to understand more of what is happening in Germany, so every day I have crossed back over the border. The guards are used to me by now. I have stopped for lunch by streams. I have turned off the metalled road onto farm tracks and bought milk from sturdy farming women. I have been greeted gaily by men and women working in the hay fields. The women play a large part in the hay-making, in turning the drying grass and stacking it. The actual mowing seems to be a male preserve, and the scythes which the men wield are monsters. All the peasants seem to be clad chiefly in black, which looks heavy and hot for the work and the weather. It is worse for the women, because they can't strip to the waist as some of the men do.

The bicycle was a capital idea for more reasons than one. It makes me mistress of my day, where I go and when; it means I can travel further than I could on foot; it allows me to travel at a speed that is ideal for looking around and seeing things; and not least, it seems to remove the impenetrable wall separating the foreigner from the German. The country people on farms and in villages have been most friendly. I have heard about their lives and their families, their hopes and their beliefs.

There was one farmer's wife, Frau Klammer. She sold me a bowl of warm, frothy milk, fresh from her milk pail, and rested from her labours while I drank it. I admired her farm – the ancient wood-and-plaster farmhouse with troughs of Geraniums in all the windows, the well-raked farmyard, and plump, golden cows standing patiently in the barn, awaiting their milk-maid. Frau Klammer lapped up my admiration like a kitten with a saucer of cream: slightly wary at first, but increasingly relaxed with me, and beaming a gap-toothed smile between dried-cherry cheeks. She looked about fifty.

She agreed with me. Ja, farming was doing well. The cows were flourishing because the fields were doing well indeed, producing good winter feed as well as vegetables and grain for human consumption.

She and her husband must work hard, I said.

Jawohl. But not so hard now as before, nor for so little reward. The years after the War had been schrecklich – dreadful. The price of everything rose with the terrible inflation. They could grow enough to eat, of course, but they had almost nothing over to sell, and what money they could bring in was almost worthless. So their children couldn't afford to work the land and went to the cities but found little work there either. It was a dreadful time. But now...

Now?

Under the Reich things are much better. The inflation has been dealt with and farmers are being reminded of their vital importance to the nation. Some of the rural festivals have been revived: there hadn't been a Blossom Queen in the Schwarzwald since her grandmother's time, but her own granddaughter was crowned in May. The children have come back to the land and the farm has a future again.

She was like a rusty clockwork doll; a little reluctant to perform at first, but once she had started there was no stopping her. The black kerchief on her head jerked up and down like a moorhen's tail as she nodded her head, emphasising her points.

Her kitchen was a tribute to her, with scrubbed floor and table, worn, comfortable wooden chairs, a large range for cooking, a dresser displaying her 'best' dishes and a whole foundry of ironware hanging amid hams and onions from the rafters. As I left Frau Klammer returned to the byre. I could hear her singing at her work as I closed the gate behind me.

Another day I ate my lunch sitting in a hay field with Hans, a real blond Aryan of twelve or so, who was taking a break from tossing and turning the cut grass to allow the sun to dry it. He was fascinated to meet a foreigner, which he claimed was a new experience for him.

Has he really never seen anyone from outside Germany? He lived near Switzerland and Austria. Had he never met anyone from over the border?

Ah, but they didn't count. They weren't really foreigners, they were part of the Aryan race.

He laughed at little at my German accent, both the pronunciation and the stresses I use. I challenged him: how good was his English?

Another laugh. Why should he learn English? He spoke German, the best language of them all. One day everyone who was important in the world would speak his language too.

As a human being and a non-German I found Hans disturbing, but in my new guise of anthropologist I found him fascinating, almost too good to be true. His beliefs were so fervent and thorough. He was, I soon learned, a member of the Hitler youth movement. "And to wear my uniform is a wonderful thing for me. I know that making hay in the sun I am untidy and not totally clean. But I always keep my uniform properly. It is clean, ironed, and polished. I should be ashamed if it were not so. When I wear my uniform I am not just Hans the hay-maker and farm-worker. I am more than that, more than myself alone. I am Hans, part of the force that is renewing our land and our people."

I would be hard to miss the overtones of ritual, power and even holiness in that speech. If religion is that which gives meaning to life, which answers the 'why' questions, then Nazism is this boy's religion. It would be hard to quarrel with his espousal of his faith. After all, it obviously answers questions for him. It gives him a reason to live and work. It gives him a sense of value and purpose and, so far, is bringing him prosperity.

Even in my short sojourn in Germany I have seen that this National Socialism does not bring prosperity and ease to everyone. People of many races live in this country: now, like my Swiss friend, many are leaving. In particular the Jews who can afford it are going. To be non-Aryan, and obviously non-Aryan, is no good thing in Germany now. I have fair skin, but my hair and eyes are dark, and I have felt questioning looks directed my way on occasion. Businesses of foreigners are flagging as national pride dictates that the patriotic German will prefer to patronise his Aryan compatriot. The Jews, especially, are openly spoken against.

But young Hans is a country lad. He knows no 'real' foreigners, and quite likely has never knowingly met a Jew – they are almost exclusively an urban race. Hans may be ignorant and blinkered, but his religion is perfectly appropriate for him. Perhaps any religious belief requires voluntary (if subconscious) blinkering?

At first Sandy was amused by the intense way in which Joyce devoured the diaries. Tuesday, Thursday and Saturday evenings were their regular dates. Joyce needed other times to study. Sandy needed them to breathe. Now, whenever he arrived in Windmill Road, Joyce's nose seemed glued to a blue-bound volume. Miss Murdoch's handwriting was far from easy, and in places she had economised on paper by crossing her writing or abbreviating. If Bridget wasn't there, Joyce was good about finishing her paragraph and putting the diary aside. They would go and have a quiet drink at "Kate's", take a moonlight walk along the West Sands, or just sit drinking coffee or sipping wine, talking. Joyce kept him posted on Miss Murdoch's adventures and he spoke of the dream buildings he designed in his head, and a little of the difficulties he was running into with the partnership. He still kept to himself the idea that perhaps he would have to move away.

Miss Murdoch's Musings – as Sandy insisted on naming the diaries – he did not find more than mildly interesting. Joyce's passion for them intrigued him far more, as he sought to understand her character; what made life real and exciting for her. When he found Bridget also present in the flat, he was glad to have some idea of what Miss Murdoch had been doing and saying now, as the two women could talk of little else. When they were together, they took turns to read the diaries aloud, calling on the other to help decipher the worst hieroglyphics. His presence rarely caused them to halt their activities. Then when they had finished a session, they had to discuss every nuance of what had been said. Sometimes Sandy suppressed a smile, wondering what Miss Murdoch would say if she could see her musings being analysed and argued over like a definitive literary text. None of the august lecture rooms for the university could have witnessed a more dedicated pursuit of knowledge than was shown in Windmill Road.

Not that the diaries were, strictly speaking, literature. On this the women agreed.

"They aren't consistently written," Joyce pointed out. "Her style changes quite a lot. Sometimes she is quite verbose, as she tackles detailed descriptions of atmosphere as well as surroundings. At other times she records conversations; but often it's mere jottings. It's lively, but it's not literature."

"No, " Bridget was agreeing and disputing at the same time. "It's not literature. She didn't intend it for strange eyes. Real literary literature is written for general consumption."

This was a new idea to Joyce. "Really? Is there no literature that was found later? What about Pepys' diary?"

"How do you know what he hoped? No. he wrote in code, so that won't wash." Bridget was very merry that night, half teasing Joyce. "Well, it's a general guideline, and Pepys is the exception that proves the rule!"

But Joyce was not prepared to discuss the matter flippantly. It was a new idea and as such must be thoroughly explored. "You say literature is written for publication? All such writing?"

"Not really." By now Bridget had learned when to desist from teasing Joyce. "In one sense, yes, in that any group will talk of their own documents as their literature, as in, 'Disseminating our literature to get our ideas across.' But no, what you say about style matters, as, I think, does the appropriateness of the literary method employed to the subject matter being dealt with. But in addition, it should be written in hopes of being read by several people."

Sandy joined in the conversation. "But then, what about the Bible? As I understand it, some of the Old Testament people never wrote a word down. They had no thoughts of publication. Would you say the Bible's literature?"

Bridget thought for a moment. "You know, I've never applied my theory to the Bible before – strange, considering my job! I suppose that I don't primarily think of the Bible in literary terms, because it's more than words on a page to me. But now I come to think of it, I wouldn't deny its claims to be part of literary literature, Alex. After all, some of the various leaders and prophets may have had no thought of publication, as you put it, but someone did. Someone wrote down the words, put them into an acceptable literary form, in the Hebrew tradition. Oh yes, the intention behind the act of writing is quite clear."

"That's foreign literature, though," Joyce said. "Is foreign literature still literary in translation?" I'd say myself that that depends on how it comes out."

"Yes, and I think that most people who talk about the Bible as 'the most wonderful literature' mean King James' Authorised Version. There have been many translations since then. Some I might call literature, but not all of them."

"If foreign literature can become British literature – and presumably vice-versa – a the hands of a good translator, can poor foreign-language writing become literature with superb translation?" asked Sandy.

"Surely not," replied Joyce. "Such a translation, one that polished the original, wouldn't be true to the test, and so, ironically, would be a poor translation."

And so the conversation would continue. Bridget always left by nine, jumping to her feet, shaking back her curls and exclaiming that she must get home and kiss her children before they fell asleep. Sandy wondered what her husband thought of her frequent absences, when her job also caused her to work irregular hours. He wondered, but he didn't ask. The conversation was strictly intellectual, not personal, when they met in Windmill Road.

Sandy didn't read Miss Murdoch's diaries himself. He didn't particularly want to, and, in any case, Joyce never offered him the opportunity. But he kept track of her itinerary and her musings through the conversation. Thus he followed her southwards, out of Switzerland ("mountains and meadows, clocks and cleanliness"), heard of her journey West through the Austrian Tyrol ("These summer months spent in an alpine hut have been the most incredible experience. For the first time I have known real solitude). He followed her through Salzburg and Linz to Vienna.

There are some who say that these are the final months of this city's glory days. Certainly, life is hectic here. There is a sparkle to social gatherings that is stunning and not quite natural. In the coffee-houses, the cafés, the ballrooms, conversation is most hilarious, but with a forced gaiety. It seems that people must make noise, because they fear what they may hear in the silence."

From Vienna it was Sarajevo and then southwards, down the Adriatic coast to Greece. *"Finally, the cradle of civilisation."* The Spring of 1936 was spent travelling in the Greek islands. *"Where I am stared at for my pale skin and smooth hands. I often wonder if I am the first Scot to set foot here, but surely I can't be. After all, there is usually someone around who speaks English."*

In the summer she was in Italy, fleeing North from the heat to explore the Italian Alps and the countryside around Lake

Garda. She found in Mussolini's Italy a different kind of fascism from that of Hitler's Germany. Then in October she went south to Rome. *"I went to St. Peters. It is very impressive, but I wasn't impressed. It is impressive artistically, but ore especially politically. Here is the centre of an organisation whose overt aim is world domination. That is an end I cannot agree with, and so cannot be impressed by."*

From Italy, north to the French riviera for the first months of 1937. *"I'm not a traveller here, I'm a member of a community. I have never been an ex-pat before, just a foreigner. I find there is a great difference. As a foreigner I know myself to be (delightfully) out of place and I enjoy the differences. As an ex-patriot I am drawn into a community which seeks to ignore, no, to eradicate, the differences. Apart from the weather, they want France to be as much like Britain as possible. But their Britain isn't mine, so learning to fit in here is another experience for me."*

One Sunday in November with the rain teeming down, the sea recalling a bowl of dirty washing-up water and the fallen leaves rapidly disintegrating into a lethally slippery brown paste, Sandy and Joyce were talking.

"Do they really help you in your studies, these dairies?" Sandy asked idly.

Joyce laughed. Not directly. No. I mean as an anthropologist she is the most amateurish of amateurs. I'm not sure she had ever read any anthropology. I expect she had heard the term and decided it would sound good to adopt the title. There was no harm in that: after all, she was primarily writing for herself."

Sandy went to the kitchen and filled the kettle. "You will have coffee, won't you? If Miss Murdoch was a poor anthropologist, why do you find her diaries so fascinating? You're obsessed by them."

"No coffee. Herb tea, I think. Camomile if I have any. I think, for me it's the person. It's not good scholarly observation, and – as we agreed the other night – it's not literature; but it is the unfolding of a character."

Sandy brought two steaming mugs into the room. "It sounds like you're reading it like a novel. Unfolding character through circumstance is the novelist's business, isn't it?"

"I suppose I am – that's very sharp of you, Alex." Joyce looked startled as she shot a glance at him. "There's not much story in this novel and the character is fairly self-conscious about finding new experiences and analysing how they affect her, but the character she displays – deliberately and implicitly – is fascinating. She is talking to herself, you see, so she had no need to hide things."

"No need to hide things?" Sandy queried.

"No, Alex, why should she? She would know if she hadn't told the truth, so what would be the point?"

"But Joyce, you're an anthropologist! How can you be so naive? Don't we all hide things from ourselves?"

"Do we?" Joyce allowed the interest to drop from her tones and concentrated on her camomile tea.

"I hope we do! I don't think I'm an innately deceitful person, but I know that I do. At least I know that I have, so I suppose I still do."

"What sort of things?" Joyce asked, with greater interest. She was perhaps hoping that if Sandy talked about himself they could change the subject.

"I don't know. At least, when I was a boy I refused to let myself think that I didn't love my mother. I didn't, and I still don't, but such an idea was horrible to me. I thought it was a given that parents and children did love each other – that it was the normal, natural thing. To admit to myself that I had no love for my mother would have been to face the 'fact' that I was abnormal and unnatural."

"Same thing," said Joyce, smiling.

"Same thing," he agreed. "But the horror was greater than one word could say. I finally faced it when I was away at uni."

"Were there any others?"

"That was a big one. There were others. For years I told myself I was a linguist. I so much wanted to be a cosmopolitan man-of-the-world. I wonder if that's why I let you call me Alex? Anyway, I studied hard at French and German at school, and I got almost nowhere. That was so galling that for a while I had myself convinced that the entire language department at school was dud. That was more acceptable to me than that there was something that I couldn't do."

Joyce was laughing, and Sandy chuckled with her. "I know it's funny, but I'm not unique. What about you? You must have tried a bit of self-deceit yourself."

"Must have?"

Oh, I think so. After all, you are human, Joyce." He saw hostility in her eyes, and was about to back away, but then, on impulse, he went close to her, knelt down in front of her and tucked her hair behind her ear. "Haven't you had any secrets from yourself, Joyce? Are you really an unmysterious woman? You're a mystery to me, at any rate."

Joyce relaxed. She had forgotten what it was to have Sandy pay attention to her, caught up as she had been in Miss Murdoch's story. Reaching down she tweaked his nose. "What do you mean, mysterious? I'm an open book, I am."

"Oh really." He was bantering now, relieved that she had

not flared up or coldly withdrawn from the conversation. "If you're such an open book, why am I so full of questions about you?"

"Well, I don't know. Maybe you're nosy."

"Nosy? I don't think so. You're the one who's usually insatiably curious – though not, I now learn, about the workings of your own mind. No, I'm not nosy, but perhaps I'm more interested than most."

"More interested in?"

"You! You fascinate me, Joyce Cunningham, but half the time I don't know what to make of you." He paused, then, taking a risk, added more seriously, "Why have I never met your family?"

She stopped smiling abruptly. "They're not quite as close at hand as yours, local boy."

"No, Joyce, but really, Pitlochry's not so far away. I have a car. Why don't we go up there some Saturday? I'd love to meet your people, and I'm sure they'd be glad to see you. It must be months since you were last home."

"Over a year, actually."

"What!" Sandy was shocked. "You didn't even go home for Christmas?"

"I don't celebrate Christmas," said Joyce. "And I don't go 'home'. This is my home. Why do you want to meet my family? What have they got to do with you?

"Joyce, they're your family. They gave you both your genetic make-up and your upbringing." Sandy grinned broadly. "Nature and nurture, in fact. I want to know you thoroughly. If I could meet your family I might understand a little of where you've come from to become the person you are now. A terrific person, I may say. Your family can't be so bad if they produced you."

"Oh, can't they?" said, Joyce, darkly. Then she became brisk. "Please don't go on about this, Alex. I'm not on good terms with my family. We haven't quarrelled, but we've nothing to say to each other. That's all there is to it." There was a brief silence, then Joyce added, "Don't you like a little mystery?" The bantering tone had returned.

Sandy rose on his knees till their faces were almost level, leaned across and gave her a quick kiss. "Of course I do, Scheherazade. I'm in this for the trill of the chase. But I'm not afraid of ever catching the fox. There's enough in you to keep discovering forever.

"You're very sure of that," Joyce remarked. She looked around the flat, then glanced at the window. "Look, the rain's stopped. I need some exercise: what about a walk along the West Sands?"

Outside a gusty, cold wind was breaking up the cloud so that sunshine occasionally raced across the beach. The sea was still a dirty grey-brown, and huge waves broke like ruffles of grimy lace before rushing up the sand. There were few people about, and walking away from the town, with little sign of civilisation anywhere, it was easy to imagine yourself somewhere far more barren and remote than civilized North-East Fife. Two miles from the town they were nearing the estuary of the river Eden, when they noticed that they were no longer alone. Ahead of them two kites dipped and trembled in the wind. One was red, a traditional kite-shaped affair, with a yellow tail. Joyce knew from experience that such kites are difficult to fly, but this one was doing very well. Beside it a blue and purple stunt-kite strutted its stuff, like a Kingfisher showing off to a Chaffinch. The shrill yelps of children could be heard, and Joyce perceived that this was a family outing.

Another fifty yards and she realised that the mother of the family was Bridget. These, then, must be Ian and the two children. Joyce found that she didn't know their genders, never mind their names.

She turned to Sandy. "It's Bridget."

"So it is. Hi! Bridget! Reverend McKay!" he yelled.

Bridget turned and waved, then beckoned. Joyce and Sandy approached. Bridget was looking decidedly windswept and happy, not to say unselfconsciously scruffy in the oldest of clothes. She gestured to her husband, tall, fair like herself, but about a hundred percent tidier. Unlike his wife, Ian was thin, but like her he exuded a carefree feeling.

This is Ian, my husband," said Bridget. "And these," indicating the two children, engrossed in their kites and so wrapped up in anoraks and scarves that their faces were almost completely hidden, "are my children, Mairi and Angus. Ian, this is Joyce Cunningham and Alex Melville. Joyce was Miss Murdoch's tenant and is the owner of the diaries."

Even as he reached out to shake hands, a slight frown crossed Ian's face, and although it passed away, the carefree look didn't quite return. "I'm glad to meet you." His voice was deep, and he had a slight English accent. "I've certainly heard about you and your exciting legacy, Miss Cunningham. I just hope that Bridget isn't plaguing you too much in her obsession with the diaries."

Joyce made a polite rejoinder and Sandy remarked on the kites, but the two didn't stay with the McKays for long. The air was chilly and they weren't dressed for standing around.

As the two figures faded away down the beach, Joyce's beige jacket soon disappearing into the background, Ian turned to Bridget. "So that's her, is it?"

"That's her. It's a pity they couldn't stop on longer so you could get to know her better. She's an interesting personality – sometimes warm and open, and at other times closed-in and snappy. I think really her bouts of temper are to cover up for when she doesn't know what's going on or isn't in charge. She's insecure."

"Poor soul," said Ian with a touch of irony in his voice. He had often taken issue with what he saw as Bridget's facile, psycho-babble, character reductions of people she had just met. Sometimes subsequent knowledge or events proved her right, but, as he never failed to point out, not always; so shouldn't she reserve judgement just a little longer? He had made this point so often that now his simple comment said it all for him, and Bridget flushed with annoyance. – both at him and at herself. She must learn not to say these things to Ian, whatever she might think.

Now Ian went on, "You never mentioned him, what's his name? Melville?"

"Alex Melville. Did I not?"

"No. Is he part of the all-engrossing reading as well? Good looking fellow. Perhaps that's why you're so keen?" He was teasing her, but Bridget was aware that with Ian it didn't take much for teasing to become a matter of great weight.

"Don't be silly, dear. He's not interested in the diaries – at least, he doesn't read them. He's Joyce's friend, and sometimes arrives while we're still reading, that's all."

"Joyce's friend? Boyfriend?"

"I think so, though sometimes you might wonder. But what business is it of ours? He's a pleasant fellow, an architect, I think, and a good conversationalist. You should get to know him – you'd like him"

"I'd like that. I need to know more people who're not teachers or children," said Ian blandly. "Maybe when you're finished with the diaries, I'll ask Melville if I can come round to his place a couple of nights a week. You wouldn't mind, would you?"

"Ian! You knew when we got married that I would be working odd hours, including evenings. You knew it when we decided to start our family. Why are you so cross now?"

"Who's cross? And why are you changing the subject like that? All I said was that I'd like to get to know Melville. It's not a great complaint about the marital status quo."

Wasn't it? Bridget couldn't be sure. Ian never lost his temper, but his cool exterior didn't indicate any lack of opinions. Even after all these years she couldn't always tell when a statement masked a bitter complaint. However, time would tell. In the meantime, she would continue with her visits to Joyce. If she changed her pattern to propitiate Ian she'd never find out if he was really annoyed. Thus straightforward Bridget reasoned.

3rd August 1939 London

And so I am coming home. I had hoped to visit Spain at some time, but the civil war has dragged on and on. I have enjoyed the year I spent in Provence, waiting for word that Spain was safe, and I shall miss the joie de vivre of life lived out in public, in streets and gardens. However I have been strongly advised to come home. So I am in London and I won't stay here long. When I set out on my travels – and I didn't know then that I was leaving for years – I thought London magnificent. I remember how it thrilled me to read the street signs: Baker Street, Edgeware Road, Regent Street, Piccadilly Circus – streets whose names were so familiar from my reading. I loved being alone in a strange city for the first time: riding on the underground; gazing at Buckingham Palace, Westminster Palace, the Thames; eating in various Lyons' Corner Houses. London was freedom, and as such was bathed in the golden light of joy.

But now, no longer. It is summer, but even though the sun shines, the city seems grey, self-contained, waiting. I don't talk much about my foreign visits because something tells me not to. Instead I talk about going back to Scotland soon. Will I find there the sense of unease that is here? To me this unease is the more potent because no one else seems to acknowledge it. It's the Stiff Upper Lip, I suppose, in its true manifestation. It has been so parodied on caricatures of Empire-builders abroad, but it is right and natural here. No one makes a fuss. The only reason I notice is because I have been so long in Latin countries, spending time amongst people who love to live dramatically. The British are different: now I see it.

Practically, I have been in contact with Mr Macpherson, my solicitor, about opening up the house for me. The last tenants left in June, so that's all very handy. I shall return home next week and see how I like living in Windmill Road again after all I have done and seen and been. Now that I have accepted universal good advice and decided to do this I am looking forward to it. I have no idea how I will react, or whether I can remain the person I have become.

12th August 1939 St. Andrews

Back in Windmill Road. Actually, I've been back for three days, and very busy days they've been. First, I gave the whole place a good clean. It wasn't really very dirty, but I found I wanted it to be clean to my own satisfaction. In none of the hotels and guest houses of the past five years have I felt remotely like this. Then, if no excessive surface dirt showed, I gave cleanliness no second thought. But as soon as I got here, I fell to cleaning. I rearranged the furniture as well. The tenants had moved it around - as was their right - and it gave me ideas. Some items were too large and heavy for me, and some obviously had to remain where they were (no need for a bed in the drawing room, or a kitchen table in the bathroom!) but I decided that since I am probably here for a while, until Europe calms down – and goodness knows when that will be: I don't think it can happen without a war – I might as well have things comfortable and convenient. I've changed my bedroom. The small room over the kitchen was always dark and a bit cramped. Instead I have what was the spare room, looking out both towards the sea and away from it. I'm using the double bed which was there, and have taken mother's dressing table, which looks well in that room. It also looks better without the ruffles with which she festooned it. I've gathered together all the bookcases in the drawing room, which will be my all-purpose room, for leisure, business, study and so on. The books took a lot of moving, but they give the room a solid feel. I did think about getting rid of some of mother's books. After all, I'm scarcely likely to read her Christian apologetics and devotional manuals. But then I decided that sorting the books would take too long to be done now.

I have closed up the dining room and removed the flatware and silverware to the kitchen. As I am living alone and want no servant, I shall eat in the kitchen where the range makes it warm. I could feel mother's horror prickling all over my skin when I made that decision, but I am sticking by it.

As well as re-arranging what was here, I had to receive the good pieces of furniture which had been put in store. It was lovely to see the rosewood desk and inlaid tallboy again.

So now my house is as I want it. I don't know quite what I will do with myself all day here, but I expect something will turn up. I might see if I can undertake some informal study at the university, though of course that will have to wait until term-time.

30th September 1939

I shan't bother with studies just now until I see how this war goes. I'm not hopeful. I have seen the way Nazism has built up the military might of Germany. And in this war there's no nonsense of pretending it will all be over by Christmas.

They are talking of evacuating Clydeside children here. I have a big house, all to myself. I don't want to take children (I can say that honestly in this diary, if nowhere else). I know nothing of children and am afraid I couldn't cope. That being so, I must find some other way in which to use my house for the war effort. This is not something I contemplate with reluctance. I find that knowing I am free to make choices, and that it is my house, helps. Besides, while I should hate to hurt the many Germans who were good to me, I should also hate to see this country subjected to Nazi doctrines. I should hate that more. I remember the last war. Mother opened up the house as a hospital for wounded soldiers. We took up to twenty at a time, putting them five to a room upstairs, and removing ourselves to the downstairs rooms. Although the living arrangements were cramped, it was a fascinating time for me – the house was so full of life. Of course, I was out at school by day, but not in the evenings or at weekends.

I remember how I would try to find excuses to go upstairs. I wanted to see these men, these heroes who had risked life and, often, had lost limb to serve King and country. At first. Later, as I grew older, I wanted to see these soldiers who were young men. My mother did her best to prevent me. I was "just the wrong age" to be around the wounded. I heard her say that to one of the nurses once. I was "at the tiresomely romantic stage, ready to see a hero in every soldier's face, and give her silly affections to the first one to look back her way." Perhaps she was right. I was fourteen when that war started, eighteen at its close. I had been nowhere and had known no other boys than those I saw I the town. I attended the all-female St. Leonard's College, so had no masculine classmates. My mother had no friends with boys of my age, and so I had reached my teenage years without knowing any growing boys. Now the house was filled with young men, and I was not allowed to help nurse them.

I remember the temper tantrum I threw at first! I shouted that I wasn't a baby. I wanted to help in the war and that if I could nurse after school, another nurse could be used elsewhere. And my mother looked at me coldly and said that I was indeed still a baby, I had just proved it. She told some of the soldiers that she had a little girl, and they would send down an occasional present – a piece of chocolate or a crudely-made toy. I knew they thought I had not yet reached my eighth birthday and I burned with resentment against mother. Those tantrums were the last I threw. I never let her see the real me, the person who felt and reacted, again.

Of course, sometimes I did manage to slip up the stairs. I didn't often dare show myself to the invalids, because when it became a possibility, I found I was shy. So I would sit on the stairs or hide behind the box-room door and listen to their conversations. It was like listening to another language at first. Not only did they have their own slang, but they spoke of things so divorced from my experience. But gradually I learned to listen with some understanding and learned far more than most girls in my school about trench warfare. I learned that injury, even death, is not always to be feared. I learned that in such grotesque fear and dread, and in such horribly squalid living conditions the human spirit can be broken – or can triumph and be strengthened. I learned a good many obscene terms and what some of them meant. And I learned what many women never know – something of the mystery of male friendships: what men talk about when women are not present, and what is tabu. By the end of the war I was no longer hiding, but slipping into rooms and trying to meet the men on their own terms. Then I learned that it is a rare man who will talk to a woman as he will to the man in the next bed. And I learned that I was a sexual object, rather than a sensible, sentient being.

I learned a lot. I might learn more if I did it again. I think I may offer this house as a convalescent home for wounded soldiers or airmen. There is a lot of talk these days about doing things out of Christian duty or charity. I will do this a) to help, because I want to (so not charity), and b) to keep learning from the lives and experiences of other people. It should be better than a university course!

15th October 1939

This war is a slow starter, but I can't believe it will be any less fierce because of that. I have officially offered my house as a convalescent home, and the offer has been accepted. I am asked to hold the place ready for its possible use at some later stage. I have fitted Mother's room up with five army cots and closed the door. I shall see about more if and when the beds are needed. I chose Mother's room on purpose. This use of the house looks as if I am following in her footsteps. Mrs Marr at number 2 said as much to me. "I hear you're going to run a hospital, Charlotte? Just like your dear mother. You must have inherited her noble nature with her looks."

Her noble nature. I am not my mother, and she has no hold over me. I am doing this simply because it seems the best way I can use my property and experience in this emergency. So I will put the soldiers in Mother's room first. It is Mother's room no longer, nor will I call it so. It is my room now to name, and for now it is ward one.

I have avoided church since I came home. I might have gone, just to test my new theories and make sure my memory is still accurate, but I heard something on the radio that sickened me. A call went out, from the government, I think, or perhaps from the Archbishop of Canterbury, or even from the B.B.C, doing it of its own accord. Anyway, an authoritative-sounding call went out for the churches and people of this land "earnestly to petition God to grant us good success in this terrible endeavour." Fine language! Underneath, what does it mean? They want me to ask God, if there is a God, to help us kill enough Germans that they will have to give in.

This seems very little different from the outrage I witnessed in Cologne cathedral. Oh certainly, nothing has been said about British racial supremacy, but built into this call to prayer is a very similar assumption. I know that the Germans are also praying for "success", confident that God will aid them, because they are the chosen people. We think God may instead be swayed by our prayers. Why? Because we are in the right. Which is as much as to say that we are more chosen than the Germans are.

Are we? I remember the people I met around Bavaria, on my bicycle, and I doubt that very much. God, if there is a god, would do well to keep out of this whole affair. It is certainly infantile of us to demand that he pick sides. Can't the Supreme Being make up its own mind as to the rights and wrongs of human affairs without our childish whining? I know that if I attend a service I shall be asked to participate in these prayers for success. The church will quickly become a focus for national hope as well as a source of comfort for the afflicted. Indeed, I fear the only comfort given may be the idea of national pride. I hope not, from a humanistic point of view, I very much hope not. For then if we lose, our loss will be the greater. In a time like this some people, perhaps most people, need a religion to cling to, and that religion should not be tied too closely to the national interest.

Most people need religion but I do not so I shall not be going to church. It would be hypocrisy. I have no religion, and I will not have my national spirit enmeshed in religious twaddle. Mrs Marr and her ilk can think and say what they like (they will avail themselves of that permission, I know) but I am not going.

25th December 1939

First Christmas of this war. I wonder how many Christmases will pass before it ends? My father's cousin in America sent a lovely box of what she calls "goodies". It includes tins of meat, raisins, sweets, and chocolates. And I wonder if she thinks we are starving over here. There is talk of rationing coming in soon, but so far, though prices have risen, I can buy what I need. So when I got the American parcel I wondered what I should do with it. Should I keep it and use it up gradually? Should I have a bean feast with it and make myself deliciously sick? Should I give it away? I think it might be ungrateful to give it away, so I will eat it a little at a time. All the same, I feel odd about this package. Cousin Rosemary never bothered to send me anything before. Now she assumes that I am in need. It makes me feel like a charity case, I, who am far better off than most others. But there is a world beyond Britain, even, unbelievable, a world beyond this war. I had almost forgotten. Cousin Rosemary does not carry a gas mask when she goes out shopping. Her Christmas charity is to give to someone who needs her pity: me.

31st December 1939

Hogmany, but there is no dancing in front of the Post Office in South Street this year. You can't dance in blacked-out streets. It has been an interesting evening for me. In a sense I have given charity too, charity that cost me something – just how much I can't begin to work out now. No doubt it will make itself clear.

I went for a chilly walk this afternoon – walking gets the blood moving better than sitting by the fire and doesn't cost anything for fuel. I came home around 4 o'clock, when it was almost dark. As I turned into Windmill Road I saw young Jimmy Marr come out of number 2. He was wearing an air-force uniform. I must say, I was surprised. He was just a little boy when I went away on my travels. Actually, he must have been thirteen or fourteen, as he's nineteen now. I called out a greeting to him, and he started, as though he had been far away. When he turned towards me, I could see that his face was white and troubled. In fact, it looked as though he had been crying.

I said something about was he going away soon, and he looked in danger of bursting into tears on the spot. I must say I was curious. "After all, he's not going to the trenches," I thought. So I asked him to come for a farewell cup of tea. Over the tea (and I gave him an American biscuit) I asked about where he was going, what he would be doing etc. He answered in single words. This was silly. I obviously wasn't helping, and I dearly wanted to help: he looked so young and pathetic, sitting in his stiff new uniform. So I got personal.

"Are you afraid?"

He looked, if possible, even more hang-dog. "Yes."

"Of flying?"

"No, of course not! I can't wait to get in the air." There was more animation about him now, so presumably he did want to fly.

"Then you're frightened of dying," I stated. "Which is it< the process of dying – pain and so on – or the cessation of being?"

Suddenly he smiled. I suppose it was a relief to share his secret. "It's not being alive. I can't say this to Mum, because she gets into such a state at the thought of her boy in danger, Miss Murdoch. I'm not afraid of danger – it will be exciting. I'm not afraid of pain: all I ever wanted to do was experience life – whatever life throws at me. But I haven't experienced much yet – and I can't bear that I may not experience much more."

"But you may," I said, still briskly. "In fact, here you are, unburdening yourself to a middle-aged woman who is not family. That's probably a new experience too."

He smiled again. "It is."

Then I told him he should call me Charlotte, if I was to be his confidante. I really said that to keep the conversation flowing, but he seized on it.

"Charlotte? Can I really confide in you?"

"Of course."

"I don't have any fixed ideas about what I want to experience in life. I've always been content to take whatever came

my way." Yes, happy-go-lucky Jimmy Marr, that's how he'd been as a boy. "But there's one thing I want. I want it so badly. How can I die without knowing this?"

"And it is?"

"What it's like to be with a woman." Well, he meant that he was a virgin and didn't want to be. I poured him more tea.

"You don't have a girl?" He didn't, and anyway, he was well brought-up, which is such a handicap, and was too shy to suggest such a thing to a girl.

I thought hard: he was miserable; he was nice; he might be going to die. There was only one thing for it.

"Well, Jimmy. I've never been with a man any more than you've been with a woman, but I'm prepared to risk the experience if you are."

He was astounded. "I'm not as young as you may have had in mind," I cautioned him. "But woman I certainly am."

What can I say? He was pathetically eager. We tried an experimental kiss or two and then I put the guard on the fire, and we repaired upstairs to my room. My hopes of enjoying the experience were not high: after all, neither of us knew what we were doing. But in the event we managed quite nicely.

Jimmy went off home again at about 6 o'clock, fervent in his gratitude and with a bit more spring in his step. I am left to wonder what this may have cost me. Not my heart – I am too old and too sensible to lose my heart to a boy of nineteen. But if anyone finds out, I will most certainly have lost a bit of respectability – all my respectability, all my prestige, in fact. They won't find out from Jimmy, though, I'm sure of that. And I won't talk, so unless a baby comes – oh surely not! Even so, even if no one knows, there is a cost. I no longer think of myself in quite the same way.

Mother would call me a slut. Am I? A slut, a trollop – me? Or am I a charitable woman?

CHAPTER THREE: EHTICAL DILEMMAS

"Our virtues

Lie in the interpretation of the time." **Shakespeare, *Coriolanus***

It was a Tuesday in mid-December. In the town the shops glistened with Christmas sparkle and their lights spilled yellow from windows. Strung over the street and wound around the branches of trees were simple strings of coloured lights. A nip of frost in the air only added to the festive feel of the dark afternoon, and people smiled as they went about their business.

Joyce was in her flat, nominally at work on a chapter of her dissertation. She was still at the early stage of asking herself questions and then seeking to find the answers. As usual, her table was piled high with books, many of them brown and dusty, borrowed from the university's extensive archives. A splash of lamp-light fell on her notebook and diffused itself into the room, highlighting the sheen of an old sideboard, the glow of coloured glasses and the scarlet blanket thrown over the sofa. In the old grate, a gas fire hissed and glowed: a picture of ideal student life.

Joyce, however, was not playing the part of the ideal student. Although she sat dutifully at her books, less than half her attention was on them. Instead, she waited with impatience to hear the shriek of the front door. Now that Bridget was in the throes of Advent, and Christmas preparation was eating up her time, she couldn't come to read the diary together with Joyce. Most often Joyce gave it to her, having marked the place where she herself had reached, and she snatched five minutes here and there to absorb its contents. The last extract contained the entries for December 1939, and Joyce was curious to know Bridget's opinion. She very much regretted that it hadn't been possible for them to read these extracts together. Now she would get the minister's considered response rather than her first reaction.

Unlike Sandy, Joyce had never really accepted or understood Bridget's interest in the dairies. She had grown up with a profound distrust of religion, formal or otherwise, and couldn't quite believe that Bridget would be able to accept Miss Murdoch's life story at face value. After all, surely everything pointed to Miss Murdoch's outward religion being a sham, or at best a cover.

She had given up waiting and had gone into the little kitchen to boil a kettle for some herbal tea when at last the door emitted its usual nerve-jangling screech. The next minute there was a knock on the door, and Bridget's smiling face appeared, calling out, "Is anyone home?"

"Come in, Bridget. I'm just making elderflower tea. Do you want some?"

"I've never had that, but I'll try it, if it's hot. It's cold enough outside. Nice and cosy in here though."

Joyce poured the tea, carefully refraining from mentioning the diary. This was very unlike her, and Bridget burst out, "Wasn't that last entry a turn-up for the books? I don't know if it helps your research any – the unexpected things people do in the uncertainty of modern warfare? – but it certainly made me laugh. Good for Miss Murdoch!"

Joyce was surprised. "You applaud her? I thought you'd be shocked."

"Why?" Bridget challenged. Like Joyce she had been looking forward to this conversation, having a very shrewd idea of how Joyce expected her to respond.

Joyce busied herself removing the teabag and squeezing it out. "Well, what she did was wrong, by the church's standards, wasn't it? She was a parishioner of yours. How can you be glad about it?"

"She wasn't a parishioner of mine then," said Bridget. "She wasn't a parishioner of anyone's. By her own word, she had placed herself outside the church's authority, and outside its standards. Up till now she seems to have had very little pleasure from doing so."

Joyce ignored this last sentence. "That's true. But Bridget, are you saying that the church's teachings only apply to its members? I thought Christianity – and other religions – believed in moral absolutes."

"Yes, we do," replied Bridget quickly. "I do. Perhaps I am being a bit inconsistent. I've just finished reading the entry." She paused. "You know, Joyce, I find it very hard to recognise the Miss Murdoch I knew in the woman of these dairies."

"The one you knew wasn't the real woman," said Joyce.

Bridget shook her head. "That may be, but the jury's still out on that question, isn't it?"

Joyce was silent, realising that if she were honest, she would have to say that the jury was not still out. The jury had delivered a verdict right at the beginning of the investigation. The charge was hypocrisy, and the verdict was 'guilty'.

Bridget went on, "I suppose I'm regarding this younger Miss

Murdoch (who is already older than I am now) as a character in a novel. That's why I applaud her. Not because she sinned – and I suppose you're right, she did sin – but because for the first time she seems to have acted in a generous, disinterested manner."

"Really? I hadn't thought of it like that." Joyce was interested. "You may have a point. I'm fascinated, not by the story, but by the unselfconscious revelation of a character, as she records her thoughts. You're right. She may have thought things that were disinterested, even generous, but she hasn't done much that wasn't concerned with herself. All of her travels seem to have been simply for pleasure."

"And there's nothing wrong with that," said Bridget. "In fact, she hasn't had many acute moral choices to make so far. Now we find her making one. Technically she may have made the wrong one, but she made it for the right reasons. None of us are perfect, and sexual sin is far from being unforgiveable – though you wouldn't know that from the way the church and the press can go on about it."

Another pause when Joyce said nothing. She hated finding herself wrong-footed and badly informed. She had never heard 'sexual sin' so quickly pardoned before.

Bridget went on. "You know who Jimmy Marr is, don't you?"

"No, I don't know anyone of that name."

Bridget sighed. "You've met him. Miss Murdoch would want you to keep this under your hat, but – it's Dr. Marr."

"Dr. Marr! The one who was upset when I didn't report the death at once?"

"Yes. He said she had been good to him."

In the ensuing silence the screech of the front door sounded louder than usual. There were footsteps on the stairs and

Sandy let himself into the flat. Seeing the two women he aped surprise, staggering, and smiting his brow.

"Two of you and no talking! I thought there must be no one home, it's so quiet. Who's died?"

Joyce glared at him, while Bridget chuckled.

"Why are you here so early? Shouldn't you still be at work?"

"Dear Joyce, you are always so welcoming!"

Joyce sighed. Evidently Alex was in one of his moods. It was going to be impossible to take anything seriously. Before she could decide how to handle things, Bridget had joined the conversation.

"What you have just witnessed is the silence of stunned surprise. We have learned that Miss Murdoch was not a virgin."

"And this surprises you?" Sandy's voice held a serious note behind the banter. "Didn't you think that someone who was so determined to experience life would want to experience the pleasures of the flesh as well?" He licked his lips and rolled his eyes. Bridget chuckled again.

"Sadly, I really must be going – I've no time even to breathe this week. Joyce, I'll be in touch. Alex, I'll let you fill in your theories to Joyce's ever-open ear." With that she caught up her coat and whisked out of the door.

"Was it something I said?" Sandy quipped.

"No, she said she was busy before you came." Joyce suddenly smiled. "Sorry for your reception. Hello, how nice to see you."

She came close and raised her face to kiss him. Sandy, though, was still playful, and caught her, holding her away from him slightly, then pulling her close to run his tongue along her lips. Joyce twisted away.

"Don't."

She retreated to her chair before turning to him again. "Seriously, Alex, why are you here so early?"

Sandy's teasing grin disappeared abruptly. "There was nothing doing at work," he complained. "Joyce, I don't know what I'm going to do. I have no new contracts coming in, and I've tried for everything going within an hour's drive. There's not enough work in our office for two of us. Hargreaves is a commercial architect, and things seem to be going fine for him, but there's little doing in houses. At least, there's little I can do. No one seems to want to build unique dwellings these days; they'd rather have something by Wimpey or Barratt. I'm not a bad architect, I'm just an unknown one. Hargreaves says I should switch to designing shopping centres or office blocks, but it's not that simple. Anyway he has so much experience in that area, I could never compete with him.

He stopped speaking and swung away to the window, pulling one curtain aside and peering out into the early darkness. The window-pane showed Joyce his face, with the vulnerable look of a mirror image echoed by the determined way he clamped together his trembling lips. Compassion and contrition smote her: this could be no recent development in his life. Why was it the first she was aware of it? She must have been shutting him out, imposing her own agenda on their time and conversation. She had been so wrapped up in those diaries.

Wisdom told her to say nothing of this. This was not the time to mention herself, even in apology. This was the time to forget herself and consider Alex: what he needed and what she could give him. She recalled her recent conversation with Bridget. In a sense, she, like Miss Murdoch, was presented with the chance to do something for someone other than herself. If such opportunities had been coming her way recently, she certainly hadn't noticed them.

Sandy was speaking again. "I should have told you before, but I've started looking at the employment pages on Fridays. I think I'll have to apply to a big established firm. I might find something in Dundee, but probably it would mean a move to Glasgow or Edinburgh – perhaps Aberdeen or even Inverness. I should have told you, because if I move it will affect us both, won't it? At least, I hope it would mean something to you."

Joyce nodded wordlessly, then realising that he couldn't see her in the window reflection, made an encouraging, affirmatory noise in her throat. Sandy went on, without turning round.

"Damn it, Joyce, I don't want to leave. I belong in this part of the world. I never wanted to be anywhere else. I don't want to live in a city again: I had enough of that at university. I want to be here, using my skills to enhance my home-town and the places around it. I could, if only someone would let me, I know that I could. I just haven't had the chance. I feel so rejected, so incomplete, so powerless. If no one will hire, me, no one will know what I can do." He turned from the window, dropping the curtain. "And I don't want to be further from you, Joyce. You get so wrapped up in what is near and current. That's not a criticism – I love you for it. But I want to be part of what's near and current for you."

He stopped speaking and came across to where Joyce sat in her big armchair. She stretched out a hand and held his, while he slipped down to sit on the floor, with his back resting against her legs.

"I suppose your funny mood when you came in was a cover for all of this?" Joyce asked.

She felt him briefly squeeze the hand he held. "A cover and an anaesthetic. I've kept it at bay for a long time, but today I couldn't. I'm sorry to dump on you."

"Don't be silly." There was a long pause while the gas fire hissed and flared. Somehow the room seemed more shadowy than before. "Alex," queried Joyce, "When did you last get lucky?"

Sandy thought. "I suppose when I landed my last contract, which was eight months ago now."

"No, that's not what I meant." Joyce's free hand began to stroke his thick, black hair. "When did you last get lucky?"

Sandy turned, now kneeling before her. "Do you mean? Are you offering?"

Joyce nodded. "It seems to me it's time you got lucky."

The next day found Sandy back at work, or at the office, still trying to secure a contract, still trying to find a job elsewhere, and still very much bemused at the previous evening's events. He wasn't sure what to make of it, and so he found he could not put it aside. Truth to tell, he wasn't sure that having sex with Joyce was really what he'd wanted. He had been depressed, however, and certainly he (or his body – were they the same? Sometimes he doubted it) had wanted it enough not to bother working through his feelings at the time. Besides, Joyce was very rarely physically forthcoming. This was a huge gesture for her, and he couldn't be churlish and refuse. Not after all he's been saying about how much he wanted to be with her. The fact remained, however, that she, not he, had initiated the encounter: subconsciously this rankled.

She had been curiously inept at the act itself. He had been glad that, unlike other girls he had known, she didn't demand a performance rating afterwards. Nor did he: his ego wasn't up to it. After all, he had been offered sex 'to make it all better' as a small boy might be given a sweet. And he was aware that he had been continent for a long time – two years, more or less – up until now. If Joyce had been inept, he had felt clumsy, and that wasn't pleasant.

As for what it meant for their relationship, he had no idea. He hoped it meant that Joyce was initiating a new stage. After all, that was what women usually meant when they began to sleep with someone, or so he gathered. Women like Joyce didn't have casual flings, and so the sex act spelled some kind of commitment for them. As it happened, both these generalisations were true of Sandy – even if former commitments had been less than life-long. He hoped that in this Joyce might run true to feminine form. But she was Joyce; she was different; she might not.

That same day Joyce met Ian McKay in the supermarket. It was late afternoon and the presence of his briefcase in his shopping trolley, as well as the slightly rumpled tweed jacket and tie he wore suggested that he was on his way home from school. Full of bonhomie after a particularly profitable day's study, and the consciousness of a memorable evening the night before, Joyce broke from her usual habits and hailed Ian across a mound of oranges, chestnuts, and out-of-season melons.

"Hello! It's Ian McKay, isn't it?"

"Joyce Cunningham! How are you?" Joyce, who carried only a wire basket, and was therefore more mobile than Ian, dodged round the unnaturally glossy fruit pyramids and came up to him. As she did so she noticed that his trolley contained four litres of milk, three large loaves, two family-sized packs of margarine and several packets of cereal. Ian saw her noticing.

"Families take a lot of feeding." He looked pointedly at her as-yet-empty basket. "I remember doing my shopping with one of these." He smiled, a warm smile which showed slightly uneven teeth.

"Do you do all the family shopping?" Joyce was curious as to how a minister's household functioned, something she'd had no opportunity to ask Bridget.

"No, not all. I generally do the big, weekly shopping for basics, then Bridget pops in here when necessary to get the one-offs, or the things we've run out of. It works fairly well – and neither of us have to have the children with us. Taking children shopping is not an exercise in exemplary time-management. It's also pricey: they always spot things we just can't live without."

Now Joyce smiled. "I've never liked shopping, but I must say I agree with your children – an occasional treat makes it more bearable." She hesitated. "I'd like to meet your children: they sound most intelligent."

Ian was surprised. The little Bridget had told him about Joyce (told him objectively, not as one of her psychological 'discoveries') hadn't led him to believe she would have much time for children or family life. Glancing at her, he noticed for the first time how attractive she was. Her features were regular, her skin, hair and figure were all good, and today there was a definite sparkle about her.

"You must come to dinner, which is really tea, and meet them sometime." It was a conventional response, and Joyce smiled politely, without committing herself. After all, she wasn't really keen to meet children. Ian noticed her hesitancy and guessed at its cause. "Really, Joyce, you must. Bridget isn't to keep you all to herself. I'd better not ask you during Advent: Bridget's busy with church and I'm busy with end of term and the children. But after Christmas. Have you plans to see your family for Christmas?"

Joyce didn't answer but picked up an orange and began to squeeze it.

"You haven't, have you?" Looking up, Joyce saw his blue eyes fixed on her. "No," she murmured. "I'm not going away."

"Then why not have Christmas with us?" Ian grinned. "You'll meet the children with a vengeance then, all right. But we can sit on them if they become too much for us. We'll be at church in the morning, of course, but you'd be welcome to come home with us afterwards. Who knows, we might even find time for some rational conversation."

"O.K. Yes. Thank you, Ian, I'd like that."

"Then that's settled. I'll tell Bridget. Now I must get on and get home. I'll see you on Christmas, Joyce. I'm glad we ran into each other like this."

Joyce could not remember what she had come into the shop to get. She retreated to the entrance, replaced her wire basket, and squeezed through the crowd of people coming in, who eyed her aberrant behaviour suspiciously. Dazed, she walked home, berating herself. Why had she done that? Why had she agreed to go to a minister's house, and one with kids, for Christmas? Why had she said she wanted to meet children? She never knew what to say to them. She had planned a nice quiet day on December 25th, while the world celebrated. Now she would probably even have to go to church again. And what would Alex say? It had been hard enough convincing him that she wouldn't be celebrating Christmas and that she wanted to be alone. (And that was before last night.) How would he react to the news that she was going to Bridget's – and Ian's? Need she tell him? Yes, he was bound to hear from Bridget. And presents! Now she would have to buy presents. What do you give a minister, two children, whose genders and ages you have forgotten, and a tired-looking teacher with a sympathetic presence and blue eyes?

Sandy heard of the plans the next night. He was hurt and furious.

"Why are you going there when you wouldn't come with me to my family?"

Joyce didn't answer. There was no real answer she could give. The truth was, she was asking herself very similar questions; but she couldn't admit this to him.

The two of them had gone out for dinner at an Indian restaurant to celebrate the end of Joyce's term. "I love the vacations: they give me so much more time for my own work," was her comment. This had had an unsettling effect on Sandy, who had hoped they might have more time together. His emotional state was fragile that night. He had been turned down by an architectural firm in Dundee but was making an effort to appear cheerful for Joyce's sake. He had arrived hoping to find her full of plans to move their relationship closer – as indeed, was he – but had so far found Joyce perfunctory in her treatment of him. Closeness was particularly lacking. Now, after the Lamb Tikka, had come this bald statement of Joyce's plans for Christmas Day. It was all Sandy could do to keep his voice down and not let the whole restaurant know his humiliation.

"Joyce, I don't understand you. You told me you don't celebrate Christmas: fine, I can appreciate that. Naturally then you wouldn't want to come to my family. But now you say you're going to the McKays. Why? Did you want a religious celebration? I would have come to church with you. I won't hide that I am hurt and confused by this. I thought after the other night we were moving closer to each other. Was I wrong? It certainly seems so."

Joyce pushed aside her plate. She knew he would take it this way, or she should have known it. But she just hadn't thought. Now guilt shot through her, and she too became angry.

"If I want to change my mind, I shall, Alex Melville. Why shouldn't I go where I want, when I want? I don't like your family and they don't like me. If you think otherwise, you're fooling yourself.

"But you are a fool, Alex. You think some physical intercourse will change a relationship. Why should it? I offered you my body for a couple of hours, and used yours, that was all. It was a little pleasure, a little comfort, but not something by which the world changes. Sometimes it seems to me that you only offer me the worst of all possible worlds. You obviously don't respect my independence, nor do you pay me the attentions that other men might."

She stopped there, aware that in her anger she had probably gone too far. Sandy sat impassively through her diatribe, neither eating nor moving. Now silence fell between them, and the hum of conversation from other tables seemed to grow louder, while the whine of Indian music hung softly about their table. After a minute, Sandy turned his attention to his plate, and swiftly cleared it. "No point in wasting a good dinner," he remarked to the world, as he hailed the waiter. Requesting the bill, he paid for both meals, then rose unhurriedly, put on his coat, and without even a glance in Joyce's direction, he left the restaurant.

The Christmas season passed in a blaze of coloured lights and a warm glow of candles. Joyce was impatient to 'get on' with the diary but agreed to wait until Bridget had more time. "It will give me time to get writing at my dissertation," she said, making no reply when Bridget added, "And give Alex a chance to have more time with you."

Christmas Day was a new experience for Joyce. She had never attended a Family Service, and church that morning left her gasping. The overall impression was of colour, light, gaiety, and joy. She had fun. She laughed – everyone did. "Well, why shouldn't we have fun on Christmas? It was our festival first." Bridget would have said.

Joyce's childhood Christmases had been patterned on early

excitement, frenzied unwrapping, then lunch, boredom and bickering. The day at the manse was different. It flowed better, as she was to say later. Presents were unwrapped and admired individually, and any games opened were played at once, by the whole family, postponing all other gift-giving. The excitement was never uncontrolled but was maintained throughout the day. Joyce found the domestic life of the McKays fascinating. Bridget laughed more, teased the children, fussed over lunch, and refused to clear the table and wash up.

The children were revealed as real little personalities. Mairi was a questing, questioning child. Why and What and How were her best friends and she was not afraid to get her information from a stranger.

Angus was activity personified. He never walked but ran or hopped or bounded. His presents were nearly all sports-related. In his ebullience, once or twice his personality knocked against another's; then he would produce the most angelic grin as he made swift, rueful apology.

And Ian, Ian was there too, controlling, commanding, joking, and playing. The rational conversation he had hoped to offer Joyce did not materialize, but there would be other times for that.

Since the night in the restaurant, Sandy had not been in touch and Joyce couldn't hide from herself that she missed him. For the best part of a year her social life had been dominated by his relaxed presence, and although she had other friends, they had all left town for the Christmas break. With no attractive diversions offered her, Christmas Day apart, she put her head down and got on with her work, reading, analysing, writing, re-writing, tearing up, starting again. It was a necessary process, but not one she enjoyed. Joyce was a good teacher, an original thinker, and a dedicated researcher: she was not a natural writer.

The strange week between Christmas and New Year passed, and Hogmany enveloped the town. With no party to attend, and no group of friends to go out and celebrate with, Joyce stayed at home and watched television, curled in her armchair with wine and chocolate as her personal celebration. Windmill Road was usually quiet, but on this night of the year no street could remain aloof and ignorant of the festivities. As midnight came and went, she heard cheers from the hotels and from private parties. The church bells pealed in uncoordinated cacophony. People called out "Happy New Year!" in the streets.

Then the old front door screeched. Joyce stiffened at the sound. Alone on this night of revelry, she felt vulnerable. This could be anyone, and was she able to deal with the unpredictability of a tanked-up chance passer-by? She knew how flimsy was the lock on her door: at other times it hadn't mattered, but now she felt very unprotected. The room seemed unnaturally still as she listened to the footsteps on the stairs – more than one pair of feet. The gas fire hissed and popped, sounding as loud as an industrial furnace to her strained, responsive ears. Quickly she darted into the kitchen, seized a frying pan and tiptoed to stand behind the door.

Came a soft knock. Joyce held her breath. Then a quiet voice called out "Joyce? Joyce are you still awake? We saw your light was on." It was Bridget.

Still brandishing her frying pan, Joyce flung open the door and stared speechlessly at the entire McKay family grouped on the landing. The children were wide-eyed with excitement and all four were grinning. Still Joyce said nothing. Bridget filled the silence.

"Oh good you are still up. Want some first footers? We have the appropriate whisky and coal – though goodness knows what use you'll have for coal. None of us is really dark, so we'll send Ian first over the threshold, as at least he's tall, handsome and a man."

Mechanically Joyce stepped back, and Ian, bearing two parcels, followed her into the flat, then stooped and pecked her cheek. "Happy New Year, Joyce," he said.

Mairi saw the frying pan. "Why are you holding that? Were you about to have supper? We had ours ages ago, at the church party. You should have been there; we had great fun. I won the children's musical bumps, and Daddy lost the grown-ups one; he had to have a custard pie in the face! It was made of shaving cream, and he did look funny!"

Joyce replaced the frying pan in the kitchen. "Happy New Year all," she said, and offered drinks all round. In the kitchen, when she was spooning drinking-chocolate into mugs, she found Ian beside her.

"We scared you. I'm sorry," he said.

"That's all right." Joyce was glad he hadn't asked if she had been scared. He had seen her fear and there was no need to hide it. "I'm glad it turned out to be you."

In the sitting-room Bridget was in high spirits. "It's the first time we've let Angus and Mairi stay up to go first-footing. We're having an exciting time of it. Coming past the police station, one of the constables offered to kiss them, and me, for luck! I didn't know if you'd be here or at Alex's. Where is he? I thought that wherever you were you'd be together for Hogmany."

Just then Mairi upset her mug of chocolate on a pile of computer-printed paper. In the subsequent bustle of cleaning up and apologies, Bridget's question went un-answered. Ian decided that perhaps Mairi and Angus should be in their beds, and as it was a bit of a walk back to Martyrs' Manse, the first-footers prepared to take their leave. As they trooped down the stairs, Bridget turned and asked, "Diary on Tuesday?"

CHAPTER FOUR: MISS MURDOCH'S WAR

Abstract war is horrid,

I sign to that with all my heart, -

But civlyzation doos get forrid

Sometimes upon a powder-cart.

James Russell Lowell, The Biglow Papers: First Series, 1848

Throughout January Joyce and Bridget worked through Miss Murdoch's version of World War II. From a professional point of view, there was little in this section for Joyce. As Miss Murdoch herself acknowledged, "*No doubt it should be possible to remain objective about my own people. I can see that in a time of emergency, such as this, while some social distinctions break down, certain patterns of human behaviour are magnified. If I were a real anthropologist, I should be able to notice and delight in these as they occur. But as a poor amateur I can only live in the present, and hope to have time in some future, peaceful moment to look back and see what was really going on.*"

It seemed that the house was not, in the end, needed as a convalescent home, nor was she saddled with evacuees. Too old for the services and unused to work in a factory, Charlotte Murdoch found her place as an A.R. P. warden. This wasn't too arduous a task. She recorded how glad she was that St. Andrews escaped the bombing suffered by Glasgow, London and other cities. But then, who would want to bomb St. Andrews? *"Only a person bent on destroying one of the jewels of our British nation. It would affect morale quite badly. Indeed, now I think of it, were I Hitler, I should attack the small, historic towns. After all, that might engender real fear amongst us: fear of losing our history and thus our identity. On the other hand, that fear is one which might give rise to an even greater urgence in self-defence."*

She began to struggle with the increasingly meagre rations of a single person, and continued to refuse to go to church, or make any religious pretence. For the first two years of the war, she lived a very solitary life, having no place for regular gatherings with others except for her times on A.R.P. patrol with another local volunteer. She stayed at home away from people and knitted endlessly, producing a harvest of grey woollen socks.

"You would think that machines would be faster and more labour-efficient," commented Bridget. A few pages further on, Miss Murdoch answered he observation.

"Why do I knit? No one has utterly commanded it. Enough socks can surely be made in a mechanical fashion, and I'm not so sentimental to think that a home-made sock is worth more. The worth of a sock is in direct proportion to its ability to keep the foot warm and comfortable. So why knit? I can only think of it as a throw-back. I did this in the first war, when I couldn't get close to the soldiers. It's what women do in wars; what they have always done; they stay at home and knit for their men-folk. I have no men-folk, but still I knit."

The entries went on, a spasmodically detailed record of life in war-time St. Andrews, as seen from one limited perspective. Even taken from that perspective, there were gaps. Miss

Murdoch had been writing for herself and had felt no need to go into all the minutiae of official regulations, except when they affected her personally, one way or another. Some were sensible.

"I don't want to take evacuees and am glad I needn't, but I do see it's sensible to keep the next generation as safely as possible."

Others she found irksome.

"I am developing a small ridge on my right shoulder where the string from my gas-mask box cuts in, and have a constant bruise on my left hip where the box itself bounces around. It's nice to be prepared. Sometimes I really hope we'll have call to use them, with all the bother they are."

Occasionally she saw the funny side of a situation.

"Out on the A.R.P. rounds in the haar tonight, well wrapped-up and with a scarf round my face, for all it's August. In the dark and the mist, twice I collided with people, similarly muffled. The second one grabbed my scarf and threatened to report me as a German spy. Deciding he couldn't be in earnest, I asked why he should think so. Answer, 'Only a spy would be out on a night like this. I should know. I'm one myself!' Turned out to be Ewan Jamieson, a fellow-warden. He was livening up a shift when, as he put it, 'Every house could be shining search-lights and Gerry wouldn't see us in this weather.' We decided not to report each other if we went home early."

Hardship was mentioned only in passing.

"I have decided to live on carrots from the garden for a few days. I simply must have a break from the exhausting, everlasting queuing in the shops."

Meanwhile she lived quietly. On October 26th 1940 her entry was more dramatic.

We were bombed last night. Four bombs, they say, though only three did any damage. The fourth, for a wonder, fell in the burn. What are the odds of that happening when you compare the size of the burn to the size of St. Andrews as a whole? But the cottage at the bottom of Allison Place was demolished, and damage was done to the Bute building and St. Mary's College quadrangle. It's not my A.R.P. area, but of course I went to see if I could help. The mess was incredible, and from just three small bombs. I feel shocked and outraged and insecure, and this surprises me. I don't know what I expected, but maybe I didn't expect to meet war head-on here in St. Andrews. It was something that was really happening elsewhere. While this war lasts, I can never feel so safe again. Now I share, to a small degree, the fears known by those in the industrial cities who experience this time and again. Or do I? Perhaps, as I've heard claimed, they get used to it all. Perhaps they adapt.

I'm writing incoherently, I know. So many thoughts crowd me. I am so relieved that no real damage was done in St. Mary's. Those lovely old buildings, and Mary Queen of Scots' thorn tree – and the more magnificent Holm Oak. They have had such a close shave.

I ache with sympathy for Mr Brand whose cottage was destroyed. I am furious that our sirens gave no warning. How dare there be a failure of electricity, just when it was needed? If Mr Brand hadn't been elsewhere by chance those electricity people would have had his death on their hands.

Yet, perversely, amid it all I have a small, a very small spark of pride. As a St. Andrean I am, stupidly, proud that our town was deemed worthy of attack. This is ridiculous: the whole East Coast was affected. I believe people were killed in Cellardyke – Cellardyke of all places!

And I wonder if I have known the pilot, have sat in the same café with him, or have passed him on the street and have seen him raise his hat to me? I know the chances of this are infinitesimally small, but I wonder. I can never know, and that is why I wonder.

This war is so faceless, so impersonal. I will never know if someone with whom I have passed the time of day in a train has been sent to bomb my town. If, impossibly, he was such an acquaintance, the bomber will never know that I, the Scottish lady, am one of those affected by this.

In a faceless war, one thing is sure: chivalry is dead. There is no romance about this bombing, no heroics. Chivalry is dead, and the old high chivalric ideals, and with them something in me dies. How melodramatic! But it is true, because I will make sure that it is true. This new world is no place for a woman with no purpose in life. I shall be such a woman no more. I shall find a purpose. And when, if, people ask me where I got my commitment to whatever I end up doing, I shall say, "I found it in St. Andrews, the night the bombs fell, and the sirens failed to go off."

(Oh dear, will I never overcome my melodramatic leanings?)

This last aside delighted Bridget, who recognised in it something of the Miss Murdoch she had known: the woman who could always laugh at herself. The rest of the war got very sketchy cover from the diaries, most of the entries being mere repetition of daily routines and difficulties. Charlotte Murdoch retrieved her ambition to study and registered at the university, digging out her old school certificates to prove her competence in Latin, English, Mathematics, French, and History. She was by far the oldest student, which she found stimulating.

"I may not be able to memorise as quickly as my younger colleagues, but I can think better. I can put ideas together, make connections and express myself."

She enjoyed connecting her disciplines, tracing the mutual influences of philosophy, history, and literature. She even essayed a little theology.

"...Strictly as a philosophical and historical phenomenon; and

attitude which I find enrages other, ardent young students, proselytisers (and misogynists) to a man."

War-time conditions curtailed the number of students at the university and changed the composition of the student body. A far higher proportion of the undergraduates were female, compared with pre-war days. There were some discharged service-men, and unhappy young men, physically debarred from being called up. There were fewer students than in peace-time, but classes were larger, with younger lecturers called away, or volunteering to serve elsewhere. The range of subjects offered for study was narrower than before. But it was student social life which suffered most from the effects of the war.

"Not that that concerns me. I shouldn't be involved in parties and picnics in any case. Very few people are complaining much, apart from a few empty-headed county girls, fresh from boarding school."

As the terms passed, the diary entries became more and more cursory, and were spaced even further apart. There was a whole year's break from June of 1944 until the end of the war, recorded in 1945.

"It is over. The parties and rejoicing have begun. I will go down presently to join the throngs. But my rejoicing is not un-mixed. I have spoken thus to no one – it is not acceptable at this time – but I cannot forget the devastation of these past six years. I look at people dancing in the streets, and I wonder how they can. Hasn't that one lost a husband, that one a son? And is this little boy not now fatherless? I see a family who came to this town as refugees when a bomb fell on their Glasgow home, having nothing. I have suffered far less than most in this war. With no family and few real friends, I have not known personal loss. My home is intact, my personal history remains un-violated, and I have come through.

I have more than come through: I have gained a new sense of direction, have been trained to use my mind and am the richer for these years. I have gained so much, and it is ironic that my specific gain prohibits me from uninhibited revelry now. I have not suffered enough to know the gladness of relief. And I know that the war is never over, and that the terms of peace now will set up international tensions which will shape the world for the rest of my life. I am glad that the killing has stopped, but I am also aware of the magnitude of the problem we have created: a problem of used-up resources; of devastated cities; of displaced people; and of a country become an obsolete war-machine. I am determined to help shape a future – for me and for others. I have gained an education in this war – one I might not have had otherwise (though who can say what might have been?) There are tears I my eyes as I watch our normally reserved citizens making merry. The level of anxiety the war has generated is shown by the excess of relief now it is over. It was never displayed while life was full of daily uncertainties. There are Polish soldiers among the celebrants, and I wonder what peace will mean for them, and if they will want or be able to go home? I can't forget my reserve and join in the festivities whole-heartedly. I wish I could. But my heart sympathises with their gladness – and hope them always happy, despite the odds.

During January Joyce and Bridget participated in Miss Murdoch's war: war with her nature, her personal history, and her sense of purpose. They talked as eagerly as ever about her revelations, and about the matter which she kept to herself. Joyce, for instance, was of the opinion that if war couldn't turn Miss Murdoch to God, then nothing could. However, on other levels the two women had less to say. Week by week they sat together at the table in Windmill Road, the gas fire popping in the background and the lamplight glowing on the faint gold and glossy beech-brown heads, and always what conversation there was remained constrained, restricted to the matter in hand.

Bridget puzzled over this, as she puzzled over Sandy's absence. Joyce was particularly unforthcoming on this topic, and her silence spread in concentric circles around her, as though a vacuum was eating up the sound-waves. Bridget found a fine sense of irony in reading about the war with a woman who seemed to be waging a gently, quiet, ruthless war on her. The irony did nothing to comfort her, however. She cared more for people than for nuances of atmosphere and hated to be shut out by Joyce for no known reason. For of course how could Joyce tell her that she and Sandy had quarrelled over Joyce's Christmas visit to Bridget's home?

Bridget could not know that, and she could not know that part of Joyce's seeming hostility was caused by an assumption that as a minister Bridget would have a heightened insight into situations. She should therefore know that Joyce was mentally locked in a stand-off with Sandy. This was not possible, of course, and Joyce also miscalculated in not realising that Bridget's first concern was their own relationship. Because this relationship had become muted, Bridget looked to her own conduct to try to explain the silence. Sandy became a lesser concern.

Joyce, in her near-paranoia, did not see this. Her thought processes ran like this, starting from the conviction that Bridget had done more than note Alex's absence. She must have realised that they had had a fight. But then, she never asked about it. Surely a minister would ask about a fight. They were supposed to give advice. She didn't ask, so perhaps she already knew. How? Perhaps she had met Alex in the street? Even phoned his house? Perhaps he had consulted her (the two-faced bastard) – they always got on so well. Too well? Perhaps Bridget was seeing Alex regularly but not mentioning it? – hoping to keep them apart. In this way Joyce could relieve herself of feelings of guilt and responsibility. If all this was the case, then Alex must have been looking for a reason to quarrel with her, so that he could dump her for Bridget. For a minister? Why not? He didn't seem to want her body and kept claiming to love her mind. Perhaps he loved Bridget's mind better? Then it wasn't just because she spent Christmas with the McKays that Alex had run off. That was just a convenient excuse. Though he probably was angry enough – after all, perhaps he had been hoping to be there himself that day.

In any case, it wasn't her fault. She needn't feel guilty. And so she managed to convince herself that she was free to feel as rejected as she liked, and to admit to herself how much she missed Alex. But she wouldn't contact him. In any event, she couldn't as her phone was out of order. With this genuine excuse for not using the instrument, Joyce procrastinated on reporting the fault and having it repaired.

Deep down, Joyce knew that some, at least, of her angry fantasies were far-fetched, but it was easier to go on with the cheap consolation of speculation than confront any degree of truth. Daily new permutations on the theme presented themselves to her. Perhaps it wasn't Bridget but Ian? Perhaps Alex was gay – that would explain why he hadn't had much interest in sex. Ian was attractive, she could see that. Had Alex also seen it, in much the same way?

Sandy meanwhile was also caught up in the battle. He was not having a happy new year. There was his work, or the lack of it, and there was Joyce, or her absence. Several times he had tried phoning her, but of course had never received an answer, and the sound of what he did not know was a broken telephone ringing on and on became abhorrent to him.

He was ashamed of his outburst in the restaurant. Even with all the pressure and uncertainty that had been growing in his life, there was no excuse for such a public display of temper. Because of his shame he was unable to let himself call in on Joyce and apologise in person. He felt he needed permission to approach her, permission, and forgiveness. And the broken telephone went on ringing, until in despair he gave up trying to call.

His work went from bad to worse. His only current project was nearing completion, but he felt none of his customary pride in the job, simply numb despair of ever landing another contract. Sandy usually coped alone with his problems and since childhood had been accustomed to keeping his own counsel. Normally his placid exterior could cover any inner turmoil, but now he was growing irritable.

His grandfather was the first to notice. With true family directness he questioned the matter.

"What's wrong with you these days, Sandy? You're aye going around with a face like a cold, grey November. And you're aye here of an evening. How come you're never going to St. Andrews to see your opinionated young lady? She's never gone away, surely?"

Sandy gave no direct answer and muttered something about "trouble at work."

The old man knew he was getting only half an answer, but he didn't press his questions about Joyce. "What's wrang with work? You haven't fallen out with young Hargreaves, have you?"

With a sigh, Sandy explained the dearth of contracts coming his way. "I should have told you before, Grandad, because it looks like I'll have to be moving away. I've applied to firms in Glasgow and Edinburgh. Mind you, I'm aware I'd not be any firm's first choice. They would rather have a new graduate to guide and mould than someone who tried on his own and failed. They want someone who wants to see his designs mass-produced, who doesn't care if he only designs a cupboard in a house that is put together from bits and pieces from lots of different designers. They want someone who wants to see thousands of homes which he has had a finger in springing up all alike, in every corner of the country. They don't want someone who only comes to the mass market with reluctance, someone who would rather design a house to fit in with its location and start from scratch every time. But if I'm called for interview I'll try to sound as production-line-happy as possible, so there's a chance I may be leaving you. If I'm not, I don't know where the rent money's to come from."

The conversation ended there. Old Mr Melville had more sense than to offer false hope or cloying sympathy. All the same, he was concerned. He liked Sandy. In his opinion the boy had grown into a finer man than his father. More selfishly, he didn't want to have Sandy move out. If that were to happen, his interfering son and daughter-in-law would be here more often, if they didn't try to convince him, or the authorities, that he was incapable of living alone. Which was ridiculous.

The conversation helped Sandy a little. He pulled himself together and took a long look at how he could help himself. He was trying with work, but what about Joyce? Things were impossible as they were. Reluctantly he decided that if he didn't deserve to approach her directly, then he should stop trying to phone. Surely she couldn't have been out every time. He should, in fact, consider it over, chalk it up to experience and try to forget her. It wouldn't be easy, but it had to be attempted.

Following the war, Charlotte Murdoch set out on her travels again. This time, however, she was not travelling purely for her own pleasure. She couldn't. Although she had not lost financially by the war, the new laws restricting the amount of money which could be taken from the country made lengthy pleasure-trips difficult. That there were people making such trips, and others prepared to accommodate them, showed that it could be done; but Miss Murdoch had no interest in discovering how.

January 10th 1946

I have rented my house to two families, one upstairs and one dawn. There is a great shortage of housing in the cities and finding people to take on this place was depressingly easy. It was even sadder that no one could afford to take it in one piece and live in it as it should be lived in. I'm afraid this house's glory days are over.

What do I care? I'm off to India, and I'm going to take my first job!

"Educated lady required to teach two British children (aged 10 and 12). Skill in English, Mathematics, French and History required. The successful applicant must also be prepared to ready the children for life in England."

That successful applicant am I, and I'm off to Calcutta. I am greatly excited at the prospect of travelling once more. I am also glad that I am travelling with a purpose. I gather from Captain Lewis that his children, Susan and Christopher, have not been to Britain for eight years. A lot has changed in that time. The family will be returning here for good next year and the parents don't want the realities of life here to be too much of a shock for their children. That is very far-sighted of them. I wonder, though, if they realise that they too are likely to be surprised. So very much has changed here during the war. Somehow I don't think that things can go back to being as they were.

Tomorrow I'm off, by train to Southampton – that will be a weary journey – and there I shall board the liner for India. Although I may only take so much money with me, there is nothing to prevent me travelling well. In fact, I deem it patriotic to go First Class throughout. This will leave a little more room for people in second class and the extra money I pay will help the travel companies. I may be a governess, but that is from choice, and I needn't be dowdy.

January 14th 1946

I needn't be dowdy, indeed! I had no idea. I really thought that my collection of carefully-preserved pre-war clothes with the best of my war-time wardrobe was as good as could be found anywhere these days. Ha! This ship has been a real eye-opener. Dressed as I am I belong in the second class, not that I have any intention of removing there. The first-class passengers seem simply dripping jewels and furs, to say nothing of their sleek cashmere twin-sets by day, and their satin and silk evening gowns. Every night the first-class dresses for dinner. I had expected we might sometimes, but not every night. I have only two evening dresses with me, and both were packed with an eye to warm Indian evenings, not the North Atlantic in January.

So far none of the other guests has been more than civil to me. But this is just day two. The South coast of England is still not far away, literally and atmospherically. Anyway, come what may, I shall hold up my head and enjoy this voyage. I will look around me more at dinner tonight, and I may manage to have at least one conversation that goes beyond passing the cruet.

I am impressed with my cabin, though! I had heard that this ship was used as a troop transporter, so I wasn't expecting the pre-war fittings still to be here. But they are. Either the troops had a luxurious time, or else, more likely, the fitters have been busy of late. My cabin – stateroom, I should say – has mahogany appointments: a bunk (very comfortable), a wardrobe, a chest of drawers, an armchair, a desk and chair, and a washstand, and all have touches of gleaming brass about them. The carpet is deep-piled and very clean. And the heating works. This is a real blessing, as it is bitterly cold outside. Very few people are using the decks, although the various lounges seem well-peopled. I, however, have found the ship's library (leather chairs and doors on all the bookshelves, for use in high seas) and am quite comfortable in my stateroom with a pot of tea and "Persuasion". It is a long time since

I read any Jane Austen. They also seem to have complete sets of Dickens and Hardy, so I needn't be dull at any point on this voyage.

January 16th 1946

The weather is getting warmer. I spent some time walking around the deck today, needing a little exercise. There are a few fitness fanatics who were exercising with weights; I was surprised to see some women amongst them. This ship is beginning to feel like home, especially my stateroom. Also, I am beginning to make social contacts (I don't think I can really claim to have made friends). After so long living alone, and living in a very restricted manner before that, this communal living is new to me. I had thought it would be like living in an hotel, and there are similarities. But in an hotel people come and go. Here we are the same guests in the same "building" for 24 hours of each day.

The last two nights I have looked around and discovered that I am not in fact the only first-class passenger who has no jewels and who wears a cardigan over a summer evening gown. There are some others, and one or two men who don't seem to possess evening wear at all. It is simply hard to notice us because we don't glimmer and glow like the others, so we disappear into the shadows a bit.

Last night I was talking to one of the other plain-dressed single ladies. She was a good conversationalist, speaking of the war and her experiences, and listening with what seemed to be interest to my own war-time stories. She applauded my decision to be better educated. Then she said something about being glad to be able to return to India. I was surprised, because she didn't seem the Memsahib type. She's not. She's a missionary!

I said that I didn't think missionaries travelled first class, which was perhaps a bit rude, but she laughed and said that this was a leaving gift from her father. Usually she travelled as cheaply as possible. I told her that I think that the day of the missionary is over. Surely now we have learned to live and let live, and the last thing any Indian needed was to be bound to any Western superstition. I suppose I meant to hurt her.

She simply smiled a little and asked if I'd ever been to India. When I said, "No," she said, "Nothing you can have heard about the country will prepare you for the reality. You may love it or hate it, but you will react. India cannot be ignored. My response is to be a medical missionary. Yours will be different. But once you have been there for a while, think again about me, if you will. You may find that whether or not you agree with me, you may understand what I am trying to do."

I suppose I asked for that, expressing an opinion about what Indians don't need when I've never been there.

January 20th 1946

The food on this ship is tremendous! Right from the start it has been better than rationing could provide. Again, I suppose, money talks. But now we have had a quick stop in Morocco – though not trips ashore, unfortunately – and new provisions have been taken on board. The fruit! We are awash with tropical fruit. There is a constant supply of it available to us. Yesterday I ate so much pineapple that it has hurt my mouth. I've never had it any way but tinned before, in syrup, which is very sweet. Fresh pineapple has sweetness and tang and crisp juiciness. It must also have a lot of acid! Today I am eating mangoes, another new experience. Again they are sweet, but denser in texture and they have a richness to them. One is sufficient, so I won't be overdosing today.

I heard one of what I think of as the "Memsahib types" say, "Oh, my dear, how this fruit gives one hope. We have been in the savage wasteland. Now we are returning to civilization."

Her friend laughed and said, "Yes indeed. Real food again: lots of meat, the fruit, proper puddings, and with people to cook and serve it for one. In London I just could not find decent servants. And the wages they expected! But now we are returning to India. Dear, cheap, servile India!" And they both laughed. I wonder if my employers will be like that? Captain Lewis didn't sound that way, but I have only met him through letters. And what about his wife?

It is now warm enough not to need a cardigan by day or by night. I must say, I love the heat, even at night, when others complain about being stifled.

February 20th 1946

Calcutta. What can I say? I arrived here yesterday. As we sailed up the East coast of India, occasionally we have been close enough to glimpse the land: long white beaches backed by lush greenness; pointed roofs atop towers shining brightly in the sun; small clusters of huts gathered around rocky bays, with children's voices coming faint but shrill over the water. But all that time we were on the ship. We were still out at sea, removed, looking on. Yesterday we docked. As soon as the ship touched the wharf, everything changed.

The relaxed calm of the first class disappeared completely. There was a rustle of expectancy. Some people peered over the side, looking for friends or family. Others kept resolute watch over their luggage. Hurried goodbyes were called to ship-mates. The missionary-woman smiled at me and waved, as did Mr Brown, with whom I've had such interesting literary chats. Neither of them moved from their luggage though, old hands that they are. When I left my trunk and cases to go and peer over the rail, Mr Brown called out to me not to be so foolish. I soon saw why.

It seemed that we hadn't really docked before Indian porters flowed over the ship. They were young men who didn't wait for the gangway to be put in place but swarmed up ropes flung from ship to shore. Each headed for a pile of luggage. Had I not been with mine, goodness knows what might have happened. I mean that. I don't know. It may be that nothing untoward would have taken place, but I might have lost a bag or case or items from inside the luggage. I don't know. I looked at the thin, lithe Indian boys, with their black hair and eyes and white teeth gleaming in their smiles and I could not judge anything about them: characters, hopes, intentions, humour.

The next impression was heat. As the ship came to a standstill, the ocean breeze and the slight wind of our passage was left behind and the air settled on me like a warm, damp blanket, making me feel instantly sticky and snatching at my breath with hungry fingers. I am told that this is not the hot weather, and that I shall become used to this. I hope so. When I think that off the African coast I said that I liked the heat and thought the other passengers weaklings for complaining! Perhaps in that gentle warmth they remembered the heat to which we were sailing.

With the heat came the smells. So many smells, and not really combining at all, so that my nose was bemused by such over-stimulation. There were the normal dock-land smells: petrol fumes, stale water, damp, mould and so on. Then there were the perfumes of the various cargoes being loaded onto a ship in the neighbouring berth: a whiff of orange oil, the sweet scent of bananas, the clean smell of coconuts. There were spicy aromas from cooking, for the wharf boasted several informal cafés, where a fire was lit on the stones, and over them rice was boiled, and curries concocted. There were large, thin pale foods, looking like enormous potato crisps, which smelled of cumin and seemed very popular. On top of the cooking was the heavy scent of tropical flowers. One or two women were selling handfuls of gaudy, exotic foliage, and nearly everyone meeting the ship had a floral tribute of some kind – such bunches, formal bouquets, even garlands, wreaths and head-dresses!

If there was a smell which was stronger than the rest it was the warm odour of humanity. A sell of spicy breath, hot bodies, faeces (I might as well say so) oiled hair and sweat. The people were everywhere. When the gangway was in place they followed the porters on board, seeking family members, offering to sell flowers or food, promoting their taxis or courier services. They thronged on the wharf in coloured saris or white robes, jostling and waving like a border thick with coloured daisies, each with a black centre.

I think that I shall never forget this, my introduction to India. I shall never forget the clamour, the bemusing sounds, smells and sights. I shall never forget either the exuberant sense of welcome I received. For whatever reason (and I am aware that most people must see me as a walking source of income) I could not believe that these people were anything other than glad to have me come. It was an infectious feeling. I had been a little apprehensive at the thought of the voyage ending. I had even been a little sentimental about my stateroom (my "dear" cabin I had said to my stupid self). I had been wondering about my new location and new employment. But now all that uncertainty was swept away in the wave of warmth and greeting which flowed over and around me. After a welcome like that it will be very hard to do anything other than adore this place.

I may as well continue writing this. It's the middle of the night, but what with the heat and the unfamiliar sounds of the night, I can't sleep.

I allowed my self-appointed porter to carry my baggage, and he managed it all, tying it to a leather strap then hoisting it over his shoulder. I kept a firm eye on him and made sure no one came between us as we made our slow way down the gangplank and through the crowds to the customs office. Once or twice I had to grab at one of the bags, both to hold him back and to prevent the throng from sweeping us apart. The customs shed was incredible. It was hot and dim and indescribably smelly. People were lining up in various queues; porters and officials were screeching at each other and at us. I caught sight of the missionary lady and firmly attached myself to the queue she was in, hauling my porter with me. At length we got through. The customs officer himself was most charming, and very grand in his crisp uniform. He checked over my papers, counted my bags (though he didn't open them), wished me a pleasant stay in his country, and waved me through. As I stepped out of the shed, I felt as though I were taking my first proper steps into India.

All this insistence on beginnings and firsts intrigues me. I haven't usually been this way about new countries. Of course, I had to travel further and for far longer to get here, but I don't think it's just that. There is something about this place. It is so different from Europe that it is almost like starting life afresh.

On the other side of the customs shed was Captain Lewis, along with hundreds of others meeting the ship. All the faces were confusing to me, and I just stood and stared at them, wondering what to do. Just then I saw my name. MISS CHARLOTTE MURDOCH was written on a large piece of cardboard being waved around. Still followed by my porter I approached that part of the crowd and found that the sign was held by a man of around my own age, tall, tanned, blond but greying, wearing a white army uniform. He didn't seem to have seen me, indeed he looked right through me as I approached. I was obliged, therefore, to tap him on the arm and introduce myself.

He was taken aback, I could see that. And I knew that he had been expecting someone younger; younger and less shabby.

He recovered himself beautifully, however, and bade me most welcome. "I see you managed to find a porter," he said, seriously. I managed not to laugh, but really! I wonder if this is a British-in-India joke, harking back to the difficulty of finding porters in "Dear Old Blighty". Or perhaps he didn't know what to say. In any case, he led us both out of the crowd to a car he had waiting. He helped the porter to load up my luggage and then paid him off with small coins and strange words. I was relieved that he paid without question – as I have yet to acquire any Indian money.

That is one of the things I must see to tomorrow.

I fancy I shan't need much money, though. This is a lovely house, and I am going to be living in luxury. The house is outside Calcutta. We drove through the city to get here – incredible – but I shall perhaps describe it when I have seen it better. Anyway, here we are away from the bustle and smells and endless presence of people. This must be some kind of suburb, and a very pleasant place, with large houses set in their own gardens.

The house is relatively cool with marble floors, long verandas and windows propped open to catch any breeze that's going. I have a large room and a bathroom to myself, and a servant to take care of my clothing and clean and wait on me! She is a slim, graceful, serious girl, named Lakshmi, and I hope that she doesn't think that my poor clothes are beneath caring for.

I haven't met the rest of the household yet. They were out at a party when I got here, and Captain Lewis said they might be late. At his suggestion I had a light supper in my room, helped Lakshmi to unpack my luggage, and turned in early. The bed is comfortable but sleeping in a tent of mosquito netting is a new experience. It feels a little claustrophobic – as though the net absorbs any spare air. But I have no intention of contracting malaria, so the net stays. I will simply have to get used to it.

Thursday February 21st 1946

This won't be such a long entry. My eyelids are drooping. I think – hope – that even the warm air and the insects can't keep me awake tonight.

Just a few lines to put down my impressions of the day. Impressions of people. Captain Lewis has the imagination to know that his family must be readied for life in England. Why does he not see this must also apply to his wife?

I met Mrs Lewis at breakfast. She is beautiful – dark hair and eyes, glowing skin, lovely figure, gracious walk. She talks well too, quietly but persistently. One of the first things I gathered was that she was born here. "Calcutta is in my blood and my bones: its air was the first I breathed; its sounds my earliest lullaby." As we talked – polite nothings mainly – I made some remark about the traffic in London. To my surprise she rewarded me with a sweet smile. "I am sure you are right, Miss Murdoch, but I cannot tell. I have never been to London." In fact, she has never been to Britain; something always prevented her making the trip. If Susan and Christopher need education about life in Britain, surely their mother needs it even more. They, after all have been there, even if it was years ago. Will Mrs Lewis allow me to attempt to ready her for the transition that is coming her way.?

Susan is blonde, like her father, with a square face and a still childish body. She and Christopher (known as Kit) showed me round the house, and I found that her mind is not that of a child. She has insight and awareness of what is going on around her, and she makes and stands by moral judgements. She explained to me, very carefully, that in her view, India should be free of British rule, but that her opinion doesn't matter. The ruling nations can't force independence on the other; such independence would have its roots in bondage and would not be strong. While she would like to give India its independence, she's afraid that it would not be worth having unless it were fought for. "A struggle makes a thing more precious." Precocious child, but she doesn't seem to realise it.

Kit is probably a typical ten-year-old boy, but I wouldn't know. My experience of small boys is slender. He is not like either of his parents being possessed of red hair and freckles. He always seems to be running, has a shrill voice and a short span of attention. Teaching him will take some skill.

Saturday 23rd February 1946

I should have at least tried to discover more about contemporary

India before I came here. I believe I still had a picture of a country where the British ruled, enjoyed a superb life-style, and were loved by grateful subjects. Maybe it was like that once. Perhaps. But I find it hard to believe. Anyway, what I did not realise is that I have come here at a time of unrest. It began in Bombay, but it has spread here: mutiny on some Royal Navy ships. I knew nothing of it when I arrived. Of course, I saw some naval ships in the docks, but there was no obvious sign of mutiny about them. Indeed, there was no sign of life at all. If I had but known it, that was the sign, but then I wasn't to know that these ships are usually crawling with sailors – or so I'm told.

Today there was a lot of shouting in the streets beyond the garden. The children became curious because they said it sounded angry, not like the usual noise. Again, I'm too much of a novice here to tell the difference. We asked Ali, our Muslim steward, what was going on. (Already I'm learning that it matters that Ali is a Muslim, religion determines almost everything here.) Ali said the people were angry because the army has been called in to deal with the mutineers. "What else do they expect?" I asked. Ali smiled gravely (not a contradiction) and said, "Indeed, they expect nothing else. But they had thought that British soldiers would be used. The anger is because some of the troops were Indians. That is a bad thing, to put Indians one against another. It is insulting to both."

I don't fully understand that, but I'm beginning to see how little I understand of this marvellous country. I want to know more.

Monday 25th February 1946

All is calm again here in our leafy palace. We started our lessons properly today. I have decided to do ordinary lessons and include the preparation for a return to Britain in informal conversation. Making a formal lesson of it might actually make it seem more portentous and difficult than it will be. In any case, the children are intelligent, and they know they will be going. They naturally ask questions.

It is a pity no one knows just when the family will depart. I did ask Captain Lewis, but he said he had no indication as yet. A lot seems to depend on what Lord Wavell agrees with Nehru and the other Indian leaders. "And." The Captain added dryly, "It depends upon Atlee's agreeing to it." I gather that Atlee does not get on well with the Viceroy.

Sunday March 17th 1946

These children have hidden depths. Today Kit took a tumble and fell, giving himself a really nasty gash on the knee. The way he runs around, it's surprising this doesn't happen more often. After I'd cleaned it and put on a gauze dressing I was attempting to wrap a rolled bandage over the spot. What with the moisture, the slippery ointment and Kits' involuntary movements, the whole thing would not stay in place. I was most impressed when Susan firmly removed the roll of bandage from my hands and deftly bound everything up.

I asked her where she learned that skill. "In the war," was her amazing answer. It seems she was patriotically desperate to help in the war. Her mother, who doesn't believe in saying no when she can say yes, allowed her to join the Junior Red Cross. At first she was simply rolling bandages and learning theoretically. But casualties from the war in the East were numerous and many came to Calcutta, while others came to their warm weather base in the hills. Susan didn't ask permission, but simply went in and began changing dressings and cleaning wounds. By the time anyone noticed her – I think it must have been quite a chaotic situation – she was so well-practiced they allowed her to continue. She spent two hours a day nursing. This means that she has a lot more experience than I, who grew up in a convalescent home.

I asked if she wants to be a nurse, and she shook her head vehemently. "Not a nurse. I want to help people though. I might train as a doctor and then go to places where medicine isn't very advanced and train other people to do it better. The missionaries do that here, but I don't want to be a missionary."

That reminded me of the missionary lady I met on board the ship. Perhaps that is what she means by responding to India, though she would have done better to leave her religion out of it, I think. I suppose growing up here, in privilege, surrounded by poverty, has fuelled Susan's humanitarian urges. It does her credit though: few girls of her age would do other than take the status quo for granted.

May 2nd 1946

The heat is growing. Normally in the hot weather women and children – British women and children - would be sent to the relative coolness of the hills. But not this year. The mood here is too uncertain for Captain Lewis to be willing to be separated from his family. Oh well, the hills might be nice, but the heat will be an experience, if I'm not too limp and exhausted to do anything. The children are used to it all. In the first years of the war they went to the hills as usual; they go to school when they are there, and in 1940 they stayed for the whole year. But Captain Lewis is a family man. It's rather touching, really, because at times he seems the complete military man: stern, unyielding, disciplined, even unfeeling. He is devoted to his family, however. So when the war became more intense he kept them by him as much as possible. Of course, he had to be away with his troops, but Calcutta was his base, so the family stayed where he could best come home to them.

May 10th 1946

A day off from formal lessons and I went into Calcutta to do some shopping. I have done this several times since I came here, but it is never less than an adventure. I don't want to romanticise this city once I've moved on, so I will try to record what I saw today, just as a reminder.

The streets are busy. Cars vie for space with pedestrians – thousands of them – and with bicycle rickshaws, man-pulled rickshaws, motor bikes, ox carts and cattle. You never know where you are going to find a cow. They are holy to the Hindus, and so no one interferes with them, but lets them wander at will. Sometimes they bear fresh or faded wreaths of flowers. I asked why once and was told that the cow is the image of one of the gods or goddesses – Lakshmi is it? – and so they are honoured with flowers just as images in temples are. It strikes me it might be more honouring to take the cows out of the dangers of the streets and give them a proper feeding regularly. They are no advertisement either to the bovine race nor to any goddess, being mainly bony, covered in sores and very dirty.

With this respect for cows, the streets are far from clean. It's not just cow dung though, there's human dung too. It's quite common to see people squatting by the side of the road to relieve themselves. Men are the chief culprits, but I have seen poor, shabby women do the same, using the skirts of their saris as a modicum of privacy. Also, the Indian seems to have no concept of litter. Anything and everything is strewn in the streets – fruit and vegetable peelings, rotten and slimy, wrappings off foods, old newspapers. You name it, it's there, and the population tramps over it regardless. I find it better to be driven where I want to go.

The streets house beggars. Literally, they house them. They lie down and sleep outside shops, some in makeshift cardboard or wooden shelters, but most only in their clothing, such as it is. While none of them are anything but emaciated, they are given food by those around them. I'm told that beggars are regarded as holy in Hindu and Buddhist religions. All the same, it seems that it is chiefly the poor who give to the beggars, not the rich. Do riches erode religion? Or are those nearest destitution naturally more sympathetic to others who are already bereft in the world?

I'm writing this all down, but it's very clinical. It doesn't convey the real sense of colour and life, above all life, which pulses through everything. There is nothing dreary about Calcutta's streets when taken as a whole, even though some of the people there live in great misery.

Today I saw a man writing letters, a freelance scribe for the illiterate masses. And of course there are always travelling entertainments, often with animals. Monkey men are the most common, beating their drums and leading the crowds in a rhythmic chant, urging two monkeys to perform a rather grotesque courtship and mate.

I could write on and on about the sights and sounds of Calcutta. I believe a whole life spent collecting them would only scratch the surface of their enormous variety. But I know I will never forget, no matter what else I may come to know.

August 16th 1946

Something terrible is happening in the city. Even here at our safe distance this is more than obvious. I can see a cloud of orange smoke rising from burning buildings. I can smell it – the smell of burning decay. I can hear cries, cries of pain, of rage, of fear, of grief. The people are rioting in the streets, Hindu against Muslim, Muslim against Hindu.

Captain Lewis says the Muslims began it, by flying black flags from their properties and declaring today a holiday. I don't see myself why this should have such terrible consequences, but of course, the Hindus don't like being told what to do by the Muslims and want no part of any Muslim Holy Day. It always comes down to religion here in India. I wonder if that's true at home? Maybe we just disguise things better?

Anyway, The Muslims began to enforce this "holiday" and the result is carnage.

August 17th

The terror continues. Now I have seen some of the results for myself. Those escaping from the city have come past this house. They are dazed and distressed, clad in rags and often wounded, or helping wounded friends. I wanted to tend the casualties: Susan and I could have done something, but Captain Lewis wouldn't hear of it. He says that if we become involved then we, and other British households, will no longer be safe. We will be perceived as belonging to one side or the other; or it could be that both sides will attack us. He's probably right: he's been here for a long time. But my heart aches for those I see.

August 18th

The hardest thing is lessons. I can see it's important to keep Susan and Kit from being frightened and that the normality of lessons is good. But with such a background? The carnage has in no way abated. I have decided we will do only history these days. We will study battles and their causes, then we might find some logic in these volatile days. And studying historical battles against such a background should bring home the consequences of violence.

August 20th

No more lessons. The domestic staff has vanished, though whether they've run from the city, seeking safety, or into the city to join the rioters is unclear. I'm sure that some of them must have been worried about their families. I know I would have been.

So now we're all involved in keeping house, in every sense of the term. Captain Lewis is guarding the gates with an armoury of weapons. He is still afraid we might come under attack in the confusion. I am in the kitchen, the last place I'd have expected to find myself. There has been no fresh food since the riots began. It hadn't occurred to me what this means in a sweltering climate. We are dependent on fresh supplies being brought in daily. Now we are reduced to the tins in the larder. Mrs Lewis can't cook. I don't mean that she's a bad cook, I mean that she has never had to cook anything, ever. She can't use a tin opener nor light the stove. I have decided I must teach her and Susan what I can. I'm no cordon bleu chef, goodness knows, but I can prevent starvation. Ironically all the years of making do during the war are coming into their own now. I'm les afraid of mixing unusual ingredients than I might have been. If I knew how long the food had to last, I would enjoy the challenge, but I don't, so we're eating very sparingly.

August 22nd

When will this horror end? The glow of the fire, and the noxious cloud of smoke never grow any less. And now we see not just fugitives passing our grounds, but also their pursuers. Today I took a meal to Captain Lewis in the gatehouse: he's living there all the time now, and looking horribly haggard and tired. As I stood for a minute looking out of the window, I saw a man, a Muslim, judging by the remnants of clothing hanging on him, hurrying out towards the country. Suddenly there was a ferocious cry, "Jai Hind!" From the gatehouse roof another fellow leaped upon him and stuck a dagger in his stomach. The first man screamed, a terrible sound. His assailant jerked out the knife and struck again and again, all the time grunting his war-cry "Jai Hind. Jai Hind. Jai Hind." When the poor Muslim was obviously dead the assassin stuck the knife in his belt and sauntered off towards the city. That saunter – it wasn't even a swagger – was one of the worst things I have ever seen.

I made for the door, but Captain Lewis held me back, gripping me by the shoulders. He spoke very quietly. "Miss

Murdoch, he's dead. You can't help him, but we must be very careful if we are to avoid the same fate." I saw his point at once. Suddenly our precarious situation became very real to me.

I also saw that Captain Lewis simply had to have a break. I told him so, and offered to watch in his place for a few hours while he slept. I thought I had left war-time emergencies behind me, but I haven't. So I put on my A.R.P. hat, metaphorically speaking, and organised him. "You sleep here in the gatehouse, and I will watch. If I see anyone who even glances this way, or who does anything other than hurry past I will waken you at once." He agreed. Poor man, he had no strength to do anything else. I saw more fugitives, but no more murders. No one paid any attention to the body lying in the road, but simply hurried past.

August 24th

There are now more bodies on the road. They are covered in flies and have been gnawed by animals. It is horrible. I spend part of each day keeping watch, so I have plenty of time to observe them, unfortunately.

The children are splendid. I knew Susan would be, of course, but Kit is remaining calm and uncomplaining too, in a wonderful way. Susan and her mother are coming to grips with the kitchen and household chores. They did some laundry today. They might not have bothered, but Captain Lewis told his wife it was "important for morale" that we all have clean clothes and keep ourselves feeling neat and "civilised". Tonight I shall show them how to use the flat irons.

August 26th

It's over, thank goodness. But the end was perhaps the worst part of all. The armies, both Indian and British, came in, with trucks, tanks, and foot soldiers. They could only gain control by force and fear; they could only show how serious they were by using their weapons. More people died. The smoke is still thick over the city and the only sound is of the occasional military boot passing the house. But the quiet is not calm; it is far from peaceful. Resentment still simmers, and at any moment it could turn against us, as an army household.

August 28th 1946

We're still in some uncertainty. Captain Lewis is sure his short leave will be curtailed, and his regiment called back to active service. Mrs Lewis refuses to stay on here without him this time, nor would it be safe for her to do so, not now. So she and the children are going to Britain on the first possible ship, next week, and we have begun to pack up the house. There is a lot to do, and so far none of the servants has returned.

I saw one of them today, however. I ventured into Calcutta with Captain Lewis, as we urgently needed supplies. We walked. It is not safe to drive through streets of burned-out buildings, liable to collapse; besides, most of the streets are impassable except on foot. If it were just burned buildings and fallen masonry it wouldn't be so bad. But there were bodies still lying – bodies that no one had taken away: men and women, old and young. I saw several small children who will never grow up.

On the way home, with some fresh vegetables and naan bread I heard a loud wailing. A man was bent over the body of an ancient woman, cradling her head and crying aloud. As we drew nearer I saw that it was Ganesh, our cook. Captain Lewis had seen him too but did not approach. "Leave him to his grief," he said quietly. "She was his mother."

I have often heard Ganesh on the subject of his mother. "So old she is," he used to say. "So old and she will not die. She has gone beyond death and will live forever. She will bully my wife, that old woman. Yes, and she bullies me. I wish she was dead, I do, then

I may leave Calcutta and live somewhere quieter. But she won't leave the city, and as her son I must take care of her." He would go on and on like that, especially on the days he was most harassed. And there he was, wailing and sobbing as though his heart would break.

I can't forget it. He speaks to me. How I was with my mother was wrong, I know it. What seems worst of all was that no one grieved at her death. Ganesh was probably quite genuine about his chaffing under the maternal thumb, but he had the decency to grieve at her death. He is not so cold and detached as I have been.

I have been I say. But that is the past. I need not continue in this way. And I must not. I must change and become more caring, and less selfish. This will mean going against the grain for a while, but I am a determined creature. I will attempt it.

September 1st 1946

In one week, the Lewis family will be on board their ship, without Captain Lewis, and without me. I have decided that India has more to teach me, and I must remain for a while. My plan is to travel out of Calcutta to some smaller town and find a place, or set up on my own, teaching English to native children. British rule may soon become a thing of the past, but the language will continue to be used for a long time to come, I expect. It is the only lingua Franca India has.

I haven't told the Lewises my plans yet. I think they would try to dissuade me. They would point out the difficulties and hardships I may encounter. I know all about that. I just don't want to have to explain my motives. It's too personal to say that I have to undergo hardships to benefit others in order to cure my callous selfishness. The Lewises think I want to see something of India before I leave, and they're not wrong in that, of course. This evening they spent the whole dinner time (dinner cooked by Ganesh once more) suggesting places I should see.

Captain Lewis commented that it wasn't really "quite the thing" for a white woman to go off alone, but he had seen my courage and common-sense in action and believed that if any woman could travel in safety, it was me. I felt the compliment deeply and thanked him for it.

September 8th 1946 On a train.

Mrs Lewis, Susan and Kit left today, quite early in the morning. I went with Captain Lewis to bid them farewell. There were excited and nervous – all these new experiences – the ship, leaving India, reaching England, moving in with their Lewis relations for a while. I felt quite a lump in my throat when I saw their faces diminishing as the ship pulled away. I'm sure Captain Lewis must have. He stood still and silent, watching the ship till it was out of sight. Then he sighed, took my arm, and towed me away.

My luggage was in the car, and the station was my next destination. But as we reached the car, Captain Lewis halted, looked at me and said, "You really don't have to leave yet, Charlotte, I still have three days and I'd value your company." As he spoke he bent towards me and slipped an arm around my waist. I knew what that meant, and that it wasn't intended as an insult to my integrity but a complement to our camaraderie. I wanted to go back with him. I have come to regard him very highly. But I reminded myself that I have a higher purpose now. So I gently stepped away from his arm and said, "Captain Lewis, you were kind enough to compliment me on my common sense once. Common sense tells me it would be better for everyone that I catch my train."

So I did, but Captain Lewis kissed my cheek before I boarded and told me that I'd been a great help to his family and that he hoped we would meet again soon.

Now I'm off on my adventure. No, that's thinking of me. I'm off to be a servant. I remember the missionary lady on the ship. Perhaps my reaction to India is not so different from hers, after all.

CHAPTER FIVE: DAMAGE AND DECEIT

"I present myself to you in a form suitable to the relationship I wish to achieve with you."

Luigi Pirandello "The Pleasure of Honesty" translated by William Murray

February brought foul weather to the East coast of Scotland. First there was a Siberian cold, so intense that the edges of the sea froze, and thin blades of ice could be seen floating in the harbour, menacing the unsuspecting ducks. The extreme cold passed eventually, then the clear skies clouded over, and snow began to fall. In two days about six inches lay over everything, rendering the golf courses unplayable, much to Antipodean tourists' wrath. As the month progressed the snow melted and was replaced by gales and driving sleet. The tides were unusually high, driven up the beaches by the ferocious East winds; those hardy citizens who braved the weather and ventured down to the East Sands were treated to a spectacular display of water. The grey sea was whipped up like white-of-egg and the waves from opposing currents fought with each other and the retaining sea wall to dramatic effect. Along at the harbour the smallest pier was totally immersed, while the venerable stones of the main pier, many of which had once seen sacred service as part of the cathedral, were pummelled, battered, and drenched by the spray breaking over them.

In the town itself the cold brought burst pipes and the thaw saw those leaks flooding. The snow made untreated pavements treacherous, and the wind caused havoc. Windows were broken, branches brought down, and slates and pan-tiles were hurled from roofs to smash in the streets. Many buildings were affected, public as well as private. Plumbers, joiners, and builders became as rare as gold-dust, and worth far more. They were the only people to really welcome the upheaval and as time went on and they became more and more overworked, even these invaluable citizens became liable to snap and grumble.

Sandy was perhaps the only person to whom the outrageous month brought nothing but good fortune. He finally landed a contract.

His employer was Martyrs' Church, and the project was a complete renovation of the church halls.

Bridget made the first contact, phoning his office on a morning when he was, as usual, trying to postpone attacking the crosswords in the morning paper. He had read all the parts which might be useful to him, and they weren't. When the phone rang, he leapt for it. Even if it were for Hargreaves, it would break the monotony.

"Hello, is that Alex?"

For a second he didn't recognise the voice. His heart leapt in guilt, hope and apprehension. It must be Joyce! Who else would call him Alex?

"Yes it is."

"Oh good. Alex, this is Bridget." His heart sank, but not all the way down. After all, Bridget was Joyce's friend. Perhaps she wanted to play intermediary. But she didn't. "I want you to re-design our church halls."

"I beg your pardon. I don't think I heard you right."

"I expect you did. I'm inviting you to submit a plan for a new-look hall, or halls complex for my church. It's just interior work, of course. Can't change the historic walls. But inside you can have carte blanche."

Sandy swallowed. "Hello, Bridget, how nice to hear from you. Can I ask a couple of questions?"

"Of course."

"Is this to be an act of charity on my part?"

"Oh no, naturally your usual fee will be paid."

"And am I being asked out of charity because you feel sorry for 'poor old Alex' who needs work so badly?"

"Do you? I didn't know. In fact, I was hoping you'd not say you were too busy."

"Oh. I thought perhaps Joyce had told you about my tricky position."

"No. In fact, she doesn't talk about you at all. I'm sorry if that's a blow to your ego." Bridget sounded both humorous and coolly ironic. "Could you have a stab at it? The thing is, first we had a burst pipe, which did for large parts of the ceiling and brought down our over-head heaters. Then four windows were broken in the gales, and the rain got well and truly into the walls. The floor was already beyond a joke, and it wasn't helped by getting soaked and having the heavy heaters fall on it."

"It sounds a mess." Sandy commented.

"It is. We were saving to re-do the halls sometime in the next few years anyway, and now it seems stupid to spend money repairing the damage and then more money re-designing it. Obviously, the insurance will help us get wind and water-tight again, but we might as well push ahead with the changes we were looking at. The Kirk Session met last night to discuss matters. I said I knew of an architect, and for a wonder, none of them did. Until last night I thought my Kirk Session had connections with every conceivable trade and profession. I never said so, but I 'm sure they could produce call girls!" She giggled. "So can you submit some ideas for our approval?"

"Very probably," Sandy replied cautiously, a smile creeping into his voice. "It's more usual to go to several firms for different quotes and ideas though, or even to advertise for competition."

"Oh, I didn't know that. Well, we may do that in the end, but if we like yours, why should we? If we like yours, mind. I'm making no promises, and my Kirk Session can be a tricky bunch at times."

"Well, I think I'd better come and take a look at your halls, see the space we're talking about. When will suit you?"

"This afternoon about two? You know where the church is, don't you? In North Street."

"I know it. Oh, and Bridget, you might be prepared to tell me the current use of the space and what you project future uses might be."

"That's easy. We have..."

"This afternoon," said Sandy, firmly. "I'll see you then." He hung up, a smile spreading over his face. The worry lines disappeared. He was at least potentially back in business, and he was also potentially back in contact with Joyce. Suddenly life looked good again.

Life looked even better when Sandy saw the state of the church halls. Here was a real challenge, such as he had never attempted. Designing houses from scratch had been his line of work, not building or renovating public (listed) edifices. He felt obliged to tell Bridget this when they met. She, being ignorant about architecture, didn't see much difference. "A wall is still a wall, and a roof is still a roof, right?"

The building was interesting, with a fairly forbidding exterior and a solid stone husk. Inside it was divided almost exactly in two. The right-hand side was given over to the sanctuary and was therefore outside Sandy's remit. On the left side was a large hall, with folding doors which could divide it in two and which all dated from the 1920s. There was as small platform at the further end. Beyond that was a modest kitchen which hadn't been re-fitted for at least forty years. And beyond that were a couple of carpeted rooms and some toilets.

The main hall had suffered the worst damage. The floor was piled with fragments of plaster and rubbish which had come down with the ceiling. Heaters lay tangled among this, with twisted metal and wires bristling about them like avant garde hedgehogs. The kitchen was grubby, and there the ceiling, while still technically whole, was bulging with damp in spots. The back rooms, which had been nice, solid Sunday School classrooms had windows broken and glass littered the floor. The wind howled in, singing through the jagged shards. The rooms were full of paper whirling about. Some was rubbish blown in from outside, but there were also scraps of children's drawings, paper models and carefully-written prayers dancing around in the draught. The wind had wrenched these from their proud places of display on the walls. What remained of the once-bright children's art gallery now writhed in tatters, straining at blue-tack and drawing pins, and flapping loudly against the plaster-work. Even as Sandy watched another fragment, containing a lurid picture of, presumably, Moses, leapt from the wall and was flung into the melee. The bright green figure, standing by a fiercely pulsating burning bush of scarlets, golds and crimsons, brushed against Sandy's legs and moved on.

Bridget slipped out of the room and closed the door. "Come into the vestry and I'll put on the electric fire. It at least has four walls, windows and a water-tight roof."

It did, and a threadbare carpet, a standing cupboard, a desk, and a few chairs which weren't quite hard.

"So what do you think, Alex?"

"Sandy." The correction was automatic.

"Sandy? Have you changed your name?"

He smiled. "No, I've always been called Sandy, by everyone except Joyce." Saying her name he flushed slightly and hesitated. Bridget regarded him steadily and made no comment. "If I'm to work for you I would rather you called me Sandy. Think of it as my professional name if you like."

"O.K. I don't mind what you call yourself, so long as we can communicate. Now you've seen it, what do you think?"

"It's great! A real challenge. If I understand you, I can re-configure the rooms, take out and put in walls (so long as they are not load-bearing walls, of course), re-do the flooring, re-decorate the walls – anything I want. I just mustn't change the exterior walls and windows. Is that right?"

"That's it. Is it an architect's dream?"

"Yes it is, or it would be if there were an unlimited budget. I don't suppose that there is, this being a church. What tiny figure are you going to name?"

Bridget smiled blandly and shook her head so that her fair curls bounced. "I don't know." Seeing Sandy's face, which had "amateurs" written all over it, she explained. "We've raised a certain amount so far, something over £100000, but that's not all there need be.

"I'm relieved to hear it. That won't go far."

"Yes, but I don't know how much more. It really depends on the plans you produce. You see, if your plans are stunning in themselves, and if they make obvious all the new things we can do in the space, and therefore all the new places we can go as a church, then the congregation will give more – probably in proportion to their excitement and approval."

Sandy nodded his understanding. This was an approach he hadn't encountered before. Bridget continued talking.

"And then there's the Presbytery. If we can use – or show intent to use – our facilities in ways which they have prioritised, then they may give us grants as well. Or loans. The General Trustees of the Church of Scotland, in Edinburgh would become involved."

"I don't really understand that" Sandy confessed. "I'm afraid I'm not as conversant with church government as I might be. I know that the Kirk Session is the ruling council of the congregation and the Presbytery is officials from a local group of churches..."

"In this case Cupar and St. Andrews, and places nearby, of course," Bridget put in.

"Right. But I don't know what presbyteries do. From what you said it sounds as though they pass out instructions to the churches."

"Well, no one would like to hear it put quite so bluntly, but yes, sometimes that happens. More often though the presbytery generates good (or supposedly good) ideas. The churches are then supposed to recognise the presbyters' great wisdom, applaud wildly, and immediately seek to carry out these ideas voluntarily. Sometimes for major initiatives sums of money are earmarked to encourage voluntary participation."

There was a short silence. Sandy could hear the wind howling through the broken windows in the other rooms. "Are all ministers as cynical as you?" he asked.

Bridget flushed, twitched her mouth, and sighed. "No. Some are young and idealistic. That rarely lasts, however. I was idealistic once, but now I'm realistic. I still have ideals, but I no longer think of the church in the hopeful, spiritual way I once did. It was a kind of naivety, I think. I haven't lost my faith in Christ, or anything like that. In fact, I still believe in the church as an expression of the gospel. But sometimes human ambition gets in the way. Its' understandable and it's forgivable. It keeps us all humble, if frustrated, which is very necessary, especially for ministers. I really think that if there are ministers of around my age who don't have a streak of cynicism in them, they're probably incurable naïve, and maybe dangerous.

"My hope, my personal hope, I mean, for the way I may develop, is what I see of older ministers. There are some – by no means all – who have come through the cynicism. They haven't left it behind, but they have learned to see beyond it. The matters which make me wry-mouthed are to them a source of gentle mirth. They are saints, of course. You can tell that because they are so extremely practical."

Sandy grinned. "I thought saints wore haloes and floated around in a most impractical fashion."

Bridget shook her head. "No, that's a false impression put about, I should think, by people who've never known a real saint. Which is peculiar: they're not so very rare, after all. I know several, and I expect you know a few yourself. They needn't be overly religious people. Oh, and they won't be wearing dinner-plates."

"Dinner-plates?"

"Oh, you must know the dinner-plate school of religious art, when all the holy people have circles, usually gold or white, behind their heads. Sometimes you can tell the relative states of holiness by the different styles of dinner-plate." She laughed a little, and Sandy joined in.

"Back to business," he said. "What is presbytery offering money for that you think you could tie in with?"

"Well, there are one or two matters, but we wondered about getting involved with their initiative on homelessness. It's a growing problem, and there's nowhere in St. Andrews trying to help people with nowhere to live."

"What had you in mind? A soup kitchen? A drop-in place? An overnight shelter?"

"If possible, all three. What we'd really like would be to start with occasional plain lunches. After we'd got to know some of the people better we'd gradually stay open longer, as a warming centre. Then, if we found there was need, we'd offer mattresses and breakfast." She hesitated. "And showers?"

"I see." Sandy's voice gave no hint of his thoughts. "What else do you want to use these premises for?"

"Well, Sunday School, of course. We actually have five groups meeting: creche, under-fives, five-to-eight year-olds, eight to elevens, and Bible Class. They all meet at the same time. At the moment the creche has one room and the Bible Class the other. The rest share the hall, with one class on the stage. It's not ideal. Then we have an evening youth group, the Guild – no longer confined to women, but no man has yet dared join; and there are various mid-week prayer meetings and Bible studies. An A.A. group meets here, we have a Scout group, a dramatic club, oh, and a support group for people with long-term illnesses, so it will have to be accessible for wheelchairs and so on. In fact, I think that's a law these days. There's a mother and toddler group twice a week, and sometimes students use our hall for meetings of societies. Here, I've got a list."

She held out a typed page, on which Sandy found details of all the happenings she had mentioned, and the ideal requirements for each. Mothers and toddlers' groups, he noticed, needed carpets underfoot and lots of cupboard space for toys (in fact each group seemed to need its own cupboards) while the Scout troop wanted easily cleaned flooring. It was – again that word – a challenge.

"All right, I'll consider it carefully and get back to you. You may as well get the windows mended since they can't be changed. At least nail boards over them. I'll just take a quick look at the church and be on my way."

"The church?"

"Yes, its architecture may inspire me. And whatever I do come up with mustn't be hopelessly at odds with the other side of the building. This isn't the sixties now, you know, nor the seventies."

Back in his office his partner could hardly believe the change that had come over Sandy. He was reborn, filled with energy and joie de vivre, scribbling doodles and sketches, cracking lame jokes and laughing unrestrainedly.

"They haven't accepted your designs yet," Hargreaves was moved to warn. "You haven't even done them yet."

"But I shall, old son, I shall. And they will be brilliant. It's a peach of a job, a dream, a gift. As we said in our youth, this is a naked, blonde nubile job. You should see the place!"

"You're crazy. And you seem to be regressing to your second childhood – or adolescence, with is worse. Naked, blonde, nubile, indeed. I don't know when I last heard anything being described as an NBN." He grinned. "All the same, Sandy, it's good to see you happy. Well done."

Later that evening Bridget and Joyce pursued Miss Murdoch over the oceans towards India. Joyce had brought the book to Bridget's rather bleak vestry, as the church must be kept open, awaiting a glazier. One of the congregation had agreed to do the work at short notice: when Bridget had phoned him after her meeting with Sandy the response had been, "No time like the present: how about tonight?" Bridget had hopes that being a church member he might also give them a discount for materials and labour – Mr Grieve was known to be a generous man, and lately his business had been booming. To that end she had vowed to be there in person, and to give him a cup of tea while he worked. She explained this to Joyce before the opened the diary.

"It's not as comfortable as your flat, I know. I could, of course, make it more inviting, but I don't want to."

"Why not?" Looking round the room, Joyce felt that almost anything would be an improvement. It was clean, but that was all that could be said for it. The bareness was aggressive rather than invitingly simplistic.

Bridget giggled. "You're not in the church, so I'll tell you, but keep it quiet. You've no idea how stories fly around this town. Only Ian knows this. The fact is I don't want it to be inviting, because then people will come in. Don't look so shocked. I can read your mind, Joyce. You're thinking that I'm supposed to welcome people, and to want to help them. You're right. I am and I do, but not all the time. I just can't be fully accessible all the time. The church finally understands about my day off, but they think I'm on call for the other hundred and forty-four hours of the week. You try that, especially with a husband and young family making demands. This is my retreating place. I can come to this horrible room and rest, relax, read, or study. There's an electric fire in this cupboard." She opened the free-standing, stained press, pulled out a small fan-heater and plugged it in. "I bring books or papers with me – if I left them here people would find out about my hide-out. I can get a cup of tea in the kitchen, or I could until the other side became a ruin. I have a flask with me tonight, both for us and for Mr Grieve. But when he comes, you'll have to go, I'm afraid. So will the fire. Oh, and if he asks about you, I'll tell him you're a friend of the architect."

Bridget held her breath. She had led up to this deliberately. She wanted to know how things stood between Sandy and Joyce. Somewhere at the back of her mind a small voice argued that it was none of her business, but she ignored it, as she usually did. Everything was her business, and if she didn't understand what was going on, how could she be a good minister? Bridget was no adherent of the 'faith-as-mystery' school of pastoral theology. She paid mystery lip-service in her spoken words, but for her this was always a last-ditch approach; it was failure. Faith was to explain and enlighten, and consequently needed as much information as possible to give best results. Bridget's was the faith of the computer age.

"I only know one architect," Joyce said quickly.

"Yes, but he's the one. Sandy Melville was here this afternoon getting all excited over the project."

"Alex was here?" The tone was indescribable – reproach, interest, reserve, and a little hostility hung in the three words.

"Of course, Alex. He said he was Sandy professionally. Strange how quickly I adapted to the new name. Maybe it fits better, don't you think?"

"No, I prefer to call him Alex."

"You don't sound surprised that he was here. Perhaps he phoned and told you? I bet he did – he was a very excited man."

"No, he hasn't phoned. Shall we set to on the diary? After all, we don't know when your glazier may arrive. Let's see if we can get her to India tonight."

Drawing a chair up to the table, Bridger sighed. The mystery still stood. Perhaps she should talk to Sandy – or Alex – instead.

Mr Grieve came at 8.30, and Joyce was duly introduced. It was frustrating to have to break off from the diary just as the ship was about to dock in Calcutta, but Joyce packed the old ledger away without complaining. She was charming to Mr Grieve, a short, stocky man in denim overalls and three jerseys, who seemed to live in a perpetual bustle. Bridget explained that Joyce had a connection to the architect and was amused and surprised to see Joyce playing along. She praised Mr Melville's skill highly and offered no contradictions when it was assumed that she was his assistant. Then she turned the conversation to the work in hand. How long would Mr Grieve take to re-glaze the windows?

"Oh, no so lang, no so lang. They're a' the same size o' glass, ye ken. A' the same size. No need to keep cutting and measuring. No need at a'. There's fower windaes, ye ken, wi' sixteen panes in each. Sixteen. It'll only tak' a couple o' oors. Me and the Rev. will be hame in oor beds by eleven, so we will. In bed by eleven. I'll just awa' and bring in my gear."

Bridget and Joyce giggled, then Joyce left. Bridget looked after her, rather surprised. She wouldn't have put Joyce down as a person likely to enjoy conversing with the glazier, nor embroidering her own slightly misleading statement. Previous experience had suggested that with Joyce most things were done to the benefit of herself alone. Obviously she had been mistaken.

If Bridget had followed Joyce along the street, she might have changed her mind. Joyce did not go West to Windmill Road. Instead she turned South, through the main streets and walked briskly to the outskirts of the town, and the solid mid-century residences of Irvine Crescent. There she rang Bridget's own doorbell and was admitted to the house by Bridget's husband. Neither she nor Ian spoke until they reached the living room, then Ian said, "The kids are asleep."

"Good. She'll be at the church until at least 10.30. There are sixty-four panes of glass to see to, though they're a' the same size so there's no need for cuttin' and measurin', ye ken."

Ian smiled. He hadn't heard Joyce mimic the local accent before and was surprised to hear that she had a good ear.

"I'm glad you could come tonight, Joyce. It's always good to see you, and I don't like spending all my evenings alone."

"Not all of them," Joyce remonstrated. "Be fair, Ian. She's not out every evening."

"No but it's getting more frequent., and it won't get any less until the renovation is complete. I know I shouldn't complain. I knew it would be like this when I married her. I just miss my wife, Joyce. I miss her company."

Joyce didn't know what to say. Since Christmas, she and Ian had been meeting once a week, or more, and were enjoying each other's company. When Ian had first suggested it, she had been very wary, not knowing what the sub-text of the invitation might be. "Couldn't you come and spend an hour some evening when Bridget's busy at church? The children go to bed and I'm left alone, baby-sitting. I'd appreciate some conversation and company." It was an invitation which could mean almost anything, and Joyce knew she hadn't enough experience of the world to know if the words meant more than they spelled out. However, she accepted the invitation. Her very lack of experience drove her to it. She wanted to know more and live more, and she couldn't do this by running away from uncertainties. Her experiences with Alex told her that. She had come and they had talked. With Ian, Joyce found herself often the listener. This was a role partly born of her own insecurity, but equally fathered by his need to talk.

Ian talked well. He spoke of his work at the Cannongate Primary school. Joyce came to know as real people some of the other teachers: Mrs Munro, Miss Wray, Mrs Lyons. Mrs Munro was older, thin and old-fashioned in appearance. She was drab and had no staff-room small talk. Her classroom was a place of light and colour, where groups of children seemed always to be doing four different things and doing them well. If Mrs Munro's children wrote stories, they were full-fledged fairy tales, or else epics of grim realism; when they did maths their sums were rooted in the every-day, or else made amusing by their sheer impossibility. Mrs Munro's art projects lasted all term and could be hung in the Tate. Her history lessons were more than repeated legends, and her scientific experiments were really experimental, no one seeming to know what the outcome might be. Mrs Munro was a born teacher and leader of children.

Miss Wray was new and pretty. She was nervous of the children and afraid the other staff might discover it or otherwise criticize her. She therefore dominated the staff-room whenever she could, talking of her student days, and dropping the jaw-breaking names of the most up-to-date educational theorists, knowing that no one else would have had time to read them. She was all right Ian said, but there was no getting away from her. Miss Wray was wearing.

Mrs Lyons, he claimed, was a terrible woman. She was coy and suggestive, making him feel acutely his position as the only man in the staff-room. She made innuendos and then would twitter, "But of course you wouldn't understand that, a man of the manse like you!" Ian supposed that prolonged contact with ten-year-olds had retarded her sense of humour, but he was sorry for her husband, whom he had never met.

And then there were the children in his class. Ian McKay

taught primary five, a class of eight and nine-year-olds. It was a great age, he enthused, when their intelligence was waking, and they became able to do some thinking for themselves. Joyce heard stories of Mary, Callum, James, Hannah, and other characters. That night it was Adam who had been amusing his teacher.

"He's a little chap, dark, and very, very serious. Life is real and life is definitely earnest for Adam. Today he finished his sentences early, so I let him join the handful of kids who were watching the gerbils – a reward. He trotted off happily and the room was fairly quiet again, really quite a model classroom for a few minutes. Suddenly there's an eruption of nervous laughter from the gerbil cage. I went over to investigate, and what should I find but the two gerbils mating. (And I was assured they were both female. That will teach me not to check for myself.) The children knew what they were seeing – they're not little innocents nowadays. They were laughing in embarrassment. So I told them I was a surprised as they were, and why didn't they go and sit down. But little Adam, he looked up at me and said, "I don't think they ought to laugh. The gerbils wouldn't like being laughed at. And anyway, Mr McKay, *it's not funny*." Poor Adam, he had no routine reaction to cover social embarrassment. Perhaps he's better for that, I don't know.

Earlier in their acquaintance Joyce had exclaimed, "Bridget must love your stories. Does she use them in her sermons?"

Ian had been startled. "Bridget? No, she doesn't know about most of these people. You see, she can't talk about a lot of the people she sees at work: too much of what she does is confidential. So I don't bring my work home either (except for marking!). It wouldn't be fair.

"Ian McKay, you're a saint," Joyce had teased.

The talk was not all of school, however. Ian wanted rational conversation. "I can't have it in the staff-room. I don't know what it is about women. I know they can be good conversationalists, but if you get more than two or three together that seems to go by the board. The staff-room's full of words, but few of them are stimulating. Of course, if you want to exchange recipes, discuss household appliances, or compare different brands of baked beans it's a great place to be." And so together they would discuss the news and the larger political and moral questions arising from the happenings of the moment. They talked of literature and art, of sport and philosophy. Sometimes they even talked about themselves.

In all this conversation Ian took the lead. He sat by the electric fire, one clean, denim-clad leg flung over the others, his hands behind his sleek, fair head, eyes eager and sparkling, and let the words flow from him. It was an effortless performance, and indeed seemed to be totally unconscious. Joyce always thought that were she to point out that she hadn't fully had her say Ian would be genuinely surprised and apologetic. He was just a talker.

Listening to him, and considering his life, Joyce realised that there must be times when he felt very much cut off from the masculine community. He worked with women and because of Bridget's job, he was most often stuck at home after work, unable to get out and meet with male friends. She wondered why he didn't invite such friends round for an evening, as he did her, and it was quite a few weeks before it hit her that in fact he never mentioned having any male friends. She didn't give the matter much thought, because she was too busy listening; for the first time in her life discovering that they joys of conversation need not revolve around her own brilliant performance. She listened to Ian's words because they were interesting and because she wanted to follow his thoughts.

Previously she had mainly listened to a person in the hope of finding something better to say herself – a more brilliant thought, a more amusing story. Even with Alex, when he had talked, this had been how she had listened.

Now that she was listening properly, she made discoveries about conversation. She found more pleasure in it. She found that at times her own small contributions were far closer to brilliant than they used to be – and without effort. Most of all, she discovered the incredible intimacy of converse, when two minds follow an idea this way and that, through whatever winding by-ways it might lead, with some discussion, some amusement and wholehearted dedication. Joyce did not know it, but sometimes as they spoke together Ian would watch the emotion passing over her face and find there the response that carried the conversation forward to new heights and new depths.

With such communion it would have been impossible for the two not to discover each other. They might speak of events, and people and ideas, but the excitement came from the self-disclosure that unconsciously accompanied their words. Some facts were revealed: if asked, Joyce could tell that Ian was forty, enjoyed his work because of the children, was a proud father, came from York originally, had met Bridget in Edinburgh where she was studying Divinity and he doing a one-year post-graduate teaching course at Moray House. She knew that his father was dead, and that his mother, now returned to her roots in Aberdeen, didn't seem to be coping very well these days. He had a sister in Stonehaven and a brother in Ireland, both of whom were also married, although the sister's marriage seemed shaky. Joyce herself had never put all this knowledge together, but it was there as a background none the less.

For his part, Ian was more aware of his knowledge of Joyce, because its paucity surprised him. His own eyes told him she was intelligent and attractive, and younger than himself. He had learned her age – twenty-eight – and her place of origin – Pitlochry – but little else. He gathered there were siblings somewhere in the background, and assumed that her parents were still alive. Her academic background was less mysterious. Her first degree was from Aberdeen University and now she was here is St. Andrews. But what had she done in between? She was writing a theses, but he had no idea of its subject matter.

Neither of them ever mentioned Sandy.

Neither of them even asked why or if their friendship was secret from Bridget. It had never been discussed. Ian didn't say, "You won't tell Bridget, will you?" Joyce didn't ask, "Does Bridget know I come here?" They didn't need to ask each other for secrecy, because neither wanted to tell.

And so tonight, as on any other night, when the grandfather clock in the corner of the room struck ten they regretfully surfaced from the depths of conversation where they had been exploring. Joyce reached for her coat, saying she had better be off home and put in some work before bed-time. Ian gathered up the two coffee-mugs to wash them in the kitchen, and said he'd better make the children's lunches before he turned in. Finally, he thanked Joyce for coming and she assured him she'd enjoyed the visit. "I'll be in touch, then" Ian added, opening the door for her. They did not embrace, nor touch each other in any way, and Joyce might have been surprised and perhaps uneasy had she known how far such a possibility was from Ian's mind. For her own part, she thought a hug might be nice, and harmless.

The door closed behind Joyce and the stepped off into the night, through a hedge-bound land, past Kilrymont, the junior High School, and Westward along Scooniehill Road to Largo Road and so home. It was a good twenty-five minutes' walk that way, slightly further than the more direct route she had come. But Bridget would not be on these more circuitous streets on her way home to her husband.

Two days later the phone rang in the manse. Ian answered, hoping to hear from Joyce.

"This is Sandy Melville," said the receiver. "Is Rev. McKay around?"

"She's quite busy," said Ian, discouragingly. "Can I take a message?"

"Not really – need to talk to her, just for a minute." Sandy was firm on this point and Ian went into the study to fetch Bridget.

"Who is it," she asked, wearily.

"A Sandy Melville. He didn't say what he wanted, and he wouldn't leave a message." Ian sounded disapproving but Bridget beamed with pleasure. "Oh good, he's the architect I've got working on the halls – Joyce's friend, you remember?"

Ian did remember. He had remembered the chap as being called Alex, though. So Bridget had hired him? The thought made him uneasy. What did it mean? Had Joyce suggested him? Was she two-timing Melville, or indeed, himself? But their relationship, Ian and Joyce's, wasn't the sort that could be part of a two-timing situation was it? Or was it? Basically honest, Ian left that question and its implications quickly and went to see to the children's breakfast. It was Saturday morning. "Who's going to help me wash the car later?" he asked.

Meanwhile Bridget had picked up the phone in her study. "Sandy, hello," she said. "What can I do for you?"

"Hi, sorry to ring on a Saturday, but I wanted to get you in."

"Oh, Saturday's a work day for me. Monday's my day off."

"Oh good. Well listen, Bridget, I think I'd better ask you to give me a key to the church. I'm going to have to come over quite a bit while I'm getting my ideas together and you won't always be able to be there to let me in."

"That's true. I'll look one out for you, when do you want to pick it up?" Please don't say today, she added silently, I have too much to do today.

"How would it be if I came to the service tomorrow? I want to see your church working, as it were. Then you could give me the key afterwards."

"That would be fine," Bridget beamed in relief. Her sermon-writing time was safe.

"Oh, and Bridget, just one more thing. Could you please not introduce me to anyone as the architect. I don't want people bending my ear with their bright ideas. Not at this stage."

"That's no problem. Just hang around after the service till everyone's gone. Would you like to come for lunch with the family afterwards? You remember my family? You met them on the West Sands." With Joyce, but she didn't say that. Sandy agreed to come for lunch and the phones were hung up.

The lunch party was not a success. The children were well-behaved and chattered away to Sandy in their usual fashion; they were too used to their parents entertaining strangers to be shy. Bridget did her best, seeking topics of conversation that would be of general interest, trying to help Sandy and Ian to see the best in each other. But it was no use. Ian scarcely spoke an unnecessary word to his guest. He was cheerful with his family, but he kept referring to private jokes, or turning the conversation to mundane domestic trivia, which shut out Sandy completely.

Not that Sandy was much more forthcoming. It was only as

he crossed the threshold into the manse that he remembered Christmas. This was where Joyce had chosen to spend the day. Ian had invited her, and his invitation had been enough to attract her. Sandy knew he was being silly and surly, but try as he might, he couldn't stop himself from looking around and picturing Joyce. He saw her in every chair in the sitting room, relaxed, smiling, and unreserved. He knew that where he sat at table had been her seat, and he looked at the room and the McKay family with her eyes. The room she would have thought a little over-furnished (it was a small room, made to hold a solid dark wood dining table and sideboard), but what would she have made of the family? Did she enjoy or endure them? Had she a secret soft spot for Angus and Mairi, or would she have preferred a purely adult gathering? She had agreed to come here for Christmas, and she didn't have to, so presumably she liked this family. Better than her own. Better than his. Better than him. The conversation swirled around him as Sandy's mind chased after unanswerable questions like a mad Scottie dog after rabbits. Mairi and Angus didn't take to him the way they had to Joyce, Bridget was perplexed, and no one was sorry when after the meal Sandy had offered his thanks and made his excuses.

He would have left without the church key had Bridget not remembered and pressed it into his hand. Sandy stared at it quizzically for a second, then pocketed it, smiled, and left. He needed to get away, to sort himself out.

It was the Wednesday of the following week, and Bridget was sitting at the desk in her vestry, working on Sunday's sermon. It was flowing well, which, rather superstitiously, she regarded as a bad sign. There was nothing to prevent inspiration from striking as well on Wednesday as on Friday or Saturday; but the fact remained that a sermon written on a Wednesday nearly always demanded re-writing or extensive modification later in the week. Some people might therefore have refused to waste time on Wednesday, but Bridget didn't see it that way. She didn't want to get stuck in a pattern because some weeks there was no time to write on Friday or Saturday. Besides she didn't want to allow her subconscious to dictate to her and play these sorts of tricks. This time she would preach her Wednesday sermon. It was an internal battle which she had often fought and never won, but Bridget was not one of life's quitters. As long as she fought, there was a chance that she wasn't being dictated to by some sub-conscious patterning. If once she gave in she was lost. Of course, some weeks inspiration didn't come until later: these weeks didn't count in the battle. She wanted to be free for God's Spirit to come at any time, even on Tuesdays and Wednesdays (though she would prefer not on Mondays, her day off).

Even as her pen flew over the paper, she was aware of this internal conflict and of her decision to ignore it. So deeply occupied was she that the footsteps in the corridor and the sounds of rubble being occasionally kicked, moved or dropped could not get her attention. It was only as she looked up at the end of a paragraph that she became aware that these sounds had been going on for a while. Her concentration was now broken, and the flow of ideas dried up. Looking at her notes she found she had no idea where she had planned to take her thoughts. She would have to come back to it another time. It was a nuisance.

So it was in no cheerful mood that Bridget stalked into the hall to see who was there and what was going on. It was Sandy. He had managed to manipulate the fallen beams and heaters to construct a substantial throne for himself, and there he sat at the back of the hall, gazing around him. On his knee was propped a pad of paper, and he was gently tapping his teeth with a yellow-painted pencil. He looked completely at home. As Bridget cleared her throat he slowly turned his eyes in her direction. She felt sure he was looking through or beyond her, but gradually his eyes focussed, and his lips parted in a smile of greeting.

"Hello Bridget."

"Sandy."

He grinned. "The architect at work. Not many people see this stage. I'm getting inspired."

"So was I." Despite herself, Bridget sounded gruff.

"You were. Does that mean you were writing your sermon?"

She nodded.

"And it's finished?"

She shook her head.

"Ah. You head me crashing around and inspiration flew out of the window. He can be a cagy little bird. I'm sorry."

"It's all right, really. I should probably have torn it up and started again on Friday. I generally do. I suppose now I've startled inspiration away from you?"

"Actually, no. He seems quite tame this morning." Sandy still sounded distant, then he got up and climbed towards her over the rubble. "Sorry, forgive the whimsey, won't you? Since you're here, can you tell me something?"

"If I can."

"Why is this church called 'Martyrs'? Is it a comment on the fortitude of its members?"

Bridget laughed aloud. "It can be cold here in winter."

"Yes, I can feel that, even though I came dressed for the occasion. So, do I qualify as a martyr now? Can I join the club?"

"The church. Actually, we're named for the local martyrs of the Reformation."

"You mean for specific people? It's not just a catch-all, hedge-your-bets kind of name, like 'All Saints'?"

Bridget was amused. "Don't let the Episcopalians hear you say that. All Saints' church is just along the street. To answer your question, yes, we are named for specific people. Four of them, in fact: the four who are commemorated and named on the Martyrs' Monument."

Now Sandy was genuinely puzzled. His black brows lifted towards his hair-line. What monument? Is there some other part of the church I've yet to see? Where? I thought we'd accounted for every square foot."

"Oh, it's not here," said Bridget. "It's nothing to do with this church. The town erected it in the first half of the nineteenth century. It's down near the Royal and Ancient, in fact it's actually on Witch Hill – where suspected witches were thrown into the water, though that's by the way. I know you're not from St. Andrews, Sandy, but you must have seen it. It's a sort of plain obelisk, sandstone, thrusting skyward."

"Oh, that thing. I thought it was the war memorial."

"No, that's by the cathedral. It's a monument to the martyrs." In the cold, dusty hall, Bridget shivered. "If you want to hear about them, let's go into the vestry; there's a heater there."

In the bare little room Sandy divested himself of his thick green jacket and unwound a scarf from his neck. He pulled a hard chair up to the desk, laid his notebook on its shabby surface, tucked away his pencil into an inner pocket of his tweed jacket and produced a pen. Then he sat up and looked eagerly at Bridget. At that moment she had a sudden vision of how he must have looked as a little boy at school: the same black, untidy hair, the same air of eager anticipation; the same whole-hearted absorption in his work. He must have been a joy to teach, she thought.

He was certainly flatteringly attentive to hear what she could tell him of the four famous martyrs: Walter Milne, the old priest from Montrose, converted to Protestantism at eighty; Patrick Hamilton, the nobleman burned outside the university quadrangle; Henry Forrest, rash enough to proclaim Hamilton a martyr; and George Wishart, burned by the Castle, or Bishop's Palace. Talking of Wishart, Bridget produced an old book and read Sandy his last words. "This flame has scorched my body, yet it hath not daunted my spirit; but he who from yonder high place beholdeth us with such pride [Cardinal Beaton] shall in a few days lie in the same ignominy as now his is seen proudly to rest himself."

"Of course," put in Bridget at this point, "The whole speech is almost certainly apocryphal. Burnings involved having a tight rope around the neck, which would have precluded speech. Cardinal Beaton lasted another fifteen months.

"These are the four on the monument. I like to think that this church would also remember the others."

"Others?"

"Paul Craw died near the Merkat Cross in Market Street. He was a Bohemian, so I suppose the makers of the monument were most concerned with Scots. And two others, Gourlay and Straiton, were burned together. Their names aren't totally lost. Each has a wynd named after him in the newest part of the Council estate."

"You certainly seem to know your martyrs," said Sandy. He frowned slightly and pulled at his mouth. "I don't know if this is a delicate question, but I'm going to ask you anyway. What about Catholic martyrs? Were there any, after the reformers had the upper hand?"

Slowly Bridget shook her head. "I don't know." A pause, then she added, "Isn't that terrible? I just don't know. I don't remember our Church History classes at New College touching on that. But I don't remember hearing that there were no executions. The reformers were pretty determined, hot-headed folk. Especially Knox. But I don't know. I don't know if it will be easy to find out, wither. Most Scottish histories are written by protestants."

"I'll go to the library and try to find out," said Sandy.

Bridget was curious. "Why do you want to know?"

"For this hall complex of yours. I don't know exactly why I need the information, but the bluebird of inspiration is telling me to ask these questions. At least, I think that's why. Of course, executions and tortures are always, unfortunately, fascinating. It could just be the worst side of my nature getting the better of me. It's so incredible that people walk around this town – I do myself – every day, and this quiet burgh is the same place where such terrible things happened. I've never seen a ghost, but you'd think that the passions which were unleashed here to such awful effect must have left an imprint on their surroundings. The faith and fear and anger and defiance that shaped matters then – it seems to me that there must have been emotion overflowing and to spare. It may be waiting for a chance to be of use."

Suddenly he blushed. "I'm sorry, Bridget, I was rambling. I shall now go off home, and the next time you see me I shall once more be the matter-of-fact architect, bursting with plans and enthusiasm."

"O.K. Sandy," replied Bridget. She hesitated then laid a hand on his arm, stopping him in the act of pulling on the padded green jacket. "But while you're in the mood to see ghosts, may I ask what shade or spirit you were seeing in our house on Sunday?"

She held her breath. Sandy turned away from her and shrugged into jacket and scarf. With his back still toward her he muttered, "That was Joyce. Not a real ghost, but I knew she'd been there. Silly of me, and I apologise, since obviously you noticed that I wasn't quite myself."

He made for the door, but Bridget was there before him. She placed herself firmly against it and folded her arms. Her plump figure and fair curls were never designed to look imposing, but Sandy could see the light of determination in her eye.

"Sandy, I have to ask you about Joyce. I see both of you for different reasons, and both blush and mutter when the other's name comes up. Please don't tell me to mind my own business. I need to know what's going on between you two – otherwise I'm afraid I'll keep putting my foot in it."

Sandy was not an unreasonable man. He wanted to get away and sketch some of the ideas he had been fermenting in his brain, but Bridget's speech brought him up short. He had been childishly evasive

"I'm sorry. I didn't mean to put you in such an ambiguous position. Joyce and I are no longer seeing each other. We had a silly, though sharp quarrel, and I haven't managed to get hold of her to apologise. She doesn't want to talk to me: I know that because she simply won't answer her phone to me. If she won't discuss the matter either, I suppose I can take a little hope. Obviously she's not indifferent. But that's the scenario."

"Thank you. I'm sorry it's happened, but thank you for telling me. Now let me make my position clear. I look on you as a friend, Sandy. I hope you're beginning to feel that way about me. I like you. But I also have a friendly relationship with Joyce. I don't know that we're friends, exactly, but we are allies, held together by a shared interest. I don't want to jeopardise our friendship or Joyce and my alliance. Therefore, I will not tell Joyce anything you say to me. Nor will I tell you about her. I won't be a go-between, because that would make me a betrayer of confidences. I want you to know that so you can feel perfectly comfortable having any conversation with me."

"The secret of the confessional?" Sandy lifted a quizzical eyebrow. "That's fine by me, Bridget. Friends it is, and if you are promising confidentiality, I can do no less. Your secrets are safe with me," he ended, on a teasing note. But Bridget was satisfied. She stepped away from the door and opened her mouth to say something else.

But abruptly Sandy was gone, his muse was calling him back to his drawing board.

CHAPTER SIX: FAMILY MATTERS

One would be in less danger

From the wiles of the stranger

If one's own kin and kith

Were more fun to be with.   Ogden Nash, "Family Court"

A week later, Bridget and Joyce were back in their old positions, sitting side by side at the table in Joyce's flat, with the lamp-light gleaming on one smooth brown head, and tangled in the fair curls on the other. They had set aside the whole afternoon and were caught up in Miss Murdoch's unfolding story. Together they had followed her descriptions of life in Calcutta, and of her charges.

"She's not very good at description," Joyce opined, and Bridget had to agree with her. The diaries had been written for their author alone, and the descriptions Miss Murdoch had included had been more in the nature of reminders than of blue-prints. This was both frustrating and fascinating.

"All the details I want to know is the very same information that Miss Murdoch couldn't forget. She had geography and geology imprinted in her mind, with smells, tastes, feelings, sights, and sounds. She takes for granted that she will always know the social intricacies and the architectural detail. We can't know these things from her, but they were enshrined in her memory forever."

This was Bridget speaking. Joyce seized eagerly upon the idea. "Which suggests that what she is writing down are the things she was afraid she would forget."

"Or else it's a small collection of details which she hoped would remind her of the rest. It's probably a bit of both. Some of this stuff is first impressions – she wanted to remember them, and she knew that they would soon become overlaid with daily contact and familiarity. If that was what she was doing, I hope it worked for her."

Joyce nodded. "I used to keep a kind of a diary, and there were times when I was detailed and times when I wasn't. I'd be too tired or too busy to write properly. Often, I would assure myself that it didn't matter, as I'd be sure to remember all the details of days that hadn't been monotonous. But I was wrong. Looking at my diary entries now – which I seldom do – there is no day I can remember in its minute-by-minute entirety. Many incidents are clear, and the diary helps me recall those, but not whole days. So much of life inevitably gets lost or left in the sub-conscious."

"I've never kept a diary." Bridget was curious. "Does it really help you remember? I've always thought that a danger might be that you would remember your life more as words on a page than as a series of events."

"It might. I found that was possible. But for me what value there was in being a diarist (and I don't keep one now) was in remembering the commonplace. Events that generated emotional reactions of one kind or another were less apt to be forgotten than ordinary days, when I might have made a quiet discovery or two."

"Of course, Miss Murdoch was her own person. She began this diary as an amateur anthropological record."

"Which it never was." Joyce was firm on this point.

"Quite. But she didn't know that. She seems genuinely to have believed that was what she was doing. Why did she keep on writing, though? It may have been primarily to record, but reading these last few entries, she seems to be veering towards using herself and her own reactions as a subject of study. Did it ever strike you, Joyce, reading all this, that she doesn't seem to have had many real friends, if any? She may have found that writing was a companion for her – a way of talking to herself which didn't send her voice echoing round an empty room, highlighting her solitude."

"It's an idea. Unless she tells us, we'll never know."

They turned back to the worn note-book before them and soon found themselves embroiled in the Calcutta riots. With amazement and some glee, they saw the Miss Murdoch who stood on the side-lines and observed life, become a woman of action, caught up in terrible events and becoming a participant.

They left her there that day, with the smoke hanging over a distant city and an uncertain quiet hanging over the house. "It's getting exciting," Bridget laughed. "That was more like the Miss Murdoch I knew."

Joyce nodded. "I know what you mean. She was always a woman in control. My main dealings with her revolved around the delivery of her milk in the mornings, but even in that she liked things done just so. It wasn't that she was domineering, exactly..."

"But you always knew she could be," interrupted Bridget. "That's right. The word 'domineering' was never far from my mind while I was dealing with her, although I consistently rejected it as inappropriate. The best way to describe her is that she wasn't domineering."

"You're right," Joyce chuckled. "It's one of the few instances of a negative description giving a firm and positive impression." For the first time in weeks, she looked at Bridget openly, relaxing back in her chair and grinning. "How's ministry these days?"

Caught off guard by the question, Bridget replied, "I feel more like a clerk of works than a minister, with all the work on in the hall."

"You're renovating? Does that have to involve you?"

Bridget sighed. "It shouldn't. In theory the men can stabilize and strengthen the roof without me, and the contractors can clear away the debris by themselves, but it doesn't happen that way. They ask questions. That wouldn't bother me if they were essential questions, but they're not. At least, perhaps some of them are, but these are the ones that are so technical that I never know the answer. The others – manly asked by the clearing-up men – are stupid. They want to know how it happened, or if they can get their skip to the door. Oh, just silly questions, but I keep thinking there's innuendo behind it."

"Sexual innuendo?"

"No – actually I hadn't thought of that. So many people think of ministers as sexless beings that I don't get much of that. No, I can't stop hearing the thought that I have nothing better to do than hang around and watch them. After all I get my money easy – I only work one day a week!"

She shrugged, and Joyce laughed, long and clear. Bridget was amazed. She had never heard such uninhibited mirth coming from the other woman. "What's so funny?" she asked.

"You are. I'm sorry, Bridget," Joyce became calmer, "That must have seemed rude. But you laid out your paranoia so exactly. It's nothing short of ludicrous that you should think that you don't work hard enough. No," as Bridget tried to interrupt,

"You do think that. If you didn't you wouldn't read that into other people's stupidity."

"But I've heard it in words more than once, Joyce. It's not my own idea."

"Yes, some people know so little about your life that they might say something silly like that. But you mind it so much! You mind, and that makes you see criticism where it doesn't exist. I still say you're paranoid. It's nothing to be ashamed of, you know. After all, we're all paranoid about something or other. Deep down you don't believe that you work hard. Why not?"

Bridget was silent. They were sitting facing the un-curtained window, and darkness had fallen while they read and talked together. She could see the dark shapes of the clouds, tinged orange on their undersides from the glow of the town's lighting, as they raced and reeled before the wind. Stars suddenly appeared between them, then were as quickly covered, as though some diabolical painter was concerned to conceal all light and purity. She turned the matter over in her mind, her thoughts racing and somersaulting like the clouds. Did she think that? Did she?

"I suppose you have a point," she finally admitted. As she spoke it was as though the rushing clouds were whisked away and a million quiet stars were twinkling calmly in her mind. "You see, I enjoy my work. Except funerals. So most of the time it doesn't feel like work at all."

"Lucky you," said Joyce. "But why shouldn't you relax and enjoy it?"

"Like that Chinese proverb: if rape is inevitable, relax and enjoy it?"

"Now you're being flippant and inappropriate," Joyce smiled. "Anything to get the conversation away from yourself. The question remains, why shouldn't you enjoy your life, especially when you happen to be doing a job you believe to be worthwhile, and doing it well?"

"I don't know."

"The safe and unquestionable answer. Come on, Bridget, you can do better than that."

"I *don't* know. I don't think about myself very often. Why should I think that doing a full-time job, raising a family, loving a husband and enjoying it isn't enough?"

"Protestant work ethic." Joyce said the words with serio-comic glumness. "What is good for me can't be nice, so what I like can't be good for me."

"I hope that's not it, but you might have a point. I'm going to have to think about it. I must go soon, Joyce, but before I do may I ask a question?"

Joyce was still relaxed, turned away from the window and sprawling over the table, leaning on one elbow. "O.K. After all I asked you."

"What was going on in your life when you wrote your diary?"

The effect of the question was immediate. Joyce got up abruptly and walked around the table to stand, shoulders hunched, looking out of the window. Bridget could see her face reflected back amid the hurrying clouds.

"What do you mean?" The question was challenging.

"I only wondered how old you were? Child, teenager, young adult? Perhaps I phrased my question badly."

Joyce's shoulders levelled out as some of the strain eased from her reflected face. "I see. I was in my late teens, from about sixteen to eighteen."

Bridget smiled. "Thanks. But now I have to ask it. What was going on in your life at that time?"

At once the room before her vanished and Joyce was back in that time, feeling the tangled emotions of a teenager. She was eighteen years old again. She saw herself coming home from school, happy and relaxed, laughing with her friends as they tramped down Pitlochry's narrow main street. She left them and turned off, up the hill, delighting in the crocuses flourishing in gardens she passed. Through a small green gate which fenced off her parents' land, into the solid, squat, white-painted house, up the stairs and into her own room. She still felt the shock and betrayal as her mother raised angry eyes to meet hers, eyes which had been devouring her diary. It was a kind of paralysis and again it had her in its grasp. Again, she heard her mother's voice, shaking with pain and guilt, denouncing her, up-braiding her for ingratitude. Joyce's world had changed that day. Her diary had been the place where, amongst other things, she left her frustration about the relationship with her mother – a woman who was too invasive for her adolescent tastes. Now she had read it all. *"I do wish Mum would leave me in peace." "I can't tell Mum this idea, because she will want to improve upon it." "Mum is never satisfied, no matter how well I do. What can I do to get her approval?" "As usual Mum is trying to improve me, this time my opinions are at fault." "I wish Mum would just* ***go away****."* Childish statements, but unmistakeably heartfelt. Mrs Cunningham threw the volume at her daughter and stormed out of the room. She never spoke to Joyce again, except as was absolutely necessary. She didn't ask about her life or her plans, she didn't share familiar jokes with her or ask for her help. It was as though she had no daughter, only sons.

"Joyce?" Bridget's voice, ringing with concern, brought her back to the present. She turned from the window and Bridget could see tears in her eyes. "I seem to have asked a bad question. Please forgive my inquisitiveness."

"No," Joyce's voice was thick with grief and shook with remembered pain. "It's just a bad memory. My diary got into the wrong hands. It wasn't pleasant." She pulled out a chair and sat opposite Bridget. A sudden intensity came into her voice. "They're dangerous things, diaries. They aren't a complete record. They can give a very imbalanced picture, and if they are read by the wrong people, they can cause pain. If you ever decide to be a diarist make sure you keep it where no one can see it. No one. You may think you can trust someone to respect your privacy, but you can't, Bridget, you can't. I know what I'm talking about: keeping a diary taught me that. Trust me."

She sighed. "I'm tired now and I think you said you have to go. We'll do more reading next week."

Bridget got up at once. "Yes, I'll go now. I'm sorry you were upset, Joyce, but thank you for trusting me enough to tell me why. I don't need to know the details. And Joyce," she hesitated, "Thank you for what you said earlier about work and pleasure. I think I needed to hear that, and I won't forget it."

Then she was gone. Joyce stared in silence at the door after she left, surprised, shocked even, at her last words. Then she laid her head down on the table and cried as though only tears could wash away life's pain.

After Miss Murdoch left Calcutta, her journal became extremely sporadic and such entries as there were tended to be brief. As February progressed into March and the days began to lengthen with a false hope of Spring, Joyce and Bridget followed her on her travels. At first, she did much as she had told her employers she would and saw some of the tourist sights. Broadly speaking, she followed the Ganges through the great northern plains to Patna, Benares and Allahbad, to Kampur and Fatepur Sikri. Then she left the river for Lucknow and Agra and returned to it to visit Delhi.

Her comments on this journey, which lasted the best part of a year, were certainly no travelogue. She noted the crowds of pilgrims she was at her various stops along the Ganges. As time went on the devotion of these worshippers seemed to impress her more and more. At first her comment was, *"I shouldn't care to bathe in that dirty river."* But four months later she remarked, *"It is certainly remarkable that such piety is shown. For this happens every day, it is not an annual ritual. Mother Ganges is a constant hostess to pilgrims. Spending some time watching this is impressive. I don't have faith of any kind, and if I did, I doubt that bathing (communally) in rivers would fittingly express it. However, there is no doubt of the genuine religious feeling in the acts of these pilgrims. It may be ninety percent superstition, but the ten percent which is something else is fascinating."*

While in Kampur she travelled to Fatepur Sikri, the legendary capital of the Mogul emperor Akbar. *"Quite majestic,"* was her comment. *"It is also remarkable that through the country's political upheavals of the past four hundred years, this monument to one-time Muslim supremacy has been allowed to stand, more or less intact."*

Agra, of course, brought a visit to the Taj Mahal, which left her *"Speechless with delight. I was prepared to be disappointed, after all, can any beauty survive such a build-up? But I was not prepared for this: opulence, grace and, yes, austerity combined. I find the restraint of Islamic architecture very soothing. It is probably the canny Scot in me which is a little disquieted by the showiness and riotous images found in Hindu buildings, particularly religious edifices.*

The mountains were described with a series of staccato words and phrases. *"Glorious. Majestic. Beautiful. Terrible. Cool. Magnetic. Remote. Simply marvellous."* However, by the time Miss Murdoch had reached these northern territories the political situation had become more volatile. She noted that *"I cannot be unaware of the approach of independence and the intense debate as to this region's future. Here, where there is a strong Islamic presence, the pros and cons of remaining in India or becoming a separate state are constantly re-hashed. I had hoped to spend some moths in Lucknow, but think it would be better to follow my original plan and return to the plains."*

It was on August 2nd, just two days before India's independence was established, that Charlotte Murdoch alighted from a train in Badepuri, a village near the centre of the state of Uttar Pradesh. She recorded that *"All I have with me is one (rather battered) leather suitcase and a large knapsack on my shoulder, so far have I managed to reduce my luggage on my travels."* She did not describe the village in any detail, besides calling it *"A collection of low-built dwellings, mainly painted white, grouped haphazardly around a 'village square' of trodden earth with a few trees. There is also, most importantly, a well. I am not coming here for my own comfort, but fresh water is a must. I can be of no use to anyone if I am constantly laid low with dysentery, cholera or typhoid – quite apart from the fact that I have no wish to die."*

Once arrived in Badepuri, Miss Murdoch gave few details for a month or so, except to remark on the festivities around independence. *"From midnight there was dancing in the 'square'. Great quantities of rice and curry, and of fruit and sticky sweets were eaten, everyone generously sharing with those around. I expect my insides will rebel later at the quantities of strange substances they have been asked to absorb. I had been a little hesitant about joining the celebrations – after all, I am British: they might not have liked it. But I want to stay here, so I ventured into the throng. Far from being unwelcome I found I was fêted! A garland was hung around my neck, made of glorious yellow flowers. I never lacked food and drink. I was even thanked, several times, for 'giving us our land'. It was a wonderful introduction to my new village."*

The beginning of September 1947 was when Miss Murdoch opened her school in Badepuri. This event she gave greater coverage than many which had preceded it.

September 1st 1947, Badepuri

This was day one of my school. Class met in what I think of as the 'village square', partly because I find the contrast between my mental concept of these words and the reality amusing. No doubt soon my mental picture will be of beaten brown earth, dusty trees, and the mud around the pump. We met under one of the trees.

I had wondered how many, if any, children would come, so I was pleased to find ten chatterboxes waiting for me. They were all aged between five and ten, which was what I had expected. Older children have to help their parents. Indeed, one of my pupils had her little brother, aged about eighteen months, with her. The square isn't the best place to hold lessons, there are too many distractions. We could all squeeze into this tiny house of mine and be more private, however I will stick to the square for the first few weeks. There is a lot of curiosity about what I am doing and it's as well that we don't seem to be too secret.

Today we began with the alphabet. It was all great fun, writing the letters on my broken bit of blackboard and having the children make the sound. I don't know how much will be remembered, though. They all thought it a great game, and I fear they concentrated only enough to be able to play. Several people came by to watch us, and I was amused to see some adults standing behind the children and trying to make the right noises. Most people have a few words of English (thank goodness) but none are fluent. They have had no need to be. Nevertheless, they do see that if their children can speak English, they might be able to get official jobs, one of these days. Official jobs are highly desirable, as they carry a salary, so free a person from dependence on the vagaries of soil and weather. I'm a little surprised that no one has suggested that independence might cause the demise of the English language in India, but if they have, I haven't heard it. It certainly has yet to occur to the inhabitants of Badepuri.

September 3rd 1947

I wonder if I should set up an adult class? Several mothers and some fathers have attached themselves to the class of children, standing at the back and drinking it all in. They pay better attention and learn faster than the children. Today we moved from the alphabet to words – tree, water, village, sky, earth, people, children, adult, woman, man, boy, girl.

September 5th 1947

The class is growing. I'm moving inside next week, which will deter the adults. I will also have to explain that new children must wait for a while. I will offer an adult class in the early evening.

September 9th 1947

How one thing leads to another! Of course, these children don't know their numbers, but they must. Once they have enough English (maybe another month or so – they're coming along very quickly) we will start on basic arithmetic. The adults (I hope) won't need that. But already ten more children want to start with me. I have let it be known that new children can come in the afternoons. So now I have my original class in the mornings, class two in the afternoons and the adults in the evenings! And yet I can't quite believe that it may not all turn out to be a nine days' (today) wonder, or a nine weeks' wonder. Will they persevere, or will they give up and go home? It is my hope that they persevere. I want, when I die, to have done something to enhance even a few lives.

And I am enjoying being busy. I am enjoying my simple life here. I can't help but think of Mother, with her large, elegant rooms and leisure. What would she say if she knew I was on the other side of the world, living in a two-roomed mud dwelling, sleeping on a charpoy (well, she wouldn't know what that is) and spending my days teaching an Indian village to speak and read English? Would she approve? Would she think it worth the sacrifice? I doubt it. But I can't think about it just now. I am too tired to think. One blessing of this life is that the teaching and physical labour involved in living has me exhausted: I am nearly always too tired to think.

After the storms of February, March was surprisingly calm. The month was half way through when one evening Joyce had a chance encounter with Bridget and Ian together. Her professor had offered her his ticket for a performance by the Scottish Chamber Orchestra. It seemed he had a season ticket for the whole of the winter set of St. Andrews concerts. "But I can't go this time. Damn departmental meeting. I'd send you to the meeting instead, if I thought I could get away with it, but since we're talking about funding, I have to go myself. You'd better use the ticket instead. Saint-Saëns, Mozart, Brahms – nice accessible programme, and a very good little orchestra. Watch out for the double bassist – cousin of my wife's."

Still wondering at this uncharacteristic display of generosity and devotion to duty, Joyce made her way to the Younger Hall on the specified evening. It was a building which she could not contemplate, outside or in, without wondering that such a disparate collection of architectural styles could be brought together in one place. Art Nouveau and Classical Greek rubbed shoulders, while Victorian Gothic peeped coyly over the shoulder of Presbyterian ecclesiastical stones. All the same, it was a good hall for a chamber concert. Joyce found her seat, high up and quite far back, which had been selected with attention to the amount of leg-room: the professor was a tall man.

She gained her place with little time to spare, and it wasn't until towards the end of the Saint-Saëns that she was aware of her fellow concert-goers. She had paid close attention to the double bassist, who was altogether unmemorable, and amused herself with the antics of the percussionists. Then for a while the music carried her away from herself and her seat. Wafting back to the present she saw familiar fair curls a few rows in front and to her right. She craned her neck. The hall's lights had not been designed to dim, so it was quite easy to pick out Bridget, with Ian sitting beside her. They were holding hands. Annoyance rippled through Joyce like a wave; she liked to go to events alone and be anonymous in the crowd. She turned her head slightly that she might not see them and concentrated on the music and the orchestra. Mozart's light, brittle brilliance fell around her, making her uneasy even as she delighted in the sounds. There was something about Mozart she distrusted. He made his genius too obvious. She felt now a little as though he were showing himself off and contrasting himself with her. "See, I am brilliant," he said. "There is nothing I can't do with my music, and do easily. It's a game. I can make you feel things – things which perhaps you don't choose to feel. You can't do anything so wonderful."

It was silly to feel inadequate: history taught her that Mozart's personal life had been far from successful. But listening to the clarity of the Nachtmusik, Joyce wondered how much that had mattered to Mozart himself. Perhaps it is worth losing every other facet of human life and experience to be sublimely good at one thing. It was a moot point, she remembered, as she joined in the applause. She wasn't supremely good at anything, and not even normally skilled in many of the relational aspects of life which other people appeared to find so easy.

Thinking like this, she had forgotten about Bridget and Ian. She was therefore completely off her guard when a hand tapped on her shoulder and Bridget's voice hailed her. "Hello, Joyce, I didn't know you were coming. They're good, aren't they? You remember Ian from Christmas, don't you?"

Joyce gasped. "Oh hello, you startled me. I came at the last minute: my professor had a meeting. He's the last person I can imagine enjoying Mozart, but he seemed really sorry. Hello Ian."

Bridget's smile was teasing. "I wouldn't have put you down as a Mozart fan yourself, but he seems to have totally discombobulated you. We're enjoying a rare evening out together." She lowered her voice. "We went the whole hog and got a babysitter!" Joyce couldn't see why this should be a joke, but Bridget obviously found it very funny. Still laughing, she towed Ian away, calling over her shoulder, "I never get this man to myself, so you won't mind if I'm selfish and don't share our time with you. I'll see you on Thursday." Ian smiled back at her and winked, then the two of them vanished through the curtained door which led to the stairs. They were going to find a drink.

This incident confirmed to Joyce her belief that Ian had told his wife nothing of their growing friendship. Surely this could mean only one thing: that what he understood them to have was illicit within a marriage.

The next evening Ian telephoned to tell her that Bridget has a Session meeting and to suggest that Joyce might come round at eight thirty or nine. Joyce decided that this time she would cycle to the manse, and it was only when she was on her bike, forcing her unaccustomed muscles to carry her up-hill against the evening breeze that Joyce herself began to think about the moral dimension of these meetings with Ian. Was it just a friendship, or was Ian planning sometime to take it further? And if the did take it further, to use her own euphemism, what would that do to Bridget and the children? The thought was such a new one to her, that she stopped pedalling. Dismounting and pushing the bike ahead of her she reasoned with herself. If Ian wanted her and if she wanted him, was that all that mattered? This was the nineties, after all, and that was what society seemed to say.

If she wanted Ian. Did she?

Yes, she did.

But how much? And why?

Why, because he treated her well, made her feel like a pleasant person, seemed to want to spend time with her, that was why.

That was all? Run over that reasoning again. You want Ian because you think he wants you and that's good for your ego. You don't love him for himself.

I do. I'm fond of him. I like being with him.

But you don't love him, any more than – in fact less than – you loved Alex.

Joyce was not accustomed to dealing with herself so honestly. Her normal way was to drift through life on vague feeling and assumption rather than turn her considerable intellect on herself, as Sandy had seen. Now her conclusions shocked her. If there had been one thing she believed it was that she loved her Alex. This had been the excuse for all sorts of self-indulgences. Even when they were together she had allowed herself the indulgence of feeling misunderstood, of testing him with moods and strange demands and of trying to re-fashion him more after the pattern of her ideals. Now that he seemed to have left her life, she allowed herself to be comforted by friendship with Ian, by self-pity and the active cultivation of a broken heart.

Self-analysis need not take a long time. Joyce had covered a lot of ground when she arrived at Martyrs' manse. The red curtains of the sitting room glowed warmly, pulsating with the light behind them. No other window showed signs of life. Ian welcomed her quietly and cheerfully, as ever, and drew her into the room. He closed the door.

"Did you enjoy yourself last night?" he asked, as she sat down at one end of the couch. He hesitated, then sat at the other end himself. This was his usual place, but Joyce was accustomed to enthroning herself in an armchair.

"Yes, thank you. And you?" A demure smile hovered about Joyce's lips, something Ian had never seen there before. With a start he realised that she was playing on her femininity, subtly displaying herself before him. This was a new Joyce, not his eager, self-forgetful companion in conversation.

"It was marvellous," he agreed. "The whole thing was good. Apart from anything else, I had an evening away from this house. And I saw my wife. And I enjoyed the music."

"In that order?" Joyce asked.

"Maybe."

A short silence fell. The grandfather clock in the corner struck nine. A car passed, driving slowly round the crescent; from inside the quiet house they could hear the beat of the music it was playing. Ian found that he couldn't end the quiet, for all he was such a good talker. Joyce wasn't herself tonight (or perhaps, finally, she was) and he waited to see what would happen. Eventually she spoke, and her words took him by surprise.

"Ian, I have two things I need to say to you." She looked him full in the face, daring him to turn from her gaze. "Firstly, I cannot and will not sleep with you, and secondly, I think we should tell Bridget."

Ian still found nothing to say for a few seconds, so, blushing now and with downcast eyes, Joyce continued, "You must see that we can't go on in this way, meeting in secret, and we can't move on to a more physical relationship, because I don't want to. And really, there's nothing for Bridget not to know, is there? I mean..." she tailed off and Ian took his chance.

"Where did all that come from?" Who ever said anything about sleeping together?"

Joyce flushed deeper and continued to look down. Then she raised her head abruptly and again looked Ian full in the face. He tried to look bemused and concerned, but before her angry eyes he turned away. He looked into the fireplace as he said dully, "I think you'd better tell me what's on your mind. But don't shout. Don't forget the kids."

"Oh, I won't forget the children." Joyce spoke in a furious mutter, only half-voicing her words. "I have been thinking about your children, and your wife. And you needn't come over all innocent with me, Ian McKay, I saw you last night – you didn't want to acknowledge we were friends. I didn't think you had told Bridget, and so I never did because I thought that should come from you, her husband. I assumed you'd just never found a good time to tell her that we'd been getting together. But last night she gave you your chance on a golden plate garnished with parsley." Despite himself, Ian grinned at the metaphor. "Yes, smile. What was I supposed to think? You hadn't told your wife, and you weren't going to tell her. Now, if a man conceals a relationship with a woman from his wife there's usually a good reason: what else could I think but that you might be planning or hoping to change our agenda and initiate a physical relationship? And I'm not having it. Bridget is also my friend and, to be honest, I can live without having sex with you." She stopped speaking, but Ian made no reply. "Well, say something."

Ian smiled, a joyless grimace which contorted his face. "You're all the same, aren't you? Women."

"I don't know what you mean," Joyce was suspicious now, on the defensive.

"I mean that after all you would fit in well in the staff room. I had thought you were different, that you looked at things more openly, more broadly. But it turns out that after all you are as stereotyped in your thinking as any other woman. You don't know much about men, and you certainly haven't understood me, Joyce. You think because I'm a man I always have sex on my mind."

"I do not! But I know what I'd think if I were your wife and found that you'd been meeting another woman secretly. It's the secrecy that would make me suspicious. I'd be suspicious if you were meeting a man on the sly too. In that, yes, perhaps I am like all women, but I'm not apologising for it. I'm just telling you how Bridget will think, and therefore we should be more open."

"That's not all you were saying." Ian seemed to have shrunk into himself and looked pursed, not only at the mouth but in his very body. "You seemed to think that I wanted to sleep with you."

"And I was wrong? Put aside your anger and think honestly, Ian. Was I wrong?"

With a sigh Ian turned his whole body so that he was facing her. "It never occurred to me that you'd go thinking along these lines."

"Let me get this straight. You mean you were not intending we should sleep together?"

"I wasn't intending it, no."

"But if it happened you would go along with it?"

"I hope not. Perhaps. I don't know. I oughtn't."

"No. But you didn't tell Bridget."

"I know. I told myself, and maybe it was true, that I didn't want her to know that I had something she feels she has to deny herself: a confidant. I wanted her to think we were both still in the same unsatisfactory boat."

"That's what you told yourself?"

"Yes."

"So you never thought of me as a woman. You never reminded yourself that you are an attractive man?" The coyness Ian had noticed earlier in the evening had returned.

Ian shook his head. He had always enjoyed being able to bowl a girl over with compliments. He had always known that women found him attractive in a mild, unthreatening way. But these matters had been far from his mind when he was with Joyce, even though, as he noted now almost for the first time, she was very pretty, and feminine in a strong-minded way. Surely he hadn't subconsciously equated her strength of character with a masculine turn of mind? Surely his long years spent in female company should have freed him from such chauvinism?

"You are attractive, Joyce," he said now, firmly. "And one of your attractions is your forthright way of speaking. You are right in saying we shouldn't be more than friends. I hope we never would have, but I shouldn't have put us in such an ambiguous position. I don't believe adultery is O.K., even if, impossibly, no one is hurt by it. But you weren't to know that. So we'll just stay friends, can we?"

"If we tell Bridget."

"What? Why?"

"Oh Ian, I've just told you! She mustn't think we have a secret from her, or she'll suspect the worst. Besides, I don't believe that you could never have been tempted to stray off the straight and narrow. Talking the way we do is very sexy, very intimate. We should tell her, because then it will help to keep us friends," Joyce said, a little incoherently.

"But Joyce, that will let her see how alone she is."

But Joyce insisted. "Would you trust a relationship from which you were excluded? Wouldn't you feel a little paranoid about it? Bridget's paranoid anyway, always thinking that people are watching her every move, as a test or an example. I think what I'm saying is that she needn't be excluded, Ian. She's your wife, she's my friend. We shouldn't keep her out of our *platonic* friendship." Joyce's sense of humour was recovering, and there was a smile in her voice as she said these words. "Surely if she knows she's welcome when she's around, she won't resent or suspect us if we spend time together when she's busy?"

"I hope not." Ian got up. "Coffee?" He walked towards the kitchen without waiting for an answer. With his back to her he said, "I don't think it's disloyal to my wife to say I enjoy your exclusive company at times. Why not? We all react differently to every other person, and you help me to feel adult and relaxed in a unique way. With you I'm not just a father and a teacher."

"And a husband," Joyce said, firmly. She too scrambled to her feet. "No coffee for me thanks, Ian. I'm going home. You'll speak to Bridget?"

He turned to her. "Yes. Yes, I will. Of course, I'd far rather you did, but I can see I must. Thank you for tonight, Joyce. Part of me is cursing you for spoiling my favourite toy, but I'm sure that eventually I'll come to see that you're right."

"Bye for now, then. This toy is returning to its toy-box."

Despite Ian's misgivings, Bridget seemed to take the news very well. The next evening, Thursday, she met with Joyce for a short session with the diaries. Her comment on Ian's revelations was, "It seems the laugh was on me the other night, asking if you remembered Ian, when the two of you have become friends. However, Ian tells me you weren't laughing, Joyce, so I'd better tell you not to worry. It's fine by me." Then they turned to the text.

Ian, however, found that he couldn't laugh the whole thing off so lightly. He had always been so sure of his fidelity and his single-mindedness, but now, as he relived the conversation and thought about what Joyce had said, he began to wonder. Conversation could be very intimate: the act of converse, no matter what the subject. He had thought of Joyce as a substitute for his long-gone male friends of his student days. So there wasn't any danger was there? It was all a storm in a tea-cup.

But gradually, as he repeated this to himself, it broke in upon him that this was all very well, but the fact was that Joyce was not a man. She was Joyce. He had assumed that she saw the friendship in the same way as he did, but how was that possible? She was a woman. Her relationships with men had to be coloured by this. Although she had, on the whole, reacted and responded very much in the role which he had marked out for her, yet in the end differences must have shown up. And then what? Denied the pure intellectual friendship he craved, how might he not have responded to the woman whom he had come to know so well? He must face the fact that he had been deceiving himself. He had been deceiving his wife as well, yes, of course, but he had been able to take himself for a ride. It shook him.

Most of this thinking was done in his walks to and from school. If at all possible, he avoided accepting lifts from his wife or from other members of staff, as he truly enjoyed the seventeen minutes each way between Irvine Crescent and the Cannongate. On his morning journey he passed a steady stream of junior secondary school pupils making their reluctant or eager ways in the opposite direction. Some would be former pupils whom he would greet: he enjoyed discovering which children would return his salutation gladly, and which would squirm and avoid his gaze. However, for a week after his conversation with Joyce, he found it hard to think about anything else. Could he in fact trust himself? Was it in fact possible that he could deceive both himself and Bridget to such an extent that he might be tempted into an affair? He knew he was lonely, and though he thought that loneliness was for male friendship, was it possible that he might ever be prepared to substitute a sexual affair? How did he know? Should he perhaps deliberately arrange a series of tests? But that wouldn't work – not if he knew he was testing himself. He had never been too impressed by accounts of those ancient Christians who tested their celibacy and restraint by sleeping beside a naked woman. If you knew something was as test it was so much easier to perform. But that wouldn't tell him much about his daily self. His class found him less lively and creative during these days.

It wasn't just in the classroom that his preoccupation impinged on his normal demeanour; at home too his normally placid temper began to show signs of fraying. He took to snapping at Angus and Mairi, and at Bridget. Then, if they looked at him questioningly, he would apologise forcibly, abasing himself before his family in a most uncomfortable manner. After a week of this, Bridget called him to account for it.

"What's got into you, Ian? You're preoccupied, you're bad tempered and you don't seem to think you deserve to live and be part of this family. What is it? Don't say nothing, because I certainly wouldn't believe that."

"It's not nothing. I'm a bit ashamed, and I don't seem sure of the sort of person I am."

"Ashamed? What of?" Bridget was genuinely puzzled, then her voice rose in disbelief. "Surely you're not still thinking about Joyce?"

Ian nodded.

"But why should that shame you? You've done nothing wrong."

"But I might have. I might not have. I didn't think of it at the time, but who knows?"

"Oh Ian, you're making a rod to beat yourself with. I never knew you had such masochistic tendencies."

"Nor did I, but then there's a lot I didn't know and don't like about myself." Ian was unbearably morose.

"If you go on like that I'll begin to wonder if I ought to have been worried about your meetings with Joyce. Ian, all you did was keep it a secret, wasn't it?"

"Yes."

"Well, that might have been a mistake, but that's all it was. A mistake. Something silly you did without thinking it through. If it had been done on purpose you would have seduced Joyce in pretty short order."

Ian gasped slightly.

Bridget smiled grimly. "It is unfaithfulness we're talking about here, isn't it? That's the 'it' that's giving you shame. You weren't unfaithful, you just had a secret. So it was a mistake if it was anything at all. Let it go."

"It was Joyce who pulled me up short. If she hadn't seen where it might be heading who knows when or if I would."

"You would have." Bridget was certain. "Even if, which I don't believe for one minute, you had gone as far as getting into bed, the act of doing so would have reminded you. Actual adultery is never just a mistake: it's always deliberate. But whatever you might have done, the fact is, you didn't. And I trust you completely and always have and always will. Now can we put this behind us, please. I don't want to have you moping around the house, wondering if I should still be able to trust you.

March continued its erratic journey into Spring. The snowdrops and crocuses were in full bloom before the next snowfall. Undaunted, the trees began budding and a southerly wind blew the snow away, bringing squally showers in its place. On the Kinness Burn, winding its way through the length of the town, the ducks began to pair off, with much quacking and fighting, churning the brown waters with the beating of their wings. Soon pairs of honeymoon ducks could be found wandering in a happy daze far from their burn-side roosts: in streets, gardens, and parks, on low roofs, even in the cathedral grounds. No one could be unaware that the ducks' time had come round again. In the houses near the burn green-eyed cats licked their lips and waited in hope for the advent of the first ducklings.

Now that her friendship with Ian was out in the open, Joyce began to attend Bridget's church. She had been thinking of doing so since Christmas Day, when she had enjoyed the service. At first her attendance was sporadic, and when she did come, she was frequently late. It was not easy for a person of her strongly-held religious assumptions to open herself up to another possibility. But Miss Murdoch had attended this church. The woman whose life-story she was reading seemed to have little to do with the routines of Church of Scotland worship, but she had gone, and gone faithfully, for years. Joyce had tremendous respect for Miss Murdoch, and even if she didn't know yet why her mentor had posed as a religious believer, yet she had faith that there was a good reason for it. So, Sunday by Sunday she at least thought about attending herself, and sometimes she actually did so.

Meanwhile Sandy's ideas for Martyrs Church were going well. Bridget tried to discuss them with him, but found that this he would not do. When they were finished she would see them. When would that be? Soon, very soon. In time for the April meeting of the Kirk Session? When was that then? Oh yes, he thought he could promise them by then.

With this Bridget had to be content, though, as she pointed out, it didn't help her to answer the many enquiries parishioners put to her on the matter.

Joyce and Bridget were making steady progress through Miss Murdoch's diaries, though once again Joyce had gone quiet when it came to discussing what they were reading. She would talk happily enough about anything else, except Sandy of course. At this time Bridget learned more about her upbringing in Pitlochry, her family, and her delight in the hills, which she missed. She even finally heard Joyce speak about her studies, although without total enthusiasm, and with a certain vagueness in her manner.

Having no Joyce or Sandy with whom to discuss the diary, Bridget turned to Ian, and he now became familiar with Miss Murdoch's doings. He was ignorant of most of the story, so his wife filled him in on the salient points to date, as well as offering her reflections on her current readings. Ian was fascinated, and privately stored away some of what he heard for future consideration.

The reason that Joyce had become shy of talking about the diary was a sense of inadequacy. She could reason, argue, theorise, and discuss with the best, but as she read Charlotte Murdoch's story, she could not help but contrast herself with the woman. It seemed that Charlotte had not appreciated her mother. When she had gained her freedom, she had spent it on selfish pursuits, and had travelled to gratify herself alone. Joyce, who did not get on with her own mother, wondered if her studies were not a similar indulgence to Charlotte's travels. She studied, not for its own sake, but for hers. She had no ambition to enlarge the sphere of human knowledge: she just wanted to know more herself, and if she had any further ambition it was that her studies might make her name known at least to one section of academia. Such troublesome self-knowledge was a painful thing for Joyce, and the unpalatable idea hit her with the full impact of a first experience. It left a bitter tase in her mouth. She felt that she measured up badly compared to Charlotte, because her mentor – and she was coming to regard Charlotte in this way – her mentor had gone on to do useful things, while Joyce could see little that was useful in her projected future. Wild ideas filled her mind. Perhaps she shouldn't finish her degree? Perhaps she should follow in her land-lady's footsteps and go off to India, or some other poor country? But what could she do there that someone else couldn't do better? It was perhaps fortunate that she did not get as far as deciding that her possibly second-rate attempts to help might be better than no help at all. Had that thought occurred she would probably have disappeared without warning, so keen was she to make amends for what appeared to be unforgiveable selfishness and uselessness.

As it was, Joyce brooded, squirmed, and was silent. She wondered if Bridget had noticed the parallels she found between her life and Miss Murdoch's earlier writings, but nothing would have induced her to ask. Lest any of her inner turmoil and guilt came out, it was better to preserve an absolute silence on the matter. She decided that she would make no decision about her future until she had finished reading the diaries. They were more than half-way through now and Joyce's inner self shrank from the thought that they couldn't be made to last so very much longer. Charlotte Murdoch in life had been her landlady. In death she had become her mentor and was fast becoming like family. It was a mark of her mentor's effectiveness that Joyce was able to see this. Not since the time of the ill-fated adolescent diary had she been so given to introspection as she was now.

Charlotte Murdoch was family. What kind of family was she? Logically, by age she should be like a grandmother or a great aunt, such was their chronological separation. But through the diaries, Joyce knew Charlotte as she had been in her thirties and forties, so that wasn't it. A mother then? Or an aunt? Again, she rejected these analogies; that wasn't the feeling. No, she was like a sister, a close sister. At first she had been like an older sister, able to give younger siblings the benefit of her experience. Lately, however, Charlotte seemed to have been growing younger, or else Joyce was aging fast. Now it felt as though they were close in age, very close, and close in emotion and reaction too. Joyce wouldn't be surprised if soon she discovered that they were twins, fraternal and then even identical.

She had never known and enjoyed knowing another person as she did Charlotte Murdoch. As a child growing up she had, of course, never really thought about people, or wondered how well she knew them. They were there and that was that. You know, for instance, that Dad didn't like company in the mornings until he'd had some tea. You knew that older brother John wouldn't wear a vest, or anything brown; that younger brother Simon was fiercely territorial, and that Mum couldn't stop asking questions. At school you knew that Mr Reid had a passion for neat handwriting, while Miss Cameron preferred good spelling, and Mrs Fairnie prized a well-exercised imagination. You knew that Anne couldn't sing but could draw, and that Isobel loved her maths, and her favourite colour was green. These things came by osmosis.

As she grew up her knowledge of people became more complex, but always the nuances of her understanding were self-centred. She knew if she liked a person and why, she knew if a person liked her; the 'why' wasn't often asked in such cases. All this, had she known it was the common experience of human development. With her growth in understanding, Joyce also began to be more consciously aware of how to get certain people to please her. Dad was a sucker for the helpless-daughter act; male teachers responded to a carefully-played femininity; her peers preferred people who were funny and independent and a little radical. Joyce never questioned whether she was these things: automatically she took on whatever guise most suited her purpose. She was the perfect teenage chameleon.

That all ended the day her mother read her diary. In one way Joyce grew up that day: she learned not to trust. She also learned to fear herself. She was afraid of the thoughts that raced through her mind. She was afraid of what they said about her. She was afraid lest unwittingly she display herself to others. When she was eighteen, Joyce froze, preventing herself, by effort of will, from thinking deeply about herself or others.

When she first left home for university this had been no hindrance. She had freed herself from most of the late adolescent anguish and posturing which could have sapped her energy. Instead she found it easy, even a relief, to plunge herself into her studies, giving her stressed, analytical brain something to become involved with. Outwardly she was self-possessed and friendly. She had many acquaintances, some of whom called themselves her friends. But when she froze her self-knowledge she had also frozen her ability to regard others objectively. She could not invest in other people since she could not invest in herself. None of her friendships lasted, nor her romantic experiments. As a physically attractive girl, she found there were boys who wanted to count themselves as her boyfriend, and some of these relationships she gave assent to. The most successful were those which were primarily physical in their expression. But even then, when she gave up her body willingly to her partner's pleasure, it quickly became clear that there was no emotional bonding available, and once again the boyfriend would cease calling.

While she must still return home in the vacation-times, this was how life had to be for Joyce. It was only when she mentally left home for good and came to St. Andrews as a doctoral student that Joyce's icebergs began to melt. She began to feel to feel human, a little. She met Alex and the process advanced. She met Bridget and another few ice-cubes dissolved. Now she was meeting Charlotte and had begun to feel the warmth of an Indian sun.

As March wore on, and the days of Lent grew shorter ahead and longer behind, Joyce and Bridget basked in that Indian sun. The pages of Miss Murdoch's diary with their now fairly infrequent entries, recorded the life of a happy woman. She said so herself, in explaining why she didn't write so often, as an aside to herself, which she seemed to think was required.

30th May 1948

Happy days need no recording. It is enough, it is more than enough to live them. I have nothing but happy days now. How I love my Badepuri life! My work may be demanding, but it fills me with such satisfaction. It is something worth doing. I revel in the sunshine, my simple house, food and life-style. I am communicating in more than English now: and why not? I always enjoyed language, and this is so different from related European tongues. I am at home here and at peace. The rhythms of the village suit me: this is what I was born for. And there is no need to record or reflect, just to be.

When I was growing up, and worse, when I was stuck at home with Mother, what volumes I might have written then! But I could not write, for I had no privacy. If I wrote, she wanted to know what and why and expected to read it. And what a coward I was! I couldn't stand up to her but allowed myself to fade and wither and live in her shadow. Look at me now, Mother! It's ironic that she'd probably like what she would see now. My meekness was so irritating to her, but in her presence I could be nothing else.

I scarcely think of these days now. As I travelled round Europe before the War they were constantly on my mind. Of course, I was closer to them then, but also I had to point the contrast. My freedom would not have been so deliciously precious had it not had the piquant contrast of my former bondage. But now I don't need to search for happiness, to remind myself that life has changed. The sun rises on my joy and sets with my contentment.

Small changes in her life came in gradually, slipping into her journal with a naturalness which precluded trumpeting.

1st September 1948

End of the first year, and I'm still here. I handed over my beginners to Maha today; since she has children of her own, she can teach them in the morning and attend adult class later.

2nd November 1948

Madhur has read a complete story without asking for help. She wants to work hard on writing, though I told her never to forget that she will write best in her own tongue. "The language you dream is the language of your soul," I told her. She nodded gravely. "Yes, teacher Sahib, and the language of your prayers." I don't pray, but I still dream in English with a good Scots accent.

15th December 1948

The festival of Diwali. It is a beautiful occasion. The whole village glows with light from dusk till dawn. Classes are suspended and we feast a lot. The temple is very popular during these days. It's not a big or spectacular place, but it is filled with wonder for these people. Their devotion is very real, and even the poorest give priority to finding food and flowers to make offering to Vishnu, to Shiva, to Ganesh, to Brahmin, to Sarawati, and to the ancestors. I'm never sure which deity is the object of veneration, or if it is a matter of personal taste. Ganesh, the elephant god, is the god of education and learning (amongst other things). Some of my pupils have painted a little Ganesh on the wall of my house.

14th January 1949

My sari stayed put all day. No quick fumblings and pullings necessary. This is a first no one will notice but myself.

10th March 1949

Madhur asked me to go with her to the temple to perform puja. This is different from wandering in to look around. I brought some sweet rice and flowers (I still don't know the names of most of the flowers). I had thought it would be hard to pray, and indeed at first no words came. But then I tried my pidgin Hindustani, and I found I had quite a bit to say to Vishnu. Too much for Madhur's liking, actually. The offerings and our presence apparently say more than words. Or ought to. Hmm. Westerners are very wordy. Now that I think about it, every morning and evening when I see people making private puja, lighting lamps, making ablutions, I don't recall that these actions have a form of words accompanying them.

20th May 1949

I am still an outsider here. Perhaps I should expect nothing else. Sunburned as I am, I am still pale compared to everyone around me, and my larger bones are undoubtedly non-Indian. Besides, I teach English. But I should like to fit in. Perhaps I shall start paying attention to the rhythms of religious life. I know it exists, and I have observed it, but it doesn't pulse through me as I'd like (or would I?). The question is, can I be in touch with the religion without subscribing to it? It's not a question I can ask anyone. My Hindustani isn't up to it, nor is even Madhur's English. Besides, I have a feeling that it may be one of those questions which demonstrate the East West divide. I doubt if it would be heard, no matter how eloquently I phrased it. I may be wrong, but I doubt any Indian would see the distinction. For them, it would appear, to perform the rituals is to be a part of the religion. Faith is action. But if that is so, can I join in? Because God or gods, I still don't subscribe to deism.

1st July 1949

Panji and Benaswati have found government jobs! They were fourteen years old when I began teaching them. Now they are sufficiently bi-lingual to compete with city youths – and be successful. Of course, they will be the lowest form of clerks, but they, and I, are still very proud. Tomorrow they move to Bombay. Panji has an uncle there, so they won't be totally adrift in a strange environment. Tonight there is to be a feast to honour them.

Later: It turned out the feast was also to honour me! "You did it, Miss Murdoch, Mem. We are so happy that you have come to our village." Benaswati's mother said that to me, even as the tears ran down her face at the thought of losing her son. Train fares may not seem expensive to me, but she can't afford them and nor will he at first. So it is a hard parting for the mothers, not knowing when a reunion may happen.

I pointed out that it wasn't only my doing. I taught the boys English, but their general education and their own determination were also important factors in obtaining this blessing. (Everyone calls it a blessing.)

9th August 1949

Very hot. I have spoken to Madhur about puja. I asked her to show me how the ritual washing is done as I want to offer my ablutions to Shiva. Do I? Not really. But it was all I could think of that she might understand. She was pleased. In her pleasure she reminded me of that missionary woman I met on the boat here. I almost expected Madhur to exclaim about lost lambs returning to the fold. She didn't, of course. In stead she praised Vishnu that her friend Miss Murdoch Mem loved his people so. Perhaps she sees that I am doing this to become one with my Indian neighbours? Or does she equate Indian life with piety? I don't know.

Really, it occurred to me that as I must and do wash daily anyway, there would be no harm in doing it in a certain way. Then I would show solidarity with my friends, but for me it would just be washing. I couldn't delude myself that leaving offerings of food, flowers or light for the gods was anything but religious; but washing – that's part of daily life. So from now on I make a little ritual of my morning wash – something still private to me, but I think of the religious spirit of India as I wash. Whoever dreamed up these rituals had some notion of essential hygiene.

21st August 1949

Letter from Mr Macpherson, the St. Andrews solicitor. It is over two months old, and says one of my tenants is moving out. He assumes it will be my wish that he find another occupier at the same rent, but he will allow nothing to be signed without having confirmation from myself. He assures me that the house is being well-maintained and hopes I am in good health and spirits. Will I be returning to Scotland in the future?

Shall I? It's hard to imagine. This is my life now.

15th October 1949

I suppose it had to happen. Washing has ceased to be a ritual and has simply become washing again. I told this to Madhur who was anything but surprised. "You washed before," she said. "You still wash. How can your body know you are doing anything different?"

I said that I had hoped my mind might realise it, and she laughed. "The mind is full of tricks. We don't trust our religion to our minds in India. It is too important."

I asked what else I could do. She replied that it must be something which I would never normally do. "Perhaps you should offer food to the gods. When I am eating with you, I see you always eat everything given you." I pointed out that I had been brought up to believe that this showed mannerly appreciation.

"In Europe, perhaps. In India it gives your host reason to doubt you have been given enough. But this is not my point. When you are eating alone, is it also your custom to consume everything?"

I said that it was: I don't cook more food than I am able to eat.

"Then I suggest you cook no more than previously but leave a little aside to offer to the gods."

I have seen the villagers do this, of course. Every house

has a little shrine of some sort, usually with a statue of one or other of the gods. Krishna is probably the most popular. It has often puzzled me why people who rarely get quite enough to eat themselves give a portion to their shrines. I told Madhur as much. She gave me a puzzled smile.

"Truly, you know little of Indian pride, Mem. We should be poor indeed if we could not give to the gods. We give from our poverty and Krishna, or Shiva, or the ancestors, they in return give us dignity and a place in the ordering of the world. If we could not do this we would truly consider ourselves worse off than the sweepers in the streets."

Then she offered to help me purchase a fine god.

I don't know about this. I find my strict presbyterian upbringing rebels. "Idolatry" whispers a voice in my ear. But is it? If I don't believe in God – or not actively: if, at least, I'm unsure about God can it be idolatry to keep a statue? Can't I just have it as a work of local art?

But if it were just a work of art I wouldn't give it rice. So if I make an offering to the statue I am saying something, even if I don't believe the statement I am making.

17th October 1949

I have asked Madhur about the ancestors. They have no statue: usually they are represented by the gods. Why was this, I asked.

"So many questions," she replied. "Only Westerners have so many questions: more than a child." I pointed out that she had grown up here, and that if she were to come to Scotland she might have as many questions as I. This idea delighted her, but once she had finished laughing she answered my quest for information.

It is to do with Karma. We do not know where the ancestors are in Samsara. They may be all around us in people and animals, or they may be enjoying life far from here. But it may be that they have had their Samsara interrupted – we say that they have achieved Moksha and have escaped to Brahman the eternal. If this is so, they are no more but have become part of that of which the gods are also a part. So when we worship the gods we remember our ancestors and hope that they too may be in Brahman."

This took some thinking about. But I have decided that I shall offer a little rice daily (a very little) and keep a sacred flame burning in my house. These are things I wouldn't normally do, so they shouldn't lose their significance. And a flame could be useful.

If I make offerings to my ancestors, does that mean to Mother? I suppose it does.

CHAPTER SEVEN: MARTYS REMODELLED

"Vision is the art of seeing things invisible."

Jonathan Swift, "Thoughts on various subjects"

Lent was ending its course as a brave flourish of daffodil trumpets heralded the approach of Easter. Ian was busy with end-of-term activities: projects to finish, a parents' night, reports to write and next term to plan for. Bridget was caught up in work, a couple of funerals adding a sense of hysterical impossibility to the scheduling of her days. Joyce saw little of either friend and was herself taken up with assessing some of the students and marking belated papers.

Sandy was also busy. He was adding the finishing touches to his plans for Martyrs church halls. The luxury of the last few weeks had been incredible, as he was able to give his whole attention to the project. Time enough to dwell on the "what next?" when the building work started. It never really occurred to him that the people of Martyrs church would not accept his plans, as he lost himself in his work. By day he drew plans and sketches, both by hand and on the computer in the office and he spent his evenings constructing a scale model of the new church premises, as he saw them. This he built with the East wall removed, so that people could see into the model. The wall itself, containing the windows, would not be undergoing external change.

Bridget had asked if the plans could be ready by Easter Sunday morning. The church was serving a breakfast after the traditional sunrise service in Kinburn Park. ("Why not the beach?" Sandy had asked. "No one wants to have to fuss around with tide tables finding out if it's possible," was the answer.) Breakfast on Easter Sunday had a fine sound to it and was popular. But as Bridget explained, in reality it was rather tricky. After all there were three hours to fill between 8 a.m. and 11 a.m. when the main morning worship began. Eating and clearing up took no more than an hour. They couldn't bring forward the main service, because of the many who didn't attend the breakfast and would be put out to have their Sunday routine disturbed, and because of the even more who came to church only on this and Christmas Eve, and who would assume that church could only happen at eleven. These latter would be the most vociferous in their complaints should they find themselves caught out by sneaky time changes. So, year by year, something had to be found to help fill in the time. They had had Easter egg hunts, quizzes, games, a walk out the pier and back; all manner of things. This year breakfast would be served in a hall bearing the marks of wind and water damage, and cooked and cleared away in an apology for a kitchen. What better way to fill the time and point forward to a better future than to have the new design getting its first airing? Discussing the plans would more than fill the awkward time.

Sandy listened to Bridget posing the problem to him and agreed that this could be the solution. So taken was he that he offered to attend the breakfast and chair a discussion-cum-meet-the-architect session afterwards.

Bridget was overcome. "Sandy, would you do that?"

"I've just offered."

"You won't mind? Some people may be less than complimentary, you know. We've our fair share of folk who pride themselves on their plain speaking, unfortunately."

"That's O.K. My grandfather is of that breed, so I'm used to it."

This reminded Bridget of another concern. "What about your family? You won't be disrupting their plans for Easter, will you?"

"I will, and I want to. They take too much for granted, my family. I don't like their Easter. Grandad's all right, he's a church-goer, one of these stiff, unbending old elders who always wear black. He would be going to church anyway. But for quite a while now I haven't liked my mother's insistence that the whole family go to church on Christmas and Easter. It's hypocritical. Coming to your breakfast will give me the perfect excuse: work. My parents know the importance of employment and earning pennies."

"So you'll come to Martyrs to avoid going to church?" Over the phone Sandy could hear the laughter in Bridget's voice.

"No, no. I'll probably stay for your service, actually – that will get me out of family lunch. It's not church I object to, it's making a big family holiday out of something we don't give more than lip service to. It's form without content. I don't object to the content if you happen to believe that way." He was sounding hot and bothered now, and Bridget's laugh stopped his words.

"Don't worry, Sandy, and don't feel that you have to justify yourself to me. I'm very grateful if you can come on Easter Day. And now, when am I going to get a glimpse of these plans of yours?"

When Bridget did see the plans and the model (it's very existence a surprise to her), a week before Easter, she was rendered speechless. She had come to Sandy's office for what had jokingly been named "the great unveiling" and had been amused by the slight air of ceremony which met her there. Sandy had her sit down in the main office while he went into a large cupboard to bring forth the fruits of his toil. Hargreaves was on hand, ostensibly working at his slope, but in reality keeping a sharp eye on Bridget's reactions. He had seen the plans and had been impressed. Nevertheless he was intrigued as to what "the client" might make of Sandy's wholesale, visionary approach.

From the depths of the cupboard Sandy's voice sounded muffled. "I'll bring out the model first. That will probably be easier to understand."

Bridget said nothing. The sun burst through the clouds, glinting off the brass detailing of the old furniture, glowing in well-tended mahogany and spotlighting the table which was waiting to receive the model.

Staggering slightly, Sandy emerged backwards, and still with his back to Bridget he made his way to the table. There was a slight thump and a slithery noise, then the sound of Sandy taking a deep breath. He turned away from the table and the model stood revealed.

It was incredible. As a model, as a miniature work of art, the thing was amazing. Quality and attention to detail sang in its lines and colours. As a plan for the church halls, it was unlike anything Bridget had imagined.

For one thing, it was bright. It glowed in the sunshine with the rich colours of jewels or velvets. Church halls, Bridget might have said, are brown, pale blue or cream. But this, Sandy might have answered, is not a church hall.

It was not. A church hall has a high ceiling, a wooden floor, and a draughty air about it. It is a functional edifice. This building had a low ceiling and attics, comfortable, carpeted attics. The main room was large, but had a tiled floor, rather than wood. Its walls had been given a softer feel by rounding the cornices, so that ceiling met wall in an unbroken curve. A cross-section showed items stored in the spaces thus constructed. The kitchen had been moved to one of the rooms at the back of the building and the toilets had been extended into the other, allowing for showers to be installed.

Where the kitchen had been was a comfortable, carpeted room with easy-chairs. The floor level had been lowered to match the rest of the building. The six upstairs rooms were of different sizes and had been variously furnished. One had bunk-beds; another children's' toys and couple of cots; one had a table and chairs; another miniature bean-bags. The fifth room, above the kitchen, held a washing machine and dryer, and a miniature ironing board, while the sixth was empty, save for a tiny notice "Use Your Imagination."

But the colour! Sandy Melville had not contented himself with designing the shell of the building: he had done the interior decoration as well. This was to be murals. On the model they were suggested by drawings of the main figures of each picture, painted brightly to give the overall effect. The murals were to be on all four walls of the main room and yes, on the ceiling. There were pictures in the corridor, in the stair-well and one each in the rooms upstairs. All seen at once, the effect was kaleidoscopic. When life-size the suggestion of the kaleidoscope might be less, as they would not all be seen together. But leafing through the accompanying book filled with the details of the murals, Bridget could not think that the effect would be anything less than explosive.

She had been silent so long that Sandy began to doubt her approval, to doubt his vision for the first time. He had worked on this project with the single-minded devotion of inspiration, and it had not occurred to him that his work might not be approved. Nervously he coughed.

"Shall I explain it to you? Perhaps I should show you how various people could use this? It's not too bad, is it?" he ended pathetically.

Bridget didn't look up. "It's brilliant," she whispered. "It's simply brilliant."

Brilliant was the word she used again when Ian asked her about the plans. "It really is the only word. He's given us all the space we could ask for, some specific to certain purposes, but some left nicely flexible. But he's made it all glow and shine. It will be like walking into a stained-glass window when it's all decorated."

Ian lifted a spade; they were gardening at the time. "Brightly coloured walls? Sounds like the seventies."

Bridget sat back on her heels with a handful of weeds. "Nothing like the seventies. And its' not just coloured walls, it's the most amazing murals. And before you say anything, they are bright but not crude. Far from it. You'll just have to wait until Easter Day like everyone else."

"Fair enough."

They worked on in silence for a while. This was the first day of the year that their own commitments and the weather had come together to allow gardening. Thankfully, as Ian said, the bulbs came up every year whether or not they had done anything to help them. But apart from the glowing patches of crocuses, grape hyacinths and early daffodils, there was a lot needing done. This first session they devoted to tidying. They pruned, pulled out dead plants from last autumn, dealt with the mouldering leaves which covered the flower beds and through which fresh green shoots were poking. Ian was turning over the soil before digging in compost, already preparing a seed bed for the packets of annuals awaiting planting. As usual, Bridget had bought more seeds than they could hope to grow. She couldn't help herself. The shops displayed these beautiful pictures of flowers on seed packets in February, just when she was most longing for some warmth and colour. It was no wonder she went overboard. And they could always give some away.

Now she looked up from the sack she was filling with weeds and asked, "Have you seen much of Joyce lately?"

Ian flushed then silently cursed himself. Was he never to hear that name without guilt? It wasn't even as if he had anything to hide. "A couple of times, but not for long. The kids were there one time."

"That's not why I'm asking, idiot. I just wondered if she mentioned Miss Murdoch's diary to you?"

"No, not that I can remember. Why? Interesting again, is it?"

"Well, it is, but Joyce won't discuss it with me. We read, and then she carefully turns the conversation to other things."

"Why? What's she writing about now?"

"As a matter of fact, she seems to be thinking seriously about becoming a Hindu. Miss Murdoch, I mean, not Joyce. That's why I'm so surprised. At the beginning Joyce seemed so determined that Miss Murdoch would prove that at least one of my flock wasn't the devout Christian she appeared. At this stage in the story – it's like a story – events seem to be bearing her out. The Joyce I first knew would certainly have pointed that out to me, probably many times. I was wondering if she had something else on her mind."

"You weren't just wondering," smiled Ian. "You were hoping I could tell you so you could interfere. Don't meddle, Bridget. If

Joyce wants your help, she's quite capable of asking for it."

Bridget threw a weed at him. "I am not interfering. It's my job to help."

"But it's not your job to go poking your nose where it's not been invited. Come off it, Bridget. You know you have to earn the right to meddle."

"I don't like your vocabulary. 'Meddle, interfere, poking your nose.'"

Ian grinned. "I know. I only do it to annoy because I know it teases. There must be something in it or you wouldn't get so mad. O.K." as his wife glared at him and brandished a trowel, "I'll leave off. Actually, I think with Joyce you are earning the right. What does she talk about?"

"This and that. The weather, her students, her professor, my work: it's nothing to get hold of."

"Then you'll have to wait and see. Meanwhile tell me about Miss Murdoch becoming a Hindu. I find that hard to match up with the formidable old lady who once told me she doubted I had enough responsibility to be either a teacher or a man of the manse! I can't see her in flowing draperies, offering sacrifice."

"Well try. So far, she's not a Hindu, but she is wearing a sari and yes, she is making offerings, though at home, not in a temple."

"How do you know she's not a Hindu? I mean, how do you become a Hindu?" Ian was busy filling the wheelbarrow with compost, so didn't see the worried frown on Bridget's face.

"She says she's not a Hindu. She seems to be trying to assimilate culturally while withholding her faith from the whole thing."

"Doesn't believe in it? Then why do it?"

"Like I said, cultural stuff. Apparently she wants to be more in touch with the villagers and the spirit of India."

Ian broke into hooting laughter. "To be in touch with the spirit of India! This wasn't the sixties, was it?" He laughed again.

"No, the late forties. Do you mean she was some sort of proto-hippie?"

"What does it sound like? Bridgie, I am delighted. I never knew I could be so surprised by anyone or anything. Old Miss Murdoch the archetypal hippie. Miss Prim and Proper getting in touch with the spirit of India and finding herself. It's marvellous!"

Bridget was silent. Savagely she removed her gardening gloves and hauled her sack of weeds to the shed. Ian straightened up and watched her. "Are you O.K.?" he asked.

"Since you ask, I'm cold. The air is damp. I'm going in."

"The air is always damp in March. It never worried you before. What's really wrong?

Bridget glared at him.

"It's not something I said about Miss Murdoch, surely? Come on, Bridgie, can't you take a joke?"

"Miss Murdoch was my friend."

"I know. But she did have a sense of humour under her unbending manner."

Bridget stalked to the house. "It was a mistake telling you about the contents of the diary. I might have known you'd just make a joke." The door closed firmly behind her.

Ian stared at its blank, green façade. Damn! What had happened here? One minute they were as chummy as you like, and now... Of course, Bridget was always tired at this time of year, but he worked hard too. Was it the mention of Joyce? But she'd brought the subject up. Should he have mentioned their recent meetings? But they had said they would be open and talk. How could he do that if this sudden temper was to be the result? Women!

Not all women were like that, of course. His mother now, she never erupted into temper or dissolved into sulks. Ian smiled thinking of her. She lived in a retirement home outside Aberdeen these days, and could not wash or dress herself. Her mind was still clear, however, and her love still gracious. He wished he could get to see her more frequently. It was difficult, though. Bridget always worked on Sundays and nearly always had important commitments on Saturdays as well. He could take one child for a visit but not two, not by himself. They disliked the home, and small blame to them; after all it was not designed for children. As with any unfortunate experience, singly they could endure it properly, but together their mutual discomfort fuelled them to acts of rebellion. It took both parents to control them at the home. Or else Bridget had to baby-sit in St. Andrews. Ian's sister and brother-in-law lived nearby and one or other of them popped in to see his mother nearly every day. This was good, of course it was. It kept Mum happy. Even to himself Ian found it hard to admit that he felt usurped, an outsider who only came for occasional visits, not a proper family member.

Perhaps because of this unacknowledged pain, Ian most often thought of his mother as she had been when he was growing up. Such a wonderful mother to have! Never angry, never cross, yet such a sensitive, feminine woman. Unpleasantness could not come near her. More than once Ian and Moira, his sister, would be engaged in fierce sibling sparring. Usually their battles were verbal and noisy rather than physically violent. Ian remembered his father's habit of coming upon them and with quiet tones and flashing eyes ordering them to be silent "Or you'll upset Mummy. You don't want Mummy to cry, do you?" No, he didn't want that. He'd seen it only once in his young life, and once was enough. Mummy must be protected. If her darling children weren't quite perfect, she must never know it.

Later in adolescence, how much he owed to his mother. He could come in from school full of angst and rebellious anger after a trying day and rant about the injustices of his life. This teacher didn't like him, that one was dumb; the whole school system was out-dated. His mother would look at him with these gentle eyes and say, "Now, Ian, you don't really think that." If he insisted, "I do!" She would soothe him, saying "No, you don't. That's not my son speaking. That's a conglomeration of hormones. My son doesn't think that at all." And time had proved her right. He didn't really think that. Mummy had guided him through that sticky patch and now look at him: married to the church (as it were), a respectable father and even a teacher in the once-despised system. Mummy knew that teenage rebellion was just a waste of time and energy. She had refused to argue with him or show emotion and now he thought she had been wise.

You knew where you were with Mummy. You knew how things were. There was order in her world and certain inviolable truths which would always be so. Her purity and innocence were her strengths, for no one would want to bring dubious humour, crude language, or any other unpleasantness into her world. She was consistent and expected consistency of behaviour from you. Life was pleasant with her. But now she was frail. Now she seemed both precious and far away.

Ian caught at himself. Yes, but his life with Bridget and Mairi and Angus was good too. He smiled wryly. If he had to remind himself ad protest this it said something, he knew. He might as well admit that he missed the security of his mother's predictable world. He didn't know why he couldn't recreate it in his own life. But, whispered his subconscious, his mother's world would not last forever, and already he was being squeezed out.

Slicing his spade down hard in an effort not to hear this last thought, he found he had sliced the heads off his favourite budding red tulips.

Easter Sunday was a pearly grey day. There was no glorious golden sunrise at the ecumenical dawn service, but a faint silver mist shimmered imperceptibly about the bushes in the park. Sandy noticed it with appreciation. He might have been the only one to note it, being more detached from worship than the rest of the crowd. Only the religiously committed attended the dawn service: most people thought it more civilised to have an extra couple of hours in bed. Perhaps they were right. Gazing about him and philosophising to himself, Sandy wondered where the idea of dawn worship originated. No doubt these faithful people, trying not to shiver in the chilly air, would say they met at first light because in the Gospel stories that was when the resurrection was first discovered. But time zones questioned the logic of that position. After all, dawn in Israel was when? Probably around 2 a.m. British Summer Time. If they really wanted to be in tune with the timing of the story shouldn't they be gathering then? Of course, it wouldn't be very practical, but should faith baulk at a little difficulty like that? Wasn't it more likely that this tradition of sunrise worship was just that, the worship of the rising sun? A pagan spring ritual, perhaps, or even a custom displaced from the mid-winter solstice? Or it could be some residue of an equinoctial rite. The equinox wasn't so long past after all.

The people lifted their voices in a hymn. "Christ the Lord is risen today" they sang, louder and louder. This final hymn seemed to be some sort of competition in showing zeal: the louder you sang, the wider and more glazed your smile the more genuine and heartfelt your joy on this day. Or perhaps they were just cold and hungry and glad that the service was drawing to a conclusion.

A benediction was pronounced, and the members of the various congregations greeted one another with hearty, if brief, handshakes, led by the assorted clergy. The Roman Catholic priest and the Episcopalian rectors in their bright red and white robes looked far more festive than did the four black-gowned representatives of the church of Scotland. Bridget was at least wearing a glowing scarlet and cream embroidered stole. Beside the robed clergy were a couple of men in lounge suits, one with a clerical collar. They had no way of showing festivity at all.

The clergy soon broke ranks and then the people dispersed. Bridget had sported Sandy hanging around behind the crowd and darted over to him. "Sandy! I didn't expect to see you here. You must have had an early start. So come on. Let's go for our breakfast. The ladies will have it ready."

Sandy raised an eyebrow and grinned.

"What?" said Bridget. "Have I said something strange?"

"The ladies will have it ready," quoted Sandy.

Bridget gave him a dubious look then laughed. "You surely didn't think all the roles had been reversed because a woman is the minister? No, no. One change at a time is enough. Anyway, the ladies do a great breakfast, so I'm not sure I'd want that tradition to change."

"Will the ladies have had first squint at the plans?" asked Sandy, relenting. He had delivered plans and model the day before.

Bridget shook her head and flapped the sleeves of her gown to keep warm. "No. After you left yesterday I thought about that, and I realised it would never do. I don't want a few half-formed opinions doing the rounds before everyone has a chance to make their own judgement. So I pushed the trolley into the vestry and locked the door. They can all wait until breakfast is eaten and cleared away. Curiosity might get some habitual non-helpers to do a hand's turn for once." She sounded fierce. Suddenly the wind twitched her stole from one shoulder. Clutching at it she caught Sandy's eye. The next minute they were both laughing helplessly, and neither could have said why. The expectancy of the day was upon them, and excitement coursed in their veins. Hurrying along North Street they chuckled and giggled like school-children on an unexpected outing.

At the church there was no great air of excitement. Sandy felt crushed. Perhaps it had been unreasonable of him, but he had assumed that the congregation's interest would be as intense as his own and Bridget's. Instead, all energy was focussed on getting everyone seated around the long trestle tables which were set for a festive breakfast. There were five of these tables, covered in crepe paper and festooned with flowers, chocolate eggs, and pastel decorations. Sandy guessed that the decorations were traditional, kept from year to year, and had not been deliberately chosen to show up the dilapidated state of the wrecked hall, as they did. He wondered how it would look next year if his designs were accepted. Despite confusion in the kitchen, a hot breakfast appeared, with coffee or tea. This soon dispelled the dawn chill, helped along by a battery of portable fan heaters valiantly blowing warm dry air into the dank room.

At first, they ate largely in silence, but as the chewing slowed the conversation increased. Bridget had introduced Sandy to those seated near him at the beginning of the meal, but they had paid him little attention. Now the woman to his right, what was her name? Mrs Simpson? Turned to him and said, "So, you are our architect, Mr Melville? Tell me, how did we come to choose you for the job?" Her blue eyes were glacial, and her best puce suit mirrored the weather-beaten face above it. A diamond brooch winked at him, and the whole aura of the woman proclaimed 'I am a Grande Dame. I am Someone To Be Reckoned With.'

Inwardly Sandy quailed. The woman reminded him of a most terrifying maths teacher he had had at school. Although maths had been one of his best subjects, he had come close to failing it that year, being too cowed to learn anything at all. Stammering slightly he replied, "Well I'm a local man, you know. Office in Cupar."

"That surely cannot have been your only recommendation?"

"Your minister had heard of me. I suppose she must have seen some of my work." He was not going to tell this woman every detail. She had no right to pry into his private life, although to be fair – Sandy was usually fair – she didn't know that was what she was doing.

"You have done many public buildings as renovations, I suppose." Mrs Simpson wasn't giving up so easily.

Sandy looked her in the eye. "No, I'm a domestic architect. But I have enjoyed the challenge. Of course, the Session need not accept my plans if they don't like them. Are you on the Kirk Session?"

"My husband is. I look forward to seeing your designs." The glacial eyes swivelled from him to their right and a puce-clad shoulder was turned his way as Mrs Simpson launched into conversation with her other neighbour. Just as Sandy was reflecting that if this was a fair sample of the congregation he might as well leave now, the young woman on his left turned his way with an engaging smile. "Well done!" she whispered, her eyes dancing with delight. "You won!"

"I beg your pardon?" It was a feeble reply, but really it was too early in the morning for all of this. Sandy felt like Alice at the Mad Hatter's tea party.

"I said you won. Old Dorothy Simpson won't make trouble for you now."

"She won't? You mean she could? And why won't she? I'm sorry, but I've forgotten your name."

"Emma, Emma Farquharson. And you're Mr Melville."

"Sandy, please. Sandy to my friends – and allies?"

Again that dimpling smile. "Allies it is – unless I hate your plans of course. But friends in any case, I hope. As for Dorothy, she's constitutionally a problem. She can't agree with anyone about anything. You bet she came here this morning gearing up for battle."

"Do I take it you're old enemies?" They were still whispering, and Sandy gave a glance over his shoulder. The puce back was still in his face.

"Enemies with Dorothy? Of course not. She means well, you know. Her negative attitude is just her way of making sure that nothing goes wrong. She looks for the bad points because she wants things to be as good as possible. Every church needs a Dorothy. But she can be formidable to strangers."

"I believe you." Sandy wiped his bow in exaggerated terror. "And just how did I vanquish the dragon?"

"You asked her if she was a member of the Session. She would love to be an elder and be allowed more involvement in the running of the church. Her husband can stand up to her so there's nothing in her implication that she can influence things through him. Dave has a mind of his own."

"If every church needs one, why is she not an Elder?"

"You're not a church person, are you Sandy? There's more to being an Elder than administration. Each Elder has a certain area of the parish assigned them and they are supposed to offer pastoral care there, with the minister, of course. We take that element of the Eldership seriously here and poor Dorothy's just not cut out for it."

Sandy had been engrossed in this conversation with Emma, so that he hadn't noticed the tables being cleared and the floor being swept. He was surprised therefore to notice a hush falling on the room. Bridget stood up and said quietly, "And now if I could have someone to give me a hand – no, perhaps Mr Melville should be the volunteer – we will bring in the model of the proposed new church halls. I know you're eager to see them, and Mr Melville is here to answer any questions you may have. Mr Melville?"

Sandy scrambled to his feet and went with Bridget into the vestry. As they carefully wheeled out the trolley on which his model stood, he found his heart was beating faster and his knees felt less than steady. Bridget shot him a knowing look. "I know," she said, "It's as though they're going to look into your soul. Some of my sermons feel that way. It's O.K., Sandy. Your soul will survive. In my experience they are more apt to comment on the weather than anything else."

In the hall the hum of conversation died away as the model was brought in. The silence became uneasy and at first no one moved, although Bridget invited them to come and inspect it for themselves. Then Mrs Simpson's large, puce shoulders could be seen to rise up ominously. Immediately there was the sound of chairs scraping over an uneven floor, and four or five people made their way to where Sandy stood, almost running in their eagerness. They were led by Emma Farquharson, who gave Sandy a friendly wink and jerked her head at the lumbering Grande Dame. Clearly, he was being protected. Fleetingly he felt grateful for such charity yet simultaneously annoyed that he should be considered in need of protection. But both emotions faded as every person in the hall flocked in his direction. This was the moment of dread: his work was being inspected.

The babel of comment was incomprehensible. Just now and then a phrase would drift clear of the other voices and float anonymously round the hall.

"That's never our halls!"

"Where's the kitchen gone? Oh yes."

"Isn't it colourful?" "Gaudy." "Cheerful."

"All that space. Here, what are they mattresses in aid of?"

"I wonder if there are enough cupboards."

"Showers, how marvellous!"

"What's he done with the Sunday School supplies?"

"What would we need showers for?"

"Will the walls support an upstairs?"

"It doesn't look like a church hall at all."

"What are those pictures?"

Bridget stood with Sandy surveying the scene. After a few minutes she said quietly, "Are you ready to do some explaining?"

He started, having been straining his ears to hear the reactions. "Yes, yes of course," he stammered.

Bridget clapped her hands for attention, but no one took any notice. She shouted, but her contralto voice made no impression. She poked Sandy and grinned, but he shook his head in alarm. So Ian was discovered, and using his best teacher's voice he shouted, "HOY! QUIET!"

In the startled hush Bridget indicated Sandy's willingness to answer questions. A wheat-field of hands waved in the air.

Most of the questions were easy to answer: What about storage space? Had this to get planning permission? Would the walls support two floors?

Some Sandy referred to Bridget. Why did they need showers? What were the mattresses for? Were so many rooms necessary? He was interested to note which of the people knew of Bridget's hopes for expanding the use of the building. These he labelled the inner circle. Some were obviously taken aback by the idea of offering shelter to homeless people, and these could be subdivided into those who were interested but cautious, and those who found the idea incomprehensible. Mrs Simpson was one of the latter, her ruddy face turned pillar-box red, and the pudgy features assumed an expression of outrage. It wasn't clear whether she was most angry that she had heard nothing of this plan (although her husband must have known about it for months) or that 'these sorts of people' would be encouraged to 'hang about the premises.' Her splutterings were the loudest comments on this matter and the most prolonged. However, Bridget handled everything competently, saying that the whole church should have a discussion on the matter later. For now they were concerned with the plans themselves, not the uses for the building.

These practical matters were now dealt with, and Sandy began to relax, sensing a general approval for his efforts. Then Emma Farquharson raised her voice.

"I think the whole thing is splendid in design and I like the bright effect of the decorations. But I wonder, Mr Melville, if you could explain the pictures to us? What do they represent, and why did you think of murals for decoration?" There was a murmur of interest.

Sandy took a deep breath. "That's quite a story, but I'm happy to tell you. However, it might be more comfortable for everyone if you sat down to hear this." He produced his sketchbook of pictures. These are larger versions of the murals than the really tiny scale impressions on the model, and I think I can explain them better using this book than with us all straining to see as we crowd round. "

There was a minute or two of bustle ad chair-scraping and then he found himself confronted with fifty upturned faces, waiting for his explanation.

"I had the idea one cold day in February when I had come here seeking inspiration for the project. Your minister had already outlined to me the uses this space is currently put to, and her hopes for the future. So I knew what had to be achieved space-wise. The general plan for that was already in my mind, much as you see it today. It seemed obvious to me that much space could be gained by cutting this room in half horizontally. After all, it seems it's no longer used as a sports hall, which, presumably, is why it was built with such a high ceiling in the first place. But I came here seeking inspiration – I was looking for that certain something that would set your premises apart from any others. Something that could make the various rooms unique and yet unify them as parts of a whole. I'm not a great church-goer" (Mrs Simpson sniffed) "but I remember enough from my Sunday School days to be aware that a church is a body made up of individuals with different tasks to perform." His grin transformed what had been a formal countenance. "I said something of the sort to your minister the other day, and she told me I was close to being Biblical! Apparently St. Paul had the idea first." The audience laughed politely.

Anyway, that February day I was freezing in here when the Reverend McKay came in. I happened to ask her about the name of this church – Martyrs – and what she told me sparked off the whole idea for the murals in my mind. I remember I rushed back to Cupar and shut myself up in the office making rough sketches, lest I forget the idea.

"The church is called Martyrs, and I gather it is named for the protestant martyrs who are also commemorated on the Martyrs' Memorial. I have used them as my starting place, and these are the pictures in the main room – what this hall will become downstairs.

"On the back wall." His out-flung hand indicated the northern wall, "will be Walter Milne." Sandy opened his sketch-book at the first page. "He was an old priest who dared to change his mind. You can see that I have tried to show this in the smaller pictures surrounding the main figure. In the top left is Walter as a conventional Catholic priest. Top right shows his adopting the garb of a Reformed cleric and clutching his vernacular Bible. Then the main picture is his execution at the stake; the man helping him is the executioner – he was too aged to walk alone. With this picture as with all of them, I have tried to imitate the style and colouring of old stained glass. This is a church and that seemed appropriate.

"Behind where you're all sitting will be Patrick Hamilton. Again the smaller pictures tell his story. First we see him in colourful luxurious dress with his family: he was of the nobility, and you can see the coat of arms in the background. Then he appears in the traditional red gown of the St. Andrews student. The third scene shows the rather gaudily-dressed Catholic clergy pleading with Patrick, now clad in reformers' black, to change his ways. You see they are holding out a scarlet robe to him. Finally his execution. You can see there is more smoke than fire as apparently they didn't handle his burning efficiently. I've shown St. Salvator's tower and chapel and the face appearing in the tower stones which legend says happened as he burned.

"Over here," he indicated the smaller south wall, "Will be

Henry Forrest. It's a smaller space and a different story. For Henry there are two pictures of similar size. In the first he points back to Hamilton, proclaiming him a martyr – I've used a simpler version of Hamilton's main picture for that. In the second he himself is at the stake. He was killed to the north of the cathedral. This bulk is the cathedral wall, and you can see the monks filing past and the sea behind.

"Finally, behind where I'm standing would be George Wishart. His smaller pictures show him preaching in a church and in a market place. His main picture shows his execution by the castle. You can see the castle stands behind him and this is Cardinal Beaton watching from a window. Wishart's hand is still upraised as we are told that even at the stake he spoke out. The script running round the outside of this picture is the words tradition ascribes to him. 'This flame has scorched my body, yet it hath not daunted my spirit, but he who from yonder high place beholdeth us with such pride shall in a few days lie in the same as ignominiously as now he is seen proudly to rest himself.'"

Sandy took a deep breath and surveyed his audience. "Any questions so far?"

Two hands were raised. First a middle-aged man spoke. "I would like to know what your criteria for using halos are. It seems a little haphazard. Is it just artistic license?"

Sandy smiled at him. "It's a very good question, but, if you'll excuse me, I'd rather leave it till later. I assure you it's not haphazard, those halos follow a definite pattern. But if you'll bear with me, I'd rather we looked at all the pictures before I explain it. If, by then, I still need to. Actually, I hope it will become clear to you as we go along."

Mrs Simpson was, of course, the second questioner. "All this blood and fire!" she exclaimed in fruity horror. "Do you really think such subjects are suitable for decoration? I should have thought a few nice prints would have been better. The Impressionists maybe? Dear Van Gogh's sunflowers or Monet's waterlilies, for instance. Your subjects are so very grim."

"Yes, aren't they." Sandy was bland, his face showing nothing of his inward irritation and trepidation. He had been afraid of just such a remark. "Of course, in the end the suitability or otherwise of any of my ideas will be a matter for the Kirk Session." Mrs Simpson bridled. "Let me just say this. What I was trying to achieve was more than mere decoration. I have been doing a lot of homework on matters relating to this project, and I have come to see these pictures in much the same way that mediaeval church artists did. They are not entertainment but instruction. Historical instruction, in part, but also moral teaching. The question is: what's the message? And the answer to that has a lot to do with the gentleman's question about the halos. There's a clue for you, Sir! In the meantime, shall we go on?"

The crowd nodded and craned their necks to see the next illustration.

"There were more than these four protestant martyrs killed in St. Andrews. Your minister told me about the others. Their portraits belong in the small counselling room, where the present kitchen is. This room is more intimate in feel and purpose, and so I have muted the colours slightly although I continue using stained-glass style. This one is Paul Craw. He was a Bohemian – see the flag – and was executed at the Mercat Cross. This is the Market Square as it was, where that ghastly fountain-cum-plant-stand is now." Heads nodded in amused comprehension.

"On the wall opposite Craw are Gourlay and Straiton, two men at one stake. In the background there are modern houses and street signs. This is to indicate their present-day memorials, not the place of execution.

"If we move upstairs there are six rooms. These are the pictures I should like to use in them, though not necessarily in the places I have put them. What I mean is, once you have decided what room will have what purpose you may decide a different mural would be appropriate."

There was a restlessness in the audience, and Sandy saw Bridget rise from her seat at the back and indicate her watch. Glancing at his own he realised that the service began in half an hour. Hurriedly he said, "I didn't notice how late it is. Quickly then, this is a representation of the murder of Archbishop Sharpe on Magus Muir, killed by covenanters, which runs into a picture of the battle of Bothwell Bridge, when the Covenanters' rebellion was put down. And then a picture of Culloden. This is for the stairway.

"Upstairs are these six pictures. You will see these show modern St. Andrews – the harbour, South Street and Market Street but peopled by the Dominican, Cistercian, and Benedictine monks of the past.

"Then these two are different. In them I have tried to show the passing of time through architecture (after all, that's my job). One has a modern view of the Market Square with mediaeval buildings ghosted on it. The other shows the mediaeval monastery of the Blackfriars with the High School of today ghosted in, complete with pupils and bus stop.

"Finally, we have a last judgement. That's a traditional idea: every church once had one. This shows the scene before the judgement actually begins, with a blazing throne and people before it. If you look closely, you will see figures from the other pictures are in that expectant crowd."

He drew a deep breath. "That's it. I see the minister has left us, and probably some others need to make preparations for worship. The rest of us, quickly, what about those halos? Any ideas?"

The sense of urgency against the clock was just what his audience needed to goad them into spontaneous response. The original questioner took it upon himself to answer.

"They're no on the usual heads, they halos. It's the executioners who have them, or the oppressing side. I saw it with your covenanters. The murderers on the Muir are wearing them, but no the covenanters at the battle. If it wasn't for that I might have thought you were just a Catholic bigot." The rest laughed, though uneasily.

"And what do you think now?"

Emma Farquharson butted in. "It's showing how things looked then. We're called Martyrs, and we believe Hamilton and the rest were right, but the men who killed them did it because of their own fervent beliefs. So they got the halo. At the time, they thought it a holy deed."

"Yes, yes," the speaker was an excited teenager with a stammer. "These, these pictures with the m-m-m-monks. And the ghosts of building. They say things were dif-different once." He blushed and subsided. The church bell rang out.

"I'm not going to tell you what I thought about the pictures," said Sandy, running an abstracted hand over his hair. "You're doing a good job yourselves. Besides, that's what they're for – to be considered and discovered and then perhaps understood. Now I think it's time we were moving. Thank you for your patience and understanding this morning."

He sat down and the people swept around him on their way from the hall. Thanks were expressed, and praise, but Sandy was only half listening. He had worked with obsession on the plans, and now, with the first presentation over, he felt inclined to sleep or weep.

Instead, he followed the last Sunday-suited back from the

hall. It was as well for his peace of mind that he didn't know that Joyce had become a worshipper at this church. She was not there that Easter Day, however, keeping herself away purposely to avoid Sandy. Not knowing to miss her, Sandy went calmly into the sanctuary and watched the faithful worshipping another man who had had an obsessional idea.

CHAPTER EIGHT: ENLIGHTENMENT

"if we're not foolish young, we're foolish old."

Chaucer, "The Knight's tale" as translated by Neville Coghill

1st January 1950

With a new year a new excitement has come to Badepuri. A holy man, a Swami, has come amongst us. He is not like some of the other holy men I have glimpsed in my travels in that he is neither emaciated nor dirty and he doesn't seem to be given to unusual physical practices – rolling instead of walking, tying his body into yogic knots, and so on. He's a slender, dark-skinned man of middle height, wearing white robes, and with the most charming smile imaginable. His name is Swami Krishnanya. I know that I'm becoming an accepted part of life here when I am no longer the village wonder. Krishnanya has that role now, and even should he leave here tomorrow I would not be quite so strange again. There is no going back, and his coming has changed something I have long wanted to put behind me.

15th January 1950

Swami Krishnanya is still with us. Badepuri has become a centre of pilgrimage for people from a radius of up to thirty miles away. He teaches people when they come to him, or when it feels appropriate to him. He has no schedules, nor does he do other work in the village. He sleeps where he may and eats what is offered to him. I shouldn't be surprised to find that a people which offers from its poverty food to the gods should also undertake to feed a holy man.

The reports I hear of him are only good. He teaches with wisdom and talks of restraint. I haven't heard him yet myself. Somehow I think I should wait until I'm invited to one of his sessions.

21st January 1950

Madhur has asked me why I don't attend the Swami's meetings. I said something about being quite busy teaching and preparing lessons. She looked at me sombrely and shook her head slowly. "But, Mem, this is not right. You should not be working so hard that you forget to attend to your soul. No one wants that from you. So you will stop working and come with me tomorrow. We will give the school a holiday and everyone will be very happy for you."

Cornered! So I'll have to go. Now it comes to it, I find I'm very reluctant. What am I afraid of? I have my own mind and will, and no one can take them over without my permission, which I should never give. I won my independence from Mother at too high a price ever to present it to anyone again.

24th January 1950

There was no need to write about the Swami's meeting, as, from my perspective, it was unremarkable. The most significant thing was that I could follow most of what he said without difficulty, so my language skills must be growing. I went to another meeting last night. There's no harm in it, and it is what the village does these days. Why should I hold myself aloof? I like to look at Krishnanya: he's a very handsome, well-made man.

3rd February 1950

Still Swami Krishnanya makes his home amongst us, and still people flock to hear him. They say that really he is a hermit: he speaks to no one as a private person, but only when he is teaching them. That's what they say, but I know differently. He has spoken with me. I met him as I came back from the well today. He was walking away from my little house towards me, and said he's actually been looking for me.

"I have seen this English Mem in the village, and I wish to know more of her, so I seek for her house. It must be this house, for here I see no sacred image, although the flame burns brightly." He spoke in good, though accented, English. That is to say, he has a different accent than the Indo-Scots of my students.

I invited him in and asked what I could do for him. He seemed to find the question perplexing.

"I do not come seeking favours, English Mem. I do not wish you to do anything for me. I come only to learn."

I decided that if we were to have a conversation I should tell him my name and stop all this 'English Mem' business. I did so, adding that I am Scottish. His smile was at its brightest as he spread wide his hands and exclaimed, "Scottish! But I was educated at a Scottish school, Dr. Bell's college in Madras." It was out of pure curiosity that I told him that Dr. Bell had also founded a school in St. Andrews and named it 'Madras College'. I was curious to see how much more excitement he could convey without bursting. What he did took me totally by surprise: he bowed to me salaaming with his palms together. "Then we are brother and sister. We share a common bond." He took this so seriously that I hadn't the heart to tell him that I hadn't attended Madras College, but St. Leonard's.

He asked what I was doing in Badepuri and why. He asked about my sacred flame, and I told him. He listened and made no comment. Nor did he tell me anything about himself. But when he left I felt as though I had found a friend, a real friend, who understands me as no one else has ever done. Friendship has been scarce in my life, but not so scarce that I can't recognise it.

10th February 1950

I have now had three talks with Krishnanya. That's his real name. Swami is just a title others gave him, "And who am I to reject a gift when it is offered?" But I still know little of him. I know he is from the south of India, and that he has been travelling for several years. I know a little about his education. That's all, really – the externals at any rate. But I feel as though I know more. I can sense things which words can never share: he is kind, humble, wise, and caring; he is selfless in his life. And he is understanding: he understands me. It is so strange to meet like this, across continents and cultures, and yet with a sense of complete inevitability.

28th February 1950

I haven't written because my life has been too full. Full of my usual work and routines, full more than ever of the wonders that India is showing me. And now my nights contain these wonders too: Krishnanya has become my lover.

It was inevitable. I knew from our first meeting that I could deny him nothing for which he asked. And he asked for me. He asked if I knew the joys of the flesh. I told him about young Jimmy Marr. "You have much to experience," was his comment. Then he explained the Vedas teach that carnal pleasures are a stage of growth through which a person must travel. "It is a duty to your development and your understanding, and it is a way of great delight." How true that is. I feel a different person, yet not different at all: in a strange way I feel more intensely myself than before. I am aware of my body, and I delight in it – my middle-aged body. It delights me because Krishnanya says it delights him.

15th March 1950

Still nightly we enact the great wonder, the union of two into one, the unison of the soul with the Brahman, the union of all things on earth. And now by day I perform other rituals. I have a little Shiva in my holy corner, with my sacred flame. And I do my puja each morning and evening. In the morning I also mix oil and pigment together and place Shiva's mark on my forehead. Krishnanya taught me how. In the same way he has taught me to look at the world as a place of myth and miracles. Each night he tells me another story to shape my view of the world.

Last night it was the story of Ganesh, the elephant god who is painted on my house. It is a charming story and full of human truth. Shiva and his wife Paravati didn't always see eye to eye. One of the things which annoyed Paravati was her husband's habit of surprising her in her bath. A wife must have some privacy to perform her captivating toilet. So Paravati took the oils and unguents she used for her bath and fashioned a boy from them, rather like a soap sculpture. She scattered holy water from the Ganges on it and gave it life. Ganesh was endowed with great strength and was bade guard Paravati's private quarters against any callers.

Along came Shiva, and found Ganesh blocking his way into Paravati' s bathroom, denying him a conjugal right. Previous guards had been easily dealt with, but the only way Shiva could defeat Ganesh was by cutting off his head.

Paravati was inconsolable and demanded Shiva return her Ganesh to life. But Shiva is the destroyer and cannot restore life as easily as he can take it away. Paravati wailed and bemoaned her loss. So terrible were her cries that the gods woke Vishnu, the Lord Protector, from his eternal sleep. Vishnu could not resurrect the boy but took the first head that came to hand – that of an elephant. With Shiva he replaced the boys' head with this, and now Ganesh was a new being he could be given life.

Paravati was quieted and Shiva promised never to force himself where he was not wanted. And Ganesh is the gate-keeper in temples and homes all over the world.

There is a lot of truth in that: the eternal misunderstandings between men and women, the irreversible power of destruction, and the need for a new being if one is to have new life.

I have a new life – so I have newness in my being.

22nd March 1950

More teaching from Krishnanya is chiming with the notes of my soul. He has been telling me about the god Vishnu, who is compassionate. He is the mediator between Brahma, the creator, and his creation. And he has come to earth several times when a sense of duty declines and wrong-doing is on the increase. He has come as a fish, a turtle, a boar, a man-lion, a dwarf, a hero, and as Rama and Krishna, the legendary examples whose names are invoked and whose stories are depicted everywhere. This speaks to me. It sounds like what I was taught about Jesus – that he was really God. But it is more than that. Jesus was a man. Vishnu has identified with different aspects of the creation (and helped mankind each time). He has also been the founder of a whole new religion (which actually ignores the gods, for the most part). I like this. I like this all-embracing acceptance. No one need feel distanced from Vishnu.

22nd April 1950

A month has gone by. Another month of living and loving and learning, and, of course, teaching. I am not working any less hard, but there is so much more in my life now. Krishnanya – how am I to begin to count up all he has done for me? I am amazed, and yet I can't help laughing. It's so delightfully ridiculous that at my age I should have found love in my life; and that after everything I have known and done (and not done) I should be able both to give and receive that love.

1st May 1950

A terrible thought. Madhur said something about "When Swami Krishnanya goes." Apparently, no one expects him to stay. His is essentially a nomadic role, and I know that I can't be nomadic with him – it wouldn't be acceptable. But won't he want to stay with me? There are Swamis who don't travel but stay put and let people come to them.

8th May 1950

He's going. He says he must leave soon, by the end of the month. His work here is finished. He told me tonight as we lay together, and I was too stunned to say anything. Now I can't sleep. I can't sleep and I can't cry. I just want to find him and ask one question: is his work with me also finished?

10th May 1950

The answer is yes. I tried not to get upset. But I couldn't help a tear falling when I told him that it didn't feel finished to me. He was so gentle. He took my face in his hands. "Ah no, it never does. This is why I must leave. If I do not, you will never move forwards. You and others. I have brought you to a place which you like, but you can't stay here forever: you must grow through this stage." I was confused and it must have shown, because he went on, "Charlotte, at the beginning I told you, sensual pleasure is but a stage in development. A good stage, but just one. It's over now.

If you grasp it and try to keep it past its time, will it not become rotten and stink and become a burden to you?" I don't think he could ever be burdensome to me and said so. "That is good. Then you will only have good memories of this time."

Will I? I curse myself for an old fool. I fell in love with a holy man. I fell in love with a man who could never put me first. But I thought he would, I thought he did. Now I wonder – was I the only one in this village? Even if I was, what of all the places he's been and those to which he goes forward? Who was there before? Who will erase me from his memory in the future? I have been a fool. But oh, I have been happy.

19th May 1950

Krishnanya has gone. I bade him farewell and thanks with a smile on my face. My only consolation just now is that he has no idea how he has hurt me. Nor, I think, has anyone else. I have never told of our special relationship, naturally. Even if I wouldn't have thought it in the poorest of taste, I had no wish to. I hugged the secret to myself.

But he's gone and now I hope no one knows because I am ashamed. How could I, Charlotte Murdoch, the daughter of Amelia Murdoch of Windmill Road, how could I have let this thing happen? How could I have so forgotten myself as to enjoy it? And why is my pain also loss and grief, not just shame?

25th May 1950

I have extinguished the sacred flame and banished the idol from my house. No longer do I perform puja and anoint myself to express devotion. How could I have been taken in by all that? How could I have been taken in by that self-pleasing, smiling little man? How I hate him! He has ruined India for me. It can never be the safe, innocent pace it was before. I look at my students and now I wonder – what are they really like underneath? How do they think?

What motivates their daily lives? Suddenly the faces which were so bright and attractive appear sinister and mysterious. I know, I know that they haven't changed. It is I who have altered. I who have been altered, disfigured, abased. I used to trust, but he has killed good faith in me. All I hope is that his constant wanderings may show him incapable of finding happiness. How dare he be happy when he has ruined everything for me?

1st June 1950

Madhur came to see me. She is my closest friend here and I have been avoiding her. I didn't want her to know my hurt, my anger, my horrible disappointment. I suppose I didn't want her, or anyone, to know my human frailty.

I might as well have told her: she knew anyway. The whole of Badepuri has noticed that I have given up on religion, and of course they weren't slow to connect that with Krishnanya's departure. If I hadn't been so caught up in myself I'd have seen that. They have also noticed that my Hindufication corresponded with his presence. They knew what was between us. And I thought it was my (then delightful now shameful) secret. I blush just thinking of it. How can I face them again? All that keeps me from rushing off blindly, by night, is Madhur's assurance that no one thinks any the worse of me for it. She shook her head and hands at me in protest, earrings and bangles flashing and glittering, as she said, "No, Mem. It is natural. The Swami took you through experiences he saw you needed. Our only fear here in Badepuri is that now he is gone you may find yourself with child."

I smiled at that. They obviously don't know how old I am.

Madhur doesn't understand my shame. No one does. But that doesn't make it any easier.

5th June 1950

I haven't been to my school for five days now but sent word I was indisposed. I suppose they all think I'm pregnant, but I don't care. All my ideals are in the dust: my ideals about India, about life, about people and about myself. India is no paradise, life is not just waiting to be experienced, in sweeter and sweeter mouthfuls; people are corrupt, unable to solace each other because they are unable to see beyond their own noses. And I? I am as corrupt as any. All this time I have been living a lie, wearing a freedom I pretend I was denied, pretending to myself that nothing could ever have been different.

7th June 1948

Madhur came around and forced me to let her in. She also forced me to eat some rice and vegetables. I suppose I haven't eaten much lately. She stayed with me and tried to get me to talk. Then she talked. She spoke about other holy men who have come to the village. She spoke about some who came with a message of austerity. "They were never so welcome as those like Krishnanya, who preach joy and pleasure. But I wonder if those who would have us fast and meditate may not be best for us. No one mourns when they leave, at least. No one loves them."

I started crying then. Madhur was lovely to me. She told me she was sorry she hadn't realised my heart was broken. "I was so slow, Mem. I did not recognise the look of the widow in your face: the look of one who would be glad to die also, to perform Sutti. I did not think a Mem could love a Swami."

Then I told her how I feel cheated and stupid. "If he could treat me like that, then how can I trust anything he said? He's a philandering swine." Madhur didn't understand 'philandering', and by the time it was properly explained we were both inclined to giggle a little.

I agreed to return to my teaching tomorrow. She's quite right – I shouldn't give myself too much time to brood. "There you have an advantage over many Indian widows: you have work to do which has nothing to do with your family."

10th June 1950

Madhur came to see me again this evening. It was very hot today, even by Badepuri standards. I was trying to prepare lessons when she came, but I was too warm, and the insects dying in my light were distraction enough tonight.

She brought me cold minty tea which was very refreshing. "Mem" – I don't know why she won't call me Charlotte – "Mem, I have been thinking about what you have said about the Swami Krishnanya. Mem, I am puzzled. Why do you say that because he brought you sorrow his words may not be trusted?" I was taken aback. It had never occurred to me to think otherwise. You don't recognise your cultural heritage in operation in moments of crisis. I explained that I had been brought up to think that a wise man would have wisdom enough to realise what would be painful to another and avoid it. Krishnanya had mis-judged my reaction to his programme (his full programme, including its end) for me; therefore he could not be as wise, nor as good, as had been thought.

Madhur heard me with a small frown creasing the red anointing on her forehead. "But Mem, he is a Swami. He does not claim to see all ends. He simply tries to teach the wisdom he has found. He cannot *see all ends. Particularly he cannot understand how he may affect the emotions. How can he? He is a Swami. The holy life must come first for him. But Mem, in the matter of the holy life, he is an expert. He should be listened to."*

"What about the teaching of other Swamis?" I asked. "You said that some came teaching austerity, others pleasure. How can you tell which is right?"

Again that small crease folded the crimson on her forehead. "But must one be judged against the other? Oh, Mem, we do not think like this in India. Both ways are true and holy, and others besides these. We are all in different places within Karma, and so different truths speak to us. But Swami Krishnanya, his truth spoke to you, I think?"

Did it? I don't know. Was it his truth or something else?

11th December 1950

I am leaving Badepuri. I have laboured on through the hot summer weather and my classes flourished. But now they are dwindling away. I am told this is because I have succeeded. My students now know enough English to get by – in a country which will, I assume, increasingly turn to the Indian languages native to it. My students know enough, and they will teach the children, quietly, informally. So I am no longer needed.

But it is more than that. For six months (I find, now that I've returned to my old diary that it's exactly six) I have looked at myself and my life, and at life here, and I have questioned. For almost the first time I have asked myself what I am doing, and who I am, and where I am going. And I have forced myself to answer in positive, rather than negative terms. Yet the answer that affects my actions is negative. I am not Indian. I no longer have a purpose here. I am going nowhere if I stay here now.

I have learned in my years here. I think I have lost a lot of my romantic naivety. People may approach life from different perspectives, but in the end you get the same mixed motives and complex personalities wherever you go. It is simply that as an outsider it is not immediately obvious. As an outsider I thought there was simplicity and humility about this land and its people, and I wanted to be part of it. So I allowed myself to be drawn in and found that on the inside it was not quite so facile. I found squalor, physical and spiritual, and I found the beauty and purity I expected: I found complexity built of a multitude of simplicities; I found humility in which great pride was taken, and arrogance of assumption which left me breathless.

But this is not a unique discovery. I am sure that any society will yield up such paradoxes, given enough experience. Experience is not to be gained by objective scrutiny. To experience one must allow a place and its people to enter the heart. It was only when I forgot to observe and began to live and love, to laugh and cry, that I found India.

Where am I going? I am going home. I will return to Windmill Road and take up the connections and neglected relationships of my life. I will live there, not pining to be somewhere else. And because that's my place, I may learn better, and I may be more complete there than anywhere else. Six months ago Madhur told me to follow Krishnanya's wise advice. I never told her what that was.

When Krishnanya left, he told me I should leave India and go home. I remember the conversation so well. We were in my bedroom, sitting on the floor and gazing at the sacred flame. Because we had been together, he wore only his dhoti and turban. I was in an old nightie. The dim light cast golden shadows on his dark face.

I said, "If I return to Scotland it will be difficult to be a Hindu. There is no temple there that I know of."

He shook his head vigorously. "No, no. You must return fully to your country. You will be a Christian."

"But I don't want to be a Christian. I gave that up long ago. I'm a Hindu now. Why would you tell me to do this?"

"Listen. Listen. Listen." He tapped my arm lightly. "A good Hindu accepts that all religions bring us to Brahma."

"Really? Then why do you bother?"

"After all this time, you ask that?" He sounded hurt. "I

look out for people whom I may help, that is all. Then I help them as best I may. I do not strive to instill orthodoxy into a soul which needs individuality. I simply seek to help that soul onwards. So many people have become stuck in their Karma. You say you gave up Christianity a long time ago. You were stuck. I helped you forwards. Now you can go on."

"As a Hindu."

He sighed. "There are some even among the Hindus who would consider your obtuseness a triumph. I do not. Yes, you will be a Hindu. There are so many ways to show the gods devotion. You will simply do it in the Christian way. You cannot be an Indian. It is not in your soul. But you can still show devotion. The worship we offer is localized. Even from region to region the gods are different. Ours is not a great world faith; we see too easily the argument that we may be wrong. But I tell you that you will embrace your religion, in the spirit of the Hindu gods. And so we shall not be divided."

I have puzzled over this for months now. Sometimes it makes sense, sometimes not.

15th December 1948

I have let it be known that I am going. There was some gratifying dismay, but mainly people are unperturbed, though they wish me well. It is only as the news of my departure has gone round that something has dawned on me: I don't seem to have any enemies here. When I reflect that I arrived at a volatile period in India's history, a member of the nation which was leaving, and which had not always been beloved of the Indians, this is remarkable. Either these are very generous people or very polite. In my earliest days here, especially, I expect I wasn't always tactful, but no one has been hostile or rude to me. I honour them for that, although now that I am going, I wonder if that was partly because they never really expected me to stay.

I put the burden of Krishnanya's advice to Madhur. I thought I owed it to her faithful friendship to allow her to have one last chance of explaining things to me. She did a good job.

"Mem, I know something of the Christian religion. I have a Great Uncle in Kerala who is of the church of St. Thomas." That's hardly the Church of Scotland, but I let it pass. "Krishnanya is not saying you must be a Christian as these people are. He would not urge you to think something which does not sing with the truth of your life. We Hindus believe in a different way. We need not have a belief in the reality of the gods for their stories to speak to us, to help us, to guide us. Ours is a very ancient tradition, Mem, and one which only an old and wise people can grow to. When we are young, in body or in Karma, we may need to believe in the reality of the gods in the world. But we grow. And as we grow we realise that the truth is deeper than that. These stories are symbols and helpers on the journey. The truth is deeper.

But the truth must be worshipped, for that keeps us growing on our journey. We must honour that truth. Krishnanya is saying that you may use the rites of Christianity to pay homage, Mem, just as I may use the rites of Shiva or Vishnu. You can honour the truth and we will reach Brahma when the time is right."

Madhur is a good teacher as well as a good friend. When I look back at this short but important time in my life I wonder if it will be she, rather than Krishnanya, whom I will call my Swami?

CHAPTER NINE: SUMMER STORMS

Death is a thing of grandeur. It brings instantly into being a whole new network of relations between you and the ideas, the desires, the habits of the man now dead. It is a rearrangement of the world."

Saint-Exupery, "Flight to Arras", translated by Lewis Galantiere

Bright June sunshine had brought the visitors to town. During the week the streets hummed with foreign voices: American, French, German, Australian, and Japanese. They wandered among the cathedral ruins and wondered at their majesty and the fact of their ruination. Some were puzzled that such a great building had been allowed to fall into disuse. Others questioned why the crumbling walls and broken arches had not been cleared away long ago. St. Andrews in June was a very cosmopolitan place. During the week.

At the weekend the warm weather brought in the local Fifers. They thronged the streets in search of ice-cream and novelty. They descended on the more accessible beaches: the East Sands and the first quarter mile of the West Sands. The broad Fife accents overwhelmed the loudest American or Australian drawl, and proclaimed proudly that, after all, this is first and foremost a Scottish seaside town.

Tempted outside by the fine weather, Joyce carried the latest volume of Miss Murdoch's diary to the manse garden. She made her way swiftly, avoiding the crowds as she slipped through less populous lanes and side-streets. Ian had taken Mairi and Angus to Kinshaldy beach, eight miles away - "Which is ironic, with the East Sands so close, but it will be a lot quieter," said Bridget – and the back garden was still and quiet. The McKay's work in the spring had paid off, and now the place was ablaze with colour and sweet with perfume. Joyce was no gardener, but she could not ignore the display before her, and expressed her admiration to Bridget, who smiled but said nothing on the subject. Instead, she offered refreshment.

There, in the temperate warmth of a Scottish summer day, with the sun and the breeze bringing out the glow and light fragrance of the garden flowers, the two women read the entries for 1950. They read in silence, being by now quite accustomed to waiting for each other at the foot of each page. Each was patient when the other wanted to go back and read an entry again. Yet the quality of their quiet was very different. Joyce sat at the garden table, her head propped on one hand and a smile on her lips. She read quickly and eagerly, her eyes skimming the text to see what would happen next. When she reached the bottom of a page she would read parts again, waiting for Bridget to catch up.

Bridget read more reluctantly. A slight frown marked her forehead and she sat very straight, putting physical distance between herself and the writing on the page. At times she would look up and stare blankly at the bed of Sweet Williams just beyond the table. Then she would lower her eyes and continue with her task. There was an air of purpose and duty about her, but none of the pleasure which could be read in every line of Joyce's body.

December 1948 finished that volume of the diary although

there were a few yellowed pages left blank at the end of the book. It was obvious that a chapter in Miss Murdoch's life had come to an end, and she was determined to mark it. Quietly Bridget closed the battered green covers.

"How many more volumes are there?"

"Just the one," Joyce answered. "And I don't think it's been finished, though I haven't read ahead. We must get to it soon, though. Isn't she marvellous?" Her voice sounded young, even naïve, in her excitement, and she ended her question on a squeak.

There was a long silence. Overhead a seagull let loose its forlorn cry. Turning, Joyce saw that Bridget was gazing away from her, staring into the clumps of herbs and bright flowers in the rockery. She touched her arm. "Bridget?" Slowly the blue eyes focussed and returned to the present. "I'm sorry, I was far away."

"In India?" Joyce was teasing.

"Not so far in geographical terms, but less accessible." She said no more for a while, and Joyce found herself loth to break the silence, for all that she was full of things she longed to say. It was ironic, she reflected, that while Miss Murdoch had been growing in importance to her, she had been unable to talk about her. Now she felt for some reason the identification was complete. She had learned what she wanted to know and was eager to share it. But Bridget wouldn't talk.

Ian came home, whistling round the corner of the house and driving two tired, damp, and dishevelled children before him. Bridget rose and began to talk about swim-suits and sandy towels, while Angus and Mairi chattered to her about the huge waves and the family of rabbits they'd seen in the woods beyond the sand-dunes. Their shrill voices grew muted and distant as they disappeared into the house, carrying their mother in their wake.

Ian sank into his wife's empty seat. "Hello Joyce," he smiled. "You were very quiet till we got home. Nothing wrong, I hope?"

"Nothing," replied Joyce crisply. "Silence can be a communication at least as powerful as words, you know."

"Ah." Ian tried again. "How's the diary getting on? Is old Miss Murdoch still espousing the hippy movement ahead of its time?"

His flippancy grated on Joyce. "I don't know where you got that impression, but it wasn't from Miss Murdoch herself." It was a put-down, and even as she spoke the words Joyce wondered at herself. The time had been when she thought she could talk about anything with Ian. They hadn't said much about the diary, true, but that had been her choice – she always could have done. But now the revelations went too deep. She wanted to share them, but not with Ian: with Bridget. Only someone who had actually read the diary could possibly understand. Through all her own silent weeks, when she had insisted they converse about anything apart from their joint reading, Joyce had known that this ban originated with herself alone. Now she was equally clear that somehow Bridget had withdrawn herself. The thoughts and events which had seemed to open a door on the sun to Joyce had also spoken to her friend, but obviously the message had been a different one.

She stood up and lifted the diary from the garden table. Ian stood up with her. "I'm sorry if I said the wrong thing, Joyce."

"You did, I'm afraid. But you couldn't know. I must go home now, Ian. Say goodbye to Bridget for me, will you? And tell her I'll be in touch."

Once Joyce had gone, Ian sat down again and remained in his place for a while, relishing the peace of the garden, admiring the beauty he and Bridget had created together. It was six years since they had come to St. Andrews, and the garden now bore no resemblance to the jungle of weeds and overgrown roses which the former incumbent of the parish had left. He had been an old man, and frail, and even in his younger days had been more of a scholar than a gardener. In the rare peace, Ian let his mind wander back to their early days in the town. When they had arrived, the church people had been very welcoming. Visitors were always calling round with a baking of scones or cakes, hoping in return to learn something about the new manse family.

Miss Murdoch was one of these, or so it had seemed at first. It was only later, when the novelty of a young family in the manse had worn off, that Ian realised that Miss Murdoch was different. The others ceased to call, except with pleas for help or to lodge a barbed complaint: Miss Murdoch always came to encourage. Sometimes she brought a gift, - food, or more often, flowers, or some cuttings from her garden (the very Sweet Williams flaunting their deep red and pink flowers under Ina's nose had come from the garden in Windmill Road), but always she had brought a kind word or an uplifting anecdote. Her sense of humour was keen, and she was direct. You knew that if she were to complain it wouldn't be in cryptic utterances. But she never did complain, except that the hill to Irvine Crescent seemed to be getting steeper. Ian could picture her in the garden, on the doorstep, in the hall, but not often in the living room: she would not let herself impose for long enough to come in properly.

Over the last two years she hadn't been able to visit, as she gradually stiffened with age. Her gardening had to cease, which must have been a sore trial. She had been a good old woman, the best, thought Ian, but he would never have guessed that she might have been anything but a life-long church-going spinster. It made you wonder about other people, he reflected with a smile. Human beings held so many surprises, like his children at school. He found it delightful.

In the kitchen Bridget was also meditating on the unknown and unknowable factors in the human spirit.

Later that week evening sunshine glowed through the west windows of the still-desolate church hall, sending a million motes of dust dancing around the assembled group. They hovered over bald heads and grey perms, over sensible crew-cuts, and a couple of elaborate French braids. They hovered before alert and weary eyes; caressed furrowed and smooth brows. The Kirk Session of Martyrs Church was holding its monthly meeting. At the head of the long trestle table Bridget was the only person in shadow, like a lone spectator in a brightly lit theatre.

The hall was still dishevelled and bare because the builders had yet to start work. The Session had approved Sandy's plans wholeheartedly in April. It had been hoped that the work might be done over the summer months, but now June had run half its course and nothing had happened. The subject was under discussion by the assembled elders of the kirk.

"What exactly is the cause of the delay, Mr Reekie?" It was a retired school teacher who spoke, unable to smooth years of sharp questioning from her tones.

Mr Reekie, the elder in charge of the fabric of the building, rubbed his already tousled grey hair. "There's more than one cause. First it was a matter of getting quotes from various firms. We did that, and, as I told you last month, have decided to go with Hewitts. They're not the cheapest, but they weren't by any means the most expensive, and they're local. We know they do good work. I know it, anyway. They did my extension a couple of years ago." He smiled hopefully.

"Yes, you told us so last month." The woman was persistent in pursuing her point. "Could they not take the contract?"

"They've taken it. They couldn't start the very next day, of course, but they got in touch with Mr Melville, the architect, and began to get matters sorted out. They should have started a couple of weeks ago. But," he hesitated, "We thought it better nothing irrevocable happened before this meeting."

Bridget stirred. "Why was that?" she asked.

Mr Reekie started, turning in his seat, and eyeing her with astonishment. "But Mrs McKay, you know. They told us you said so."

"Who told you?" Bridget was confused but stuck to the essentials.

"The Women's Guild, of course. They weren't sure about moving the kitchen, and Mrs Simpson said you thought it best to consider the matter again."

Bridget opened her lips to deny having said any such thing, but few heard her words. The naming of Dorothy Simpson had unleashed something in the gathering and a sudden hubbub arose.

"Dorothy Simpson, she aye has to hae a finger in the pie."

"But it's not proper procedure. They had a time to comment or complain earlier."

"Dorothy wanted her nephew to get the work, and him a proper Gerry-builder."

"But I'm on the Guild committee. We said no such thing."

"The ladies liked the plans. My wife said so."

"Well, I didn't care for some of those murals, but the kitchen would be far better in the new position."

"That Dorothy's an interfering old bizzom."

"Are we always to be held up and hindered by that crazy woman?"

"She should be put off the rolls!"

The voices rose in pitch as each one thought of some former offense by the said Dorothy.

"She's aye pretending to have some sort of authority around here."

"Not even a real local, she isn't. Came here ten years ago from Edinburgh."

"She'll think she can question the last judgement, that one."

"A right poke-nose, that's what she is. I've caught her going through the Sunday School cupboards and throwing things out. She'd no right to do that, either."

"She re-arranges the choir music."

"When I put up a flower list, she takes it down to re-write it what she calls 'more clearly'."

"She's a flamin' nuisance. Probably wanted to design the halls herself."

"No asset to the church, that one."

Bridget noted that Emma Farquharson was sitting in shocked silence, while Dave Simpson, Dorothy's husband, had turned white and was gasping at the hatred scattering the calm golden dust motes in the air. She stood up suddenly and brought her palm down hard on the table. The noise ceased, but the anger still surged around the room. Quietly Bridget surveyed them.

"Emma, thank you for your restraint. What remains of the meeting won't be relevant to you. Please be so good as to leave now. I'll phone you tomorrow." The girl who had been a support to Sandy on Easter Sunday still looked stunned as she gathered her papers together and slipped from the room.

Again, Bridget glanced around her. Now she addressed the appalled husband. "Dave, I apologise to you that you should have had to witness this abuse, no, to *suffer* this abuse here in a church meeting. I know you must feel deeply hurt because Dorothy is your wife, whom you know better than anyone else here does, and whom you love dearly. Because of that I think perhaps you should stay for a little while longer."

Mr Simpson was a small man who ought to have had a twinkle in his eye. Now he merely bowed his head in bemused acquiescence.

Bridget turned her attention to the other thirty people in the now-silent room.

"And you call yourselves Christians." Scorn laced her tones and ice was in her blue eyes. "Christians! And not just Christians but elders, church leaders, spiritual guides and examples to the rest of the congregation. Spiritual guides – you! And examples – ah, but that's just what you are, what you can't help being. Perhaps no one actually asks you for spiritual advice – before I'd have said that was a pity, but tonight I thank God for it – but they do look to you, yes, and listen to you for an 'example.'

"But, you may be thinking, I wouldn't say these things before other people. Oh no, not these things. But other little things you would say, or else you would say nothing when you ought. You can't deny what is in your heart. If you are Christians God's love should be found in your hearts. Tonight I have seen only hatred and spite. Didn't you hear yourselves? Didn't you hear the evil in the air? Did not one of you sit appalled, as I did, or raise your voice in protest?

"Each of you owes Dave a personal apology. If you were my children – and you have acted like children, and ill-natured, vindictive children at that – if you were my children I should force an apology out of you. I can't do that to you. Nor does

Dave deserve the muttered half-truths of coercion.

"Even worse, God is very much wounded by what happened here tonight. God is wounded and the church is damaged. God's love has been rejected by you, and you have mocked and railed against one of his creatures and your sister in Christ. Christ died for Dorothy. How dare you to be so presumptuous as to condemn her and write her off as you have done? By the very act you have shown yourselves far from perfect, and in no position to condemn.

"Not only have you sinned against Dave and against God, but you have totally undermined my confidence in you. How can I trust you to lead this church? How do I know you are not working for your own convenience and benefit? How am I to be sure of your true commitment to Christ? It may be that tonight was an aberration," now she was speaking more quietly, as if to herself, "But it may not. How am I to know if the normal Christian behaviour of some of you is a sham, and this the reality? It seems I have no way of telling."

She stopped speaking and thirty stunned faces stared at her. The thirty-first, that of Dave Simpson, was scarlet and buried in his hands: this outburst of the minister's was far more embarrassing to him than the original tirade against his wife. He was used to people reacting badly to Dorothy, he did it himself at times.

Bridget herself was somewhat appalled by the amount she had found to say. Usually her anger was expressed in short sharp outbursts, ending in tears. Now that she had stopped speaking, she felt incredibly depressed. The silence in the room weighed on her. Why didn't they walk out? They were under no compulsion to listen to her words. She suddenly wondered if this was what Ian felt when faced with a class of chastened mischief-makers. Her similarity to a stern teacher was heightened for her when she spoke again.

"This meeting is adjourned. You can all go home now."

It was three days later when Joyce telephoned Bridget. Another fine summer's day had the children and Ian outside once more, while Bridget wrestled with a reluctant sermon. The church newsletter had advertised the coming Sunday's topic to be "The Church as the Body of Christ." Now she wondered what she could say about this. The ringing of her phone was not the unwelcome interruption it might normally have been.

"How are you, Bridget? It's Joyce. Am I interrupting anything?"

"Nothing important. What can I do for you, Joyce?"

"Well, we never decided when to have our next diary session. I think it may be the last one, there's so little left to read. When would suit you?"

Bridget was silent.

"Bridget? Are you there? When shall we see what Christian Hinduism looked like to Charlotte?"

Still there was no answer.

"While you're looking up a time, I have to tell you that I found the last entries quite incredible. She was so ill-used by the Swami, and yet she was able to try to be fair to him and his teaching. It must have been hard to decide to come home to a blank future as well. She must have felt so betrayed by India, by that Swami, and by his religion and yet I got the impression that when she returned she followed his advice, didn't you? She has such strength of character I can just see her doing it."

Bridget found her voice. "You can just see her doing it, can you? She struck you as deceitful and untrustworthy, did she? I thought you liked her, Joyce. This is Miss Murdoch, your landlady we're talking about. She didn't appear untrustworthy to me as I knew her. So I'm surprised by all I've read. You are not. You can 'just see her doing it.' I thought better of you than that, Joyce. I thought you had liked Miss Murdoch, that you had trusted her. Obviously not. If you had, you would share my sense of disappointment. Miss Murdoch has failed me. Or my trust in her has failed. And you didn't share that trust. I thought you did. She must have thought you did, or why would she leave you her diaries? It seems you are not who I thought you were, Joyce. No, I don't want to read the rest of the diary with you. I can't trust you either. Goodbye." And the phone slammed down.

Joyce stood by her table eyeing the receive in her hand with disbelief. It hadn't sounded at all like the controlled, humorous, sensible woman she'd come to know and rely on. In her bewilderment it became instantly clear to her that if Charlotte Murdoch had become her spiritual alter ego, her guide and companion, then Bridget had become a maternal figure. She it was whom Joyce counted on to be consistent and calm in the vagaries of life. Bridget had been so sensible about Ian's friendship with herself, so matter-of-fact about her calling and ministry. Where had this wildly accusing woman come from? Joyce's only hope was that she could find Ian and he would be able to reassure her. "After all," she said aloud, as she replaced the receiver, "It may be bad hormones. I hope so."

She stared unseeingly out of the window and addressed the absent minister. "There had better be a good reason for all this, that's all. Otherwise I shall be asking how you dare to treat me in this way. And right now, I can't think of an answer which will be acceptable."

CHAPTER TEN: THE CONSEQUENCES OF CONVERSE UP A CLOSE

"Wherever there are great virtues it's a sure sign something's wrong."

Bertholt Brecht, "Mother Courage" translated by Eric Bentley

The days passed. Joyce did nothing about contacting Ian, hoping he would get in touch with her. She was simply afraid to phone the manse in case Bridget should answer and launch into another strange tirade. But Ian hadn't been in touch. The school holidays had begun, so Ian was busy with Mairi and Angus all day, and Joyce no longer had the option of contacting him at school.

When they did meet it was by chance, and, like their first conversation, it was in the supermarket. Again, Joyce carried her wire basket, while Ian was in charge of a laden trolley, pushed this time by Mairi and Angus working in tandem. The shop was busy, full of locals with grim faces struggling past the brightly-clad holiday-makers, large arms or thighs erupting in mountains of white or scarlet flesh from gaudy cotton tops and shorts. The town-centre store wasn't built to deal with such throngs of human traffic, and there was no room for the company to think of building an extension.

Ian was standing in a queue for the check-out when he saw Joyce wriggling to get near a display of dairy products. He waved, but she didn't see him. It wasn't until Mairi, turning her eyes in the direction of her father's salutation, cried out, "Look! There's Joyce!" in her penetrating young voice that Joyce turned round and saw them. (Ian often sighed in mock-despair over Mairi's tones, saying that as the product of a teacher and a preacher, they shouldn't have expected a soft-voiced child.)

It was impossible for Joyce to make her way up-stream against the determination of those forcing their way further into the store, so she gestured to Ian to wait outside. He looked puzzled at first, but then grinned, so she had to hope he understood, and wasn't just being politely friendly. She decided to forget about the other items on her shopping list, thus condemning herself to another battle with the shelves, and made her way to a check-out. As usual the queue she joined seemed shortest but turned out to be the slowest. Hopping from foot to foot impatiently she found she couldn't see Ian hovering outside the windows as she had hoped she might. Eventually she paid for her milk and yogurt and was disgorged onto the pavement. She turned her head anxiously this way and that. The human river was only marginally less deep here than in the store. He must be gone. There was no sign of him.

"Hello, Joyce. Did you want to talk to me? It's horrible in there these days, isn't it? I've yet to discover when the quiet time is. Eight in the morning, I expect, but I refuse to try then. I'm on holiday."

He had lost the children temporarily, having in fact sent them for ice-cream, and was standing tucked into a narrow close between the shops. Despite his errands and his words he seemed very calm and relaxed. "So," he went on, "What did you want me for? It seemed more urgent than a friendly hello."

Joyce greeted him and briefly told him about Bridget's sudden out-burst. "I don't know what I've done, Ian. I certainly didn't mean to hurt or betray her. I don't know why she thinks that's what I've done, anyway. She was too overwrought to be clear. Has she told you?"

Ian shook his head, an expression of bewilderment in his eyes. "No. No, she hasn't. She hasn't mentioned the diary since the last day you were round. And I hope you won't take this the wrong way, but we haven't mentioned your name either. It just hasn't come up." He frowned thoughtfully. "When you had that session in our garden, that time when I came in and disturbed you, you looked pretty upset."

It was a question and Joyce answered it as such. "I wasn't really upset, more stunned by what I'd read. I was probably pretty rude to you, wasn't I?"

Ian waved this away as he pursued his own line of thought. "I've been meaning to ask Bridget about that session. What stunned you? Was it anything which would explain why Bridget said that Miss Murdoch had betrayed her?"

Standing there in the stuffy close, oblivious to the old fruit crates and empty bread trays stacked round them, Joyce tried to give Ian an idea of the events of 1948 as recorded by Charlotte Murdoch. As they strove to understand the events of those turbulent days and their possible effect on Bridget they ceased to be aware of the crowds pushing by on the pavement at the end of the close. Ian forgot to keep an eye open for Mairi and Angus, and neither realised the picture they presented to the rest of the world, pressed into physical proximity by the narrow space, lost in conversation. More than one passer-by noticed them and spared a sympathetic smile for a pair of earnest lovers.

Mairi and Angus returned with their ice-creams and failed

to locate their father. Certainly he wasn't outside the supermarket as he had promised to be. It took some time to search through the thronged part of the pavement, especially as Mairi refused to let go of her little brother's hand but clung to him like a dutiful limpet. They were still staring around them in confusion when they heard their mother's voice. Looking round they saw Bridget and made their way to her. She seized them by a wrist each and marched them away. Nine-year-old Mairi waited for the expected question, "Where's Daddy?" It never came. Feeling it's lack, she decided to ask it herself.

"Mummy, what about Daddy?" she panted, her words jerked out of her by the effort of licking her ice-cream and striving to match Bridget's furious pace.

"Never mind Daddy, Mairi, he'll find his way home." Mairi thought her mother sounded rather peculiar and very unhappy. She was not to know that just before catching sight of the children, Bridget had glimpsed her husband, apparently engaged in a secret and intimate meeting with Joyce. She tried to control her pain and her anger, but the tears she would like to shed wept in her voice, and her hurt desire for solitude cried aloud in her walk.

Much later Ian and Joyce agreed that perhaps Joyce should avoid Bridget for a few days while Ian should seek an opportunity to approach his wife on the matter and try to find out what was wrong, and how to help. Ian promised to phone Joyce when he had done this, and if he hadn't managed it in a week's time, he would phone anyway.

Relieved by this common-sense approach and soothed by sharing her concerns and some of her reflections on Miss Murdoch's revelations, Joyce slipped out of the close and serenely made her way back to Windmill Road.

Left alone, Ian suddenly remembered his children. He glanced at his watch and saw that almost an hour had passed since he last saw them. Alarmed, he blundered his way out of the close, falling over boxes and sending piles of crates clattering around him. Not surprisingly there was no sign of the children in the street. He looked into the still-crowded supermarket: they weren't there. To make sure, he asked the manager. No stray children had been reported. Ian imagined that the man's polite smile mocked his futility as a father and left abruptly.

Next, he tried the ice-cream shop. They weren't there, and when he could get the attention of the staff they were sorry, but they couldn't help. So many wee bairns came in on a nice day like this. Indeed, the shop was full of them. For another hour Ian scoured the streets in a panic but found no trace of his missing offspring. Eventually he made his reluctant way to the police station. He would like to report two missing children please. The sergeant at the desk asked a few questions. Were they holiday-makers? No, local. Local? And when did the children go missing? Ian gave details. The sergeant was an older man. Now he looked over the top of his spectacles at the worried father before him. "I'm assuming they haven't gone home," he said. "You've phoned to check, haven't you?"

The phone was answered by Bridget. Shortly she told the sergeant that she had taken the children home and suggested her husband return himself and stop wasting police time. The sergeant conveyed this with a smile to Ian, who stammered out his relief, thanks, and embarrassed apologies.

"Don't you be worrying about that," the older man replied. "I mind myself how hard it can be to keep track of them. I used to wish I could tie my own ones to my belt. Away home with you and be glad they're all right. I'm awful glad myself: I hate a lost child enquiry."

Bridget was witheringly scornful. "A fine father you are, unable to keep your children by your side for an hour. How do you manage with a whole class? I imagine you wouldn't notice if all the desks were empty, just as you didn't notice your own children. They did what you told them, and they expected you to keep your side of the agreement. They've been let down, and by their own father. And I've been let down too. I thought I could trust you to take care of them. I thought they were important to you, but oh no. No, you lightly let them go wandering among strangers in the streets. What would you have done if they hadn't turned up at home? How would you know how to begin finding the person who had abducted them and was abusing them? But then, you wouldn't know if they didn't turn up. You didn't bother waiting for them, anyway."

She turned to sweep out of the room, but Ian snatched her upper arm and held her back. His worry and relief might have served to humble him, but such a wild attack turned any meekness to blazing rage.

"Just you listen to me, Bridget. I'm not going to have to listen to your accusations without making reply. How dare you accuse me of not caring? How dare you say that I don't worry about my children? Yes, I was a little late at the rendezvous, but not as late as you seem to think. It's more than two hours since I discovered that they were gone. Where do you think I've been since then?"

"Up a close." The answer flashed back, but Ian hadn't been expecting any reply and barely heard it.

"I've been wandering the streets looking for my children. I've been asking for them from shop to shop. I was so worried that, as you know, Bridget, I went to the police. I don't care, don't I? I'm the one who thought my children were lost. You haven't had to go through that. You don't know how it feels.

In fact, you ae the one who put me through it. Didn't you ask where I was? Didn't you give the children a chance to explain? Obviously not. If you had, you'd have stayed with them till I returned. You wouldn't have taken them off and left me to believe the worst. What kind of action is that? What kind of wife would do that?

"Now we've both had our say and I think we've said enough. I would like to be left alone for the rest of the day to get over my fright and my anger. I'll just see the children first and apologise to them for being late."

Before Bridget could draw breath, Ian quit the room. His wife was left burning with wrath and astonishment. Unlike herself, Ian was rarely angry. Usually her rages served to make him humbly placatory. Never before had she received such a scourging from his tongue. Her world turned upside down. If Ian didn't react the expected way any longer, then where would she find constancy and security in her life?

"Only in you, Lord," she whispered, sinking to her knees as the quiet tears began to flow. "You're the only one I have left to trust. You won't let me down." Her tears continued to fall, but the sense of anger and betrayal left her. As she cried the evening sunshine shone into the kitchen. Glass jars and cupboard doors caught and magnified the glow; the geraniums in the window and the clean dishes stacked on the draining board shimmered with it; white formica surfaces and cabinets turned to living gold in the light. The beams touched Bridget's head and her shoulders, bringing a faint but real warmth.

"Thank you," she whispered now. God had her in his hand, and all would be well, she was sure of it. Quietly she rose to her feet and set about preparing the children's supper. She would eat with them. If Ian needed time alone, he would have it. Conscious of the wifely forbearance and virtue she was displaying, Bridget felt the divine glow warm her heart and soul.

The summer moved on with a succession of cloudless or rainy days: the brightest sunshine would on occasion be suddenly smothered by a cold haar off the sea, while on other days only the most fitful rays of sunshine filtered through a brownly overcast sky; the weather was pleasantly warm or unseasonably cold, dry or damp but never calm, and always worthy of comment. The east wind came steadily or gustily ashore as it always had. Golf tournaments were played on the Old Course and television commentators dug out the usual St. Andrews clichés. "The sun is shining brightly, but it's a strong, cold wind which will be the chief factor in today's game." Or, "St. Andrews, the little grey town nestling on the coast of Fife and battered by a constant wind: the Mecca of the golfing world."

From her flat in Windmill Road Joyce could catch glimpses of the first and the eighteenth hole (although she could see neither the tees nor the greens), and sometimes she looked up from her thesis to watch the crowd, denser than ever, which thronged in surprising quiet around the golf course. She was working hard these days and had high hopes of completing two chapters of the thesis before the summer was over. She wrote steadily, pulling her scattered notes into some sort of order around her. Every two hours she would take a break and go out for a breath of air and some exercise.

Most often she walked up to the Kinburn Park where she could watch people playing tennis, bowls or putting and could enjoy the relative quiet of the gardens. Few visitors discovered this park because, except to the native, St. Andrews is about two things: golf and the seaside. In pursuing these goals visitors may discover the ruined castle and cathedral, indeed they are hard to miss, and they may even climb St. Rule's tower and view the town, but they seldom go inland. Kinburn park was a haven. If Joyce felt like walking further afield, the Lade

Braes walk offered an even surer sanctuary from bustle. The aged trees hung their shining leaves over the Kinness burn, dappling in the sunlight and giving a walk of coolness and shelter.

On Sunday mornings Joyce still made a practice of going to church, though in these summer weeks she had avoided speaking to Bridget after the service. Once or twice she slipped out during the last hymn, but that felt pointed. After all, Bridget had caused the rift in their friendship, so why should she act furtively? Soon she discovered it was possible to slip out while Bridget was talking to another member of the congregation.

She still admired Bridget. Indeed, that summer many of the congregation found much to admire in Bridget's sermons and prayers. A new fervency seemed to possess her, and she spoke with eloquence and passion about God's faithful, steadfast love. "Chesed" she said, using the Hebrew word so frequently that it began to seem a part of the normal vocabulary. Chesed was the defining characteristic of God that summer. He (Bridget's God was traditionally male) was faithful when all the world turned away. He would never forget a person. No one else was faithfully, constantly, loving like God. Chesed should define the Christian as well. God's people should grow in steadfast love, till they became rocks to which others might anchor in the storms of life. God's Chesed was shown in the cross, where Jesus went because of God's love. "It was his love, not the nails, which held him to that tree" she quoted. We must repent our lack of Chesed and ask God that we might be filled with it.

They were fine sermons. Listening and watching Joyce admired Bridget more than ever. She seemed so calm and sure. Her very face radiated her faith and her desire to be loving. It never struck Joyce as anomalous that after hearing such sermons she still felt constrained to avoid the minister at the church door. She simply drank it all in, and was glad for Bridget's sake, that Martyrs church was well-patronised that summer. People talked about the Rev. McKay and long-lapsed members came curiously to see what was happening. With them came others who had no formal connection to the church, and more than the usual handful of summer visitors took places in the pews each week. So Sunday by Sunday the sanctuary of the church was warm with the heat of close-packed bodies.

Ian had phoned Joyce to say that he hadn't yet approached Bridget about the diaries. At first their mutual anger had prevented him and now he rarely saw his wife. More often than not she was absent from the manse, engaged in her usual parish work, or closeted, had Ian known it, in her vestry studying and praying. She returned home for bed and sometimes for meals, but even then she seemed engrossed in her thoughts. The children noticed her absent-minded behaviour, but fortunately it amused rather than disturbed them. They had Daddy, and it seemed he was always glad of their company these days.

Ian continued to phone Joyce, and sometimes they met up. He never went into details, but Joyce understood that the time remained "unpropitious" for tackling Bridget about the diaries.

Bridget herself was only too happy to forget Miss Murdoch and her journal. In the back of her mind she couldn't forget her sense of betrayal, extending from Miss Murdoch to Joyce, to Ian, and somehow connected to the Kirk Session. The Session usually took a break in July, a habit which dated from years gone by when that was the month in which everyone took their annual holiday. In fact, nowadays this simply was not the case, and it was very rare indeed when one of the other eleven monthly Session meetings came round and no one sent apologies because he or she was to be away on a trip.

The break from a Session meeting in July brought such a sensation of reprieve that Bridget began to wonder about the custom of monthly meetings. Was it any more than a habit? It was not laid down in church law, and it wasn't a Biblical ordinance either: the Bible didn't deal much with the way a church was run, except in terms of the underlying qualities of grace and love and the Holy Spirit. She quite agreed with St. Paul that everything to do with public worship should be conducted "decently and in order" – that watchword of reformed ecclesiology. But surely there were other ways of being in decent order than a monthly meeting of a somewhat unwieldy, hidebound, and unreliable body. This tradition of monthly plenary meetings was presumably what had once been the best way of doing things, but now? What if the Holy Spirit had other ideas for Martyrs Church? It would be a far worse sin to contradict God's Spirit than to break a human tradition. Perhaps they need only meet every three months? The elders themselves would probably be glad to have only four evenings in the year when they must come out. Or they could meet every four months, or even biannually. Bridget thought long about this matter and prayed fervently. It continued to seem a good idea. Perhaps they could start with four meetings a year, then move it through three to the final goal of six-monthly meeting. After all she was available to advise and direct the elders individually at any time. The church was doing so well now, it was vibrant and growing, and people were coming to her to talk about their lives, not waiting at home for an elder to make a duty visit and discover their needs.

Thinking about all this, Bridget knew it was time to tell her Session Clerk about her plans, so that he could get his administration in line with her new ideas. She phoned Mr Downie one Saturday morning.

"Hello, Jack, it's Bridget McKay here. Have you a minute to talk?"

"Aye, naething too important happening here, I was just going to cut the grass."

"Well, listen, I have been thinking and praying and planning about how we run the church. You know that the June meeting of the Kirk Session was a bit of a disaster, and we haven't missed out by not having a meeting in July, so I'm beginning to think we don't need to meet so often as a whole Session."

"Aye, June was not good. Of course, if I can just mention it, although maist of us were out of line about Dorothy, there's a feeling abroad that you were also out of line and a bit over the top the way you told everyone off, like they were naughty bairns."

"What?"

"Aye, but that's the past now. I just thought I would mention it, because it might not be a bad idea to have a quiet word to that effect at our August meeting, just to clear the air, if you know what I mean."

"No, I don't know what you mean." Bridget was coldly angry. "And what I was phoning to tell you was that I don't intend us to have a meeting in August. I think we can run just fine with quarterly meetings instead of monthly. In fact, I think that would be just a temporary stepping stone to having even fewer plenary meetings in the year. After all, most of the work is done by the smaller committees."

"Aye, but they have to get approval from Session for their ideas. I don't think that cutting down on the Session meetings would be a good idea. It might make thing slower to get done. Do we not have to have a certain number of meetings in the year?"

"No, Church law is not specific on that point. I checked. I would like to try it this way. Maybe if need be we could give the sub-committees powers. And I will always be available to them, so they can operate under ministerial authority. Now listen.

"Finances will need regular processing, especially with the work in the hall, and of course the property group will need to keep an eye on that. I have lots of ideas to feed to the outreach committee – they're going to be busier than ever – and to the Sunday School and the Youth Group. Matters pertaining to worship can of course be left in my hands. Life is going to be too busy to have too many time-wasting meetings."

Mr Downie coughed. "Aye, but our meetings are not time-wasting. It is important that all the Kirk Session kens what each wee committee is doing, so that we can get a whole picture of the life and work of Martyrs church. I ken that sometimes the meetings are no so very exciting, but that doesn't mean that they are not necessary."

"Well, I think we'll try it my way," said Bridget, determinedly bright and cheerful. I will send a letter to the Session."

"Should that no be my job?"

"No, I'll do it myself. I won't trouble you. After all the buck stops here. Now I'll let you get to your grass-cutting. Bye."

And so Bridget thought and planned, not only for the finance and property groups, or the outreach group and the Youth work committee, but also for new initiatives which she would spearhead herself, to reach out to the un-churched in the town. It was as well that the work on Sandy's halls was going on apace: they would need the space. Life was busy, too full to need so many meetings. So she drafted her letter and sent it to members of the Kirk Session. Their next meeting, they were told, would be in September; thereafter they would meet in December, March, and June.

(Of course, December was usually far too busy for a meeting, but she would deal with that nearer the time.)

Bridget pursued her newly refreshed ministry enthusiastically.

Ian watched this activity from a detached distance. He was glad Bridget seemed to be so happy in her work. The old cynicism had gone completely. Ian devoutly hoped that this was a step forward, through negative experience, and not backwards, hiding away from it. He hoped too that once the new regime was more settled at the church he would get his wife back. He didn't mind running the house and being the primary carer for the children, but he missed his wife. All her energy was channelled away from him. He told himself that this was not done because he had changed and become repugnant, but because Bridget had a new (temporary) priority. His head agreed, and he could even joke about being a church widower; his heart felt rather more bruised than his words admitted. After all, the church had been present in their marriage from the first, but this withdrawal was new.

Sometimes he phoned Joyce for a chat.

"Can you listen to an old married man's woes? "

"What are friends for? But what woes can you have? You have a lovely wife and kids and a job that you are good at."

"Yes, I do. But I worry about Bridget these days. She has made herself so busy that we never see her and when we do, she is not thinking about us but about her work. It's not good for the kids."

"Are they complaining? Do they resent Bridget's busyness? She really seems to be doing a power of work in the church and the town these days, but surely that should make you proud."

"Do the kids resent it? Actually, now you mention it, no. Ha, I hadn't looked at it from their perspective. They just think that Mum's busy, which is true. I think that as long as she is there, physically, they won't worry. I should remember that my kids are just like my pupils."

"What do you mean?"

"I am so often shocked when something happens in the family life of one of my pupils and I see them cope, because of the strength and importance of their interior world, compared to what is going on around them. I suppose my children are not any less than normally observant for their ages, yet they seem to find very little difference in family life. If Bridget (or I) were to physically leave they would notice, and mind terribly, but this new family dynamic seems to be readily accepted. "

"So the worry?"

"Is mine. I worry about the family. And I realise that I have sacrificed so much for the sake of the family: friendships, evening activities and hobbies, visits to my own mother, all to help Bridget fulfil her calling. I guess it's me who is resentful."

"Well, try not to be. She really is an amazing woman."

"But not, currently, an amazing wife and mother. Our lives are going on, and Bridget only knows the surface of the events that are important to us, to me and to Mairi and to Angus. Surely a mother should be deeply involved. My mother was."

Joyce chuckled. She couldn't take all this seriously, because she admired Bridget so much, even though she had less to do with her these days. "Ian, never compare your wife with your mother. I may not be married, but I know that this is lesson number one of being a husband! I'm sure things will work out."

"I hope so. Anyway, thanks for listening."

The matter of internal family communication did worry Ian, though. Bridget had the broad outlines. She knew Angus was going to have the same teacher for the next school year, while

Mairi had a new one – her first male teacher. She knew that Mairi's best friend, Linda, was moving away, and that Angus had spent a lot of this summer on the beach with a family from down the street.

But she wasn't there when Mairi wondered about the new teacher, alternating between believing that he would never be as good as Daddy, and thinking that he had to be better than any other teacher "in the school, no in the town, no in the world!" an exclamation invariably accompanied by a flow of giggles. She wasn't there when Angus cried, because he didn't like his teacher and had previously been led to expect he would have a new one this year. She wasn't there to hear Mairi's sobs after the farewell to Linda had been said, nor to help her write her first faltering letters to anyone, aside from the duty "thank yous" at Christmas. She didn't hear Angus' hilarious comments on the picnics their neighbour provided for her family: "No sandwiches at all, just a big, thin roll-thing and some cheese, Daddy. She says it's the French way. What does that mean? James (his friend, the neighbour's son) says that the French do everything best, even kiss. How does he know?"

No, Bridget wasn't there. And a family that was never really together, present in mind as well as in body, well, it was a family heading for problems.

When the work on the church hall had started Ian had agreed that there could be no going away on holiday that year, at least not in the summer. But then Bridget had promised lots of family days out to make up. They had been to the beach, to Craigtoun Park, to the Hermitage near Dunkeld, to Deep Sea World and even to the Isle of May, but the outings had been father and children alone. Now that school was starting again Ian regretted that he had been so accommodating to his wife. She had a duty to the family, after all.

He was also feeling guilty about his own mother. It was almost a year since he had seen her, and he had promised a visit that summer. Now summer was far gone, and he was due back at work. After the term was a week old he decided to tackle his wife on the subject. She was out at a church meeting, a course she was running for those who were interested in finding out more about the Christian faith, and it was after ten when she finally came home. She looked as though she might drift past Ian, up to bed, but he called her name, and instead of passing by the living-room door, she came in. Ian looked at her with mild alarm. Her hair wasn't designed by nature to look tidy, but now it was in wild disarray. Her eyes looked tired, with purplish black shadows beneath them, while her familiar face was unfamiliarly thin. She had never shown her cheekbones before in all the years he had known her. How long had she looked this way? When had he last really seen her?

"Bridget you look tired. Was it a difficult meeting?"

Her eyes brightened a little. "Difficult – yes and no. There was real spiritual warfare afoot tonight, Ian. It always seems difficult, but of course there's no real doubt as to the outcome. Christ has fought the battle for us."

It was not the answer his purely social question had expected and Ian was a little thrown. "Oh, that's good. But listen, Bridget, I want to ask you to take a day off this weekend."

"A day off! I can't! There is so much to be done these days that only I can do."

"Only you? Come off it, Bridget, that's why you have elders to help you. I don't mean Sunday, you know, just Saturday. I want to go and see Mother."

"Ian, you don't understand." Tears gleamed in his wife's tired blue eyes. "God has set me apart for a special work, here and now. I can't dictate His timing in this matter. But I must do the work He gives me with all my strength."

"All your strength? Till when? Till you collapse?" Fear at her words brought hostility to his tones.

"Have faith, Ian. God won't let that happen. He won't let me down. When He thinks I need a break He'll provide one."

Ian stared at her for a moment. "How do you know He's not using me to provide one? You need a break and I need to go up north. We're family, Bridget. That's important."

"It is, but the Lord's work is more important. He doesn't want me to take a break yet; there is still too much to do."

Ian raised his eyebrows in an unspoken question.

"Yes, I know you're wondering how I can be sure, how I can know when to take a break. It's quite simple: there will be a sudden window in the work. Don't worry, Ian, I'm not expecting to hear voices or anything strange like that."

"Actually, that's not my worry. For all I know, voices might be a good thing. I'm glad your work is going well, Bridget," – he could say no more before she interrupted.

"No, no, Ian. It's not my work that's going well. It's God's. The Gospel is finding an open ear in St. Andrews. This is not my work but something I am privileged to be part of, as are you."

"I? How am I part of this? I don't even know what's going on, not properly."

"But that's not your part. You allow me to be free to play my part. You look after the children and the house. I am so grateful to you." She yawned suddenly and sat down in an armchair. Looking at her, Ian stretched his mouth into a smile but hardened his heart. She thought he would have to allow things to continue after that emotional appeal. But it wasn't good.

"Bridget, I'm glad you've found me supportive. I hope you'll never find me anything less. Nevertheless, I need *your* support just now. Just for one day. I have a duty to visit my mother, as real, as God-given, if you like, as your duty to the events in the parish. We both, Bridget, have a duty to Mairi and Angus. On Saturday will you please come with me to Aberdeen, on a family day out; or else will you undertake to spend the day at home with your children, while I go alone? I would rather you came, but I'm giving you the choice."

He spoke firmly but not unpleasantly and was unprepared for Bridget's response.

"Who are you to tell me what to do? You give me options! You're so hide-bound, so determined to side-track me from the work that you can't see all the possibilities. Take the children with you! Your sister will look after them, if your mother can't bear them, or they her. I don't blame them for not wanting to see her, the bloodsucking, demanding old harridan. Or leave them at home and get a babysitter. I will not be side-tracked from the work, and so I say to you, in Jesus' name, 'Get behind me, Satan!'"

She stormed to the door but stopped suddenly, disconcerted by the sound of Ian helpless with mirth. Her cold blue eyes turned towards him and read in his face an invitation to recognise that she was being ridiculous. She turned it down and quietly left the room.

Ian laughed on for a while before stopping abruptly. She was serious. She had passed the point of being able to see herself objectively. This was no progress in saintliness but a regression to the deadly earnestness and self-importance of adolescent faith. Meanwhile he must do what he could for the family, whether Bridget would help him or not. Late as it was he made for the phone and was soon speaking to his sister. However he was doomed to disappointment. Saturday was no use for her. She wished she could help him with the children, the more so because their mother had been asking for

Ian often of late, but she had other commitments this weekend which could not be put off. Cursing silently, Ian hung up.

CHAPTER ELEVEN: SOUNDS AND SILENCE

"Half the results of a good intention are evil; half the results of an evil intention are good."

Mark Twain. "Europe and Elsewhere."

Summer moved into early autumn, with its distinctive sharp tang in the mornings. The days grew shorter and colder. Hallowe'en was heralded in bakeries and on school walls and windows. Then it was over; forgotten turnip and pumpkin lanterns lay rotting on door-steps and in gardens; the guising sweets were hoarded or gobbled down, and the rolls of black and orange crepe paper were replaced in stock rooms for another year. Guy Fawkes night passed without much public display, although bangers and rockets could be heard echoing through the streets for days beforehand, and teenagers sent their pocket-money and Saturday earnings up in smoke.

The days turned damp and misty. Martyrs church halls were finished and opened. Sandy attended the ceremony and was well thanked by all and sundry. Joyce, guessing that he would be present, stayed away, though she continued her faithful morning attendance.

Still Bridget hadn't spoken to her, and in her pride, she would not force the contact, but grew ever more skilled in avoiding the minister. This was not hard to do, because numbers attending Sunday morning worship continued to rise. By the end of September a second morning service was added and now there was serious talk of a Wednesday evening service for the benefit of those who had to work on Sundays.

Bridget continued to proclaim her message with unabated zeal, telling people what to do, what to think, and how to show God's love; calling people to repent and believe the good news of her gospel. She was decidedly thinner now than a year ago and walked with a more measured pace and less bounce to her step. But it was only those who had known her for a while who noticed this. "The old stagers" she called such people, now that each week brought more new faces to her church. Dr. Marr tried to have a quiet word with her about the need to slow down, but although she was very polite with him, he knew that he might as well have saved his breath. "She's fair possessed," he reported to his wife. Bridget would have agreed: she was possessed, she believed, by God's Spirit.

Meanwhile Sandy was a busy man again. The conversion of Martyrs halls had attracted attention. The "St. Andrews Citizen" had written about the project and shown pictures of his model before any of the work took place. The feature was seen by someone in "The Scotsman" offices and they too had sent a reporter and a photographer to check out the story. The results in Sandy's life were seen almost at once, and from the end of June he was able to pick and choose his work to suit himself. Of course, most of the contracts he was offered now were for conversions, rather than for the domestic new builds he considered his forte.

He mentioned this to his grandfather and received some very sound advice. "Conversions is where the money is going to be, Sandy. Folks aye look for quality work if they can afford to be doing up an old building. And more and more folks are sticking with the old, and not the new, because they believe in what's been tested by time, wind, and rain. You work on conversions – private as well as public – and if you offer quality, you'll never be short of a job."

This made sense, so, weeding out such offers as would have taken him too far from Cupar, Sandy settled down to be busy: visiting buildings, getting to know their history and atmosphere, and drawing up plans for their new life. By November he was delightfully harassed with a barn in Kirriemuir, a community hall in Cupar itself, some farm cottages on the north Fife coast and an old church in the Bow of Fife. The barn was every converter's dream: an empty shell with good strong walls, and an inside which could be carved up and re-built at will. The community hall was more of a challenge, not that it was difficult as a project, but because every idea had to be passed by an inefficient committee. Sandy realised now how Bridget had smoothed things for him at Martyrs church. The farm cottages were another battle, as the owners wanted the interiors to be large, light, and ultra-modern, while the place spoke to Sandy of quiet corners and small windows.

But his delight was the church. It had been out of use for twenty years or so but had not fallen into terrible disrepair. The people in the hamlet had used it for flower shows and other displays a few times each year, allowed to do so by the presbytery, which had long despaired of finding a buyer. But now the impossible had happened. It was to be a home.

Sandy had often passed the church, just three or four miles out of Cupar, and had given it no thought. The outside was a plain, sandstone, Gothic structure, Victorian in date, so he was not expecting to find anything very exceptional within. He couldn't have been more surprised. The interior was remarkable, with well-carved wood at the ends of the roof-beams and beautifully delicate woodwork on the pulpit. But the crowning glory was undoubtedly the stair-case: it was fit for a Georgian mansion. The first broad steps were central, but then the stairs branched into two elegant half-spirals, meeting again on the balcony. Again, the stair was of polished wood, each balustrade carved a slightly different pattern from its neighbours. There could be no doubt about it: the staircase stayed. So would the roof-beams, and Sandy hoped, the pulpit. He had yet to think of a domestic use for a pulpit but did not despair of finding one.

With all this work on hand, Sandy was happy. His creative mind was being well exercised, as well as the more technical skills of his craft. He was working at full stretch, often spending his evenings in the office, or taking papers and plans home with him. Hargreaves was delighted to have retained his partner and pleased too with the prestige Sandy's name now brought to the partnership. Old Mr Melville was secretly very relieved to know he need fear no immediate change in his living arrangements.

Sandy told himself all this more than once as he drove from office to site, or back again. He reminded himself of how his good fortune was causing pleasure elsewhere as he sat in the evening seeking elusive inspiration. As Christmas approached he found himself repeating the mantra more and more. He wouldn't allow himself really to notice this, however, as he didn't want to analyse the phenomenon. He didn't want to remember last Christmas and the hurt it had brought him.

A couple of times he had tried to contact Bridget for a friendly chat, but each time Ian had told him she was out at church, and though he promised to pass on the message, Bridget never phoned back. It seemed as though all his ties with St. Andrews, and therefore with Joyce, were severed. And he would not telephone Windmill Road. By now he had left it far too late. There was nothing to be said to a year of silence.

And then, one evening of the week preceding Christmas he

found himself back in St. Andrews. The clients with the Bow of Fife church had asked for a meeting there, since they were currently based in Edinburgh, but had occasion to be in St. Andrews for other reasons. They met over drinks in the Rusacks Hotel, a location which Sandy found thoroughly unnerving since it was but a stone's throw from Joyce's flat. He hardly touched his drink during the meeting and afterwards he was thirsty but satisfied. An hour's persuasive talk had seen all his plans accepted and given him more time to consider the pulpit. The combination of a dry throat and an elated heart called out for a drink, but not where he was. The Rusacks was too formal to cater for a solitary celebration.

In sudden defiance he decided to go to the Featherie. "Kate's Bar" it had been when he had met Joyce there, and "Kate's Bar" it had remained to them. But now he gave it the new name and set out to walk there. The air was bracing, not to say icy, and accorded well with his sense of purpose. With each step he took he felt that he was putting the past behind him and accepting a new persona: that of the successful man of business, walking with confidence into his future. His shoulders were back and his head up. It doesn't take long to pass from one stage of life into another. From the Rusacks to the Featherie was a journey of about three minutes. In that time Sandy came to terms with his hopes and his disappointments over Joyce, and accepted them, and, he told himself, he put the situation behind him. He had been ashamed of himself; he had been angry; he had both felt and denied his pain; but now that period of his life was over. He wished Joyce well, but he must move on.

All the same it was gratifying to be greeted as a long-lost friend by Tam, the barman. Perhaps it was this flash of pleasure at being recognised which most clearly said that Sandy had moved on. Before, had he dared to enter the bar, he would have avoided all those he used to know. But now Tam's greeting was a pleasant continuity. If he asked after Joyce, Sandy would be able to handle that as well. This took less than no time to pass through his mind, while Tam was still speaking his name. He thought that nothing could alter his mood that evening. The sequel to Tam's greeting proved him wrong.

"Hi Mr Melville, it's good to see you. I should have known you'd be on your way. She's over there. I hope you can do something, because she's doing nothing for trade." He dropped his voice. "A bit dismal for Christmas, poor lassie. I suppose you know what's wrong, though. Not a lover's tiff, I hope. She's crying ower much for that to be reasonable."

As he spoke he had come out from behind the bar, leaving "the boy" in charge, and had been piloting Sandy over to a dark corner. Sandy allowed himself to be led, as he seemed to have no option. The words "lover's tiff" caused him to start, and gave him some idea of what he was about to find. All the same, when he saw Joyce he was shocked.

The brown hair, usually so neatly held in place, was pushed anyhow over her head. The Alice band was adrift and caught up in the tangles. She was wet, soaking in fact, and was clad only in torn jeans and a t-shirt. Sandy could see no coat. Her grey eyes were swollen and bloodshot, and her face was white and blotchily veined, like poor-quality marble. Most distressing of all was her manner. She sat hunched up in her seat, almost as though she were afraid and was trying to hide behind the small bar table. Her eyes darted from side to side, and her hands moved at random, as though possessed by a life of their own. Now she would pluck at her hair or parody smoothing it, now pull at her mouth, or fling her arms wide. As Tam approached, both hands were held in front of her in what would have been a gesture of defence, had not the backs of her hands been towards the man and her fingers hanging limply down. As Sandy drew near he could hear her teeth chattering.

"She's all yours," said Tam grimly. "All I can say is I never gave her any drink." He left quickly, and Sandy stood quietly, his heart full of horrified pity, his mind still calmly assessing the situation.

He was inclined to believe Tam's parting statement. Something was far wrong, but not, he thought, caused by alcohol. He'd once seen Joyce a little drunk, and she was nothing like this. Besides, although the air of the pub was full of the warm smells of beer and spirits, it didn't seem to be emanating from the woman before him. It wasn't drink. But if that were the case, why had she come here, to a pub?

At that moment Joyce's eyes, which had passed over him more than once in unseeing movement, looked him full in the face.

"Alex." Her tongue mumbled his name through lips that scarcely moved. "Alex. You would be here. Is Mum with you? She should be with you. Mum. You. Bridget. People who can't be trusted. People." She was slavering slightly now and it was all Sandy could do to keep from turning away in disgust and embarrassment. It was all wrong that he should see Joyce like this.

There was a short silence, then he spoke. "Joyce. What's wrong? How can I help?"

Now she turned her head away. Her eyes began ceaselessly to swoop around in their sockets, sometimes turning up so that only the mottled whites could be seen. Frightened, Sandy took hold of her shoulders and gave her a little shake. Joyce!" his voice was sharper now. "Stop it! Tell me what's wrong."

Unexpectedly she began to weep, heaving loud sobs and gasping for breath. She made no effort to hold or comfort herself and wriggled away from his touch.

"Bridget," she gasped. "Bridget. She shouldn't. She shouldn't." Again she looked at Sandy. "You shouldn't" she added, almost calmly. Then the sobbing began again, louder than ever.

The other patrons couldn't hep knowing something was wrong. They shuffled their feet and averted their eyes, too embarrassed to acknowledge Joyce's presence, but unable properly to relax. Drinks were downed and people began to leave. Still Sandy stood helplessly looking down at Joyce. A hand tapped his shoulder and he jumped. It was Tam. "You'll hae to tak' her awa', Mr Melville. We can't have that sort of thing here. It's no fair on the rest. Tak' her home, can't you?"

Home. Well perhaps. Joyce was crying so bitterly now that she seemed unaware when he gingerly laid a hand on her shoulder. His grip tightened while his other arm circled her waist and pulled her up, steadying her against his chest. She continued to cry blindly while slowly he led her though the bar to the door, himself blushing beetroot as people glanced at them then looked away. It was with relief that he felt the cold air of the street on his face.

Take her home. But she had no bag, and he couldn't search her pockets. She seemed half-fainting by now. Sandy made up his mind, braced himself, and picked Joyce up in his arms. Then, staggering under her weight, he made his way back to his car, still parked outside the Rusacks Hotel. He would take Joyce home.

"For a modern young man, you're remarkably naïve," stated old Mr Melville. It was past midnight, and the two men were standing together in the doorway of the spare room. Joyce was tucked up under the flowery candlewick bedspread which had been Mrs Melville's delight. The rest of the room also showed the old-fashioned feminine hand which had brought its elements together. The dressing table and chest of drawers, plainly made of a dark wood, sported frilly mats on their flat surfaces, while the dressing table also wore a flowered skirt.

Every surface – chest, dressing table, window sill and bedside table – displayed a collection of china figurines, all damsels in Victorian dress. The drawn curtains and the shade of the bedside lamp, which was the only light currently lit, matched the dressing table skirt, while the carpet showed signs of hard use and repeated scrubbing. The guest room had been seldom used since Mrs Melville had died.

"What do you mean, naïve?" Sandy demanded. They were whispering, maintaining the unspoken fiction that Joyce might be disturbed by their voices. Neither would admit that she seemed beyond disturbance.

"That girl's taken drugs." Old Mr Melville was gruff, as was to be expected from one who had been roughly disturbed from sleep. He wore a plain blue dressing gown over shabby pyjamas, faded by repeated washing from an unguessable colour to pale grey.

"Drugs? Surely not. I think she's ill." Sandy was tired and dishevelled. Carrying Joyce upstairs, removing her shoes, and putting her to bed had turned out to be the easy part of his task. Keeping her still and preventing her from jumping blindly out of bed again was wearisome. Afraid to leave her, and reluctant to call his grandfather he had been unable to summon medical help. Eventually the vague thumps of his struggle and Joyce's occasional wordless cries had woken the old man.

"Drugs," he repeated. "Don't forget I lived through the sixties, though I was a bit old for the goings on then. She's having a bad trip. We should call a doctor."

This advice Sandy thoroughly agreed with. His grandfather marched downstairs and presently his gruff tones could be heard, then the tramp of his returning feet, causing the stairs to cry out in protest. As he returned to the doorway, Joyce began to battle the confining sheets and cry out again. Sandy crossed to her side and held her wrists firmly.

"No Joyce, he said. "It's all right. You're all right. Be quiet. Rest. Be still."

But still she struggled. Her left hand broke free of his grasp and she began to pull at her hair, tugging with such force that a clump came away by the roots. Horrified, Sandy struggled to hold her again, to stop this self-mutilation on which she seemed intent.

It was while this was going on that the doorbell rang. Old Mr Melville thumped off down the protesting stairs again and returned with another man who seemed almost as old as himself. Neither of the Melvilles knew him, but had Joyce been able to recognise anyone she would have known his face. The recent decision that doctors in Cupar and St. Andrews should pool their night call-outs had brought Dr. James Marr to Joyce's bedside.

"What's her name and what's she taken?" He rapped out the question even as he came through the door.

"Joyce Cunningham. I don't know that she's taken anything." Sandy's answer was gasped out through the physical effort of keeping Joyce still.

"Oh? I thought it was reported as a drugs case. Well, let her go and let me take a look at her."

Sandy withdrew from the bedside to stand beside his grandfather. At once Joyce's hands went to tug at her hair, while she writhed and moaned. The doctor watched attentively.

"Was she like this when you found her?"

Sandy explained the circumstances of his meeting with Joyce, and how at first she had been capable of speech, albeit slurred and not obviously rational.

"In a pub? Had she been drinking?"

"Not there, and I don't think anywhere else either. I couldn't smell it on her."

"Hmm." Dr. Marr seized the wrist and felt for a pulse. "Very fast," he muttered. Still observing Joyce closely he questioned Sandy further.

"Do you know where she lives? Alone? With a friend? Is there someone we could contact who might know something?"

Sandy gave the details, adding that he didn't know her parents' address. "Though we could find out: they live in Pitlochry."

"Windmill Road. Is this the girl who was Miss Murdoch's lodger? I thought I'd seen her before – at church too, I think. Neurotic subject. I've always thought so." The doctor was talking chiefly to himself.

"Can you stay awake and watch her?" He turned his head to put the question and Sandy saw anger in the old man's eyes. "She has taken drugs of some sort. This is a bad trip, a bad reaction. But I can't give her anything, not knowing what she's taken. I think she'll come through. Can you watch her?"

"Yes." Sandy didn't think twice. "What am I watching for?"

"Hold her still when she's restless in case she hurts herself and watch to make sure she doesn't go into a coma. Restlessness is better than inertia. Phone at once if you think she's sinking. We could risk an injection if it were life-and-death. But I don't think she's that bad," he added, seeing Sandy's face. "If she falls asleep naturally, that's best. If she comes to herself, get her to drink some water." He prepared to leave. "Someone will come and see her tomorrow. She's from my practice, so it may be me. I hope so. I want to know what the idiot's done, and where she got it, and why."

He left without further speech and Sandy took up his station at Joyce's bedside.

It was almost twenty-four hours from the time Sandy found her in the pub that Joyce was able to give any account of herself. Towards daybreak, at perhaps 7 a.m., she had ceased to struggle and mutter and had fallen asleep. By this time Sandy himself was almost too tired to panic or worry. He calmly checked her breathing, felt her pulse and then, satisfied, lay down on the rug by the bed and enjoyed a nap himself.

His sleep was relatively short. He was awake again by 10 a.m. and at the office by half past. There was a client coming to see him and he must be there. Business was picking up, but he could not afford to alienate a potential customer. As he shaved he asked his grandfather to relieve him at the bedside vigil.

Returning at one o'clock he found the older man sitting by the bed, watching Joyce as she slept. The colour was coming back to her cheeks, but she still looked far from healthy.

"I think we might leave her while we have lunch," Sandy suggested.

"Mmm? Oh, yes. Yes. The doctor came, you know, and he says she'll be all right now, but he wants to know when she wakes up." Mr Melville rubbed his nose. "I didn't recognise her at first, you know. Even when you were talking about her flat, I just wondered how you knew. I thought you weren't seeing her anymore?"

Sandy sighed. "I'm not. I'll tell you all about it over lunch."

After their meal Sandy had stayed at home, never far from the spare room. He was actually sitting by the bed when Joyce opened her eyes.

However, after the drama of the previous night and the patient waiting through the day, both the Melville men found it to be quite an anti-climax when Joyce was finally able to speak to them, because she simply wouldn't tell them anything. She drank the water they pressed on her and thanked them for taking care of them. She declared herself to be a nuisance to them and promised to move out as soon as she might. More than that she would not say. She tried to get up but found herself too weak to walk, so was forced to remain in that old-fashioned feminine room with her returning memories for company.

She wished now that she had never met Bridget McKay. She wished she had never gone to live in Windmill Road. There had been a flat in South Street which she had thought of taking, but Windmill Road had seemed like a quieter location. Quiet! Her life had never been in such turmoil since Miss Murdoch died and left Joyce the diaries. And Miss Murdoch had led her to Bridget, Bridget whom she had come to respect, to admire, to take as a role model. Even although the minister hadn't spoken to her since the summer – and that was tied to Miss Murdoch too – still Joyce had excused her and had persisted in almost slavish admiration. At another time she would have bitterly resented the slight. But, like Charlotte Murdoch, she had taken the Hindu Swami's words to heart. She had begun acting as though she were a Christian, hoping to discover any reality or truth that might be there.

To act like a Christian she needed a role model, and of course Bridget was the obvious choice. Not only did Joyce know her quite well, but she was a public Christian, she was supposed to be a model for others. So Joyce had gone week by week and taken her place in Bridget's congregation. At first the routine of worship had bored her, being unfamiliar. She couldn't see its purpose and sat impatiently, waiting only for Bridget's sermon to speak to her and stimulate her.

But after a few weeks she found that the simple pattern of Reformed worship was beginning to hang together for her. If you accepted the basic tenets of Christianity (and Joyce was academically aware of these), then the routine made sense. You praised God in a hymn or a Psalm; you prayed; you listened to Scripture; you gave an offering in thanks rather than as dues or a bribe. And there was teaching for children and for adults: first for the children, as a matter of logistics, of course, to enable Sunday School to start on time. This facile assumption was challenged one week when the Gospel lesson included the statement "Unless you become as little children you cannot enter the kingdom of God." Perhaps, Joyce marvelled, there was also a theological or exemplary reason for talking to the children first. The talk to the adults came later, at the end of the service, except on Communion Sundays. That made sense too. You led up to the most important thing and sacrament – not that Joyce understood sacrament, but she realised its importance – sacrament was more important than instruction.

And so as time went on the ritual of worship took on a life of its own for Joyce, and she found herself able to relax into it. She never felt quite at home singing hymns, for fear that those around might hear and perhaps scorn her less-than-musical voice, but she found the words interesting. Still, the highlight was the sermon. In these months of her inspiration Bridget had a commanding pulpit presence. Watching and listening to her, Joyce both excused her strange unfriendliness, on the grounds that the minister was impossibly busy, and forgave her, on the newly-discovered grounds that Christianity involved forgiving others as well as accepting the divine pardon.

New as she was to the church, Joyce was deaf to the murmuring and muttering of the congregation. She didn't know about changes in administration and ministry. It would never have occurred to her that those involved in the physical organisation of the church, or its financial dealings would consider their tasks as God-given ministries. She didn't know that getting this idea to take root had been the major accomplishment of Bridget's six years with the congregation. This ignorance prevented her from realising how deeply hurt people were to have their tasks taken over or undermined. Joyce, like many of the new church-goers who flocked to Martyrs in these months, knew nothing of church government. If she had heard the word Presbytery that was as far as it went. She had no idea what a presbytery did, nor how far its powers might extend. She didn't know that a Presbytery is also a court to which church members may appeal over the head of their minister. Like most of the new congregants, she had no way of knowing that this is what had happened at the November meeting of Presbytery. The fact that Bridget had given up attending the body as a "waste of precious time" made things all the easier for the disgruntled parishioners and elders, who had written a letter of complaint to the Presbytery Clerk.

Lying in Mr Melville's spare room, Joyce had no knowledge of what had happened since that meeting. Naturally she knew nothing of the telephone call from the Presbytery clerk to the minister of Martyrs church, suggesting she take a couple of weeks off and then set about mending her fences, with her elders especially. She had not seen the letter sent to Mr Downie, the Session clerk, from the Presbytery clerk telling him of the conversation and asking him to keep in touch if Bridget showed no signs of taking that time off or of dealing with the elders in a more conciliatory way. Joyce only knew that Bridget must have felt under a lot of pressure and that there must have been a lot of unpleasant discussion for her to act as she had done.

Again, she relived that past Sunday morning.

The service had begun as usual, with a hymn and a prayer

and a talk to the children about God's love for them and for everyone. The Sunday School had then left the sanctuary for the main hall. Scriptures were read by the appointed elders. Although it was near Christmas, half-way through Advent, the readings chosen were not particularly seasonal. From the Old Testament they heard Psalm 1 which talks of the righteous being like a tree planted by streams of water, while the wicked are dry as dust and about to vanish as chaff blows away in the wind. From the New Testament it was the parable of the two builders, the one who built on sand and the other on the rock.

And then Bridget stood up in the pulpit for the sermon. But instead of her usual words of hope and love and assurance, instead of words about preparing for the coming of the Lord, she announced that the Presbytery of Cupar and St. Andrews had not seen fit to rejoice in the workings of the Holy Spirit at Martyrs church. In this they were like the wicked, dry as chaff and as useful. And they were like the one who listened to Christ but did not obey him, and so built their lives on the unstable sand. "Since I cannot go against the Spirit of God, I am unable to fall in with the Presbytery's request to let the church revert to the deadly, hide-bound status quo of past years and centuries. I cannot let those of you who would chime in with the Presbytery's opinions take us backwards. Therefore I have today withdrawn from the presbytery."

Her final words still rang in Joyce's ears. "This means that I am no longer the minister of Martyrs church. I withdraw myself from the establishment and will follow no human tradition, but only the Spirit of my God. Any of you who still wish to remain tied to the letter of the dead law, remain here. Those who wish to follow our Lord Jesus Christ, follow me and together we will build a community of love and God's power against which even the Church of Scotland cannot stand. I am going now. Choose swiftly and follow me in the way of holiness."

She had stepped down from the pulpit, marched regally down the aisle, her head held high and looking neither to right nor left, and disappeared into the church porch. After a startled silence a few people scrambled after her, but not many, perhaps ten. Then Mr Downie, looking greatly shaken, rose to his feet and proceeded to lead the congregation in prayer.

Since Sunday Joyce had re-lived her incredulous shock over and over. Had Bridget committed suicide she could not have been more outraged. Bridget was her mentor, her helper, her teacher, her ideal mother-figure, giving understanding and sympathy such as her own mother had never been able to provide. In the days of their companionship, Bridget had made her accessibility and concern obvious, without demanding confidences in the way which Mrs Cunningham had so annoyed her daughter. This might have been the approach of a growing, equal friendship, but in fact had been no such thing. Bridget had rarely – only once – wanted Joyce to be a listening ear to her own troubles. Joyce recognised this now. It had been very much an adult and child situation, with Bridget poised above Joyce in that realm where secure children believe that adults live: that place where personal worries are a thing of the past. She had set herself up to be worshipped and placed herself on a pedestal. And Joyce now cursed herself because she had fallen into a blind, childish attitude and had not noticed it.

Joyce's thoughts were savage both towards herself and her fallen idol. Her big mistake – or was it Bridget's mistake? – was to go to church. She had been able to adore her divinity there, for she had seen her pedestalled before her. But she had also absorbed something of the creed which Bridget served. Even in a Church of Scotland, with little in the way of formal liturgy and rites, where the minister seems to be in complete control of the contents of the service, even there Joyce had not been able to keep from knowing that humility and obedience were Christian virtues. Her mind knew that there were others: love, tolerance, patience, and goodness; but humility and obedience appealed to her. She fancied that she heard them extolled from the pulpit more frequently than the others, and they offered her what she most wanted: rest. She need not push for herself or think for herself. She need not make sense of her life nor of the theological tangles of the Christian creeds. She need only obey, submitting her will to do what the minister told her. In her emotional tangle over family, Sandy, and Ian, and in her lonely lack of other deep friendships such unthinking obedience sounded very sweet.

But she hadn't quite succumbed. She recollected this with triumph. She hadn't been pulled in so far that she couldn't see some inconsistency. She might be hazy about the body called Presbytery, but she was sure that Bridget had a responsibility to heed its advice. She believed the minister might even have taken vows to that effect. So when Bridget had proudly declared her own truth to stand in defiance of the church's governing bodies, Joyce heard her vaunting and her disobedience speaking.

Disgust wracked her, there in the pew, now in Mr Melville's spare room and many times in between. Disgust at her own near escape, at her own gullibility; disgust at Bridget's hypocrisy; and disgust that so much of her world was tied up in this thing. Without following the connections to their conclusions she could not rid her mind of the idea that there were three traitors – her mother, Sandy, and Bridget. Worse, she could not rid her mind of the idea that she had betrayed herself.

Not that she had been so upset as to try drugs. Seeing the anxious looks that Sandy was giving her each time he entered the spare room to see what he could do for her, Joyce realised that this was what he feared. She felt that she couldn't tell him all the hurts that she had had stirred up, especially since he was one of them, but she should tell him about Thursday night. That Thursday when she could not bear to be with herself and could not escape. So she had decided, against her first intentions, to go to an end-of-term bash at the Student Union, just to be with other people, and be lost in a crowd.

"Alex," she said, when on the Saturday morning he had again asked what he could get her. "Alex, I understand that you are worried about me. After all, I seem to have had some drug-induced illness. But I didn't take them on purpose, you know. You don't have to worry about me or that it could happen again."

Sandy was unspeakably relieved to hear four consecutive sentences coming from Joyce's mouth. Up until then she had spoken only in monosyllables. "Can you tell me what happened?" He asked. "Do you know?"

"I know a bit and I think I can guess the rest," she said. "I went to a party at the Union, just to stop having to think about things that were worrying me. And it was wild and noisy, quite unnerving, really. So I got a coke, just a coke, nothing more and went to sit in a corner for a while to watch. But there were three girls in that corner, and I knew one of them. She had been in my introductory tutorial, but she dropped out of anthropology. No wonder, if she was often at these parties. Anyway they made room for me, and then they went off to dance. And the last thing I remember is looking at the drinks on the table and wondering which had been mine, because they all looked the same."

"So you think that one of them had put something in her drink?"

"Maybe. Maybe if she was used to taking the stuff it wouldn't affect her so badly. I mean, it must have a good effect on some people, or no one would take it, whatever it was."

"You don't think one of them put it in your drink for a laugh?"

"It's possible, I suppose. Or that someone else had put it in one of their drinks, without them noticing and they hadn't drunk it yet. I think I downed the whole glass in a oner, because it was hot and stuffy, and I was thirsty."

"You don't know how you got to 'Kate's Bar'?"

"Kate's? Was I there?"

"That's where I found you. I went in for a drink after a work meeting and Tam assumed we were together and told me to take care of you. You were in a pretty bad state, Joyce. I was worried."

"I'm sorry. But you don't need to worry now. I feel stronger today and I expect I can go home."

"Can you tell me what was worrying you, that you felt the need to go to that party, which doesn't sound like your scene, to be honest?"

"No. That's private." Joyce turned away her face, then after a pause said, "Well, I expect you will hear one small part of it, which is public. Maybe you know already – about Bridget?"

"Bridget? What? What's happened to her?"

That's a good question. But on Sunday she walked out on Martyrs church. I will confess that I found that shocking. Maybe it stirred up some other stuff."

That was enough to tell. Gradually Joyce was having other memories fleeting across her tired mind. She remembered sniffing the glasses on the table expecting her own to be the one which did not have an alcoholic smell and being surprised that it was not. She remembered how after she had drunk the glass and sat for a while she felt unbearably thirsty again. She remembered her decision not to return to the Union bar, and how when she looked at it across the room is swam out of fucus while the barman seemed to leer at her. She remembered reaching the fresh air and realising that her jacket was left behind, and not caring, while the cool rain fell on her. And she remembered the thought that "Kate's" was just across the street.

Lying in the spare room, and later, in her own bed, Joyce was appalled at herself. Yes, there must have been narcotic in one of the glasses, which she had drunk, and that was sheer chance. But why had she been there at all? How low had she sunk in despair and self-involvement that another woman's choice in life could so affect her? Why had she never mended any of the broken fences that looking back she seemed to see strewing her way? Why had she identified so strongly with people that she could not see them as anything but extensions of herself? At the Melvilles and once she returned home to rest, Joyce was very silent, but her mind was not inactive.

Had Ian known of Joyce's condition, he might have envied her. She was safe and secure, able to lie still, drift in and out of sleep and to look forward to the resumption of her former life. Life before Bridget. He had none of these luxuries, and he was furious.

"You might have told me," had been his first words when, at last, Bridget had returned home that decisive Sunday. "You might have told me what was going on. I thought, once upon a time, not so very long ago, we were a married couple, trying to share our lives. I thought I promised to support and cherish you."

"Yes, I thought that too!" Bridget's anger was not quiet or controlled as his was. It flared out with the noise and violence of a machine gun, each word distinct from the others, yet the sentences pouring forth relentlessly. "I thought you offered, promised, to support me. So where were you today? When I turned to see who had followed me, where were you? Rooted to your pew. Great support, Ian. And I thought you were a Christian. You claimed to be. Where were you today, Ian? Where were you? Your support! It's just as well I didn't tell you anything beforehand. It saved me from having to hear your excuses."

She turned to leave the room. For a moment Ian hesitated before her rage, then deliberately he seized her shoulder, swung her round, and slapped her blazing cheek.

"Listen to me!" he shouted, shaking her. "Just listen. For the past few months you have taken yourself away somewhere. Some holy place, perhaps. But perhaps not. Let me tell you what it looks like from outside – from the outside, Bridget, where you've deliberately relegated me. No," as she opened her mouth. "You listen. Then I'll hear you, maybe."

"For the past few months you have become increasingly aloof. I've felt it, the children have felt it – and while we're on that subject you might as well know that your children don't respect your attitude: they laugh at you. Your own children mock you. You're immersed in church, in preaching and so on. You've slept here, but that's all. You have distanced yourself from the Kirk Session and other long-standing church members. You have cut yourself off from your past. When did you last contact your parents? You even ended your friendship with Joyce."

"Joyce! Let me tell you..."

"No. Listen. You were friends with Joyce. It was a good thing for her. It was. But you hurt her, just as you've hurt everyone who knew you. Now you've cut yourself off from Presbytery. You've stepped out of your job. Well, Bridget, come off your holy hill for a moment and tell me: how long do we have before we must move out? Where shall we live? Are you going to be earning? If not, how do you think we can hope to buy a house in St. Andrews on a teacher's salary? And even if we could, why should I finance your latest stupidity, which can only cause further hurt? Do you hear me, Bridget? Are you listening? I'm not on your holy mountain – you've forbidden me to come there. I'm down with all the other people you've managed to hurt and alienate. It's not very holy behaviour."

"Hurt!" Snapped Bridget. "You're hurt. You whine, Ian and you whinge. What do you want? An apology? Don't think you'll get it from me. I am doing God's work, and if you or other people stand in my way, then they may get a little bruised. It's a pity, but then, if you were sensible you wouldn't try to stop me. If you're not with me, you're against me, and this is a battle to the death. So move aside and come with me, or I'm afraid you may be hurt again."

"Listen to yourself." Ian spoke quietly but then began to shout. "You are not God, Bridget, whatever you may think. You are not Christ, and I will not follow you. Who are you to condemn anyone who happens not to be infected by your madness? You're not infallible."

He shook her once more, then dropped his hands from her shoulders and stepped back, never taking his eyes from her face. That face was now pale as, their tones reversed, Bridget spoke with quiet fury, her slow words dripping like an icicle in the sun.

"That's just words, Ian, and I know where they come from, from your real concern: Joyce. I hurt Joyce, you said, and she was my friend. Your lovely Joyce. I know about Joyce, you see, Ian, so you can't pretend to be the injured husband with me. It was in the pages of that diary. Miss Murdoch took a lover. Joyce echoed Miss Murdoch in everything she could – she has no mind of her own, your Joyce. She took a lover too. She took.

She didn't share or give herself. She took. My husband she took. I know. I saw you. I saw you embracing up a pend while your children, your children, were seeking you in the street. Don't cast the children up at me, Ian," she added with a flash of her former fire, "Because you've not been the perfect father."

Again her tones iced over. "I hear your questions, but they are your concerns, not mine. I don't have to answer your questions for you. I'm sure you'll find a way, if you want to. As for me, God will provide. If you support me, I'm sure He'll provide for you too. Now, if you don't mind, I must get some rest. I have to build up a church tomorrow, on the foundation of Christ's word, not the dead stones of the past."

Ian was left alone in the room, with his anger still pulsing hotly through his innermost being.

Now, a week later, nothing had changed, nothing had been further discussed, nothing resolved. Bridget had, if anything, held herself more rigidly aloof from her family than before. Sunday had come round again, and she had left the house very early: it was only six o'clock when Ian heard the front door click shut. Lying in bed he considered what to do. He had to decide about going to Martyrs church or staying away. Mairi and Angus were expecting to go. They had been talking about Sunday School just the night before. Today was the last rehearsal of the Christmas pageant, scheduled to be presented on Christmas Eve. Both children were involved and delighted with their parts. This year, Angus had been promoted from sheep to littlest shepherd, while Mairi was to be a somewhat diminutive archangel Gabriel. It wouldn't be fair to pull them out now.

But if he went to Martyrs (which was, after all, his church: he was a member) then what would it say? It would tell the world that he dissociated himself from his wife and her actions. It would smack of disloyalty. And if people questioned him, what could he tell them? He had no desire for his rift with Bridget to become public property. But if he went it would.

And if he did not go, what then? They would assume that although he had not marched out last week, yet he supported Bridget now. They would think – and have every right to think – that he was as committed to his wife's new-style religion as she was.

Of course, he could keep a foot in both camps by sending the children but staying away himself.

Even as this thought crossed his mind he heard the first morning stirrings from his offspring. Mairi was singing the angels' pageant song, "Angels from the realms of glory". Her true, high voice decided him. The children deserved better than to be sent where he dare not go himself. He would go with them. Any conclusions people drew would be no less than the truth, and any questions put to him directly he would do his best to answer. He was going to church after all. It should be a place for truth-telling.

Christmas came and the year wound down towards it close. Joyce spent Christmas with the Melville family. Sandy had insisted on this, but still found it ironic, considering the source of their quarrel the year before. He had offered to be a listening ear for Joyce's distress, but this offer had not been taken up, nor had he pressed her. But he was a shrewd, observant man. A short paragraph in the local paper to the effect that the Rev. Bridget McKay had stepped down as minister of Martyrs Church, St. Andrews, had confirmed what Joyce had told him. He knew nothing of Joyce's regular attendance at the church, but he wondered about the state of her friendship with the minister. In any case, he was quite sure that Joyce shouldn't be alone at Christmas, and she was still quite definite that she would not be returning to the bosom of her family. When he had suggested this she had blanched and shuddered. "No. Go and see my mother? Now? No, Alex, I couldn't."

"Sandy," he corrected patiently. He had no reason to accept another name from her now. "In that case you're coming to us. Yes, you are. It's a dangerous day for people to be left alone. I wouldn't feel able to relax for worrying. You're coming. I'll pick you up at eleven."

"You still don't really believe that I didn't take drugs on purpose, do you? All right, I will come to stop you from feeling bad. I will come because you think I am a weak-minded woman who can't be trusted." But she put no energy into the gibe. She smiled. "All right, I'll come. But don't expect much in the way of presents."

At Martyrs manse festivities were even more dismal. Mairi and Angus were no longer amused by their mother's defection. It was all right to be vague and busy at other times, but this was Christmas and still she was never here. It was ridiculous. She wasn't minister of the church any longer, so why wasn't she around more? Mairi sadly asked Ian to help her bake mince pies and biscuits. Ian, smitten by her pathetic desire to keep Christmas as festive as ever organised a Christmas cooking night, when both Mairi and Angus spent a few hours mixing, rolling out and eating raw dough. "Mummy will like this, won't she?" asked Angus, when at the end they surveyed three trays of lop-sided mince pies. Some of the pies had mincemeat spewing blackly down their sides, while others had concave lids, fallen in over a hollow base. The biscuits were works of non-representational art: Christmas trees of lime green or dark blue, pointless stars, and angels with broken wings.

His son's question smote Ian anew. "She ought to Angus, she certainly ought to," was all he could say.

But Bridget had never commented on the baking, had never tasted even one bite. She could hardly have been expected to come to the Christmas pageant – although this was not readily understood by her own offspring – but she had absented herself for nearly all of Christmas Day. Leaving early, before even Angus had opened his stocking, she didn't return until early evening. She admired presents and opened the small pile which were marked as hers, carefully left for her under the tree. But she was pale and drawn-looking, with black-circled eyes blinking dully at her family, while in her blonde curls, Ian saw the first signs of fading.

When the children were at length sent to bed, Bridget made to go up as well.

"Give them a minute first," Ian advised. She sat down again in her chair. Ian came over and stood behind her, running his hand over her hair.

"It's not going well, is it?"

She shook her head. "I'm tired, that's all. Christmas is always a killer for clergy. You know that." Her voice managed to sound lethargic and edgy at the same time. "In case you're wondering, we met in the town hall supper-room today. The hall-keeper wasn't pleased, and he charged us double, but he couldn't claim to have other bookings. But we can't always do that. I must find a space. There's an old church at Bow of Fife. I must find out about that. Turns out the majority of my flock aren't from St. Andrews, anyway." She got up and slowly left the room.

Ian, looking wearily round him at the jumble of presents, torn paper and crockery waiting for his attentions, could never remember feeling lonelier. Even Joyce had failed to contact him. He had hoped she would at least wish him a Happy Christmas; he had counted on seeing her at church. But she hadn't been there since Bridget left. Perhaps after all she had stayed with Bridget? For his wife's sake, he could almost hope so.

He might, of course, phone her. But to do so would reveal that he wasn't trusted. If she was with Bridget's group – or if she wasn't – a trusted husband would know that.

As he tidied up, removing the physical remains of that disastrous Christmas Day, Ian allowed himself to feel. At once his anger burned up, ever ready to heat his blood. This time he did not suppress the feeling but let the anger flood over him and ebb away. He wanted to know what was behind the pain which was knocking around in his mind, gnawing at his tear-ducts, demanding recognition. It was not just the practical difficulties Bridget had landed them in. It was deeper. It was this issue of trust. She didn't trust him. Well, obviously. But now it was clear that this lack of trust was no new thing. She had ceased to trust him that day in the summer when she had entirely mis-read his relationship with Joyce. (No, Joyce wouldn't be with Bridget's group: even if she wanted to join the door would be closed to her.)

Now Bridget's behaviour made more sense. Not her quickening sense of the religious, but her treatment of him. She didn't trust him, she thought he was deceiving her, so of course she would not feel able to confide in him. Of course she would feel cut off and alone and would tread her own path. She was mistaken, but in some ways it was magnificent of her. How else was she supposed to react?

As he thought this through he felt simultaneously better and worse. He never liked to think ill of his wife, partly for her own sake and partly because it reflected upon him; and so being able partially to understand Bridget's actions and reactions eased his pain and anger. But, on the other hand, she still didn't trust him, nor would she listen if he protested his innocence. How could a marriage with no trust continue? How had he failed to realise the misunderstanding at the time? Now the idea had

had time to put down deep roots and Bridget seemed lost to him.

Sighing, he sat down. So much of the responsibility for the family had always rested on him that now he found it easiest to take this burden on his shoulders too. Somehow this was his fault. His self-esteem plummeted. Shame, never far from him, now seized and overcame him. It did not occur to him to question why Bridget was so ready to believe the worst of him. Inclined only to think the worst of himself, this seemed only natural.

CHAPTER TWELVE: PASSIONATE WORDS

"Talk does not cook rice." Chinese proverb.

It was on the second of January that Bridget and Sandy met again for the first time since the opening of Martyrs halls. Traditionally a Scottish Holiday, both were impelled to work. Sandy was now too busy to think of taking the whole New Year's break, while Bridget was burning with the urgent need to find a meeting place for her tiny flock. She drove through Cupar to the Bow of Fife, blind to the frosty beauty of the morning, hoping only to find some indication that the old church was still available "For Sale or Let."

When she arrived the first thing that she saw was that the hoarding had vanished from in front of the building. Did that mean it was taken? Or had the authorities simply given up trying to get rid of it? Getting out of her car, and finding the gate locked, she climbed over the low wall and tramped through the overgrown grounds. Frozen twigs and the bareness of winter bracken left frost dust against her legs, and once she turned her ankle on the pitted, iron-hard ground.

When she reached the building she noted there was a broken window and took this to be a hopeful sign. Surely any new owners would mend this first thing. Then she realised that the door was standing slightly ajar. She pushed it and was surprised by the noiseless ease with which it swung open.

Inside there was almost a sense of déjà vu. There, sitting a few steps from the bottom of the magnificent staircase was Sandy, wrapped up against the cold, a pad and pencil unused in his hands and his eyes blank with visions. For a couple of minutes Bridget stood still, taking in the simple dilapidated grandeur of the place, and wondering at Sandy's presence here. Then suddenly he sneezed, shivered, and looked around him with eyes once more shrewd and present.

"Bridget!" His surprise was obvious. For a moment he stared at her then he chuckled. "You have a habit of walking in on the artist at work."

"Sorry," she replied.

"That's all right. It was my silly nose disturbed me, not you."

"If you're working, I suppose that means this place has been bought?"

"That's right. I'm to make a home from it." His tone was deliberately light-hearted, although his mind was filled with speculative questions. Why was she here? What was she doing these days? What had she done to hurt Joyce? Could he get her story out of her? Was she still sane?

"A house! Oh, but you won't destroy these lovely stairs or the pulpit, will you?"

"Not the stairs, no. The pulpit – well, I was thinking about the pulpit when you came in. I don't want to destroy it, or even take it out and sell it. It belongs here. But the new owners don't want to keep a structure with no purpose. What can it be used for?"

Bridget bent her mind to the problem, anything but think about her own disappointment. "Add some shutters and make it a cupboard?" she suggested. "Or how about a puppet theatre? Fill it with water and make a waterfall into the sitting-room."

"Possibly. I hadn't thought about a theatre or a pool, though I don't know that my clients are into puppets."

"But it should really be preached from." Bridget's voice was passionate and tense.

"That's why you're here." It was a statement. "You wanted to find a church you could use."

"Yes, but I can't. Not this one anyway, not now it's sold. It's a shame. It was never meant to be a house, it's a church. It would be perfect for my congregation. We can't go on meeting in houses: they don't give the feel of a church. I know the place doesn't matter, but it does to them, and they left Martyrs church because they trusted my lead. I have to find a place for them." The eyes she turned on him glittered in the cold sunshine. "You don't know of any other church buildings near here?"

"No. And," said Sandy, bluntly, "I don't understand you. If having a church and a church building is so important, why did you leave Martyrs? You used to be so full of hopes and plans for its future."

"Of course, you're not a believer: you couldn't understand." Bridget spun around and disappeared through the doorway. Sandy heard her stumbling over the undergrowth, then a car door slammed, an engine was revved up, and gradually the holiday stillness returned. For Sandy the calm was gone, however. He was afraid, afraid for Bridget, for what she might do or discover, achieve, or fail to manage.

All the same, a water feature might be a real possibility. With the height of the pulpit it could be a focus on two floors, flowing form one level to the other. It was an idea worth playing with. Sandy headed back to his warm office and his drawing board. Now that he thought about it, he realised that he was numb with cold.

Three weeks later the phone-call came. For Sandy they had been busy weeks, but happy. He had managed to complete stunning designs for the Bow of Fife church, designs that included a T-shaped upper landing, stretching from the double staircase to the pulpit. A waterfall trickled from the pulpit to the hallway below. There were ways in which the wood could be made impervious to water, and the crystal flow would highlight the delicate carving admirably, with maybe some gentle hidden lighting to add to the effect. Various rooms would open off the upper landing, while the ground floor, apart from the cloakroom and utility room, would be fully open plan. These designs were enthusiastically received by Sandy's clients. Moreover his barn conversion had reached the point of actual building work being done, while the community hall had involved him increasingly with committee work. In his activity he had almost forgotten his conversation with Bridget, or that she had given him the idea for the pulpit.

So he was completely taken aback when one day his office phone rang and a high-pitched voice declared, "Sandy, I want you to know that you were right. You're not a believer, so how did you know? But you were right."

The words were run together at speed and Sandy had to ask, "Who is this please?"

"It's Bridget. Bridget, Reverend McKay. But you were right. A church and a church building. And I gave them up. Now who am I? What have I got? But I thought you would like to know that you were right."

The phone was hung up.

Worried, Sandy reached for a phone directory and dialled the number for Martyrs manse. There was no reply. There was no phone number listed for the church and he remembered that he's never seen any sign of a phone about the place. Anyway, she wouldn't be at Martyrs, would she? Well, he would get hold of Ian. He was a teacher – primary, if memory served. Looking up the Fife Educational Authority in the directory he discovered three primary schools in St. Andrews. As luck would have it, he tried both Lawhead and Langlands before he got the secretary of the Cannongate school. She informed him that Ian was with his class, in a voice which implied 'end of story.' Clearly she was about to hang up.

"This is important," said Sandy quickly and forcibly. "It is family business which can't wait. I must speak with him."

The secretary coughed unhelpfully. "I will see what I can do, but it may take some time. His class must not be left alone, and it is no part of my work to sit with them."

Sandy was sure the children were glad of that.

It did take 'some time'. It was fully ten minutes before a breathless voice said, "Ian McKay here."

"Ian, this is Sandy Melville, the architect. I've just had your wife on the phone. She sounds completely distraught and I'm very worried about her. I tried your home number but got no reply. She wasn't phoning from a call-box. Do you know where she could be? She needs help."

The tense sentences conveyed Sandy's urgency. To Ian's over-sensitive ears they conveyed more. Shame, never far from him these days, engulfed him once more.

"I don't know where she is. I haven't seen her since Sunday. That's two days. She could be anywhere. I'm just trying to keep the children going and find us a place to live. We have to move out of the manse soon." The monotone died away.

"Ian," Sandy was insistent. "This is serious. Where might she go? Think man, you've got to think."

There was a pause.

"She might go to her parents, I suppose. They live in Edinburgh." He gave the number. Can you phone them? If she's not there, how can I admit I've lost their daughter?"

"How can you keep them in ignorance of this crisis in her life?" Sandy retorted. "Yes, all right, I'll phone them. Don't go back to your class. I'll phone again in a few minutes."

He hung up too quickly for Ian to protest that with his class was where he should be.

Ten minutes later the school phone rang again.

"She's there." Sandy was abrupt.

"And is she all right?" Ian questioned.

"That depends. I spoke to her mother. She said Bridget is very tired."

"Which I can well believe," put in Ian.

"Yes. And a good rest and a return to the true faith is what she needs. That's a quotation: 'Rest and a return to the true faith.' It's Greek to me."

Ian sighed, his breath hissing over the phone lines. "It's not Greek to me. It's what she left behind when she joined the Church of Scotland. I'm a fool not to have seen that all her behaviour of late has had her up-bringing shining through it. I don't think her parents' home is the best place for her, but at least she's safe. You were afraid she would harm herself, weren't you?"

"Yes." Sandy was brief.

"Thank you for getting in touch. I'll have to go and see her."

"Let me know how it goes, won't you?"

"I owe you that. Thanks, Melville."

Ian knew he couldn't take the children to Edinburgh. Goodness only knew in what state he would find their mother, and he wanted to protect them as far as possible. But who could babysit? There were many church people who had always said they would, but that was then. Sandy had managed to shake Ian up but not to dispel his sense of shame: it was alive and well and able to transfer itself to any part of his life at a moment's notice. He couldn't turn to the church for help because then they would know that Bridget had run away from him. If Miss Murdoch had been alive, he might have turned to her: she had been a woman who knew how to keep her own counsel, but there was no use thinking of that now. Even as the memory of Miss Murdoch passed across Ian's mind, he thought of Joyce. What Bridget would conclude if she heard of this didn't bear thinking about, but perhaps she needn't know. In any case, a baby-sitter must be found soon. Ian knew nothing of Joyce's experiences of the past month, and so saw nothing surprising in the calm way she expressed herself willing to help when asked.

As he drove to Edinburgh, he reflected on what he knew of Bridget's up-bringing. Her parents were deeply religious people and church was their life. It was the centre of their energy, bringing a social element into their days as they participated in Bible Studies and organisational committees, as well as being a source of spiritual nurture and teaching. It was no Church of Scotland which they attended, but an independent congregation, founded by a group which had broken away from a traditional church. Mr and Mrs Wallace had been a young married couple when the split occurred and so their emotional attachment to the group ran deep.

It was a conservative group. Little had changed since the mid-fifties, when it was established. Preaching a 'gospel' message was central to worship, and success was counted by the number who came forward to the weekly 'altar calls'. Women had no place in governing this church, or in leading worship. They might, and did, serve as caterers, cleaners, flower arrangers and Sunday School teachers, but that was all. Decisions were made by men. It was not the sort of place where one could drop in on a Sunday morning just as the mood took you. Worship was a formal affair for which one dressed. Anything else was seen as disrespectful to the Almighty. Nor was worship something one came to once in a while. Membership was taken seriously, and member or not, if someone who had been a regular attender (having perhaps been present at three services in a row) failed to turn up, enquiries to their health were put out. Again, the Almighty deserved regular worship, whether you felt like it or not. Worship was not for the benefit of the people in the pews, but a discipline reflecting God's importance.

In this church the old-fashioned taboos were still strongly in force. Not just the relational taboos on pre-marital sex, homosexuality, and the like, but also the sinfulness of smoking, drinking, dancing, and playing cards (gambling) were hammered home.

Bridget had broken away from it all before Ian met her, but she had talked about it often. She had regarded her joining the established church as a great escape and had never experienced the bounds of Presbyterianism as anything other than real freedom. She had delighted in the structure of the system and in the differences between churches which were yet united under one denominational rule.

Her parents had not been happy at her desertion from their brand of faith. They had never refused to be present at the important events of her ministry: Graduation, ordination, inauguration into a new charge, but there was no parental delight in the unfolding of a daughter's life. Bridget had always felt the need to be circumspect in what she told her parents, lest a complaint over some difficulty bring forth the idea that this would never happen in their church.

Ian felt he had been blind and foolish not to see the seeds of her upbringing in her fevered work of the past few months. The exclusivism, the paramount importance given to preaching, and the very content of these sermons had all told of it. The simplistic spiritualising of life's experiences both in preaching and in conversation pointed to it. If Ian had had more direct exposure to his in-laws' church himself, he might have seen it sooner; but as a minister's family, visits never took place on Sunday, so most of his knowledge was second-hand only.

And it was to this environment that Bridget had fled when, presumably, it all became too much for her. Like a child she had run home. Ian wondered what were his chances of getting her to leave that crippling security and risk the reality of the world again. He was far from hopeful. Why should she even listen to him? He was her husband, but she thought him unworthy.

This thought inevitably led him back to Joyce, whom he was accused of loving. It wasn't true, but he did admire her and enjoy her company. Admiration had been strong today. She had been calm on receipt of his panicked phone-call and had been cheerfully normal when she arrived to look after the children. "Do they know about Bridget?" was her question, and she had agreed to abide by the half-truth that Mummy had gone to Granny's for a rest, and Daddy was going to see her. Ian had been full of nervous instructions about supper and bed and household organisation, but Joyce swept this aside.

"Mairi and Angus know all about that, and they'll tell me. Off you go, and don't worry about us." There had been a new quickness about Joyce today. If this was how she rose to cope with a crisis then Ian's admiration of her soared to new heights.

By now he was driving through the Edinburgh streets, empty of people after the busyness of the day. He skirted Holyrood Park and the University and drove down the broad streets to Liberton. On either side glowed the pink, yellow, green, or blue windows of middle-class houses and flats, all keeping the world at bay with carefully drawn curtains. Only occasionally could Ian glimpse the interior of a brightly lit room, and these were invariably empty. Occupied rooms were discreetly veiled.

Now the final traffic light turned green, and he was turning into the street and nosing along, looking for a place to park among the cars which lined up nose to tail along both sides of the road. Finally, Ian threw caution to the winds and drew up in a bus stop. Number 25 was brightly lit, every window shining opaquely a different colour. Something was going on.

Getting out of the car, Ian slipped on the icy pavement. He didn't fall, but the incident did not help his frame of mind. More than ever he felt a fool. But a determined fool, he reminded himself, as he rang the doorbell.

Mrs Wallace could be seen through the frosted glass of the inner front door. She hurried forward, trilling, "Come in, come in," in her brightest manner. The door was opened. For a moment Ian saw the most warm and welcoming smile on her face, and then it was gone, sponged off like the chalk from a blackboard, and leaving as little trace.

"Ian. I had no idea you were coming."

"Bridget is here, isn't she?" asked Ian.

"Yes, of course. Oh dear, you'd better come in. The thing is, Bridget's busy this evening. You should have warned us you were coming, you really should."

"I thought Bridget was here for a rest. What is making her busy? Perhaps, after all, she could rest better at home." Ian was sparring now, hoping to find out how much of their personal affairs Mrs Wallace knew.

"Don't be silly and don't pretend." The older woman spoke severely. With her stature and despite the lines on her face, Ian could see Bridget as she might be in years to come. Suddenly he realised how very important it was that he should know her and have her in his life between now and then. With that realisation came the concomitant knowledge that he was in great danger of losing his marriage altogether. If that happened he would lose Bridget and, quite possibly, Mairi and Angus as well. The idea took his beath away and he steeled himself to fight.

"I know perfectly well that you haven't been getting on," Mrs Wallace was saying. "Bridget feels betrayed by you, Ian, and as her mother I must say I'm bound to view you with some suspicion. However, you are her husband, so I will tell you that we have a prayer meeting here tonight. Naturally Bridget will be attending. You are welcome to do so yourself, but you may not otherwise see her until it is all over. She needs spiritual strength if she is to speak with you."

There was no venom in the woman's tones. The poison she spoke seemed to her a matter of common-sense expediency. These were her priorities and these her natural assumptions. She had no insight to realise that they might not be shared by all the sensible world. Ian considered carefully.

"Thank you," he said. "I should be glad to come to the meeting."

There were about twenty people gathered in the Wallace's sitting-room, so that as Ian glanced around looking for Bridget, at first he didn't see her. But there she was, sitting by the velvet curtains which masked the stately Victorian bay window. Her thinness and pallor were heightened by curtains' hideous shade of green, which reflected onto her face and hair from the light behind her head. She did not look up as he came in, and Ian knew that she had not been told of his arrival. The sitting-room was upstairs, after the manner of these houses, and conversation by the door would not be audible above, especially given that the other occupants of the room all seemed to be talking at once.

They were a mixture of people, old and young (although no children or adolescents were present), male and female, even black and white – there were a couple of Kenyans present. They were a mixture, a variety, but what struck Ian at first was not heterogeneity but homogeny. They seemed startlingly similar. It was a similarity expressed most obviously in dress. Not that there was anything approaching a uniform, but these people were all dressed in conservative, clean, casual clothes. The younger people wore jeans and sweaters, the jeans pressed into knife-edge creases, the sweaters in shining bright colours. The older people, men and women, wore slacks and lambswool jumpers in pastel colours. Most of the women wore jewellery while apart from an occasional wedding ring, none of the men were in any way bedizened.

The homogeny extended from dress to expression. All of these people were cheerful. They were not merry or raucous; they were not exuberant nor elated: they were cheerful. No face frowned or looked sad, yet no face beamed more brightly than any other. The careful regularity of expression, far more conscious than any similarity of apparel, extended to the intangible mood in the room, which was one of disciplined, hopeful expectancy.

Ian wondered what of this Bridget had picked up. Was it by accident or design that she sat slightly apart from the others? She alone was silent and unsmiling, and this circumstance was more noticeable because of the foil with which she was provided. Watching her, Ian's heart was wrung with love and pity as it had not been since first he knew her. Then these emotions had sometimes been called forth by her gallant battling to put her up-bringing behind her and taste her freedom. Now the contrast could not have been greater. To Ian's eyes she seemed defeated.

The meeting began with prayer. Mr Wallace, tall, balding, grey-haired, and slightly stooped, thanked the Almighty for His presence, for their "including those who are not usually part of this group," for their confident expectation that the deity would speak with them and for their assurance of salvation.

After this there was singing. The songs awoke memories in Ian: memories of the Sunday School he had attended as a child. Singing over, Mr Wallace read a passage of Scripture: John's Gospel chapter ten. "*Very truly I tell you anyone who does not enter the sheepfold by the gate but climbs in by another way is a thief and a bandit.... He calls his own sheep by name and leads them out... They will not follow a stranger... Whoever comes in by me will be saved... I am the good shepherd, I know my own and my own know me... I have received this command from my Father.*"

Now Mr Wallace addressed the company. "As many of you know, my daughter Bridget left the fold, tried to climb the wall. She has been wandering in the desert for some time now, but the Good Shepherd has been merciful and called her. When we pray, I ask that we pray for her and give thanks for her salvation."

Ian looked across at his wife. Bridget's head was bowed, her eyes cast down, her cheeks scarlet with – what? Shame? Embarrassment? Anger? Contrition? He realised he had no idea. He knew he ought to save her from this. He was her husband. He loved her. He should rise up and remove her from this phantom of her past which now threatened to re-engulf her. He should. But then, he should also have made an effort to communicate with her for the past four months or more. He should have fought to keep in touch with her on her journey of faith and conviction. He should have been less angry and more sympathetic. He should have been able to find her here without Sandy's help. Sandy, a comparative stranger, had shown Bridget more concern than he. It was to Sandy she had telephoned when at breaking point. All these recriminations swept over Ian and he, like Bridget, lowered his eyes and felt hot blood rush to his cheeks.

Now the psychological moment had passed, the fervent praying had begun, and the meeting would unfold in its normal pattern, unhindered.

It was almost ten thirty when the intercessors sang a final hymn and left. In all this time Bridget had neither opened her lips nor raised her eyes.

"Very well, Ian, we'll leave you with her now," said Mrs Wallace. Only then did the curly head fly up and startled red-rimmed blue eyes met Ian's from across the room.

"Ian, how long have you been here?" She sounded very much herself, and Ian took heart.

"I arrived just when they were about to start. Your mother thought you would rather attend the meeting before we spoke."

Bridget raised her eyebrows. "Oh, did she?" she commented, dryly. "And what did you think?"

Ian looked embarrassed. "Well, I wasn't sure either way, not really. I've never been to your parents' meetings, remember. I didn't know it would be like that." He tailed off.

"No," Bridget spoke quietly. "I suppose you weren't to know what to expect. But didn't you hear them, Ian? Did you hear my father? I am a lost sheep, you know. Did you hear the others? I am to repent of thwarting God's will and wantonly insisting on ordination. Apparently I have discovered the futility of selfish behaviour. I am to accept my humbling as from Christ. I am to be meek. I am to submit. I am to be prayed at and talked at and interpreted to myself until I don't know who I am. Didn't you hear them?" Her voice rose louder.

"I heard them."

"Then why did you let them? Why didn't you stop them? Why didn't you get me away from them?" She was crying now, sitting huddled once more and letting the tears course down her crumpled face. Choking on sobs she whispered, "You're my husband. How could you let them do that to me?"

Silence fell. For the first time Ian was acutely aware of his comfortable surroundings: the deep red carpet, the yielding chairs and sofas, small antique tables, bookshelves filled with hardbacks, and in one corner a stately grandfather clock, now noisily telling the passing seconds.

"I don't know. I've been asking myself that. I've been a poor sort of husband. I'm sorry." He too was on the verge of tears. His voice quavered.

Bridget looked up at him and saw his distress. Her voice was a little stronger. "You've not been the best husband lately, no. I suppose I've been a poor wife too. I can't really tell. But now, Ian, you can't help me. I think you want to, but you can't. I need someone to bring me out of this, and though I know I still love you, it can't be you. I'm sorry."

Ian bowed his head in acquiescence as his interior voice told him he deserved no better. "Who can help you, do you know?" he asked.

Bridget shrugged her shoulders. Again there was a pause. "At least come home with me," Ian begged. "Think of the children."

"I am thinking of them. They shouldn't see me like this. No, I'll stay for a while." Suddenly Bridget stood up and came over to her husband. "How did you find me?"

"Sandy Melville tried to return your phone call, got no answer at home and tracked me down at work. I suggested you might be here, and he phoned to find out. Whatever you said to him this morning really shocked him, Bridget."

"Sandy. Sandy might help me. Can you ask Sandy to come and see me please, Ian?" She turned away from him again. "Now you'd better get back. Who's babysitting?"

"Joyce."

Bridget froze. Then she said angrily, "As I said you'd better get back. I can't come. Send Sandy if he will come here. I'll be in touch when I'm ready."

Ian left, driving home in greater perturbation of spirit than before. Joyce greeted him with the news that his sister had telephoned to say his mother had died early that evening.

Sandy received the message at work the next day, indeed, he heard more from Ian than he either wanted or needed.

"Sandy, this is Ian. My mother has died. I wasn't there and she died. I didn't even know it was likely to be soon. She's gone, my mother, the most wonderful woman in the world. My God, Sandy, I'm one of the older generation in my family now – and I'm just on forty. Do you know how that feels?"

"No," Sandy slipped in an answer quickly, and before Ian could draw breath he continued, "How about Bridget? Did you see her? Or did the news about your mother stop you?"

"I saw her. I should have been driving north to be with Mum, but I didn't know that, so I went to Edinburgh. Bridget wants to see you. She said she couldn't come home with me yet, but she would like to see you."

After Ian eventually rang off, Sandy found himself alarmed about another member of the McKay household. Ian seemed to have gone to pieces and sounded completely wretched. Sandy rightly assumed that this was because of the news about his mother, but not knowing how it felt to worship the woman who brought you into the world, and not knowing what Ian had endured the night before he was inclined to think that the older man was a bit of a jellyfish. He needed some self-respect, Sandy thought, that would give him backbone. However, he had assured Ian that he would do all that he could, so he leaned back in his chair and gazed unseeingly out of the window. It seemed that he was always being cast in the role of rescuer these days. He had had Joyce thrust upon him by Tam, the barman. That had turned out all right so far. At least he and Joyce were talking, though she had yet to help him understand why Bridget's actions had affected her so deeply; and that reticence and her unspoken gratitude to him put barriers in place, as seemingly impregnable as any they had built with absence and mutual pride. Now Bridget had summoned him, and he was also finding himself wondering how to rescue Ian. It was too much. He had better go and see Bridget, he supposed, but Ian had not asked for his help, and he was a grown man. He could help himself or find someone else.

Meanwhile, what about Bridget? Sandy was shaken by a brief description of the prayer meeting which Ian had managed to give him, it was so far beyond any religion he had encountered. Well, he couldn't, he simply couldn't go today. Tomorrow evening was the earliest he could make himself free.

So next evening saw Sandy in his bashed old Mini driving to Edinburgh. The Mini was a sign of his former poverty rather than his burgeoning affluence. One day soon he should get a newer, larger car, he thought. Rattling up to sites or meetings in this tin can couldn't really inspire confidence in potential employers or fellow-workers. A middle-range Fiat might be nice, or even a smaller Rover. With an effort Sandy wrenched his mind back to the matter at hand. Bridget, he reminded himself now, how to help Bridget.

But he still had no idea how this was to be accomplished. She was the one who made helping people her business, not him, not until lately it had been forced on him. How would Bridget help someone in her position? But he didn't know. He had never seen that side of her and realised that giving psychological or spiritual help (he wasn't sure of the boundaries there) must essentially be such a private matter that few could witness it. Bridget was a minister, so presumably she prayed about things. He found himself wishing he could pray about it; that he knew an appropriate form of words, and that he had faith enough to believe that it would help. To bring a human being out of chaos and despair and help them find a pattern in their world was such a responsibility. "God, help me!" he exclaimed aloud, unthinkingly.

He smiled. There was his prayer, he did know the words it seemed, and it had prayed itself. Faith or no faith he couldn't take it back now. Just as he couldn't really prepare to meet Bridget because he had no idea what he would find. Motorway signs indicated the approach of the Forth Road Bridge and neon lights flashed to warn him that he might find its surface icy. Sandy concentrated on his driving.

Bridget herself opened the door of the house and Sandy's first impression was of welcome. Steeling himself for anything as he had been, this came as a great relief, and immediately he relaxed. Looking again at Bridget as she sat opposite him in the first-floor sitting room, he decided that she was even thinner than at their last meeting. Her blue jeans hung loose and her jumper seemed too large for her, while her formerly rounded, dimpled cheeks showed slight hollows under the cheekbones.

The silence lasted a bit too long, and like Ian, Sandy was aware of the ticking of the grandfather clock. Bridget was looking at him expectantly. He cleared his throat.

"How are you, Bridget?" Bland, conventional stuff, mocked an inner voice. Surely she wouldn't say Fine.

"You know I'm not doing very well, Sandy." Her voice was level. "Thank you for coming to help me. You have come to help, I suppose?"

"If I can. But to be honest, Bridget, I don't see what I can do. I don't share your faith, and I don't understand the religious life. I don't know what happened to you."

"That's why I wanted you, Sandy, because of what you don't know, and because you care. You found out where I was – Ian told me. You made him find out too. He hadn't bothered."

"If you're going to start comparing me with Ian I'm leaving now," Sandy warned. "He's your husband, and he's had more than enough to cope with of late, what with you having a crisis, and now his mother dying."

Bridget ignored this last piece of news. "He's my husband and he loves me, just as I love him, but he's too close to help me. He can't help thinking about how what I do affects him. He's right to, of course. But you're not really personally involved. I can trust you to be impartial and listen. Oh, Sandy, I need to talk. I need someone to listen, to really hear me. I may want your advice, but I do want your intelligent ear."

"What do you want to say, Bridget. Go ahead. I hear you."

Again there was silence. This time Sandy was determined not to break it. A coal fell out of the fire, and he bent to take the tongs and replace it. While he was doing so Bridget began to speak.

"That's like me, that coal. I've fallen out of the fire and I need someone to come along with tongs and put me back." She laughed bitterly. "No, I'm not dramatizing myself, just making an analogy, and a pretty corny, hackneyed one at that. It's a habit we ministers have, you know. And whatever my parents say, and whatever I've done, I'm still a preacher. You don't have to be good or faithful to be able to preach."

"Naturally," commented Sandy. "It's a question of intelligence, nerve and dramatic ability isn't it?"

Again that bitter laugh. "Yes, it is. It's harder than straightforward acting though, because you have to write the script yourself and hold people's interest even though you are giving a message. I think it used to be easier than nowadays. Being a minister – a man of the cloth – was a respected position in society, not too badly paid nor too hardly worked. Do you know, Sandy, when the parish system began it averaged out at one priest for four hundred people. Now it's more like one to ten thousand, in some places even more. I was lucky: I only had four thousand or so in my parish."

Her voice lost some of its bitterness and some of her old enthusiasm returned as she spoke about the work in abstract. Obviously it was still dear to her.

"Nowadays – what was it? 'Intelligence, nerve and dramatic ability' aren't enough. Now that people are more reluctant to listen you will find that almost all minsters have a deeply personal faith. We don't all have the same faith, even though we're all Christian. But now that it's not such a desirable job, with average pay, long hours and so on, no one could stick it who hadn't been touched by the whole thing – message – church – or whatever in some deeply personal way."

"Where did it touch you?" Sandy found he was fascinated.

Bridget shrugged. "Oh, lots of ways. When I was a child here I heard a lot about Jesus' redeeming work on the cross. I knew I wasn't always a good girl, and the promise of forgiveness went deep. I remember how very comforted I could feel lying in bed and reminding myself that although my parents scolded, God forgave.

"And then I grew up a bit and began to question the rigidity of my parents' faith. I never doubted the basic tenets of it – God's love, Christ's redeeming death and so on – but I wondered about being so far out of the world. You don't know their church, of course, but believe me, you'd think they lived on a desert island for all the notice they take of Edinburgh and its problems. They don't even support foreign missions, as you'd expect from such a group, unless one of their own congregation goes overseas. They say 'We don't know if he's sound' of everyone else. And yes, they mean he.

"At university I studied Divinity, though my parents couldn't see why – unless I was going to teach Religious Education. But you see, even living in this environment I had felt the urge – or call – to preach. I'd never had a chance to try, but I knew I could do it, and that I should do it. I can't describe how I knew, but you'll understand that with my up-bringing it was a very powerful knowing: after all, I was programmed to reject the idea.

"After my first year of studies, I joined the Church of Scotland, moved away from home and met Ian in a social action group. I applied to be a minister. Some people have difficulty getting the Kirk to accept their call, but everything went smoothly for me. I was a candidate and attached as a student to various churches. Then I was a Probationer, and then a full minister. Martyrs was my second church. I enjoyed my work. I enjoyed the contact with people. I was allowed into their deepest joys and sorrows. I offered consolation and counsel which people found helpful. I preached sermons which they said were challenging and inspirational. I thought I understood people."

"And you didn't?"

"Apparently not. You see, there was Miss Murdoch. I really

thought we spoke the same language of faith. I thought she was a devout old lady, sustained by her love of the Lord. But reading her diaries it turns out she was either involved in some sociological study or a covert Hindu." Bridget squeaked in genuine outrage.

"And then I found I couldn't trust Ian. He was seeing Joyce behind my back, and maybe it was harmless, but it was still, as I say, behind my back. But, I thought, I can still trust God. I had another moment of certainty and assurance in the kitchen last summer. It seemed God was saying that in the face of everyone's duplicity, I must preach His trustworthiness. So I did. I felt filled with new Spirit-led energy, and I preached as never before. And people came and kept coming. It was so exciting. And as the church grew it seemed that God was telling me to change the way it was organised. But Presbytery didn't like that. I spent whole days in prayer over the matter, then it seemed I must pull out of presbytery. I thought the church would follow me, but they didn't. You see, in the end, even God deceived me. Or I deceived myself.

"Either way, I was wrong to leave. And now how can I trust any of the ways God has spoken to me before? How can I know it's not self-delusion? And why am I asking you this? You're not a man of faith, anyway."

Sandy was stung by this. "Bridget, you are one of the most arrogant people of my acquaintance," he thundered. The firelight glowed rosily in his face and sparked in his angry eyes. It was hardly the reaction Bridget had been expecting, and her temper rose to meet his.

"Arrogant! How can you say that? Haven't I been humiliating myself telling you all about my bad decisions, my doubts and my disappointments?"

The alliteration was unconscious, and Sandy smiled grimly. The ring of the pulpit could not be kept at bay.

“Arrogant,” he repeated, quietly. “Not consciously, I’m sure, but arrogant none the less. If you could hear yourself with my ears you’d recognise it at once. As that’s impossible, let me explain.

“It seems to me that you are your own only touchstone. You talk of how your religion touches or has touched your life. Now that’s important. I can see that, even though I’m not a ‘man of faith.’ Incidentally, that’s another arrogance. You insist on setting yourself against me because of this, as if we had nothing in common. I would contend that our common humanity is more of a bond than any religious difference which divides us. Your experience is human experience. So is mine. Yes, I may not have the faith you have, but that isn’t to say I am so alien – and you seem to imply inferior – that I can’t empathise with your faith. I know what it is to have important things in life and lose them.

“However, that’s by the way. In all your long telling you never gave any indication that you took other people into your consideration. It was all you and God, God and you. Now I’m not qualified to judge the validity of your religious experiences. Valid or not, they took you where you should be. You were a good minister, Bridget. You fit that role in society. If your religious experiences took you there, then you have reason to believe in them. If I were in your shoes, I certainly wouldn’t jettison them whenever you hit a small hurdle in your triumphant procession through life.

“That’s what you’ve done. You seem to expect life to be laid out before you like a plush red carpet along which you can stroll at ease. You’ve had it remarkably easy up till now, but it seems you haven’t the character to negotiate a small hazard on the way. You reject the whole thing rather than do that.

“Well, you can’t do that, Bridget. You haven’t the right.”

She would have interrupted him, but he swept on.

"Other people may have the freedom to chop and change in their careers and their lives, but you don't. You have acted, as I said, in arrogance, because you have forgotten that you are a priest."

"I'm not!" Bridget burst out, finally getting a word in. "I'm a minister."

"Is there a real difference?" Sandy was polite but caustic.

"Yes, there is. A priest's function is to stand between God and the people as a channel or an intermediary. A minister is a servant, smoothing the way for the people to come to God directly. There's a great difference."

"Theologically, maybe, but practically, not really." Not in terms of what I'm talking about. Minister or Priest, what you do affects your congregation. If you up and leave suddenly, then many people are hurt."

"It looked like it, didn't it? Hardly anyone came with me. Not even Joyce."

"Joyce?" Sandy was startled. Suddenly he saw the answer to a puzzle. "Bridget, had Joyce taken to coming to your church?"

"Yes, off and on since Easter and quite faithfully from about the time I received my special anointing."

"The summer?"

"Yes."

"The time when you began to lose faith in people because of Miss Murdoch's diaries?"

"Yes, from about then. Of course, because of Ian and the diaries we weren't as friendly as we had been, but she kept coming."

"Well, that explains it." Sandy was completely matter-of-fact. "You walked out of church a couple of weeks before Christmas?"

"Yes."

"And later that week I found Joyce completely gone to pieces, burbling about betrayal and linking her mother, me, and you in her accusations. I know how I betrayed her – or how she thought I had – and I know a little about her mother. But what about you?"

"I know about her mother. She read Joyce's diary when she was a teenager. But I haven't betrayed Joyce."

"You may not think so, but she does. She'd taken some kind of drugs when I found her – oh not deliberately, but she'd been upset enough to go to the kind of place where drugs were given to her against her knowledge. She's been living on the edge of stress for a long time and coping – just. It's no coincidence that she looked for something to distract her –if not what she found – the week that her friend and minister showed her that she didn't care. And if Joyce, what about others? Those who have known you longer, whom you have helped through hard times. Maybe now they wonder if it was all sham. Maybe they question if there was ever reality behind your words. It could be that their worlds are fast collapsing into the crater hole left by their minister's arrogance and dishonesty."

"Is Joyce all right?"

"It would seem so. She had a very bad reaction, but she's over it, physically at any rate. I think the whole thing's left her shaken."

"The drugs you mean."

"I mean the whole thing. I don't know what truths or questions she was living with this past year. We haven't been acknowledging each other, as you probably know, and Joyce is a very private person. A friend may know a little of what's been on her mind, but even a friend can't know very much. But you have been a part of this thing that has shaken her. Don't try to isolate yourself from it."

"I wasn't."

"O.K., perhaps not this time." Sandy stood up. "I must go. I have to work long hours tomorrow." He smiled briefly. "That's partly thanks to you as well. You put me in the way of getting the contract that set me up. You are involved, Bridget. You have to see it. You mustn't deny or forget it again."

"Yes, you must go." For the past few minutes a stubborn look had been creeping over Bridget's worn face. Now her back straightened and her voice was full of scorn. "I don't know why I thought you could help me, but I certainly didn't think I'd have to be so insulted by you. Goodbye."

"Goodbye, Bridget, for now. I know why you wanted my help. It was because I was right last time, remember? You phoned and told me so."

He closed the door quietly behind him and slipped noiselessly down the stairs. There was no sound in the house as he let himself out. At the garden gate he turned and looked back. As he watched, the sitting-room light was extinguished.

Sandy was tired. He felt rather extinguished himself. As he drove off he turned on the car radio. The undemanding music of Radio Two accompanied his weary, unthinking drive home.

CHAPTER THRITEEN: GOING FORWARD

The bonds that unite another person to ourselves exist only in our mind"

Marcel Proust "Remembrance of Things Past: The Sweet Cheat Gone"

Translated by C.K. Scott-Moncrieff

It was a week later. January had blown out and February had revealed a deceitfully smiling face upon the world. Shoppers making conversation as they bought life's luxuries and necessities were often heard to offer a pious hope that this good weather augured an early spring. The more sanguine and weather-wise shook their heads at such folly. There was no such thing as an early spring, old Mr Melville asserted. Any good weather so early in the year would have to be paid for later. That was how it worked. And people who'd lived all their lives in Fife might be expected to be used to the climate. That was what came of taking foreign holidays, and in the winter too. You got out of touch with your own climate and seasons.

Sandy heard him with a grin. More than the sun was shining in Sandy's life just then. His work continued to be absorbing and plentiful and he was on his way out to see Joyce that evening. This would be his third visit since Christmas, and each time they met he was struck by the change in her. She was more sure of herself, yet quieter. She listened better and no longer had to analyse absolutely everything before accepting it. It seemed hard to believe that one dodgy encounter with drugs could have wrought such change – if it had, then psychologists would begin prescribing them wholesale. Sandy had to assume that the events of the year they had been apart had mellowed and matured Joyce. To be sure, the narcotics episode – as only partially understood by Sandy – didn't bear this out, but increasingly he was beginning to think that had been the swan-song of the old Joyce. He longed to know what had happened to change her, but he couldn't ask. Instinct told him that if Joyce thought he needed to know she would tell him in her own time.

He reflected on all this again as he drove the nine miles from Cupar to St. Andrews. Getting to know Joyce all over again was like seeing the flower the bud had become or the moth that had been a caterpillar. He smiled as the clichés passed through his mind. Never mind similes, it was enough to know that he liked Joyce, and now she seemed less dependent on him, he found himself as fascinated as ever by the woman he was going to see.

The gas fire was sputtering in the old grate, just as it always had, but the piles of papers seemed more orderly than before. There was a sense of purpose about them, and Sandy knew that Joyce must be working hard at her thesis. However when he walked over to the table where she sat and whence her cheerful "Come in!" had sounded, it was to a feeling of déjà vu. Joyce was engrossed in reading, and the volume before her was unmistakable as one of Miss Murdoch's diaries. She looked up at him brightly.

"Oh Sandy," she had switched from Alex at his request, "Look what I have here."

"One of these diaries." He didn't return her smile and his tones were heavy. Joyce was surprised.

"You don't like them, do you? Why not?"

"It's not the diaries as objects I feel antipathy towards," he replied slowly, "But seeing you reading them. I always thought they should be left unread, but Miss Murdoch herself thought otherwise. I'm sure she didn't mean to cause all the trouble she has but nevertheless it happened."

"What trouble?"

"Joyce! Think! The trouble with Bridget, of course. When I saw her in Edinburgh she told me that discovering Miss Murdoch's real motives for coming to church was one of the things which undermined her confidence in herself as a minister. She left the ministry she loved and then suffered a break-down of some kind. That was triggered, if not directly caused, by reading these diaries."

"It was triggered. It was waiting to happen sometime. I can't be sorry we read them, Sandy, they've taught me so much. Charlotte Murdoch became more than a friend to me; she became a mentor. She pointed me the way to go, and though I have a long way to travel still, I'm on the right road now."

"What are you talking about?" asked Sandy, in genuine bewilderment.

"Why, about Christ, of course. Church, Christianity, and Christ himself. She pointed me to the church and the rest follows from there." She saw Sandy's face and faltered a little. "I thought you knew I was going to church these days."

"To church, yes. I didn't realise there was more to it than that.

"What would be the point in going otherwise?" asked Joyce simply. "it's not straightforward. There are things I can't get my head around or swallow unthinkingly, but it's making sense for me, Sandy. You might say it's making sense of me.

Don't you see a change?"

"Yes, I do. I was thinking about it driving over tonight. But," Sandy ran both hands through his hair, "Joyce, how could you have found faith through Miss Murdoch when Bridget seems to have lost hers? She told me Miss Murdoch seemed to think she was being a good Hindu by coming to church. I must say, that seems insane to me, but I suppose the diaries explain it. Bridget certainly seemed to swallow it."

"Yes, she did say that. But when I started going – and I went for Miss Murdoch's reasons, to see how one could be a good Hindu by worshipping the Christian God – I soon found it couldn't be done. Not by me, at any rate, though I suppose I can see how it might look possible to the Hindu, looking in from outside. But once I was on the inside, with people who really believed it, then the tenderness and truth of it all took hold of me completely. I'm surprised Bridget didn't see the basic incompatibility. Of course, I don't know how much she knows about Hinduism. But she knew more about Christianity than either Miss Murdoch or me."

"Bridget seems to have felt betrayed that a faithful parishioner could deceive her so. I think she felt foolish for being taken in."

"But she wasn't deceived. We didn't read the last volume of the diary. I haven't touched it until today, because it was something we did together, and I found the thought of Bridget was still a bit bruising. But today I had to read it. I couldn't believe that Charlotte wouldn't find what I have found. And, of course, she did. Here, read it for yourself."

Joyce pushed the green-bound volume towards him and sat back, smiling.

20th February 1951

It is two years since I returned from India. Two years of living in this small town. Yet, why should it feel small when it is so much larger than Badepuri? I haven't written anything, because what was there to write? Just the daily doings which were not new to me. At first I couldn't bear to think of India, or to realise that I was back here, back in the very house I'd sought to escape, leading a life not dissimilar to that I led when Mother was alive. I was numb at best, not thinking at all, but going mechanically through my days. I lost myself in literature whenever I could. I submerged in the classics: Dickens, Hardy, Austen, Trollope and the Brontës. I read modern detective novels: Margery Allingham, Dorothy Sayers and Agatha Christie. I avoided Kipling – India, or Scott – Scotland. I immersed myself in times and places and situations which had no connection to my life. These were my good days. I had bad days too. Days of black despair, when I couldn't avoid seeing myself: middle-aged, unloved, disappointed, living in a small world from which I knew I would never have the courage to escape again and looking forward to a bleak, bleak future. There were days when I didn't eat or crawl out of bed.

Except for Sundays. I couldn't reject the last advice of my deceitful lover and of my tender-hearted friend. So - I went to church. I didn't always sing or even listen; often I ignored those who offered neighbourly greetings and spoke to no one, but I went. And each Sunday, as I walked along North Street, I reminded myself of the paradox. "I am going to church because I am a Hindu," I said firmly to myself. Some days this seemed to make sense, other days it didn't. Mr Maclaren, the minister, found out who I was – I never spoke to him and he's new since I went away – and he came to call, several times. I never opened the door. It's an easy matter to peer through the stair window and see who's at the door. Besides, I opened my door to very few people, very few of the very few who dared to ring by bell – they were usually hawkers or tradesmen of one sort or another. The minister gave up. Or perhaps he wisely decided that his visits were not what I needed.

Or were they? They probably would have done me good, had I been in a frame of mind to appreciate him, but I wasn't, not then.

So there was nothing to record in the diary then.

Things changed, but so gradually that I didn't really notice. I didn't notice when my black days grew slightly less frequent, or when I began to admit an occasional Indian memory without tears. There was nothing to record in all of this. I might perhaps have made a note of the day when I first voluntarily spoke to someone. I don't know who she was, but she was young and harassed, coping with a young child on reins and a laden pram full of baby and groceries. I simply held open the door of Meldrum's greengrocer's shop, and admired the baby, left parked outside. I might have recorded that, but without a background of despair to set it against, why bother?

Sundays were my stay and consolation. I found I was looking forward to them. The music pleased me, and the rhythms of the service were soothing. All through my childhood I had never noticed any Presbyterian pattern to worship; I thought it plain, harsh, and boring. But there is a quiet pulse behind it, pushing through the familiar pattern of hymns, readings, prayers, and sermon. Perhaps Mr Maclaren's gentleness helped me to see it. He is no ranter as Mr Brown was in my younger days. Mr Brown preached hell-fire and damnation to frighten us, and it worked. Mr Maclaren talks eloquently of God's love and forgiveness. His is a soul filled with wonder. He wonders at the sea and the sky, at the varied lives of people, at the idea of God's incarnation. He wonders at the wickedness found in the world, and at pain and unfairness. He doesn't try to make it all fit but shares his confidence in the power of God's goodness to overcome all odds. Yes, I have started listening to him.

As I began to listen, I found it harder to ignore the others sitting in pews nearby. We had something in common, after all. Gradually I returned smiles and simple greetings. Then I asked polite questions - and listened to the answers. So I got to know a bit about the people who live in St. Andrews now. I met people living in the ever-expanding streets of Council Housing on the south side of the town. They didn't know I was a long-time resident. They knew nothing of my family's former influence and position. They never knew mother.

I went to tea. I returned invitations. I joined the Women's Guild. But all this I did gradually, not doing anything suddenly or noisily. And although my life was opening up and despair fading away, although I could think without tears of tomorrow, or even next week, still I didn't record it. My diary belonged to the past. Why not leave it there?

Today I can no longer leave what I wrote without adding something. Will I write after today? That depends on what happens. But I must not let anyone who reads my writing (who would that be? Who would I allow to do such a thing? I don't know of anyone, but of course I may be hit by a bus at any time, and then anyone might find these volumes) – anyone who reads my writing believe that I still attend Christian worship as a Hindu. "Go to your native religion and worship in its ways," said Krishnanya, "And you will be offering puja to Shiva, to Vishnu, to Brahman." But it doesn't work that way. Krishnanya knew nothing of monotheistic faiths. His religion held no claim to exclusive truth. He could worship anything in any way, even in ways that hurt others, and still believe he was doing puja. My religion, my faith, says otherwise.

My religion. My faith. The faith of my parents and grandparents; the faith which has shaped (and in externals, been shaped by) my country. Krishnanya knew nothing of Christianity except from a Hindu point of view. He could not know that it would speak to me at every level of my being. It doesn't all hold together for me, and there is much I don't understand, but in this faith I have found what most I sought: I have found compassion. Here is a faith with a Scripture that knows loneliness, pain, and despair. I find a Saviour figure who suffers, loves, and perseveres.

I find human, human people who make mistakes and are given courage to admit it and go on. And with all this I find a claim to exclusivity. The same one who said, "Come unto to me all ye that labour and are heavy laden, and I will give you rest," also said "If any man come to me and hate not his father, and mother, wife, and children, and brethren, and sisters, yea, and his own life also, cannot be my disciple." And he says, "No man cometh to the Father, but by me."

So, I have to decide.

When I was thinking about Hinduism I tried to pick and choose those aspects which were most appealing (or least repulsive) to me. It didn't work very well. I can't do that this time round. It's all or nothing and, to my surprise, I have discovered that it is all. For now, this means that there is quite a bit of blind faith and confusion, and I'll probably spend my life-time working to understand to whom and to what I'm pledging myself. That is something which I accept. Mr Maclaren himself sometimes says that things confuse him. I think more than anything else, this honesty of his has won me over.

Honesty and openness. I have always valued them and rarely lived up to the standards I have set for myself. Will I improve? "If a man hate not his father and mother..." Yes, but I'm sure it doesn't mean what I did. Can I ever be honest and open about that? Should I have to be?

Sandy looked up slowly. "She got religion."

"You could put it like that. She got it properly this time, I'd say. No experimenting or holding back."

"I don't understand this faith business." Sandy's voice was a little bitter, and Joyce saw a frown of anger cloud his brow. "Bridget has, or had a faith, now this Miss Murdoch and you do too. But Bridget's faith didn't stop her making an awful fool of herself. Does faith sap common-sense? I wouldn't have thought you were one to be taken in like that. You've always been sensible."

Joyce raised her eyebrows silently. Sandy flushed.

"Well, almost always. The thing is," he went on doggedly, "that this faith doesn't seem to have helped Bridget. Why should it help you?"

"Help me do what?" Joyce asked. "It won't help me write my thesis, or clean the flat, or get a job, or anything like that. You're right. But, yes, it does help. It helps me to think and see and even feel better – better than I did before. I mean it heightens life for me. I think I mean that, anyway. And part of it is not about what it does for me, but just about accepting what is true. It's all very new; ask me again some other time."

"Sounds like the opiate of the people," muttered Sandy. He looked up again. "And me? What does your faith help you see and think and feel about my place in your life?"

Joyce smiled. "I owe you a lot. But I don't see into the future."

Sandy looked hurt and puzzled. "So should I go? I had hoped, Joyce, that we might be able to forget this past year and get back together. But I think I can see you don't want to."

"No, I don't want to forget this past year; I've learned too much. And I don't want to get back together, not just now anyway."

Sandy rose and reached for his jacket.

"But we can still be friends, can't we?" said, Joyce, reaching out a hand to prevent him leaving.

He twitched the hand off his arm. "You tell me. You're the one who has new improved vision. Phone me when you have an answer."

Ian had been surprised when Joyce rang him asking for

Bridget's parents' address. He wasn't at all convinced that it would be a good thing for Joyce and Bridget to be back in touch, not quite yet. But Joyce was adamant. She had news that would help Bridget, and she needed to give it herself, to show there were no hard feelings. Reluctantly, Ian gave the phone number and made Joyce promise to phone first, not just turn up on the doorstep.

When Joyce phoned, Mrs Wallace answered. "Bridget's not keen to speak to people just now, she needs rest," was her stock reply. Joyce agreed with this.

"I know, she must need rest, and prayer, and understanding. But, you see, I think I've found the answers to one of her prayers, something which was really upsetting her for months last year. Couldn't I come and tell her? I won't hang around and make general chit-chat. It could make a lot of difference to her."

"An answer to her prayer – to hers, you say. Are you someone she prays with?"

"No, just a member of her congregation, or what was her congregation. I keep forgetting she left the church. But I was also a personal friend before things got busy for her, and I know what was worrying her then."

"Do you pray for her?" Mrs Wallace was sharp and specific.

"I've just started to," said Joyce, earnestly. "It didn't occur to me that she might need that until recently. I have a lot to learn."

"You admit it at least, and that's more than most folks nowadays. Very well, come and see Bridget. I won't tell her you're coming though, because she's quite capable of going out and not coming back till you're gone. She really doesn't think that anyone can help her.

So Joyce took the bus through to the capital, and then

splashed out on a taxi, as the easiest way to find the house she sought in the unfamiliar streets. Mrs Wallace met her at the door and was favourably impressed by her conservative, neat appearance. She was shown into the sitting-room, where Bridget was mooning over a book.

Like Sandy, Joyce was shocked by her former friend's appearance, although had she but known it, Bridget was looking marginally better than when Sandy had come to call. She was as gaunt as ever, and still looked drawn and exhausted, but the ghost of her old humour glimmered in her blue eyes. This was not noticeable at first, because when she saw Joyce standing in the doorway she scrambled to her feet and exclaimed "Go away!" in hostile tones.

Joyce had no intention of being so easily dismissed. She had a message to give, and she would give it. She came into the room, Mrs Wallace at her side, and sat down on the couch. "I have some good news for you," she said.

"What? You're tired of Ian and are giving him back?" Bridget seemed to have decided to ignore her mother's presence and was as nasty as she knew how.

"Nothing like that – besides, you got hold of the wrong end of that stick, as I think Ian must have told you. No, It's about Miss Murdoch."

"Miss Murdoch! She's dead. How can you have news of her?"

"Bridget, please listen and then I'll go. I just came to tell you that she was a Christian after all. You were quite right to trust her."

"How do you know?" Bridget still sounded cold and aggressive.

"It's in her diary."

"But we read all that. She said she was a Hindu."

"We didn't read it all. There was still one more volume. I'm not surprised you've forgotten that – you've had a lot to think about these last few months. But truly, I did once tell you there was one more part."

"Oh yes? Well, have you got it with you? Suppose you read it to me. Who are you to judge if she really was a Christian?"

Again Joyce bit her tongue, then opened the battered volume and read the passage which she had shown to Sandy. When she had finished, Bridget seized the volume and read it again for herself.

"You believe this?" she asked.

"Yes, yes I do."

"Why? How do you know it's not a bluff, written after she had decided to let her diaries be read by someone?"

"That's too devious. Besides, it worked the same way for me. I started coming to your church for the wrong reasons, but now I'm a believer myself. Your preaching converted me, Bridget, just as the Reverend Maclaren's converted Miss Murdoch. But it wasn't just the preaching: just like Miss Murdoch, the whole pattern of worship began to make sense for me."

Joyce would have said more, but at this Mrs Wallace, who had been most restrainedly silent though all these exchanges, suddenly threw her arms around her guest and clasped Joyce to her bosom.

"Another lost sheep saved, praise the Lord! Oh, my dear, how happy I am!"

Bridget got up and left the room. Her mother scarcely noticed her departure. She was too busy declaring her joy, asking Joyce about her life, and offering a cup of tea. Joyce allowed herself to be mothered in this way. She had given Bridget her news, and that was all she had come for. Meanwhile It was very pleasant to find someone who reacted to the news of her own new-found faith with enthusiasm. Neither Bridget nor Sandy had been exactly supportive.

Alone in her room, Bridget looked again at the diary which she still carried with her. Silently she read the relevant entry, then turned the pages and quickly finished the book. Then she sat back and thought. She thought about what she had read; about what Joyce had said regarding her faith and the effects of her own preaching; about what Sandy had said, and things said weeks ago by Ian. She thought about her parents' treatment of her, and the hopes which they could not conceal, that she would become, finally, the daughter they had longed for. She heard her mother and Joyce still talking together over their tea. Quietly she got to her feet, packed her bag, and wrote a note.

"I have gone back to St. Andrews. I need to be with Ian and the children now. Thank you for putting up with me these past weeks. I'll be in touch. Bridget."

This note she left on the hall table as she slipped out of the house and caught the next bus to the station.

It was two months later, and spring was in the air. Bridget listened to the birds and noticed the daily growth of the buds on the lime trees outside the window. They had only been in their flat for a week, so the view was still fascinatingly new to her.

The flat was in the council estate, just down the hill from Irvine Crescent, where Martyrs manse stood. The McKay family had not of course, been able to get a council let at such short notice – council houses were as rare as palm trees in St. Andrews, and those who got them tended to hold on to their houses till death wrested them away. However many, if not most of the properties in the estate had been bought by enterprising tenants in the Thatcher years, and now some of them were available for private rental. The new flat, the upper storey of a two-tiered house on Lamond Drive, was quite a bit smaller than the manse had been, but so far Mairi and Angus were too excited about having moved to complain that they couldn't run around as they had done. The road too was a busy one, quite unlike the relative seclusion of the crescent, and Bridget and Ian had daily to remind their offspring not to run out of the garden onto the street.

It had been Ian who had found the flat and persuaded Bridget that it was the best place for them at that time. She, once she had reconciled herself to being with her family once more, had wanted to move out of the town, preferably to somewhere at least fifty miles away, where no one would know anything about her. It would, she pointed out, be easier for her.

Ian had agreed that it would be easier. For her. "But we can't just consider you, Bridget. You are only one quarter of this family, and we have to consider all of us. And we must be practical. You have no job now, and if we move I must give up my job, in the face of a very uncertain climate in my profession. I know the children would get used to being in a new place if all else was stable and customary, but it wouldn't be, and that would unsettle them – more than they have been already."

So Bridget had swallowed her pride and the family had moved to their new flat. It hadn't been as bad as she'd feared. No one seemed to notice them particularly. Part of her mind found this a little galling – she had been so sure that everyone in the town knew and was talking about her every move. Now she discovered that most people had no idea who she was. When she remarked as much to Ian he just shrugged his shoulders. "It's just as well," he said. "I'd have thought you'd be glad, not put out, to discover your lack of importance." And of course that was the way to look at things. Bridget resolved to try to remember that she wasn't as important as she thought.

Now, listening to the birds and looking out of the window she remembered the resolution with a wry smile. She was determined to make things right with her family, and glad of the chance to do so, but sometimes it seemed that every little thing in her life needed examined and changed. Had she really been so selfish as she now discovered? Had she really always thought that her calling set her above others – even above her husband and children? She would never have said so, but she had acted as though this were the case.

If she were to turn over a new leaf, then she knew that one of the first ways to prove it would be to seek employment. It wasn't easy going from two incomes - one of which included the use of a house – to just the one. She could cope, in terms of housekeeping, but there were lots of little things which the family would have to do without – day trips, the occasional impetuous meal out, being able to use the car without worrying about the price of petrol and insurance. It wasn't fair to impose this on them if there was an alternative. Ian had never asked her to find work, or mentioned their lowered income now that they had moved, but Bridget, now she had leisure to be the home-maker of the family, couldn't help but be aware of their straightened budget.

It was while she was nerving herself to go into the town library and see what she could find in the newspapers – and perhaps then she would have the courage to go to the Job Centre as well – that the telephone rang.

"Hello?" she said, picking up the receiver and remembering not to say "Martyrs Manse."

"Bridget? This is Joyce. I had to phone Ian at school to get your new number. Where are you staying?"

"Lamond Drive."

"I see. Listen, I phoned you because you have a volume of Miss

Murdoch's diary. I'm leaving St. Andrews soon and I want to get them all together. They were left to me, after all."

"Of course they were. Where are you going?"

"Edinburgh. Shall I come and get the book from you, or will you come here? If you could come to me, I'd be grateful as I'm quite busy just now."

"Fine, I'll come. I've a couple of errands to do up the town first. Shall we say about three o'clock?"

"I'll look for you." And Joyce hung up the receiver.

Bridget had never had to look for work before, as seeking a Call to a church was quite a different process. So she didn't realise how fortunate she was to find three possible jobs, two listed in the newspapers and one from the local Job Centre. She hadn't given much thought beforehand to what she might do, thinking that she was versatile, and could therefore turn her hand to almost anything. She was appalled to discover that in almost every case, experience was required, even for the most menial of occupations. From the papers she copied down the addresses of two charities seeking fund raisers to work from home. She hoped that she could persuade them that her years with the church were equivalent to years in charity fund-raising. Then in the Job Centre she saw that the University Library needed a part-time assistant. She took details of that job too, although she had no idea how much it would pay.

Arrived at Windmill Road, she found that the front door had been painted, oiled and re-hung, so that it no longer screeched on opening. There was something uncanny about the smooth, noiseless way in which it opened. It spoke of a new order, and reminded Bridget that if Joyce were moving away, then the building would be sold. She heard voices in the upper flat as she climbed the stairs, so wasn't completely surprised to find Sandy there with Joyce.

Neither Sandy nor Joyce had seen or been in contact with Bridget and Ian since they had paid their respective visits to Edinburgh. Therefore the feeling of tension in the air did not strike Bridget as anything unusual. Thinking that it was of her creation and was thus her responsibility to dissipate, she smiled at them.

“Hello, Sandy, I didn’t know you’d be here. How are you? And how’s business? I haven’t seen you since you came to Edinburgh. I think I was quite rude then. I’m sorry. Forgive me?” She held out her hand and Sandy stopped looking as if he wished he were anywhere else and shook it.

“That’s O.K. I’m glad you’re doing better now,” he said gruffly.

“Joyce came to Edinburgh too, did you know? She did me a lot of good, though I’ve never told her so till now.”

Now Joyce smiled, though still in a forced manner.

“Here’s the diary, Joyce. I didn’t mean to run off with it. Let’s just say I was not quite myself that day. There’s one more entry after the one you came to show me. In some ways I found it even more helpful. Had you read it?”

“No. I thought that one was the last. The next page was blank.”

“Yes, for some reason she seems to have opened her book at random, when she was quite an old lady, and scribbled a few lines. It reads like a confession she had to make or burst. Here,” Bridget thumbed through the yellowed pages, “This is it. Her handwriting looks older now, and the ink is less faded.”

Joyce took the book and Sandy came to look over her shoulder. The entry was quite short and they read it together.

1st January 1989

Another new year. How many I have seen in. Will I see many more? Each year I wonder where the next will find me. This year I was still able to go to the Watchnight service for the passing of the old year. Will I be so fit and active in twelve months?

Not that that matters. What matters is my conscience. The Reverend Mrs McKay the new minister, preached a sermon tonight that I can't forget. She talked about confessing our sins to God at the end of the year and going into the next with a clean slate. It's an old message, though she told it well. But muttering my confession in my prayers isn't enough for me, not for this sin. I have confessed to God over and over, and while I suppose He must have heard me, I can't get free of the guilt. So am I forgiven?

I will write it down. Then, one day, someone else may hear my confession. Perhaps that will help me to go forward without this old weight dragging me down.

I was a most undutiful daughter. I know that in my writing I have made out my mother to be an ogre, but the truth is, I made her that way. I don't mean that I have written falsehoods, although I suppose I have inevitably put down only my own point of view. But if she was difficult for me to live with, that's because I brought out the worst in her. And although I hated her, I loved to hate her, and I delighted in drawing out her nastiest characteristics. She loved me, although we couldn't get on. It wasn't just for her sake that she encouraged me to leave home and get a job, since I obviously wasn't going to marry. Did she know that I turned down two proposals so that I need not be deprived of my amusement – baiting my mother? Oh, they weren't proposals I had any desire to accept, but that was my reason. I wanted to stay at home and irritate.

Mother hated herself, the self that I made her display. She would nag and rage at me, then burst into tears and beg my forgiveness, and all the time I had been angling to provoke just such a reaction. I made my mother hate herself. That is even worse than hating her myself. She was glad to die. When she was so ill with pneumonia, she made no effort to get well. I made her weary of her life. At the time I was glad, almost proud, but now, and for many, many years now, I have been sorry.

I cannot justify myself, and I will not say that my guilt has paid for my sin, because it has not. I can only confess it, trusting in Christ for pardon, and go on, seeking, with His help, to amend my life.

Joyce closed the book, and for a while neither she nor Sandy spoke. Sandy's face showed no emotion, while on Joyce's a faint smile dawned. Bridget watched them and eventually broke the silence herself.

"That's why I came back to my husband and children when I did. Thank you for letting me see that last entry, Joyce. Miss Murdoch was a negative inspiration to me."

"What do you mean?"

"Well, she showed me that if I didn't leave my parents again, we would drive each other mad."

"What do you mean?" Joyce asked again. "You have wonderful parents!"

"To everyone else, yes, maybe. But they're not ideal for me. It can happen that way, though I don't know how. You'd think the genes could organise things better, but somehow my parents brought into the world a child whom they were not the best people to bring up. I recognised the fact years ago, but I needed Miss Murdoch to remind me. That reminder was the catalyst which helped me begin getting my life back together again."

"That's not right!" Joyce was het up now, and almost shouting. "You're just saying that to excuse your unfilial behaviour. You just don't appreciate your parents."

"And they don't appreciate me. It cuts both ways, and it's no one's fault, Joyce. Why are you so concerned about it?"

"Of course it's someone's fault – yours I should think. When a family has problems it's always someone's fault. In my case my mother is to blame because she violated my privacy. You don't appreciate what wonderful parents you have."

Bridget and Sandy were staring at her now, and she went on defiantly. "Yes, I am worked up. Your mother and father have been wonderful to me these past few weeks. They've listened to my story, they've rejoiced over my conversion to Christianity – no one here did that. They've taken me to their church with them. Now they've opened up their home to me, and when I go to Edinburgh I'm going to stay with them as family. So forgive me for defending your parents, Bridget, but I, at any rate, owe them some loyalty."

Bridget and Sandy both opened their mouths, but Sandy's hung open in astonishment, while Bridget rushed into speech. "Joyce, you never told me you'd been converted. I thought you were just coming to church to get the full Miss Murdoch experience. Of course I'm pleased. And I'm glad you're going to stay with my parents, if that's what you think will work best for you. I do appreciate them as people, just not as parental figures in my life. If that's where you're going to be, we'll not lose touch completely, so I'll leave the book and go now: the children and Ian will be looking for their tea." She left the room and Sandy found himself alone with Joyce.

Now he found his voice. "You're going to Edinburgh? Why? And when was this decided? Why didn't you tell me?" He could hear how pathetic he sounded, so he stopped speaking abruptly, got up from his chair, and went to stand looking out of the window, as so often before.

"I was going to tell you today, though not quite the way it happened. I'm sorry you got a shock, Sandy. The thing is, now I'm engaged in full-time writing of my thesis, I don't need to be here anymore. I can do it as well in Edinburgh, where I have access to their university library. I want to go, to get involved with the Wallace's church and to live with them, because they care about me, and it's been a long time since anyone cared for me that way."

"I care for you!" Sandy exclaimed. "You know that, or have you forgotten it? I thought you cared for me. I thought you loved me. I know you said we couldn't start again just yet, but I thought we were finding our way back together, and I hoped that this time it could be forever."

"Forever? You mean you want to marry me?" Now Joyce was the one to be surprised.

"Yes, I do. I certainly wasn't going to mention it for a long time yet, and not in this way, but since it's out in the open, can't you marry me, Joyce?"

"Of course not." Joyce sounded rather shocked. "Surely you realise that! Before this year I might have, but now, no. I can't marry anyone who doesn't share my faith, no matter how much I may like you."

"I didn't want to marry you before this past year. I want to marry you now. I want to marry the person who has lived through this past year and learned from it. Why must you insist I share your faith?"

"Because if you don't, we will never understand each other."

"Why? Because it's something we don't have in common. But Joyce, there's so much we don't have in common. We come from different families, we have had different experiences of life and most importantly we are of different genders – and I'm a few years older than you. Differences are what make you attractive to me: if we were the same, I could just look into a mirror and talk to myself."

"But – "

Sandy would not listen to her interruption. "We have these fascinating differences – and one of them is that you have a religious faith while I do not – but what we have in common is surely the biggest thing. We are both human. All our different experiences are interesting to each other because they are human experiences, and so I have some chance of beginning to understand what has made you who you are, and who you are becoming. Surely you can see that? We need to have differences."

"Not this one. It's more than a human experience. Remember, I know what I'm talking about: I'm an anthropologist; I've studied religion. And what I learned, very early on in that study, is that from outside a religion, any religion, you can't really know it. You can only know what it does, what it looks like. I've stepped inside now, and there's a world of difference - but it's not the same world as the one where I used to live, where I knew you."

"Perhaps I could learn to step inside too," suggested Sandy.

"You don't mean that. Besides, if you did, I would never know if it was real for you or if you were only playing a part for my sake. And if you did step inside, how do you know you would still want to be with me?"

"Because I will always want to be with you, Joyce." Sandy spoke the sad words as he turned to the door. "But I can see it's no good, not now anyway. Your religion has you in its thrall and there is no place for me. Bridget spoke like that once, but in the end she let me at least try to come close and help her. She gave our common humanity a chance."

"Bridget walks on the very edge of faith. That's what I've seen since I've been with her parents' church. I want to go deep into the heart of it. If it means saying goodbyes, I know I'll be gaining a whole new family."

"Saying goodbyes. That's what we're doing, though I can't believe it. But since we are saying goodbye, and 'famous last words' sometimes stick in the mind, I will tell you that the way you're talking now makes me afraid for you as well as sad for myself. You talk as though you were about to become walled up in a convent. I know that's not the case, physically, but do ask yourself from time to time if you're not letting invisible walls hem you in, and if that was what Christ came to call you to. Goodbye, Joyce. I hope I will see you again. Never hesitate to contact me."

Sandy closed the flat door quietly behind him without looking back. So he did not see Joyce's face set into a hard mask as she turned to continue putting her books into boxes.

EPILOGUE

The future is called 'perhaps' which is the only possible thing to call the future. And the important thing is not to allow that to scare you."

Tennessee Williams, "The Past, Present and Perhaps" from "Orpheus Descending".

1st August 199-

First day of my new job, and to mark the occasion I have decided to keep a diary. I've never done this before, and I wonder that I should want to try it now, after my experience with Miss Murdoch's. Joyce told me that a diary is a dangerous thing, and I can see that. It's of no use if it isn't completely frank, but if it is so honest, then it must never be read by eyes other than mine.

It seemed a shame to go off for even part of the day during the children's holidays, but a chance comment another member of staff made about the price of child-care made me realise I'm lucky to have Ian able to take charge. I feel very confused tonight, what with everything I was told today. My mind's a complete muddle of faces, shelves, books, computers, and stairs, with an accompanying voice-over of assorted instructions. After being my own boss, more or less, for so long, I had thought it might be restful being told what to do, but not so far. And I only work mornings. I can't imagine how I'd have survived a whole day.

14th August 199-

As I was running round trying to do everyone's bidding at once this morning I suddenly remembered how I once thought a library would be a calm place to work. I laughed aloud. I should have realised they wouldn't have been looking for a part-time worker if there was any way they could do without one. Nor would they have agreed to pay me for one minute more than they knew they could fill. There is nothing calm about an academic library for the staff. Everyone is over-extended. This may be why there is so much back-biting and malicious talk amongst the staff: they seem to have no general conversation that is not centred around doing someone down. I mentioned this to Ian tonight, and he just smiled at first. So I said it again, and he remarked "No, I'm not looking forward to going back to work either." I would like this to be a mysterious remark but am afraid his meaning is only too clear: this is a normal experience for working people. I don't want to come to this conclusion. I don't want to think I was so very cushioned for so long. To think I got cross with the Kirk Session.

19th August 199-

First day of school for the family. I know we used to get through mornings like this day after day, but I think the few months when I was a housewife have dulled my reactions. It seemed incredibly chaotic. I must say though, it was easier for me to go off to my morning of hard labour knowing that no one was at home. It makes me cross when I realise how easy I had things in the church. Yes, I worked long hours, but I had respect, and people who valued and needed me. Why should they have been so appreciative? I had no idea what the world of work was like for those who weren't ideally suited to their occupation. I never even considered it. Can I really have assumed that everyone found themselves in the perfect job for them? Did I really think that the people who sweep the streets, who serve in shops, and yes, who shelve library books do it as much for love as for money? Not consciously, of course.

6th September 199-

I'm writing this in the morning, as Ian and the kids are at church. I haven't been back to church yet. I don't feel that I can go to Martyrs with them. I tell myself this is because it might embarrass people there but really, I know they would be a lot less embarrassed than me, and that's why I stay away. Besides, while I know I do still believe, I am working out just what I believe, and I'm not sure church would be helpful to me for that. It has such painful connotations.

What I just wrote isn't quite right. It's not what I believe, but how I believe it that I'm uncertain about. My question isn't

What? but So What? And I don't want to have to spend a long time on any question just now. I have enough to do with a job and a family, and a small flat to run.

8th September 199-

I am so cross tonight. The So What? I wrote about last time has become very cynical.

The phone rang this evening, and to my surprise it was Sandy Melville on the other end. He sounded very glad to get through yet at the same time harassed. I asked him if anything was wrong, and he replied that he had had to get on to Joyce to get our phone number (we're ex-directory as Ian prefers that his class's parents can't get at him, one of the joys of no longer living in a manse).

"How is Joyce? Do you see much of her?" I asked. My parents never mention her, but I know she is still living with them. This was the wrong thing to ask. He got very upset, and at the end of five minutes I gathered why. He doesn't see Joyce, or rather, she won't see him. Before she went to Edinburgh he asked her to think about marrying him, and since then she has had nothing to do with him and takes the attitude that he is bad for her faith. I can guess that my parents back her up in this. Just prising our phone number out of her was hard enough. If my parents had been in, they might have given it more easily. Poor Sandy's obviously very upset by the whole state of affairs and doesn't understand it. I told him that I didn't either, before handing him over to Ian, who was the person he really wanted to speak with.

Faith, so what? It just seems to cause pain and hard feelings.

The good, if rather surprising news is that Ian and Sandy are going to watch Raith Rovers play on Saturday. I wouldn't have put Sandy down as a football enthusiast, and I know Ian can take the game or leave it. Still, it's nice they'll be doing something together.

25th September 199-

Thank goodness it's the weekend. The atmosphere at work is getting worse and worse now that the students are back in town. It's not their fault that I can see. After all the library wouldn't be here if there were no students to use it. But the librarians (and I'm made very much aware that I am a mere library assistant) go on as though the library was there simply for their erudite and organisational pleasure. The stress and tension, and with it the cattiness and back-biting, has multiplied this week. It affects me. I wish I could keep aloof, but it's impossible. Even if I don't take sides, I am perceived as having done so. Oh well, it brings in money. I wonder if there is any job which I would find congenial?

15th October 199-

It had to happen. I'm surprised it took so long. Linda Watt saw me at my work in the library. She's one of the students who goes to Martyrs church. As I thought, I was the more embarrassed; she didn't seem phased at all, but then, it turns out, she knew I was working. "Someone at church told me," she said. I wonder who? Not that it matters. She told me I was looking well, and hadn't I lost weight? It wasn't a long conversation, but now I think about it, I'm glad it happened. I dreaded such a meeting, but now the first one's over, none will be so bad. And this one wasn't too bad either.

Ian told me tonight that Sandy phoned him again, asking him to go to another football match – they've been to three now. This time my husband had the courage to confess that he doesn't really follow football, and asked if there wasn't something else they could do. The upshot is that they're both going to learn to play golf! It will be better for them than standing on terraces (though

Ian says they sit in seats actually), but more costly. However, it's to have some space for these little luxuries that I'm working.

1st November 199-

I hate November. It always seems like a long, grey month and this year it had certainly begun dreich. The library asked me if I could extend my hours to do three full days each week as well as two mornings. I should have felt glad about that. Objectively speaking, I suppose it means they've realised that things can't go on as they are, and that there is just too much for us to do. One of the librarians has been ordered off work by her doctor for three weeks – she's suffering from nervous exhaustion. Well, I know what that's like. But the prospect of being more hours in the library does not fill me with joy. It will be a long, grey November.

20th November 199-

It's almost eleven months now since that day I stormed out of church. It seems a lot longer. I haven't been back to church voluntarily since then, though of course Mum dragged me along when I was staying with them. I feel like a different person from that harried, driven woman who was me a year ago. How could I have allowed myself to become so obsessed? How could I have so closed my eyes to the rest of the world around me? It's so ironic that it was to be in touch with the world, even to change it, that I wanted to be a minister. Could I become obsessed and closed off again?

It's this last question which keeps me from being willing to try any formal religion again, just yet. What if I lost my balance again? The answer I'd have given anyone who had asked me the same question when I was still a minister, would be that of course we have to trust God not to let us fall. But I lost my balance and fell anyway, so it's obviously not as simple as that. I suspect all easy answers now. I am so suspicious that I feel as though I am peering out at the world from behind lowered brows. How does my family manage to put up with me? How do I manage to put up with myself? What gets me down is that I know I am not naturally a suspicious person, and my enforced wariness (enforced by experience) is draining.

12th December 199-

I spent the evening mending and lengthening Mairi's angel costume. Goodness knows what she did last year to get it into such a state. But of course, I wasn't there, so I can't know. She's to be the angel Gabriel again this year, and this time she has a little song to sing. The children want me to go to the nativity play. Ian tried to shush them at tea tonight when they began asking me. But I'm touched that they still want me. I have been afraid that they might accept that there are things which we don't do together as a family, and church is one of them. I will go back. Christmas Eve will be the day I first go back. I will tell them tomorrow.

24th December 199-

I don't know what I expected tonight. For myself I mean. Perhaps that's why I'm so flummoxed, because I was thinking about myself. It was the nativity play, and that's why people came to church, not to look around the congregation and nudge and point to each other that the Reverend McKay was there. Nor did they come to church to greet or to snub me. I think I had expected some sort of reaction to my presence, and there wasn't one. I mean, I wasn't ignored, but nor was a fuss made of me, which were the two reactions I was expecting and dreading. Yes, I think I was dreading an effusive welcome even more than a total snub. But in fact, people who came across me smiled and greeted me, and commented on the play, just as though it weren't a year since I stormed out of church and left them with a pastoral vacancy which is yet to be filled. The only peculiar thing I noticed was that no one addressed me by name. I probably wouldn't have noticed this at all, had it not been for Dr. Marr who greeted me with "How are you, Mrs McKay?" Mrs, not Rev. I am no longer the Reverend Mrs McKay, just Mrs. I don't think Dr. Marr was making a point, he just likes to be accurate. And it is accurate. It's just that I hadn't really thought about it before. A change of title and a change of life. And which is the happier?

If I stop to consider that question, tonight when it's late and I'm tired with Christmas preparations, then I have to say that in some ways I am happier now. Not so much in my work, but in myself and my family. And the part of life which is not work has become more important than it was previously, when my work was very much who I was, before family, friendships, interests etc. I feel more rooted now. Work is something I do, not who I am.

1st January 199-

Over the Christmas period I've been considering what I wrote on Christmas Eve. If work is no longer an expression of who I am – my priorities and interests and comforts – then surely it's about time I began expressing these important things in some better way than just sitting at home thinking about them. I don't mean the family, of course. Sitting at home (actually, I rarely seem to sit) is the best way to enjoy my family. But what about my religion, my faith? Now that's it's not given expression by my whole life – or not obviously – what should I do? I know the most obvious answer to that, and I've been running away from it. But new years are a good time to stop running, so I'll go back to church. And this time I won't expect the heavens to fall.

But I'm making another New Year's resolution. I resolve to keep my eyes and my mind open. If I can see any way to express the So What of my faith, which has been so haunting me, then I will not run away, but try to do something practical. It's a vague sort of resolution, but, I think, for me more challenging and positive than the usual "I will give up sweets" sort of thing.

3rd January 199-

Ian was surprised when I said I was coming to church. He tried not to show it, but I knew he was, and said so. He began to splutter and try to excuse his attitude, but I laughed at him, and so that was all right. I's been a while since we really laughed together. We've smiled, we've even chuckled at the children and so on, but we haven't had a real laugh based on the intimacy of our relationship. Probably because we've been so careful with each other. In other words, we've not been really intimate. Maybe things are changing.

I liked the visiting minister today. I was quite sorry to hear he was just "supply", not someone being considered for the call. They could do worse than consider him. But that is <u>none of my business</u>!

18th January 199-

I caught myself joining in the whining at work today. I noticed it this time. How often have I done so and not noticed? And if I haven't, how long before this becomes my way of relating at work?

25th January 199-

Bitterly cold today, and snowy. Slipping and sliding up to the library I was accosted by a "Big Issue" seller. I bought the paper, as he was just a young lad, looking cold and miserable. I asked him how things were going, and he looked amazed that anyone should ask. The answer wasn't encouraging. He was cold and he hadn't managed to sell much in the past few days. People were too cold to stop, or to take off their gloves to fish for the money. He didn't blame them, but he could do with some gloves himself. He was a bit whiney about this, and I wondered if he really didn't have some stuck in his pockets. But then I always mistrust whiney requests. To salve my conscience I gave him an extra pound and told him to get some coffee.

Mentioned the plight of the homeless at work, when people were complaining about the weather. Found very little sympathy evinced. What did I expect?

26th January 199-

"Big Issue" vendor was there again today, still looking pinched with cold. Gave him another pound.

Told Ian about this tonight – after all it's both our money I'm giving away like this. He was sympathetic but said a cup of coffee wouldn't help much. "If he's as scruffy as most homeless people are – and I know they can't help it – then they'll not be encouraged to linger in cafes. The only other place to go and get warm is the public library, and I've seen them asking people to leave from there, with the excuse that it's not a large place and they need the seats for other patrons." I had never thought of that.

27th January 199-

I can't stop thinking about my homeless friend. His name's Jason. Should I invite him home? But we really don't have much room. Besides, I gather he has somewhere to sleep, in Dundee. It's just during the cold days that things are so horrible for him. If he wants to sell his papers he has to take the pitch that is allocated to him, and St. Andrews is regarded as a prime location amongst the vendors.

28th January 199-

I dreamed about Jason last night. It's too much. I think this is somewhere to try to enact that vague New Year's resolution of mine. I need to try to organise a warming centre for Jason and others. Even if it can only be when I'm not at work, that would be something. The question is, where? This flat isn't central enough, even if I dared let a lot of possibly dubious strangers in. So where? If I were still a minister I wouldn't hesitate. The church halls would be perfect – especially the way Sandy had them renovated. But can I ask to use them now? Won't it look like cheek?

31st January 199-

The bitter cold weather shows no sign of letting up. So today I decided that cheek or not I had at least to find out about using the church halls. There weren't many in the congregation this morning, and the pulpit supply person was old and out of touch, so those who were there didn't miss much (Perhaps I shouldn't say that? Am I comparing with myself? It is so difficult to sit in the pew as a worshipper when I used to be the one who put everything together and led: difficult but very good for me.) However Brian Smith, the Session Clerk was there, and so I made myself approach him and outline my idea. He was a bit taken aback, and I found myself bending over backwards to impress upon him the idea that I didn't think I was due any privileges because of who I am or used to be. I also said that I didn't expect anyone else to get involved. I would just open up when I was free, and that little would be better than nothing for those with nowhere to go.

Turns out there was a special Kirk Session meeting this afternoon – something to do with the process of searching for a minister – so after humming and hawing (Brian never says anything without a few considering sighs) he said he'd bring up my proposals.

He phoned me tonight. It's an extraordinary thing. They like my idea, all except the part which I thought would be the best bit for them: they don't want to think that no one else has to get involved. It shouldn't all devolve on me, they say, partly for my sake and partly because the church should take responsibility for the things done in its name, and not just hope someone else will do them. We're starting tomorrow, and volunteers from the Kirk Session will help me this week. Come Sunday they will make an announcement and try to get some kind of rota fixed up, but they realise that there's no time to be lost in this bitter weather.

8th February 199-

This is the second week of our warming centre. I only work half a day on Mondays, so we were open all afternoon. However, the rota which was drawn up yesterday has some projected opening times when I know I will be otherwise engaged. I said this to Emma Farquharson, who was on with me this afternoon, and she laughed. "That's all right. We'll manage."

I felt a bit put down but hoped it didn't show. After a pause Emma went on, "We needed you to put the fire under us to get this thing going. We had been wondering what could be done to help in this weather. It just took you to say that you would do it all yourself if need be to get the rest of us motivated. Motivation was always one of your gifts to us."

Emma's a dear girl, so truthful and yet kind with it. Truthful people often aren't kind.

We had ten people in at different times this afternoon. They weren't all homeless, of course, though Jason was among the first to appear. Once you get him inside it's obvious he could do with a wash and clean clothes. He smells. We have a shower, but no clothes to give. This evening I went through Ian's wardrobe, but he wasn't very happy at some of the clothing I thought he could do without, so I put it back and asked him to find alternatives. It seems he can do without the sweaters which my mother has been giving him for Christmas ever since we were married! He gave me a sheepish look when he presented the gaudy pile of wool, but I just laughed.

5th March 199-

After a dreary day at work and an evening when the kids were fractious and hard to please, the phone rang. It was Brian Smith. As ever, he hummed and hawed before coming to the point. When he did get there, it turns out that the pulpit supply for this Sunday has been rushed into hospital with appendicitis. This is doubly disastrous as he was not just pulpit supply but the person selected to preach for the Call, so that the congregation might approve him as their new minister. But what he wondered was, could I fill in?

I almost said no. Maybe I should have said no. I have no right to preach in Martyrs church ever again. Indeed, I have no right to preach at all, anywhere. As I hesitated before replying, Brian asked again, "Please, Bridget, it would be doing us such a favour." Well, I couldn't say no then. I owe these people so much, more than I knew when I was their minister. So tomorrow I have a sermon to write. It's such a long time since I did that, I'm getting nervous.

7th March 199-

I did it. I have no idea how it went. I hoped Ian could tell me, but when I asked him he surprised me by saying he had no idea either. I accused him of having not listened, but he denied it, then said, "The truth is, Bridget, I was so moved by seeing you back up in that pulpit that though I listened, I couldn't hear anything. There you were, where you used to stand, and looking so vulnerable without your robes. I just sat and thought about what you've been through since you were there last and wondering if anyone knew what it had cost you to get up there again."

I cried when he said that. I was feeling pretty emotional

anyway and it was a relief to get it all out. The children caught me at it, but for once it didn't worry them. I remember how it always embarrassed me as a child if I caught my mother crying. Have my children learned that it's O.K. to cry? I hope so.

9th March 199-

I have been reflecting on what I learned from Sunday.

Firstly I learned that it would be quite easy to go back to my former job. I can still do it, and do it well.

But if I did that I fear it would be a going back in every way, including going back, maybe not all at once, but insidiously, to all my old ways and what came of them. It would be a going back, not a going forward.

20th March 199-

An amazing day. At the library this morning I was summoned to the head librarian's office. Like Brian Smith, he's a sigher who finds it hard to get to the point. But he got there at last, and I found that he was suggesting I might like to train as a librarian. It seems I could be allowed to do the study by extension, with occasional intensive courses at Robert Gordons' in Aberdeen. He said I show an aptitude for the work, and that if I chose to pursue this option, the university would make sure I was given time off (with pay!) to attend study weeks.

So we had plenty to talk about over tea tonight.

And then the phone rang.

Brian Smith. Hemming and hawing as usual, of course but finally he asked if he and Dr. Marr might come round to see Ian and me this evening. So they came.

They wanted to see if I might be interested in returning to

Martyrs as a minister, and what both Ian and I thought about the idea. The man who should have been offered to the congregation is still very ill, as his operation didn't go so well. It seems he has withdrawn his name from the vacancy. And it seems that when I preached the other day some people got hold of the wrong end of the stick and didn't realise that I was just filling in. They thought I was the person they were supposed to be considering. (They must have been late-comers, I think, because it was all explained most carefully at the beginning of the service.) Anyway, they said they thought I would be a good person. And then others agreed.

The Kirk Session has discussed the matter long and hard and what they want to know is whether I would consider becoming a three-quarter time minister with an assistant shared with other churches. It's a good idea, and I know Ian thinks it might work, as it would still give me time for the family, which is good for all of us.

It could be a perfect opportunity. But. But it would be going back, possibly back into a trap from which I escaped only with great pain. And I know that no ministerial job can ever be kept to set hours. And I don't want to be going back, but to keep discovering how to live out my faith going forward. This is not something to be decided in a hurry.

Whatever I decide, I realise that there are two people I need to bring back into my life. I need Sandy and Joyce. Joyce I need to show me the way of fanaticism (until and unless she grows out of that stage), so that I may try to avoid it. Sandy I need to remind me of our common humanity. The world as Sandy, a decent humanist, sees it, is the world in which we all live, wherever we place our faith. Some of us may accept it, may be comfortable with it, and others may wish to change it. In some ways, living in Sandy's world while still living with faith in God is the more challenging option than living wholly within a community that agrees with me, and gives me far too much power and reverence. I was at the centre of things in that community of faith, but the call is to live at the edge of things, living with faith in a world which continually challenges my beliefs.

ABOUT THE AUTHOR

Catherine Buchan grew up in St. Andrews, where this story is set. She has worked in various parts of Scotland and elsewhere as a parish minster, a tour guide, and with projects supporting those who are homeless. Currently her home is on the beautiful Moray Coast.

Printed in Great Britain
by Amazon

22071273R00202